Screening the Gothic in Australia and New Zealand

Screening the Gothic in Australia and New Zealand

Contemporary Antipodean Film and Television

Edited by
Jessica Gildersleeve and
Kate Cantrell

Routledge
Taylor & Francis Group

LONDON AND NEW YORK

We are grateful to the School of Humanities and Communication as well as the Centre for Heritage and Culture at the University of Southern Queensland for their research support.

First published in 2022 by Amsterdam University Press Ltd.

Published 2025 by Routledge
4 Park Square, Milton Park, Abingdon, Oxon OX14 4RN
605 Third Avenue, New York, NY 10158

Routledge is an imprint of the Taylor & Francis Group, an informa business

© The authors / Taylor & Francis Group 2022

ISBN: 9789463721141 (hbk)
ISBN: 9781041185833 (pbk)
ISBN: 9781003703389 (ebk)
NUR 670

Cover illustration: Manuel Meurisse, On our way to Grampians, National park, on a moody day.

Cover design: Coördesign, Leiden

DOI: 10.5117/9789463721141

For our many students of the Gothic over the years, with gratitude for your conversations and recommendations.

For Product Safety Concerns and Information please contact our EU representative:
GPSR@taylorandfrancis.com
Taylor & Francis Verlag GmbH, Kaufingerstraße 24, 80331 München, Germany

Table of Contents

Introduction: Please Check the Signal: Screening the Gothic in the Upside Down

Jessica Gildersleeve and Kate Cantrell

Abstract

How do Antipodean films and television programmes represent their own sense of the Gothic? What does the contemporary Gothic look like on the large and small screen in productions from Australia and New Zealand? New ways of watching film and television via popular streaming services have seen a reinvigoration of this 'most domestic of media'. What does this look like 'Down Under' in the twenty-first century? This introduction to the collection traces representations of the Gothic in film and television in Australia and New Zealand in the twenty-first century. It attends to the development and mutation of the Gothic in these post- or neo-colonial contexts, concentrating on the generic innovations of this temporal and geographical focus.

Keywords: contemporary Gothic; Australia; New Zealand; screen studies

The popular Netflix series *Stranger Things* (2016–) partly derives its terror from its construction of a parallel universe termed the 'Upside Down'. This alternate dimension is a site of chaos, destruction, and invasion, a space constructed in opposition to the civilization and familiarity of the small North American town inhabited by the series' teenaged protagonists. A similar concept appears in the second season of the American series *Channel Zero* (2016–2018) in which an uncanny alternate universe is accessed via the 'No-End House'; in this subverted world, people and things look the same as they do in the 'real world', but behave, horrifically, very differently. We borrow the term 'Upside Down' because the Otherness it evokes mimics the

Gildersleeve, J. and K. Cantrell (eds.), *Screening the Gothic in Australia and New Zealand: Contemporary Antipodean Film and Television*. Taylor & Francis Group, 2022

DOI 10.5117/9789463721141_INTRO

construction of Australasia as the 'Antipodes', a space not only geographically opposite to the northern hemisphere but, in the lingering relics of colonial discourse, culturally and philosophically opposite too. In Australia and New Zealand, such an orientalist or carnivalesque construction supposes, everything is 'upside down', topsy-turvy, out of place. As the travel writer Jan Morris famously wrote of the Land Down Under, 'the water goes down the plug-hole the other way in Australia, and it really is possible to imagine, if you are a fancifully minded visitor from the other hemisphere, that this metropolis is clinging upside-down to the bottom of the earth' (470).

During the late nineteenth century and into the twentieth, this sense of reversal was coded through a colonial perspective as Gothic. The foreignness of the Antipodes, with its unfamiliar landscapes and Indigenous peoples, was cast as something to be feared, as in Marcus Clarke's famous description of the Australian bush (1876):

> The Australian mountain forests are funereal, secret, stern. Their solitude is desolation. They seem to stifle, in their black gorges, a story of sullen despair [...]. In the Australian forests no leaves fall. The savage winds shout among the rock clefts. From the melancholy gums, strips of white bark hang and rustle. The very animal life of these frowning hills is either grotesque or ghostly. Great grey kangaroos hop noiselessly over the coarse grass. Flights of white cockatoos stream out, shrieking like evil souls. The sun suddenly sinks, and the mopokes burst out into horrible peals of semi-human laughter. The natives aver that, when night comes, from out the bottomless depth of some lagoon the Bunyip rises, and, in form like a monstrous sea-calf, drags his loathsome length from out the ooze. From a corner of the silent forest rises a dismal chant, and around a fire dance natives painted like skeletons. All is fear-inspiring and gloomy. No bright fancies are linked with the memories of the mountains. Hopeless explorers have named them out of their sufferings – Mount Misery, Mount Dreadful, Mount Despair. (qtd in Gelder and Weaver 3–4)

For Clarke, the Australian bush is a gothic netherworld thronged with monstrous animals, anthropomorphized landscapes and climates, and the chaos of horrific sounds – shouting winds, shrieking birds, disembodied voices. While several writers and artists have since made progress in dismantling the idea of the Antipodes as a cultural and geographical anomaly, some residual tensions remain. Contemporary New Zealand, for example, is still subject to such constructions, Jennifer Lawn observes, because the nation's perceived strangeness or mythicism means that it 'transforms itself into fantasy spaces

(Middle-Earth, Narnia, Skull Island) that feed the latest enthusiasms of the global entertainment industry' (11). Indeed, the Land of the Long White Cloud, so often imagined as a pastoral paradise or island sanctuary, is often marketed overseas as a utopian nation, a dream destination 'needing little make-up or CGI to appear beguiling or other-worldly' (Insight Guides).

But how do so-called Antipodean films and television series represent their own sense of the Gothic? What does the contemporary Gothic look like on the large and small screen in productions financed and filmed in Australia and New Zealand? Without doubt, new ways of watching film and television via popular streaming services have seen a reinvigoration of this 'most domestic of media' (Wheatley 25). Adaptations of classic Gothic texts, like *Rebecca* (2020), adapted from Daphne Du Maurier's novel (1938), *The Haunting of Hill House* (2018), based on Shirley Jackson's novel of the same name (1959), and its sequel, *The Haunting of Bly Manor* (2020), adapted from Henry James's *The Turn of the Screw* (1898), have found a new audience in the Netflix generation, hungry for horror to 'binge watch' or stream and scream. Indeed, streaming platforms like Netflix have actively participated in what Matt Hills describes as 'the horror boom that can be traced to the rise of "quality" premium cable TV' (127). Streaming services 'normaliz[e] binge-watching' and 'individualiz[e] construction[s] of audience', he observes (125–126), suggesting an intensification of the claustrophobia and invasiveness associated with the domestic or televisual Gothic.

At the same time, new adaptations of the Australian Gothic cinema of the 1970s 'New Wave' have also found a fresh following. Foxtel's serialization of *Picnic at Hanging Rock* (2018) and the commercial television miniseries *Wake in Fright* (2017), for instance, 'domesticate and democratize the Gothic' for their on-demand streaming audience (Gildersleeve, 'Weird Melancholy'), moving away from the exclusivity of the original arthouse works. This revival and revision of the corpus of the 1970s demonstrates the Gothic's mutative ability and reveals its compulsion to make visible the social and cultural mutations of society as a whole. In this way, the renewal of earlier gothic themes, and the extension of gothic discourses, enacts what we might think of as a reawakening, a troubling provocation of arousal and anxiety. Indeed, as Allison Craven observes, the reappearance of these titles after a period of dormancy has itself 'the aura of a haunting' (46–47).

Given that these particular examples – perhaps the most well-known original instances to which the term 'Australian Gothic cinema' might be most readily applied – are both 'high-art' and more interested in 'issues of Australian national identity over genre classifications' (Balanzategui 22–23), and in light of David Punter's observation that 'the Gothic as an aesthetic, as a vernacular [...] [is] an essential – perhaps [...] *the* essential – element in nation-building' (23), what does this new 'domesticity' of the Gothic look like in the Upside Down in the twenty-first century? This collection traces representations of the Gothic in film and television in Australia and New Zealand from a twenty-first-century perspective, a vantage point inevitably skewed by the mordant outlook of a contemporary moment in which we may feel as if we are living in a horror film. All of the works discussed in this volume were produced within the last decade, providing a highly recent snapshot of the appearance of the televisual Gothic in this context.

In casting a critical eye to the Antipodean Gothic, the collection also attends to mutations of the Gothic in post- or neo-colonial contexts, concentrating on the generic innovations of this temporal and geographical focus, while simultaneously considering distinctions between appearances of the genre in each nation. New Zealand Gothic, for instance, appears to more readily engage with the Māori experience and legacy of colonization, while Australian Gothic still tends toward a narrative framed by white guilt or shame. While each chapter in this collection, then, explores a particular aspect of the Gothic Down Under, examining texts that seek to exhume or exorcize different national traumas, there are key ideas and themes that cluster around the selected texts. Moral ambiguity, cultural neurosis, and ecological devastation are recurring preoccupations, inextricable as they are, in the Antipodean context, from the illegal occupation of the land. Not surprisingly, the Antipodean inflection also manifests in new reincarnations of historical tensions and concerns: the figure of the lost child and its mythic associations with white vanishing, the spectral presences and projections of the colonial encounter including xenophobic fears of the Other, and the *unheimlich* nature of the unauthorized home built on haunted land. Indeed, the Gothic's interrogative stance lends itself to a genre that is still obsessed with the disturbances and transgressions of colonial history but still ultimately unable to resolve that trauma. If there is a common 'message' that underpins these texts, it is that the ghosts of the past cannot be banished or contained; they can only be momentarily placated or temporarily appeased.

To be sure, the Gothic has always been a political and cultural discourse, a site for the examination of and reflection on that which troubles or disturbs us most. Resolution of such problems is often wistful, nostalgic or conservative in older Gothic texts, but in the contemporary Gothic no such comfort is offered. Andrew Smith, for example, has cautioned that the Gothic 'should not be read as a form which passively replicates contemporary cultural debates about politics, philosophy, or gender, but rather reworks, develops, and challenges them' (8). In the horror story of contemporary global culture, the Gothic not only provokes visceral response, as in the Gothic of old, but responsible cultural action. In fact, the Antipodean Gothic can be seen to provoke a political engagement which precisely depends upon a discourse of upheaval and disruption, a continual uprooting of colonial sensibilities and nostalgic tendencies. This most often manifests in a desire to return to and rework the past, so that while the Gothic 'frequently functions to contest the more optimistic foundational narratives of new worlds [...] [it] often continues to give expression to lingering traumas produced by colonial life, with buried pasts resurfacing in horrific form to disturb the present' (Byron 369). In the postcolonial configurations of the Gothic, this resurfacing can take the form of what Felicity Collins and Therese Davis call 'backtracking', in which the viewer is encouraged to examine historical representation for the purpose of an epiphanic recognition of the traumas of the past (37–38). More than this, we might say that backtracking paradoxically necessitates progressive or forward movement since the narrative strategies employed by Gothic texts make us accountable, both individually and collectively, for social exclusions and invisibilities, for what has been historically silenced, discarded, or denied. When the credits roll and the black mirror of the television screen casts only our reflection, we are forced to confront our own complacency in the horrific events that have just unfolded before our eyes, such that the Gothic works to remind us of our complicity in past abuses and oppressions that still hold power today.

In this way, the Antipodean presentation of the televisual Gothic exploits the quotidian nature of the medium to establish the uncanny as the defining feature of the gothic mode. The television – a staple fixture in most Australian and New Zealand homes – transmits long-standing national traumas into the private sphere, packaging them in serialized form, in endless continuations that may stretch over years, not unlike the experience of trauma itself. The televisual Gothic, then, as a domestic genre, signals a potential threat toward the very space in which it is consumed: in other words, it 'touches upon and skews the ordinary-world dimensions of domesticity, decorative form, and psychological balance; it troubles them with aberration, with something that ought not be there' (Lawn 15). In turn, the television – the ordinary domestic object at the heart of the home – becomes a malevolent portal between human and supernatural worlds, material and immaterial realms, inside and outside zones. As a result, the home is destabilized as the membrane between the real and the spectral is breached; the private space is penetrated by external threats that compromise the safety of both its on-screen and off-screen occupants, subjecting them to abnormal scrutiny and surveillance, and imperiling them in moments of madness, episodic patterns of chaos and confusion. Watching (and rewatching) this assault is a bodily experience that is marked by anticipation and unease; it is an encounter that requires vigilance, one in which our attention to suffering – and the responsibility that brings – is obligatory rather than optional. The 'gogglebox', in this respect, is not a neutral void or a venture into vacancy; the domestic space is not a space to rest or retreat. The chapters in this collection by Ella Jeffery and Lorna Piatti-Farnell both engage with this uncanniness of the domestic space: while Jeffery considers the paradoxical unhomeliness experienced by contestants on a popular renovation television show beamed nightly into the living rooms of its viewers, Piatti-Farnell observes how this uncanniness can become a humorous construction of the precise locality of the Gothic in satirical Kiwi cinema, so that 'through a good dose of humour', vampires 'are portrayed as part of the cultural fabric of Wellington, and emerge as increasingly "human" in their habits and routines'.

Granted, anxiety pervades the gothic home, as it always has, but more than this, in its recent Antipodean manifestation, domestic anxiety is a commentary on the impossibility of a productive future. Indeed, if there is a future for the family and by extension the nation, it is one that is monstrous. In this sense, New World colonial history, as has been popular in North American literature, television, and film, can be read as a gothic history, but so too is the future configured in gothic terms. In both local and global political terms, the Antipodean Gothic reads the future as a trauma waiting to happen, dreading the days and nights to come. In the televisual Gothic, this feeling of uncanny dread is heightened not only by the disruption of realist texts but by the genre's self-conscious manoeuvres, by the literal and metaphorical border crossings that global television allows. The television programmes examined in this collection reveal that the Australian Gothic, like its New Zealand counterpart, is a hybridized and increasingly transnational genre, one that reflects national interests and concerns while at the same time aligning with international markets and viewing trends in order to secure its transnational currency. The marketing of *The Kettering Incident* (2018), for example, as 'a cross between the American cult series *The X-Files*, with a little bit of *Twin Peaks*' (Turnbull and McCutcheon 197), or the promotion of *The Cry* (2018) as a 'Scaussie-Noir', a Scottish-Australian hybrid, reflects the myriad ways in which both series deliberately combine the familiar tropes of crime drama with local aesthetics, influences, and media traditions, thereby grounding both stories in popular Gothic settings, as Billy Stevenson, Kate Cantrell, Jennifer Lawn, and Liz Shek-Noble make clear in chapters addressing the specificity of Antipodean Gothic locations:

the Tasmanian hinterland and the Antarctic topos in *Kettering*, the rural backroads of country Victoria in *The Cry*, the New Zealand farmstead in *The Bad Seed*, the famous tourist location of Bondi Beach in *Top of the Lake* (2013; 2017). In this way, the Gothic not only evolves through transmutations from script to screen, and screen to stage, but through both its spatial and temporal displacement of domestic anxieties to remote locations, and its reconfiguration of gothic motifs for both a local and global audience. In this regard, Lawn's assertion that 'perhaps the best way to describe the gothic's location [...] is to say that it *could be* anywhere' (Lawn 14) speaks to the treatment of the Gothic as a mode rather than a genre, 'as a way of doing and seeing, adaptable across dislocations of culture, time, and space, rather than a substantive category' (14–15).

Indeed, the distinctive mode of the Antipodean Gothic is its attitude to the past and its unwelcome legacies. In fact, the Gothic, in general, can be read as a 'narrative of trauma', as Steven Bruhm has observed, adding that 'it is finally through trauma that we can best understand the contemporary Gothic and why we crave it' (268). Jerrold E. Hogle, too, asserts that 'Gothic fiction has always begun with trauma' (72), while Glennis Byron, in her meditation on the Global Gothic, suggests that in the case of Australia and New Zealand (and Canada), the Gothic frequently takes, as its setting, 'a modern urban development built over a site of past trauma' (375). Ken Gelder, too, agrees that the Antipodes are often depicted as places of 'abandoned homesteads' and 'obscure burial sites' (383), improvised graveyards that represent 'not a triumph of nation-building [...] but the loss of faith and reason' (381) and, we might add, the loss of stories that might have been told. To be sure, the commemoration or memorialization of 'disputed or contested pasts', as Maria Beville notes, 'frequently relies on gothic frames' (55). For Beville, the Gothic 'serves both as a part of our way of looking back and also a part of the way in which we carry the past forward into the future' (55). This is particularly true for the Gothic as it appears in the Antipodes, since its readiness for dealing with historical complexity and the haunting legacy of colonial violence means that the genre is 'particularly suited as a structural representation of trauma and oppression in Australia's fraught historical and social context' (Gildersleeve, 'Contemporary Australian Trauma' 92). Indeed, contemporary Gothic literature, film, and television in both Australia and New Zealand finds its most powerful function as 'a site for political resistance and for social and cultural disruption' (91). Such disruptions are perhaps clearest in the gothic bodies of the screen depictions discussed in this book: the sleepwalking bodies in Cantrell's chapter, symptomatic of psychological trauma; the abused and violated bodies to which Shek-Noble attends; the stereotyped bodies discussed by Corrine E. Hinton; the angry, vengeful, and violent bodies assessed by Jessica Gildersleeve, Nike Sulway, and Amanda Howell. Thus, revenge, trauma, and grief emerge as key themes in this collection, as gothic bodies, both alive and dead, yearn for attention, for recognition of their wounds and scars. The melancholy ghosts of the Antipodean Gothic rightfully recognize their troublesome histories as the troublesome present, demonstrating how 'gothic memory comes to be first constructed, and then remediated in social and cultural terms' (Beville 66).

Thus, this profound intertwining of contemporary Antipodean film and television with the Gothic may seem unusual, given what Jane Stadler terms the incongruity of the Australian landscape with the tropes of the genre as it appears in Europe (336). Indeed, such an observation was also made long ago by Frederick Sinnett, who lamented the impossibility of the Gothic in a country dispossessed of castles, embattled inheritance, and ancient relics:

> It must be granted, then, that we are quite debarred from all the interest to be extracted from any kind of archaeological accessories. No storied windows, richly dight, cast a dim, religious light over any Australian premises. There are no ruins for that rare old plant, the ivy green, to creep over and make his dainty meal of. No Australian author can hope to extricate his hero or heroine, however pressing the emergency may be, by means of a spring panel and a subterranean passage, or such like relics of feudal barons, and refuges of modern novelists, and the offspring of their imagination. There may be plenty of dilapidated buildings, but not one, the dilapidation of which is sufficiently venerable by age, to tempt the wandering footsteps of the most arrant parvenu of a ghost that ever walked by night. It must be admitted that Mrs Radcliffe's genius would be quite thrown away here; and we must reconcile ourselves to the conviction that the foundations of a second 'Castle of Otranto' can hardly be laid in Australia during our time. (98)

Yet, as the texts examined in this collection demonstrate, Australia and New Zealand have forged their own gothic landscapes. In the Upside Down, the coastal haven and the rural idyll are inverted, so that the sun-kissed beach, the tropical rainforest, and the sedate desert are all made horrific, as in *Wake in Fright* and *Wolf Creek* (2005). Moreover, sublime landscapes often reject or absorb the figure of the stranger or the foreigner, as in *Strangerland* (2015) (see Stadler), *Tidelands* (2018), and *Top of the Lake*. The carefully maintained suburban home conceals dark secrets, monstrous creatures, and supernatural forces as in *The Loved Ones* (2009), *The Babadook* (2013), *What We Do in the*

Shadows (2014), and *The Bad Seed* (2019). Antipodean land is also scarred by 'reminders of the tremendous primal forces' that have 'shaped' it – in New Zealand's case, the 'visible volcanic cones and craters [that] [prompt] the question of what lies beneath' (Conrich 394). These tropes figure the 'gothic migrations and mutations' (Lawn 11) of the genre as it makes itself at home in the Global South, adopting and adapting their origins in the European Gothic to forms more appropriate for Antipodean stories and histories. Thus, although Byron argues that 'what is identified as Gothic today is something increasingly detached from any specific historical, social, and cultural "origins"' (371), this collection posits that the Australian and New Zealand Gothic still insists upon a cultural and historical specificity. Jessica Balanzategui's chapter on the global and local intersections of the Antipodean Gothic on screen provides a comprehensive overview of the genre's global influences and connections, as well as its unique and particular characteristics as a localized practice. Patrick West and Luke C. Jackson take this a step further, considering how global ecological concerns are made manifest as Gothic in recent Australian film.

As Jonathan Rayner has it, even 'if certain generic features of horror and fantasy are common across texts divided by their geography, their history and the medium in which they are produced, an identification of the potential national specificity of Australasian Gothicism also assumes a new, particular, and cultural importance' (91). Indeed, the growing critical understanding of the nuances of the Gothic as it engages with the spiritual and cultural practices of Māori and Aboriginal and Torres Strait Islander story is just one such site of distinction from a more general 'Global Gothic' (see, for instance, Conrich; Borwein; Lawn), since it is a 'colonial imposition' to simply read such narratives as Gothic (Byron 370). In this collection, Emma Doolan's chapter on *Tidelands* considers the uses of cultural hybridity and its intersections with monstrosity in the Australian Gothic, while Emily Holland argues, via attention to uncanny space in Kiwi film, for recognizing the importance of a 'Māori Gothic'.

Contemporary Antipodean Gothic on Screen was written prior to and during the emergence of the COVID-19 pandemic. This has meant that the collection has not yet been able to attend to the specific impacts of this highly gothic virus – global, contagious, mutating – on contemporary Antipodean film and television. There is no doubt, however, that such work will arise, giving new meaning to old characterizations of the screen as a form of image addiction or image virus. Indeed, the viral influences of the pandemic on the particular social and cultural representation of the Gothic in Australia and New Zealand will be critical to trace as transmission, in its different forms, continues.

16

JESSICA GILDERSLEEVE AND KATE CANTRELL

Works Cited

Balanzategui, Jessica. 'The Babadook and the Haunted Space between High and Low Genres in the Australian Horror Tradition'. Studies in Australasian Cinema, vol. 11, no. 1, 2017, pp. 18–32.

Beville, Maria. 'Gothic Memory and the Contested Past: Framing Terror'. The Gothic and the Everyday: Living Gothic, edited by Lorna Piatti-Farnell and Maria Beville, Palgrave, 2014, pp. 52–68.

Borwein, Naomi Simone. 'Vampires, Shape-Shifters, and Sinister Light: Mistranslating Australian Aboriginal Horror in Theory and Literary Practice'. The Palgrave Handbook to Horror Literature, edited by Kevin Corstorphine and Laura R. Kremmel, Palgrave Macmillan, 2018, pp. 61–75.

Bruhm, Steven. 'The Contemporary Gothic: Why We Need It'. The Cambridge Companion to Gothic Fiction, edited by Jerrold E. Hogle, Cambridge UP, 2002, pp. 259–276.

Byron, Glennis. 'Global Gothic'. A New Companion to the Gothic, edited by David Punter, Wiley-Blackwell, 2012, pp. 369–378.

Collins, Felicity, and Therese Davis. 'Disputing History, Remembering Country in The Tracker and Rabbit-Proof Fence'. Australian Historical Studies, vol. 128, 2006, pp. 35–54.

Conrich, Ian. 'New Zealand Gothic'. A New Companion to the Gothic, edited by David Punter, Wiley-Blackwell, 2012, pp. 393–408.

Craven, Allison. 'A Happy and Instructive Haunting: Revising the Child, the Gothic, and the Australian Cinema Revival in Storm Boy (2019) and Picnic at Hanging Rock (2018)'. Journal of Australian Studies, vol. 45, no. 1, 2021, pp. 46–60.

Gelder, Ken. 'Australian Gothic'. A New Companion to the Gothic, edited by David Punter, Wiley-Blackwell, 2012, pp. 379–392.

Gelder, Ken, and Rachael Weaver. 'The Colonial Australian Gothic'. The Anthology of Colonial Australian Gothic Fiction, edited by Ken Gelder and Rachael Weaver, Melbourne UP, 2007, pp. 1–9.

Gildersleeve, Jessica. 'Contemporary Australian Trauma'. The Palgrave Handbook of Contemporary Gothic, edited by Clive Bloom, Palgrave Macmillan, 2020, pp. 91–104.

Gildersleeve, Jessica. '"Weird Melancholy" and the Modern Television Outback: Rage, Shame, and Violence in Wake in Fright and Mystery Road'. M/C Journal 22, no. 1. doi:10.5204/mcj.1500

Hills, Matt. 'Streaming Netflix Original Horror: Black Mirror, Stranger Things and Datafied TV Horror'. New Blood: Critical Approaches to Contemporary Horror, edited by Eddie Falvey, Joe Hickinbottom, and Jonathan Wroot, U of Wales P, 2020, pp. 125–144.

Hogle, Jerrold E. 'History, Trauma, and the Gothic in Contemporary Western Fictions'. *The Gothic World*, edited by Glennis Byron and Dale Townshend, Routledge, 2014, pp. 72–81.

Insight Guides. *Explore New Zealand.* Apa, 2015.

Lawn, Jennifer. 'Warping the Familiar'. *Gothic NZ: The Darker Side of Kiwi Culture*, edited by Misha Kavka, Jennifer Lawn, and Mary Paul, Otago UP, 2006, pp. 11–21.

Morris, Jan. *A Writer's World: Travels 1950–2000.* Faber and Faber, 2010.

Punter, David. 'Trauma, Gothic, Revolution'. *The Gothic and the Everyday: Living Gothic*, edited by Lorna Piatti-Farnell and Maria Beville, Palgrave, 2014, pp. 15–32.

Rayner, Jonathan. 'Gothic Definitions: The New Australian "Cinema of Horrors"'. *Antipodes*, vol. 25, no. 1, 2011, pp. 91–97.

Sinnett, Frederick. 'The Fiction Fields of Australia'. *Journal of Australasia*, vol. 1, 1856, pp. 97–105, pp. 199–208.

Smith, Andrew. *Gothic Literature.* Edinburgh UP, 2008.

Stadler, Jane. 'Atopian Landscapes: Gothic Tropes in Australian Cinema'. *A Companion to Australian Cinema*, edited by Felicity Collins, Jane Landman, and Susan Bye, Wiley, 2019, pp. 336–354.

Turnbull, Susan, and Marion McCutcheon. 'Outback Noir and Megashifts in the Global TV Crime Landscape'. *The Routledge Companion to Global Television*, edited by Shawn Shimpach, Routledge, 2020, pp. 190–202.

Wheatley, Helen. *Gothic Television.* Manchester UP, 2006.

About the Authors

Jessica Gildersleeve is Associate Professor of English Literature at the University of Southern Queensland. She is the author and editor of several books, including *Christos Tsiolkas: The Utopian Vision* (Cambria 2017), *Don't Look Now* (Auteur 2017), and *The Routledge Companion to Australian Literature* (Routledge 2021).

Kate Cantrell is a Lecturer in Writing, Editing, and Publishing at the University of Southern Queensland. Her research interests include narrative accounts of illness, immobility, and displacement. Her short stories, essays, and poems have appeared in *Overland*, *Meanjin*, and *Westerly*, and she writes regularly for *Times Higher Education*.

Part I

Gothic Places

1. Unsettled Waters: The Postcolonial Gothic of *Tidelands*

Emma Doolan

Abstract

Tidelands (2018), the first standalone Australian production in the Netflix Originals portfolio, imports the monstrous figure of the siren from Greek mythology to the South-East Queensland coast, unsettling not only the iconic Australian beach, but also the domestic television genres of the beachside soapie and crime drama. However, while *Tidelands* innovates in Australian Gothic, it also continues to engage with – or become entangled within – some of the genre's oldest preoccupations: nation, inheritance, belonging, and colonial guilt. *Tidelands*'s spaces function as gothic heterotopias, reflecting tensions between multicultural, Indigenous, and Anglo-Celtic Australia which the series attempts to resolve by replacing First Nations peoples with the half-siren Tidelanders, imagining a future in which hybridity and assimilation erase the need for Reconciliation.

Keywords: Australian Gothic; heterotopia; Netflix; Queensland; beach; sirens

Tidelands (2018), the first standalone Australian production in the Netflix Originals portfolio, represents a new kind of Australian Gothic for an international border-crossing digital age. Filmed on Queensland's Sunshine Coast, the eight-episode series leaves behind Australian Gothic's traditional home in the outback and bush to focus on the everyday space of the beach. Importing the monstrous figure of the siren from Greek mythology to this new site unsettles not only the iconic Australian beach (as both setting and symbol) but also the popular domestic television genres of the beachside soapie and crime drama. However, even while this new gothic hybrid attempts to move beyond the genre's traditional trappings, the series continues to engage

Gildersleeve, J. and K. Cantrell (eds.), *Screening the Gothic in Australia and New Zealand: Contemporary Antipodean Film and Television*. Taylor & Francis Group, 2022
DOI 10.5117/9789463721141_CH01

with – or becomes entangled within – some of Australian Gothic's oldest preoccupations: nationhood, inheritance, belonging, and colonial guilt.

Postcolonial gothic genres, such as the Australian Gothic, typically work to critique the mechanisms and aftereffects of colonization, and to reveal the unsavoury matter of the nation's colonial past. In doing so, the genre is able to effect a kind of restitution; according to Gina Wisker, postcolonial Gothic 'reconfigures spaces and places, returning the value they had to the people who initially were the traditional owners of the land' (108). However, *Tidelands* operates in a different mode, using gothic tropes and techniques not to acknowledge but to efface First Nations peoples' experiences of violent dispossession and displacement. The series thus rewrites Australia's colonial history in terms of a violent oppression of the half-siren Tidelanders by colonial powers. Although *Tidelands* has been praised for its diverse casting (see, for example, Tedmanson; Turner), and its directors include First Nations filmmaker Catriona McKenzie and Fijian-New Zealander Toa Fraser, the series avoids explicitly addressing race or the dispossession of First Nations peoples. The supernatural figure of the siren instead stands in for, and obscures, First Nations experience.

Reading *Tidelands*'s spaces as gothic heterotopias, distorted images of the Australian nation, reveals the series' unease with questions of Aboriginal sovereignty and white Australian belonging in a postcolonial, multicultural nation. Michel Foucault defines heterotopias as 'other spaces', or 'cultural counter-sites' that reflect a society back to itself in distorted form (Foucault, 'Of Other Spaces' [1986] 24). The Gothic has a long history of projecting its anxieties into such spaces, 'invok[ing] its fearful Others by displacing melodramatic menaces backward in time and sideways in space, always over the border, always somewhere else' (Luckhurst 62). Indeed, according to Fred Botting ('Power in the Darkness'; 'In Gothic Darkly'), all the classic spaces of the Gothic – its castles, abbeys, ruins, labyrinths, dungeons, and wild, sublime landscapes – are heterotopias. The 'Otherness' represented by and contained within such heterotopias 'enables the differentiation, ordering, and policing of the limits of their own space as well as the boundaries of society' (Botting, 'Power in the Darkness' 243). However, in containing and reflecting the abject matter of a society, heterotopias expose a culture's values and anxieties; heterotopias thus subversively 'reveal or represent something about the society in which they reside through the way in which they incorporate and stage the very contradictions that this society produces but is unable to resolve' (Foucault, 'Of Other Spaces' [2008] 25n15). *Tidelands*'s heterotopic spaces reveal the nation's ongoing anxieties over belonging, race, sexuality, identity, and reconciliation.

In its heterotopic spaces and on the racialized, gendered bodies of its characters, *Tidelands* constructs a fantasy of a post-racial Australia where assimilation and hybridity can resolve the uncanny state that Ken Gelder and Jane M. Jacobs have argued postcolonial Australians occupy – simultaneously 'innocent' and 'guilty', 'in place' and 'out of place' (24). *Tidelands* seeks to resolve ambivalent postcolonial guilt and belonging by collapsing the native and foreign within the uncanny figure of the white-skinned siren. The series' protagonist, Cal McTeer, further blurs these boundaries by combining her maternal siren heritage with a paternal Anglo-Celtic convict lineage. At the end of the series, it is Cal who is chosen to lead the fictional Queensland town of Orphelin Bay and its diverse inhabitants into the future, leaving First Nations sovereignty a spectre that haunts the series' ambivalent resolution of Australian anxieties surrounding inheritance, belonging, and guilt.

Gothic Television

Tidelands belongs to a new international wave of gothic, horror, and supernatural television for the streaming era, a 'Netflix Gothic' comprised of programmes such as *The Haunting of Hill House* (2018) and *The Haunting of Bly Manor* (2020), *The Chilling Adventures of Sabrina* (2018–2020), and *Stranger Things* (2016–). Although Netflix has previously purchased Australian content and partnered in joint ventures on Australian television programmes, such as *Pine Gap* (2018) and the second and third seasons of *Glitch* (2015–2019), both coproduced with the ABC, *Tidelands* is the first Netflix Original to be produced in an Australian location by an Australian production company. The series was originally funded by Screen Australia in 2014 with Netflix rival Amazon on board (Keast, 'Netflix Announces') after it was initially turned down by local broadcasters (Keast, 'Follow the Sun' 23). The series' production company, Hoodlum Entertainment, avows an 'outward and international focus' (Keast, 'Outward Focus' 30) directed towards the European and American markets, maintaining offices in both Brisbane and Los Angeles (at Disney Studios). For producer Tracey Robertson, *Tidelands*' strengths lie in its 'supernatural elements and strong female characters' (30) along with the 'primeval landscapes of Queensland' (Keast, 'Netflix Announces'), unfamiliar to international audiences. The Queensland filming locations provide the series with a unique aesthetic, particularly among Netflix's suite of gothic television series. The novel location, as well as a cast comprised of Australian favourites, including Alex Dimitriades and Peter O'Toole, and overseas actors, such as Elsa Pataky (Spain) and

Marco Pigossi (Brazil), positions the series to appeal to a broad market on the Netflix platform.

Television is a key medium through which the contemporary Gothic is consumed, aligning with, as Eddie Robson points out, 'Gothic's heritage as part of popular culture' (249). With the advent of international streaming services, television is also 'the most accessible gothic media' (Gildersleeve, 'Weird Melancholy'). Gothic has always been a mobile and adaptable genre, crossing national boundaries to migrate all over the world; however, in the twenty-first century, television expands its territory more than ever, providing more opportunities for gothic productions, and making local products more widely available.

Perhaps paradoxically, streaming television services also cement the Gothic's position as a domestic genre. Helen Wheatley has argued that gothic television represents 'the most domestic of genres on the most domestic of media' (25), making television 'the ideal medium for the Gothic' (1). The domestic space within which television is viewed resonates with the Gothic's key preoccupations: the home, the family, the familiar, and the uncanniness of the everyday. By drawing implicit parallels between viewers' own homes and the homes on their screens, gothic television 'emphasizes a potential threat towards the very space in which it is being viewed' (Wheatley 15). *Tidelands* is domestic in the sense that it is consumed within viewers' own homes and its plot focuses on issues of home and homeliness in terms of both family and nation. But the series – despite its international platform – is also domestic in the sense of belonging to a local tradition of Australian Gothic on screen.

The Australian Gothic screen tradition is often associated with the 'New Wave' of Australian cinema in the 1970s (see Rayner 91), for example the films of Peter Weir, such as *Picnic at Hanging Rock* (1975) and *The Cars That Ate Paris* (1974). Australian Gothic is now experiencing something of a small-screen renaissance with recent television series including ABC's *Glitch* and *Mystery Road* (2018–), Fox Showcase's *The Kettering Incident* (2017), and the Stan Original series *The Gloaming* (2020), as well as television remakes of genre classics *Picnic at Hanging Rock* (2018) and *Wake in Fright* (2017). *Tidelands* differs from many of these texts in that it is, as the Netflix branding promises, original: not an adaptation or continuation of an earlier work. Instead, *Tidelands* constructs a new narrative that attempts to move beyond the traditional concerns and trappings of the genre. Jessica Gildersleeve posits that the 'tendency towards adaptation (or mutation) in the Australian gothic film [...] suggests the desire to return to and rework the past' ('Contemporary Australian Trauma' 92). However, *Tidelands*, rather than evidencing a desire to continue engaging with, problematizing, and reworking debates within Australian history and the Australian gothic tradition, attempts to simply move beyond them, constructing an alternative history that obscures and overwrites the colonial past.

As well as collapsing the distance between the gothic narrative and the real domestic space in which it is viewed, gothic television uncannily collapses borders between staple television genres (Wheatley 8). *Tidelands* unsettles the boundaries of Australian Gothic by bringing it into contact with the familiar domestic genres of the beachside soapie – in the vein of *Home and Away* (1988–), *SeaChange* (1998–2000), and *Puberty Blues* (2012–2014) – and the crime drama, such as *Underbelly* (2008–2013) and *Secrets and Lies* (2014–2016). In gothic television, the uncanny erupts where 'the familiar traditions and conventions of television are made strange, when television's predominant genres and styles are both referred to and inverted' (8). *Tidelands*'s Orphelin Bay is *Home and Away*'s Summer Bay if it were inhabited by the criminals of *Underbelly* and the monsters of the Gothic. This blending of the familiar with the criminal and supernatural is an uncanny reminder that the Australian beach has never been a site as idyllic and uncomplicated as tourism adverts would have us believe. Elizabeth Ellison has written of the Australian beach as a 'badland' (120) site where natural and criminal dangers form a seething undertow to picture-perfect sun, surf, and sand. *Tidelands* emphasizes such uncanny aspects of the Australian beach, embodying its danger and allure in the monstrous sirens that haunt Queensland's waters, and the half-siren Tidelanders who stroll its white sands.

The resulting aesthetic is unlike the Australian Gothic of *Wake in Fright* (1971) or *Mad Max* (1979) with their 'remote and [...] deranged outback locations' (Gelder 121) and is equally unlike the 'Weird Melancholy' (116) of the Australian bush evident in *Picnic at Hanging Rock* (1975) and other classics of the genre. Rather than drawing on what is weird or unfamiliar about the Australian landscape, *Tidelands* unsettles the familiar, evoking especially the idealized images of Australian tourism campaigns. The frequent spectacle of Adrielle's toned beach body striding the white sands recalls Tourism Australia's mid-2000s campaign in which a bikini-clad Lara Bingle stands on the beach to ask: 'So where the bloody hell are you?' *Tidelands* inverts this familiar image to give us a monstrous beach babe on an uncanny beach. The uncanny here emerges not from what is 'unknown and unfamiliar' (Freud 124) impressing us with terror, but rather from that which is known and familiar revealing itself to be, at heart, unfamiliar and strange.

The series' uncanny effect is intensified by its casting of actors familiar to Australians from well-known beachside soaps and crime dramas. Lead actress Charlotte Best is known for her roles in *Home and Away* and *Puberty Blues*, and other cast members are familiar from their appearances in popular series including *Underbelly, Neighbours* (1985–), *Blue Heelers* (1994–2006), *Water Rats* (1996–2001), *Stingers* (1998–2004), and *Cloudstreet* (2011). Even Spanish actress Elsa Pataky is familiar to viewers as the wife of Australian actor Chris Hemsworth and frequently appears in tabloids when she is photographed around her home in Byron Bay, New South Wales. Writing on the Australian horror film *Wolf Creek* (2005), Gildersleeve argues that the transformation of John Jarrett from the familiar symbol of 'domestic comfort and inoffensive family programming' in *Better Homes and Gardens* (1995–) into the predatory outback stranger 'constituted an uncanny turn which produced for the viewer a shock similar to that experienced by the characters, as the jovial outback stranger turns into the perpetrator of nightmarish horror' ('Contemporary Australian Trauma' 94). *Tidelands*'s casting of familiar actors in a series about murderous supernatural sirens enacts a similarly uncanny turn, unsettling both genre and setting.

Gothic Reflections of the Nation

Although the beachside location of *Tidelands* represents a fresh take on Australian Gothic and the series attempts to escape many of the genre's longstanding concerns, examining the series' central spaces as gothic heterotopias reveals the extent to which *Tidelands* remains caught up in the genre's traditional preoccupations – colonization, race, exile, and home. The series' ambivalence towards these topics, and its imagining of a new, post-racial future for the nation are not only played out in spaces that both reflect and unsettle everyday life in Australia, but also on the bodies of its characters, who can be read as different dimensions of the multicultural nation and its possible futures.

Set in present-day Queensland, *Tidelands* follows ex-convict Cal (Calliope) McTeer who, upon her release from a Brisbane prison, returns to her hometown, Orphelin Bay. Cal's late father, Pat McTeer (Dustin Clare), smuggled drugs produced by the mysterious, cult-like Tidelanders who live in a commune outside town and her brother, Augie (Aaron Jakubenko), has taken over the family business, but his hold over the gang is challenged by his own men, the Tidelanders, and a Serbian gang looking to take over. Cal means to claim her share of the siblings' inheritance, but soon discovers this entails much more than her father's boat, house, and business: Cal is a Tidelander, born of a siren mother and nameless local fisherman lured to his death, and adopted by Pat McTeer.

After discovering her siren heritage, Cal is drawn to the Tidelander commune, L'Attente, compelled to understand who she is and where she belongs. The Tidelanders are a multicultural enclave of beautiful, exotic half-sirens; the cast includes Gadigal actress Madeleine Madden, Brazilian Marco Pigossi, Asian-Australian Jet Tranter, British-Indian Dalip Sondhi, and Filipina-Australian Chloe De Los Santos. The Tidelanders are ruled by a beautiful, ageless queen, Adrielle Cuthbert (Pataky), who styles herself their 'mother', and the Tidelanders, like Cal, are orphans abandoned by their siren mothers on Australia's shores. Just as Augie's hold on Orphelin Bay is challenged both by foreign interlopers and from within his own gang, Adrielle's leadership is also contested by Tidelander Violca (Madden) and undermined by a prophecy that Cal is destined to overthrow her.

The spaces of Orphelin Bay and L'Attente can be read as microcosms of the nation: heterotopic space represents a small 'parcel of the world [that] is the totality of the world' (Foucault, 'Of Other Spaces' [2008] 20). In Orphelin Bay, a representation of the Australian nation is collected, along with its anxieties and desires. The series was filmed on location on the Sunshine Coast, Stradbroke Island, and in the Greater Brisbane area. As a result, the show's locations are homely, familiar from Australians' everyday lives and domestic soaps like *Home and Away*. Orphelin Bay includes such essential Australian spaces as the local pub, the police station, and an industrial district (where the McTeer gang runs its drug operation). It also includes iconic regional landmarks such as Queenslander houses, cane fields, and the shining white sands and pristine surf of Australia's east coast beaches.

These sites are part of what Allison Craven, writing on the 1998 film *Radiance*, identifies as a 'regional sign system' (45). In *Radiance*, which is set in North Queensland, the Queenslander house, sugar cane fields, and beach are regional icons that local audiences experience as familiar. But the film works to unsettle this familiarity by transforming these signs into gothic symbols, thereby undermining myths of Queensland as paradise and evoking 'home as gothic and dystopian' (46). A similar process is at work in *Tidelands*; Australian and international audiences alike experience the locations of *Tidelands* as familiar or ordinarily recognizable whether through experience, tourism campaigns, or domestic television products. Even L'Attente – constructed as Orphelin Bay's uncanny Other, in which its values and norms can be inverted and contested – represents a familiar element of Australia's eastern coastal and hinterland regions, known for their 'hippie' populations and alternative lifestyles (Doolan 182). But these familiar spaces are rendered unfamiliar and dangerous by the presence of the half-siren Tidelanders and the human criminals of Orphelin Bay. Even as L'Attente functions as Orphelin Bay's uncanny Other, the town itself is positioned as a deviant, distorted Other to everyday Australia: a gothic heterotopia.

Policing Permeable Boundaries

Heterotopic space is both open and closed, penetrable and isolated. Appearances of accessibility are illusory; only by having certain permission or knowledge can one truly enter. Heterotopias' boundaries of inclusion are linked to ideas of purity and hygiene: only 'family' can belong; others can only ever be 'passing visitor[s]' (Foucault, 'Of Other Spaces' [2008]). Both Orphelin Bay and L'Attente are seemingly open spaces – one a seaside tourist town and the other an open-air commune – but both strictly police their boundaries, setting up divisions between who belongs and who does not.

Orphelin Bay is bounded by extensive cane fields, and the bus from Brisbane stops seven kilometres shy of town. Cal, arriving home from prison, must make her way on foot until she is picked up by a passing police cruiser, driven by her childhood friend, Corey Welch (Mattias Inwood). Although Corey is not fully inducted into the secrets of the corrupt local constabulary, he polices the town's boundaries as an agent of the white, patriarchal, colonial law that holds sway in Orphelin Bay. At the town's boundary, visitors are greeted with a sign, set against a backdrop of white sand, gum trees, and paperbarks, that reads 'Orphelin Bay: Queensland's Best Kept Secret'. To a casual outsider, the town appears to be a welcoming seaside getaway, but only locals are permitted access to its criminal and supernatural secrets.

L'Attente is similarly separated from the comparatively ordinary space of Orphelin Bay, and it too polices its borders, but in a far more violent fashion. In episode three, Cal attempts to reach L'Attente but the commune is located on the other side of an estuary. The path overland is blocked by a locked gate hung with dead owls and charms, and a sign warning trespassers to 'Keep Out'. Instead, she steals a boat and approaches L'Attente by sea, an action that reaffirms both her convict and siren heritages. The commune is a labyrinth, its buildings a mix of shanties, caravans, cabins, and beached boats serving as living quarters. Its winding pathways, lit by strings of lanterns, blend into forest and sand. At the commune's heart is the Queen's mansion, a gothic reimagining of a Queensland beach house.

Although Adrielle's house is open to all Tidelanders, and is the location where guests are received, announcements made, and punishments meted out, Adrielle's quarters are strictly off limits. Trespassing here results in violent punishment – one young Tidelander's eye is gouged out after he enters to spy on Adrielle ('Orphans of L'Attente'). A further inaccessible space is located via Adrielle's quarters, where a secret door leads to the dungeon where Adrielle keeps the former queen enslaved as her seer. This is also where Adrielle stores the fragments of an ancient horn she is covertly engaged in reassembling. The horn can be read as a symbol of the multicultural Australian nation: an artefact whose pieces have been scattered all around the globe, and which, once united through blood and sacrifice, will be able to call home the siren mothers. Only through the return of the sirens will Tidelanders gain a sense of legitimacy and origins, and with them the right to belonging they crave.

Only with difficulty is Cal able to enter L'Attente and gain knowledge of Adrielle's plan; as a hybrid figure she can cross between Orphelin Bay and L'Attente, but she struggles to find a sense of belonging or acceptance in either space. In episode five, 'The Calling', Cal tells Tidelander Dylan (Marco Pigossi) that she does not 'belong' in Orphelin Bay, to which Dylan responds, 'You don't belong here [in L'Attente]'. Cal counters: 'Well, I need to fit somewhere'. She learns that although the commune may be physically accessible, she cannot access its secrets or attain acceptance. For instance, while she can walk straight up to the jetty, at the threshold of the commune she is attacked by Adrielle's lieutenant, Leandra (Jet Tranter). When Cal is allowed in, she finds the other Tidelanders hostile and secretive. As Adrielle, speaking of Cal, insists in a later episode, 'She's not one of us. She might be a Tidelander, but she'll never be one of us' ('The Prophecy'). To be sure, Cal, a perfectly hybrid figure, remains not 'one of us', but in the end she is shown to be a figure for 'all of us', collapsing the boundaries between insider and outsider that L'Attente and Orphelin Bay work to maintain.

Spaces of Deviance

As well as differentiating insider from outsider, heterotopias also function to contain those peoples and behaviours that are deemed 'deviant in rela-tion to the mean or required norm' (Foucault, 'Of Other Spaces' [2008] 18). Orphelin Bay and L'Attente both contest the 'normal' status of the other – and the Australian nation they reflect – through the different ways that criminal, sexual, and racial difference are positioned as deviant in each space. Criminal and sexual activities that are conducted under partial cover in Orphelin Bay are pursued openly in L'Attente, and each space also reflects, to different degrees, the nation's multiculturalism. Whereas Orphelin Bay is a predominantly white, Anglo-Celtic space with a few characters of First Nations, Asian, and European heritage, L'Attente is a far more diverse space where characters of European, Latin, African, South Asian, and East Asian appearance mingle and speak in a variety of accents. The tension between the two spaces hinges not only on what is considered 'normal' or 'deviant', or on who is an 'insider' and who an 'outsider', but also on who is 'native' or 'foreign'. Tidelanders, the offspring of Orphelin Bay townsmen and the monstrous sirens, blur the boundaries between these categories. Although their accents and ethnicities mark them as 'foreign', their siren heritage positions Tidelanders as 'native', elementally at home in Queensland's waters.

Sexuality is one locus of *Tidelands*'s anxiety over questions of deviancy and normality, and the show was released in the wake of Australia's divisive marriage equality debate throughout 2016 and 2017. In Orphelin Bay, sexuality is patriarchal, heteronormative, and monogamous. Extramarital affairs are conducted secretly: Augie's liaisons with Adrielle and the wife of one of his gang members occur out of the public eye. Likewise, the homosexual and interracial relationship between corrupt police sergeant, Paul Murdoch (Alex Dimitriades), and Adrielle's lieutenant, Lamar (Dalip Sondhi), is kept secret. In L'Attente, however, sexuality is openly explored. Homosexual, bisexual, and polyamorous relationships are the norm, and sexual activity takes place not behind closed doors, but in the open – on the verandah of the main house and on the beach. For example, in episode one, the Tidelanders celebrate Adrielle's return from an overseas trip by staging an orgy in the common area outside the mansion. Sirens possess power over water, and this also affords them the power to make a person's 'blood rise', an ability that can be used for either pleasure or pain. Like their mythical forebears, sirens can lure men with song and sexuality. Part of Cal's journey is learning to master her siren powers. Her own sexual affairs with both Dylan and Corey signal not only her 'deviant' Tidelander nature, but also her position as a hybrid figure suspended between L'Attente and Orphelin Bay.

Similarly, in Orphelin Bay, Augie's criminal enterprise is undertaken secretly (under the cover of the family fishing co-op) even though it is implicitly sanctioned by the police on his payroll. Augie's criminality is not wholly deviant in an Australian context, where criminality is to some degree endorsed by a nationalist tradition of reverence for the nation's convict roots and for criminal heroes such as Ned Kelly (indeed, Augie can be read as an analogue for Kelly, as I will discuss shortly). The criminality of the Tidelanders, on the other hand, is deviant in the way it is openly conducted – it is monstrous and out of control. In L'Attente, drug production is not covert, but is the Tidelanders' acknowledged occupation. Each week, the Tidelanders line up in the open to receive wages for this work. And whereas Augie uses violence only as a last resort, Adrielle regularly employs both physical and sexual violence, as do the Tidelanders under her command.

The spaces and bodies showcased in the series' opening scenes demonstrate Tidelanders' violence, monstrosity, and sexual allure, as well as pointing towards *Tidelands*'s ambivalent racial discourse. Episode one, 'Home', opens with a quotation from Longfellow – 'My soul is full of longing for the secret of the sea' – superimposed over shots of the turbulent waters of a stormy nighttime ocean. Beneath the waves, a woman swims past. Her body is seen in close-up fragments (a technique mimicked in the opening credits, which reveal glimpses of a siren's ghostly white body underwater). The woman untethers a collection of barrels bobbing near the sea floor and rises with them to the surface. This is the Tidelander, Leandra, Adrielle's lieutenant, retrieving a stash of drugs to sell to the McTeer gang. But on a nearby fishing vessel, Zach Maney (Sam Foster) – one of Augie's men – is spying in order to learn where the Tidelanders keep their drugs. Leandra and Dylan spot him, but before he can flee, the ocean roils up and causes Maney to smack his head against the cabin wall. A moment later, Leandra is in the doorway, naked except for a pair of bikini bottoms. Immediately, she mimics the punch delivered by the ocean, landing her own hit on Maney's face: she and the sea are perfectly attuned. She overpowers Maney, then mesmerizes him, so that he kneels before her while she carves out his eyes with her fingernails.

The Longfellow quotation, inscribed across the surface of Queensland's coastal waters, acts to claim or colonize the ocean as a European, even English, space through the connection to a Romantic poetic tradition (despite the fact that Longfellow was American). It also establishes the ocean as a gothic space of secrets and mysterious allure – a trope Emily Alder identifies with the tradition of 'Oceanic Gothic', in which the sea is an ambiguous, unknowable space of 'gothic potential' (2), whose alluring yet dangerous 'depths conceal monsters, secrets, bodies' (1). Leandra, just as dangerous and alluring, is linked elementally with the ocean through the connection of her naked body with the water and through the synchronicity of her movements. She is beautiful, inhuman, and merciless: an embodiment of the monstrous feminine and the ocean itself.

Leandra is played by an Asian-Australian actress, and in the image of her emerging from Australian waters to attack the working-class, flannel-clad

Anglo-Celtic Maney, there is an implicit link with Australia's historically xenophobic fears of Asian migration and takeover. In this way, Leandra can be read as a 'sinister Asian' figure who threatens Australia from across the ocean and from within. Marion Decome sees such figures as 'the embodiment of the fears and anxiety of the Western world, losing power on the international scene' (119). Sinister Asian figures are often constructed as 'inscrutable and violent' (Riwoe), and women may be ethereal, or exotic and erotic (Decome 127). Leandra encompasses all these tropes, but Tidelanders come from a range of racial and ethnic backgrounds and therefore signify a diverse range of national prejudices and anxieties.

Like all gothic monsters, Tidelanders and their siren mothers have a complex signification. As Jack Halberstam argues, 'gothic monsters are overdetermined [...] open to numerous interpretations [...] because monsters transform the fragments of otherness into one body' (92), making this 'available for any number of meanings' (2). Sirens and Tidelanders are not simply 'foreigners' or immigrants; they are also constructed as indigenous through their elemental connection to the sea. Leandra is *at home* in the ocean, a 'native', whereas the Anglo-Celtic Maney is overcome because of his failure to be similarly attuned to the sea's movements. Sirens' and Tidelanders' claim to 'native' status is further illustrated in episode four, 'Don't Trust Humans', when Adrielle teaches Cal about her Tidelander heritage. The scene takes place in a rainforest gorge beyond the commune – a heterotopic hinterland that functions as a 'gothic repository' (Doolan 175). In heterotopic space, time undergoes an 'absolute break' with traditional or outside time (Foucault, 'Of Other Spaces' [2008] 20), and in L'Attente, the past lies very close to the present. For instance, when Adrielle directs Cal to touch the ground, Cal sees visions of the past – visions literally contained within the landscape, as Ross Gibson argues is the case in 'badland' spaces, and in Queensland in particular, where colonial and contemporary times are 'coeval' (53).

In Cal's vision, colonial and contemporary time telescopes, and she sees uniformed police and others in colonial settlers' garb shooting at men, women, and children fleeing through the gorge. These are Orphelin Bay locals in the late nineteenth century, driving out Tidelanders. Conspicuous among the Tidelanders is a young Adrielle, fair-skinned and fair-haired. Most of the persecuted crowd are also of European appearance, and yet the scene strongly recalls instances of colonial massacres of First Nations people. Adrielle tells Cal, 'It's an old story every continent knows, of men coming in the dark before dawn. Herding up the people they hate, they fear, and killing them all' ('Don't Trust Humans'). Only she and two others survive the massacre and live to establish L'Attente and continue rescuing the sirens' abandoned offspring.

This moment collapses the series' gothic storyline and characters into the monstrous material of Australia's own colonial history, and also constructs a victimological narrative underpinning the Tidelanders' right to belong. Ann Curthoys has shown how white Australia has constructed its belonging via a canon of victimological narratives beginning with convict history and the experiences of colonists on Australia's 'hostile' (8) frontier and continuing through narratives of the ANZAC soldiers and even the death of Phar Lap (10). The sufferings of white Australia's forebears, their victim status, serve to 'warrant' (4) and obscure their aggression against others – namely, First Nations people. The victimological narrative of the Tidelanders is not used to justify aggression against First Nations people, but to entirely overwrite and efface that aggression by replacing Aboriginal victims with (European) Tidelander victims, thereby according Tidelanders an ersatz native status.

Adrielle demonstrates the Tidelanders' uncanny native and foreign coding. With her Spanish accent and British surname, Adrielle Cuthbert becomes a sort of hybrid or generic 'European'. In episode four, 'Don't Trust Humans', she reveals to Cal that her father was 'a young naval lieutenant, assigned to a convict vessel', and that she picked up her accent from the Tidelanders' former queen, who raised her. Adrielle, then, is a direct descendant of colonizers, yet through her siren blood she can also claim 'native' status and sovereign rights. Her unageing body connects her directly to the victimization and persecution of Tidelanders, asserting her right to belong through suffering (Curthoys 3). Her body also connects her to another tradition of white Australian belonging: her blonde beach waves and toned, tanned body position Adrielle as the quintessential Aussie 'beach babe', part of the class of 'strong, fit, well-muscled, and racially pure white body' that Aileen Moreton Robinson sees as staging a perpetual colonization of the Australian beach ('White Possessive' 37). Adrielle is frequently seen strolling the shoreline, and the beach is also the space where her sovereignty will be legitimized when she calls the sirens back. Her claims to belonging in this space are multiple and conflicting.

Adrielle's mansion in L'Attente likewise reflects this complexity. Its weatherboard exterior and position on the water's edge evoke the classic Queensland beach house; however, its slate-tiled roof and wood-panelled interiors recall the architecture of a Victorian Gothic mansion, while the dungeon beneath connects it to an even older European Gothic tradition. The building also draws in imagery of the sea to assert an essential connection between the two spaces, conveying a sense that both the house (and its inhabitants) belong 'naturally' to the place. A timber beam above the front door resembles the spar on a ship's prow, and the mansion is painted in underwater colours of deep blue and green. Stained-glass panes throughout depict images of mermaids and the ocean. The décor is 'exotic' and colonial: seashells, peacock statuettes, and communal cushioned lounges in a vaguely Eastern style contrast against gilt picture frames and mahogany stair-rails. Adrielle's house is simultaneously the familiar Queensland beach house, and the castle of the foreign, colonial power, the European queen – both native and foreign.

The Orphelin Bay counterpart to Adrielle's mansion is the McTeer Queenslander. In contrast to the opulent formality of Adrielle's mansion, the McTeer house is homely and lived in. Its walls are hung with family photographs and shelves overflow with well-thumbed books. The house backs onto a private jetty, and surfaces throughout are cluttered with oceanic artefacts: seashells, nautical instruments, models of ships. Pat McTeer's study resembles a ship captain's quarters, with a drop-leaf desk, old radio, stacks of documents, and a battered tobacco tin containing his pipe. Cal's own connection to the sea, through both her maternal siren and paternal sailor's heritage, is asserted through her comfort in, and her right – via inheritance – to this space. As with Adrielle's mansion, the house's connections to the ocean claim its inhabitants' belonging and right to place.

However, the McTeer Queenslander does not mix in the foreign elements that Adrielle's mansion includes, and it was filmed on location at a real house in Shorncliffe (Moon). In comparison, Adrielle's mansion, constructed over a period of nine weeks for the show (Dunn), appears fantastically unreal. Unreality and artifice are key elements of gothic aesthetics and plots; the genre repeatedly and deliberately stages acts of fakery, often presenting fakes that are themselves based on fakes. Jerrold E. Hogle argues that such gothic 're-faking of fakery' (500) animates both nostalgia for, and revulsion towards, the counterfeit original; it uncannily 'feels the draw of what the past counterfeit seems to promise and yet rejects many of the cultural conditions or beliefs that once offered that promise' (506). Whereas the McTeer Queenslander appears as purely and authentically Australian, Adrielle's opulent yet fake mansion, with its foreign trappings, is an uncanny gothic counterfeit that serves both to animate desire and nostalgia for the colonial past that Adrielle represents, while also drawing attention to the falseness of this picture and the conditions it entails – domination by a violent, autocratic foreign power. The fraudulence of Adrielle's house points towards the illegitimacy of her claims to sovereignty over the Tidelanders and the futures of either L'Attente or Orphelin Bay.

The name Orphelin Bay phonetically resonates with the word 'orphan', and L'Attente, likewise, means 'waiting'. Tidelanders, like the townsfolk, are orphans and exiles. Tidelander Bill Sentelle (Peter O'Brien) tells Cal they are 'stuck there' ('The Calling'), waiting for their siren mothers to return and bring a sense of legitimacy and belonging. He also tells Cal that she may be different, because she was not raised a Tidelander. Cal represents a new generation of hybrid Australians, able to resolve the nation's racial fissures by uniting the diverse elements of Orphelin Bay – and the Australian nation it reflects – within one character. Cal's hybrid – yet still white – body offers a means of moving forward into a new, unified future. But in order for the new future to be ushered in, the past and its agents of power must be defeated or left behind.

Figures of Alternative Power

Botting argues that gothic heterotopias are inhabited by figures of alternative power, represented as threatening because they are images of an 'authority that must not be recognized [...] power that cannot be sanctioned' ('Power in the Darkness' 258). L'Attente and Orphelin Bay are replete with such figures, each representing a different kind of Australian belonging and a future authority: Adrielle, the colonial Queen; Augie, the 'native born' Australian son; Violca, the First Nations Tidelander; and Cal, the figure who mediates between them. Adrielle, Augie, and Violca are each shown to be unfit to lead; at the series' end, it is Cal, who unites in one body all the fragments of *Tidelands*'s society, for whom the sirens come home.

Augie McTeer's right to belong to and lead Orphelin Bay is asserted through his connection to Ned Kelly: white Australia's 'secular saint' (McGrath 33) and 'native son' (31). With his criminal and Anglo-Celtic heritage – Gaelic surname, fair skin, reddish hair, and blue eyes – Augie is easily read as a modern-day Kelly. Ann McGrath argues that Kelly is a symbol of Australian belonging, 'asserting the possibility of white Indigeneity' (31), and even able to transcend divisions of ethnicity and race to stand for all Australians. Kelly's armour and mask associate him with nobility through the romantic iconography of the knight, while his criminality, larrikin masculinity, and Irish heritage connect him with immigrant tales of exile, political oppression, and anti-authoritarian attitudes. Deborah Bird Rose has shown that Kelly even functions as a mediating figure for some First Nations people – a Christ-like 'moral European' (178) and friend to the dispossessed (183). Augie replicates many of Kelly's characteristics and thereby shares his claim to native status.

Furthermore, Augie is capable heir to his father's business, loyal son to his mother Rosa, and protective older brother to his sister Cal – a situation and characteristics shared by Kelly. And like Kelly, who was at 'home' in the bush (McGrath 21), drawing on local knowledge to escape colonial authorities, Augie – on the run from the Serbian gang – relies on his knowledge of Orphelin Bay to stay hidden. When Augie is betrayed by, and forced to kill, Jared, the youngest member of his gang, the scene recalls the killing of Aaron Sherritt (Joel Edgerton) in the 2003 film *Ned Kelly*. As Rebekah Brammer argues, this moment 'is presented as an emotionless act of violence, one that is morally justified by Ned Kelly (Heath Ledger), who believes Aaron betrayed the gang' (132). However, tellingly, in terms of *Tidelands*'s attitudes towards leadership and race, Jared is played by First Nations actor, Hunter Page-Lochard. His lust for Augie's mistress, Laura (Annabelle Stephenson), has prompted him to betray his mates to the Serbian gang. Jared embodies racist stereotypes of 'oversexed Aboriginal men' (Konishi 87) lacking morality, work ethic, or willpower to resist physical temptations (Moreton-Robinson, 'Imagining' 70). Such stereotypes, Moreton-Robinson argues, are a strategy of patriarchal white sovereignty, used to deny Aboriginal people the right to self-determination (77). Jared's personal weakness and failure to live up to the standards of mateship and loyalty, as enshrined in the white masculine tradition, prove his unfitness and confirm Augie's right to lead. However, his death at Augie's hands – although framed as righteous – precipitates the disintegration of the gang. The failure of the codes of loyalty and mateship suggests that the time for Augie's brand of leadership is past. Augie himself finally acknowledges this: in the final scenes of episode eight, 'The Queen's Knife', Augie is shot, and so is the young Tidelander, Bijou – who shares the former queen's ability to see the future. As Cal hesitates between the two, Augie tells her to 'Save the girl. That's why you're here'. Cal's purpose is to protect the children, the Tidelanders' future. 'But you'll die', Cal cries. Augie only nods, accepting his fate and acknowledging that it is to Cal and Bijou (played by Filipina-Australian Chloe De Los Santos) that the future belongs.

Augie's claim to 'native son' status is contested by Adrielle's 'native' siren heritage, and her authority also contests Augie's egalitarian ethos – hers is a monarchy to Augie's democracy. Whereas loyalty, mateship, and trust bind Augie's gang, Adrielle secretly uses the Tidelanders' funds for her own purposes and rigidly controls the dispensation of both money and information. And whereas Augie hesitates to use violence against his own people and does so with his own hand when he must, Adrielle routinely relies on the might and cunning of her lieutenants to enforce her will, as well as exercising her own power when she chooses. The uncanny and phallic nature of Adrielle's power is vividly illustrated in episode one when she pins Augie to the ground and crushes his genitals with her vagina. This ability seems linked to the Tidelanders' supernatural strength and ability to control bodily fluids, but it is also irresistibly reminiscent of vagina dentata, that phenomenon through which '[t]he object of pleasure becomes the agent of violence' (Miller 312). Sarah Alison Miller shows how vagina dentata is linked to the figure of the siren via the ancient Greek sea-monster, Scylla, who is represented as a beautiful woman with canine heads below her waist, signifying 'the alluring but perilous nature of feminine charms' (317). In *Tidelands*, these charms are also persistently linked to the sea itself. Adrielle's power is represented as unnatural and cruel; but likewise men bespelled by sea sirens or devoured by Scylla's teeth signal their 'impotence' (317). Adrielle's uncanny power and Augie's helplessness before it mark both of them as unfit, illegitimate figures of authority. Cal, in contrast, cannot be bespelled by another siren and wields her own power more judiciously; she condemns Augie for killing Jared, denying his claim that he 'had to' do it with the flat reply, 'No, you didn't' ('Don't Trust Humans'), and using her own siren power only in self-defence.

Augie and Adrielle both represent power past its prime, power entrenched in the illegitimate authority or outdated traditions of the past – the colonial power and the Anglo-Celtic Australian masculine tradition. Adrielle's real challengers come from within: Cal, and the First Nations Tidelander, Violca. A postcolonial Australian Gothic may be expected to restore the nation to its traditional owners by placing sovereign power in Violca's hands. However, Violca, like Jared, proves herself unworthy of leadership. While representing herself as a symbol of 'hope' ('Don't Trust Humans'), Violca is repeatedly shown to be a sly and ambitious character, frequently sowing seeds of dissent in L'Attente. One of her key actions is to kidnap the young seer, Bijou, and hold her hostage in order to manipulate another child, Gilles, into spying on Adrielle. When Gilles is caught, Violca stands by while Adrielle has Gilles' eye gouged out. Violca is established as a 'bad' mother figure, concerned with her own ambitions rather than the safety of her children or subjects, and therefore equally as unfit for leadership as Adrielle. The bad mother is the guiding trope of *Tidelands*, and a familiar one in both Gothic (see, for example, Rogers) and Australian cultural and literary traditions (see, for example, Schaeffer). In positioning Violca as a 'bad' mother figure, the series also plays into enduring Australian stereotypes about the delinquency and unfitness of Aboriginal parents, discourses that led to the Stolen Generations and continue to affect First Nations communities today.

However, Violca is offered redemption of a sort when she falls pregnant to Augie's best mate, the Anglo-Celtic Colton. Tidelanders are thought to be infertile, so Violca's child is a miracle, a perfect hybrid – like Cal – of the discordant racial elements of Orphelin Bay. The impossible conception of Colton and Violca's child fits with the other Biblical elements of the series' final scenes – the Jesus-like sacrifice of Augie, the pietà in which Dylan holds Adrielle after she is stabbed by Gilles. 'That's for my eye', he tells her, invoking Hammurabi's Law ('The Queen's Knife'). Gilles and Bijou, the next generation, are with Cal. Violca's sovereignty is an impossibility – a 'power that cannot be sanctioned' (Botting, 'Power in the Darkness' 258), but which must be explored in order to be expelled. When Colton dies at Adrielle's hands, Violca is forced to flee to save the life of their unborn child. She is literally removed from the picture, a disharmonious note that cannot be neatly resolved. It is Cal who saves Bijou, and Cal to whom the sirens finally show themselves: 'They're here for you', the young seer tells Cal.

Conclusion

Reading the spaces of *Tidelands* as gothic heterotopias exposes contemporary Australian anxieties around belonging, race, sexuality, identity, and Reconciliation. While Orphelin Bay mirrors the power structures and cultural norms of hegemonic white Australia, L'Attente represents an alternative space that celebrates diverse sexualities and ethnicities. Individual sites in both locations – such as the McTeer Queenslander and Queen's mansion – assert belonging through connections with the sea and its association with 'native' status. Yet ultimately, the brand of English colonizing power encoded in the hybrid space of Adrielle's mansion is found to be illegitimate, and it is the power of the white 'native-born' subject, symbolized through the vernacular architecture of the McTeer Queenslander, that is upheld as legitimate and used to overwrite and efface First Nations sovereignty. The series uses its heterotopic spaces to stage a drama of legitimacy and illegitimacy, native and foreign, playing out different possibilities of postcolonial Australian identity and belonging and rejecting those versions of power that cannot be countenanced – the European and colonial, but also the Aboriginal.

Within the series' heterotopic spaces, bodies are also coded with complex significance in relation to racial and national identity. Rather than existing as the absolute Others of the inhabitants of Orphelin Bay, Tidelanders emerge as an overdetermined projection of mainstream Australia's anxieties and desires. Tidelanders monstrously encapsulate Australia's anxiety over its ethnic complexity and hybridity, over the questions of who belongs, who is native and who foreign, and over the breakdown of boundaries between these categories. Tidelanders are simultaneously sinister 'foreigners' threatening from without and unassimilated 'natives' threatening from within; they are also native-born Australians of the Anglo-Celtic tradition who can claim belonging through suffering. Tidelanders share white Australia's desire to belong as well as their fear of being exiles in a foreign land – orphaned, motherless, separated from origins and home by a wide, merciless ocean.

Within the bodies and body politic of the Tidelanders, a range of postcolonial Australian identities are represented. But ultimately, it is not the First Nations Tidelander Violca, the Anglo-Celtic larrikin Augie, or the colonial queen Adrielle who is fit to inherit the heterotopic spaces of *Tidelands*, its microcosmic Australian nation. It is Cal McTeer – combining a criminal Anglo-Celtic heritage with the Tidelanders' uncanny blood – for whom the sirens return, bringing with them a sense of legitimacy through their connections to the past and their elemental belonging to Queensland's waters. Through Cal's white body, the series asserts a fantasy of a post-racial Australia, in which the fissures of multiculturalism and the competing claims to Australian belonging disappear. Cal's legitimacy is consolidated by Augie's heroic sacrifice, Adrielle's flight, and Violca's banishment. Only Violca's child represents a potential rival to Cal, an equally hybrid mix of First Nations, Anglo-Celtic, and native/foreign Tidelander blood, but this unborn child is banished off-screen along with its unworthy mother. The child's possibility – the possibility of First Nations sovereignty in any form – remains only a disquieting note at the series' end, where Cal, standing for the entire nation, looks out across the sand as the alien sirens emerge from the sea. Ultimately, *Tidelands*, despite its innovative beach setting, subversive challenges to heteronormativity, diverse international cast, and streaming digital platform, is unable to leave behind Australian Gothic's traditional concerns. The unresolved matter of colonization, race relations, and the postcolonial desire to belong form an inescapable undertow to its hybrid gothic plot.

Works Cited

Alder, Emily. 'Through Oceans Darkly'. *Gothic Studies*, vol. 19, no. 2, 2017, pp. 1–15.

　　Better Homes and Gardens. Created by Peter E. Fox, Seven Network, 1996–.

Blue Heelers. Created by Hal McElroy and Tony Morphett, Southern Star. 1994–2006.

Botting, Fred. 'In Gothic Darkly: Heterotopia, History, Culture'. *A New Companion to the Gothic*, edited by David Punter, Wiley-Blackwell, 2012, pp. 13–24. doi:10.1002/9781444354959.ch1

Botting, Fred. 'Power in the Darkness: Heterotopias, Literature, and Gothic Labyrinths'. *Gothic: Critical Concepts in Literary and Cultural Studies, Volume 2*, edited by Fred Botting and Dale Townshend, Routledge, 2004, pp. 243–265.

Brammer, Rebekah. '*Ned Kelly* vs *The Proposition*: Contrasting Images of Colonialism, Landscape, and the Bushranger'. *Metro Magazine*, no. 158, 2008, pp. 132–135.

'The Calling'. *Tidelands*, written by Stephen M. Irwin, directed by Catriona McKenzie, season 1, episode 5, Netflix, 14 Dec. 2018.

The Cars That Ate Paris. Directed by Peter Weir, British Empire Films, 1974.

Chilling Adventures of Sabrina. Created by Roberto Aguirre-Sacasa, Netflix, 2018–2020.

Cloudstreet. Created by Tim Winton and Ellen Fontana, Austar Entertainment, 2011.

Craven, Allison. *Finding Queensland in Australian Cinema: Poetics and Screen Geographies*. Anthem P, 2016.

Curthoys, Ann. 'Expulsion, Exodus, and Exile in White Australian Historical Mythology'. *Journal of Australian Studies*, vol. 23, no. 61, 2009, pp. 1–19. doi:10.1080/14443059909387469

Decome, Marion. 'The Rise of the Chinese Villain: Demonic Representation of the Asian Character in Popular Literature (1880–1950)'. *Intercultural Masquerade: New Orientalism, New Occidentalism, Old Exoticism*, edited by Regis Machart, Fred Dervin, and Minghui Gao, Springer Higher Education P, 2016, pp. 119–134.

'Don't Trust Humans'. *Tidelands*, written by Stephen M. Irwin, directed by Emma Freeman, season 1, episode 4, Netflix, 14 Dec. 2018.

Doolan, Emma. 'Hinterland Gothic: Subtropical Excess in the Literature of South-East Queensland'. *eTropic: Electronic Journal of Studies in the Tropics*, vol. 18, no. 1, 2019, pp. 174–191. doi:10.25120/etropic.18.1.2019.3679

Dunn, Justine. Interview. *Ordinary Artisans*, 14 May 2019. <www.ordinaryartisans.com/tag/set-decoration/>.

Ellison, Elizabeth. 'Badland Beach: The Australian Beach as a Site of Cultural Remembering'. *International Journal of Media & Cultural Politics*, vol. 12, no. 1, 2016, pp. 115–127. doi:10.1386/macp.12.1.115_1

Foucault, Michel. 'Of Other Spaces'. *Heterotopia and the City: Public Space in a Postcivil Society*, edited and translated by Michiel Dehaene and Lieven De Cauter, Routledge, 2008, pp. 13–29. doi:10.1111/j.1467-9787.2010.00696_9.x

Foucault, Michel. 'Of Other Spaces'. Translated by Jay Miskoweic. *Diacritics*, vol. 16, no. 1, 1986, pp. 22–27.

Freud, Sigmund. *The Uncanny*. Translated by David McLintock. Penguin, 2003.

Gelder, Ken. 'Australian Gothic'. *The Routledge Companion to Gothic*, edited by Catherine Spooner and Emma McEvoy, Routledge, 2007, pp. 115–123.

Gelder, Ken and Jane M. Jacobs. *Uncanny Australia: Sacredness and Identity in a Postcolonial Nation.* Melbourne UP, 1998.

Gibson, Ross. *Seven Versions of an Australian Badland.* U of Queensland P, 2002.

Gildersleeve, Jessica. 'Contemporary Australian Trauma'. *The Palgrave Handbook of Contemporary Gothic*, edited by Clive Bloom, Palgrave Macmillan, 2020, pp. 91–104.

Gildersleeve, Jessica. '"Weird Melancholy" and the Modern Television Outback: Rage, Shame, and Violence in *Wake in Fright* and *Mystery Road*'. *M/C Journal: A Journal of Media and Culture,* vol. 22, no. 1, 2019. <www.journal.media-culture. org.au/index.php/mcjournal/article/view/1500>.

Glitch. Created by Tony Ayres and Louise Fox, ABC and Netflix, 2015–2019.

The Gloaming. Created by Vicki Madden, ABC Studios and Stan, 2020.

Halberstam, Jack [Judith]. *Skin Shows: Gothic Horror and the Technology of Monsters.* Duke UP, 1995.

Haunting of Hill House. Created by Mike Flanagan, Netflix, 2018.

Hogle, Jerrold E. 'The Gothic Ghost of the Counterfeit and the Progress of Abjection'. *A New Companion to the Gothic*, edited by David Punter, Wiley-Blackwell, 2012, pp. 496–509. doi:10.1002/9781444354959.ch34

'Home'. *Tidelands*, written by Stephen M. Irwin, directed by Toa Fraser, season 1, episode 1, Netflix, 14 Dec. 2018.

Keast, Jackie. 'Follow the Sun'. *Inside Film*, no. 183, 2018, pp. 22–24.

Keast, Jackie. 'Netflix Announces First Original Aussie Series, "Tidelands"'. *Inside Film*, 16 May 2017. <https://www.if.com.au/netflix-announces-first-original-aussie-series-tidelands/>.

Keast, Jackie. 'Outward Focus'. *Inside Film*, no. 183, 2018, p. 30.

The Kettering Incident. Created by Vikki Madden and Vincent Sheehan, Showcase Australia, 2017.

Konishi, Shino. *The Aboriginal Male in the Enlightenment World*, Routledge, 2012.

Luckhurst, Roger. 'Gothic Colonies, 1850–1920'. *The Gothic World*, edited by Glennis Byron and Dale Townshend, Routledge, 2014, pp. 62–71.

Mad Max. Directed by George Miller, Roadshow, 1979.

McGrath, Ann. 'Australia's Occluded Voices: Ned Kelly's History Wars'. *Narratives of the Occluded Irish Diaspora: Subversive Voices*, edited by Micheál Ó hAodha and John O'Callaghan, Peter Lang, 2012, pp. 7–36.

Miller, Sarah Alison. 'Monstrous Sexuality: Variation on the *Vagina Dentata*'. *The Ashgate Research Companion to Monsters and the Monstrous*, edited by Asa Simon Mittman and Peter Dendle, Ashgate, 2012, pp. 311–328.

Moon, Ra. 'The *Tidelands* Location: The House Where the Series was Filmed in Australia'. *Atlas of Wonders*, 17 Dec. 2018. <www.atlasofwonders.com/2018/12/tidelands-filming-locations.html>.

Moreton-Robinson, Aileen. 'Imagining the Good Indigenous Citizen: Race War and the Pathology of White Sovereignty'. *Cultural Studies Review*, vol. 15, no. 2, 2011, pp. 61–79.

Moreton-Robinson, Aileen. *The White Possessive: Property, Power, and Indigenous Sovereignty*. U of Minnesota P, 2015.

Mystery Road. Created by Steven McGregor and Ivan Sen, ABC, 2018–.

Ned Kelly. Directed by Gregor Jordan, Universal Pictures, 2003.

Neighbours. Created by Reg Watson, The Fremantle Corporation, 1985–.

'Not One of You'. *Tidelands*, written by Stephen M. Irwin, directed by Emma Freeman, season 1, episode 3, Netflix, 14 Dec. 2018.

'Orphans of L'Attente'. *Tidelands*, written by Stephen M. Irwin, directed by Toa Fraser, season 1, episode 2, Netflix, 14 Dec. 2018.

Picnic at Hanging Rock. Created by Beatrix Christian and Alice Addison, Freemantle Australia, 2018.

Picnic at Hanging Rock. Directed by Peter Weir, British Empire Films, 1975.

Pine Gap. Created by Greg Haddrick and Felicity Packard, ABC and Netflix, 2018.

'The Prophecy'. *Tidelands*, written by Leigh McGrath, directed by Daniel Nettheim, season 1, episode 7, Netflix, 14 Dec. 2018.

Puberty Blues. Created by Imogen Banks and John Edwards, Network Ten, 2012–2014.

'The Queen's Knife'. *Tidelands*, written by Stephen M. Irwin, directed by Daniel Nettheim, season 1, episode 8, Netflix, 14 Dec. 2018.

Radiance. Directed by Rachel Perkins, Mongrel Media, 1998.

Rayner, Jonathon, 'Gothic Definitions: The New Australian "Cinema of Horrors"'. *Antipodes*, vol. 25, no. 1, 2011, pp. 91–97.

Riwoe, Mirandi. 'That Sinister Asian'. *Peril*, 15 June 2016. <www.peril.com.au/back-editions/that-sinister-asian/>.

Robson, Eddie. 'Gothic Television'. *The Routledge Companion to Gothic*, edited by Catherine Spooner and Emma McEvoy, Routledge, 2007, pp. 242–250.

Rogers, Deborah D. *Matrophobic Gothic and its Legacy: Sacrificing Mothers in the Novel and in Popular Culture*. Peter Lang Publishing, 2007.

Rose, Deborah Bird. 'Ned Kelly Died for Our Sins'. *Oceania*, vol. 65, no. 2, 1994, pp. 175–186.

Schaffer, Kay. *Women and the Bush: Forces of Desire in the Australian Cultural Tradition*. Cambridge UP, 1990.

SeaChange. Created by Deb Cox and Andrew Knight, Granada International Media, 1998–2019.

Secrets and Lies. Created by Stephen M. Irwin, Network Ten, 2014–.

Stingers. Created by John Wild and Marcia Gardner, Nine Network, 1998–2004.

Stranger Things. Created by Matt Duffer and Ross Duffer, Nexflix, 2016–.

Tedmanson, Sophie. 'Elsa Pataky, Charlotte Best, and Madeleine Madden on *Tidelands*, Netflix's Answer to Mermaids'. *Vogue*, 14 Dec. 2018. <www.vogue. com.au/culture/features/elsa-pataky-charlotte-best-and-madeleine-madden-on-tidelands-netflixs-answer-to-mermaids/news-story/114905030f4d27fb88c 249995aa3f177>.

Tidelands. Created by Stephen M. Irwin, Nathan Mayfield, Leigh McGrath and Tracey Robertson, Hoodlum Entertainment and Netflix, 2018.

Tourism Australia. 'So Where the Bloody Hell Are You?' YouTube, 12 May 2007. <https://www.youtube.com/watch?v=Y-ZLr9ePuj8>.

Turner, Adam. '*Tidelands* Struggles to Stay Afloat in its First Series'. *The Conversation*, 18 Dec. 2018. <www.theconversation.com/tidelands-struggles-to-stay-afloat-in-its-first-series-108751>.

Underbelly. Created by John Silvester and Andrew Rule, Nine Network, 2008–2013.

Wake in Fright. Created by Stephen M. Irwin, Roadshow, 2017.

Wake in Fright. Directed by Ted Kotcheff, Group W/NLT, 1971.

Water Rats. Created by Hal McElroy, Tony Morphett, and John Hugginson, Nine Network, 1996–2001.

Wheatley, Helen. *Gothic Television*. Manchester UP, 2006.

Wisker, Gina. 'Postcolonialisms'. *The Palgrave Handbook of Contemporary Gothic*, edited by Clive Bloom, Palgrave Macmillan, 2020, pp. 105–122.

Wolf Creek. Directed by Greg McLean, Roadshow Entertainment, 2005.

About the Author

Emma Doolan lectures in creative writing and literary studies at Southern Cross University. Her research explores Gothic representations of place, particularly in writing about Australia's hinterland regions.

2. 'When I Died, I Saw the Whole World': Uncanny Space and the Māori Gothic in the Aftermath Narratives of *Waru* and *Māui's Hook*

Emily Holland

Abstract

This chapter considers the applicability of gothic elements to the indigenous culture of Aotearoa New Zealand by addressing how uncanny space manifests in the aftermath of death in two recent Māori films: *Waru* (2017) and *Māui's Hook* (2018). These films present a tension between western gothic parameters and distinct elements of Māori culture, yet also foreground a possible co-existence between the two. This relationship can be identified in a mode of the uncanny that reflects the historical and contemporary experience of Māori in postcolonial New Zealand society. This reworking of the uncanny, in which estrangement is turned back on itself, takes on a political function in articulating the experience and process of overcoming historical trauma through a Māori cultural framework.

Keywords: Indigenous Gothic; Māori film; New Zealand film; postcolonial; haunting

This chapter considers the applicability of gothic elements to the Indigenous culture of Aotearoa New Zealand by addressing how uncanny space manifests in the aftermath of death in two recent Māori films: *Waru* (2017) and *Māui's Hook* (2018). While gothic conventions of uncanny haunting can be identified, these films nonetheless present a tension between western Gothic and Māori beliefs, voices, and values that do not typically align with gothic parameters. I argue, however, that the temporal emphasis on aftermath in

Gildersleeve, J. and K. Cantrell (eds.), *Screening the Gothic in Australia and New Zealand: Contemporary Antipodean Film and Television*. Taylor & Francis Group, 2022

DOI 10.5117/9789463721141_CH02

Waru and *Māui's Hook* enables a culturally specific mode of the uncanny to manifest. The construction of uncanny spaces where characters are haunted by tragic events of the past foregrounds an experience of cultural estrangement connected to the oppression and repression of Māori perspectives in postcolonial New Zealand society. The reworking of the uncanny in these Māori films facilitates an Indigenous vocalization of recurring historical trauma through the oppression of Māori voices in the postcolonial present. In the opening sequences of both *Waru* and *Māui's Hook*, death acts as a catalyst for the unfolding narratives; as such, gothic templates might seem readily applicable, but they also highlight the conundrum of analysing Indigenous cultures of postcolonial contexts within gothic parameters. In the opening of *Waru*, we hear a voiceover of the eponymous character, a young boy who has died from adult neglect: 'When I died, I saw the whole world'. This phrase propels the film's portmanteau narrative as we are invited to observe eight Māori women on the day of Waru's *tangi* (funeral), examining their responses to his death, which range from repressed guilt to activism, with each segment directed by a different female New Zealand filmmaker. *Māui's Hook,* a blend of documentary and narrative fiction that highlights Aotearoa New Zealand's youth suicide crisis, also begins with death. The film opens with the text: 'In ancient times, "Hine-nui-te-pō", the Goddess of Death, guided lost souls back to the resting place of the ancestors'. This opening frame transitions into a crosscut sequence between a *tangi* and protagonist Tama's suicide at the edge of a river while dark clouds form in the sky. This event sparks the film's documentary portion where families discuss the impact of losing loved ones to suicide and partake in a therapeutic *hikoi* ('parade/march/journey') from Parihaka in Taranaki to Cape Reinga, led by Māori psychologist and the film's director, Paora Joseph.

While gothic characteristics can be noted in the ghostly presence of a dead boy through voiceover in *Waru* and through the brooding landscape that serves as a backdrop for the protagonist's death in *Māui's Hook*, the event of the *tangi* in both films, and the allusion to ancestry and the Māori goddess of death in *Māui's Hook,* already marks the films as Indigenous works foregrounding *Māoritanga* ('Māori culture'). These beliefs, values, and voices are typically demarcated from western gothic conventions. Previous analyses have delved into the identification of 'settler' and 'postcolonial' gothic modes (Kavka 227; Mercer 111) where the Gothic effectively expresses traumas of 'repressed colonial violence' (Kavka 227), and where the 'New Zealand Gothic is most commonly associated with Pākehā artists exploring extreme psychological states, isolation, and violence' (Mercer 112). The bulk of cinematic works labelled 'Kiwi Gothic' have centred on non-Māori characters in fraught and often violent familial scenarios, frequently in an equally fraught relationship with oppressive and threatening spaces. The tendency of the Gothic to manifest in relation to Pākehā (non-Māori New Zealanders]) as opposed to Māori fiction appears to support the argument that it arises in subconscious colonial guilt. But how might Māori perspectives articulate the same process of being haunted by the past? How might we interpret the presence of gothic components in Māori cinema that evoke a tension between *Māoritanga* and the Gothic, while also hinting at a possible coexistence between them? How do we make sense of an Indigenous film that exists separately from a gothic framework but nonetheless *'feels* like a Gothic film' (Kavka 225)?

Finding the Uncanny in the 'Māori Gothic'

Waru and *Māui's Hook* display characteristics of what we might tentatively term the 'Māori Gothic'. Previous discussions of this term by Jennifer Lawn, Geoffrey Miles, Ian Conrich, and Misha Kavka have addressed the slippery nature of examining Māori narratives through a gothic lens because in Māori culture the supernatural is integrated into everyday life. For instance, Lawn explains that while 'the ghost *ought not to be there* within a western rationalist perspective, spiritual presences are expected and socially acknowledged in the Māori lived-world, through the intertwining of past, present and future in every moment' (18; original emphasis). While the marrying of Māori spirituality and the Gothic might be contentious, I argue that *Waru* and *Māui's Hook* foreground how the experience of the uncanny, a common feature of the Gothic, might resonate with the temporal overlap of past, present and future as experienced by Indigenous communities in postcolonial New Zealand society. Thus, as Andrew Bennett and Nicholas Royle summarize:

> The uncanny has to do with a sense of strangeness, mystery, or eeriness. More particularly it concerns a sense of unfamiliarity that appears at the very heart of the familiar, or a sense of familiarity that appears at the very heart of the unfamiliar. The uncanny is not just a matter of the weird or spooky but has to do more specifically with a disturbance of the familiar. (35)

In its connotations of ghostly haunting, the uncanny does not align with Māori spirituality, in which the spiritual world and the physical world are conjoined (Kavka 230). However, as 'a disturbance of the familiar', the uncanny can be seen to estrange the self and even a community from a once homely and familiar place, producing a sense of disconnection and displacement. In examining how something close to haunting might occur within Māori culture, Kavka reflects on Jacques Derrida's concept of 'spectrality' or 'hauntology', in which 'haunting is an ontological condition because it depends on that which is existentially present and absent at the same time' (231). This simultaneous presence and absence of the dead lies at the heart of the narratives of both *Waru* and *Māui's Hook*. Even Waru's declaration in voiceover at the film's opening captures this paradoxical presence and absence of the dead child. This paradox colours both films, but not through explicitly ghostly or supernatural disturbance. Rather, it informs the way that those in the present are pervasively haunted by the past, an absent presence that also characterizes colonial aftermath. Kavka suggests that 'the only form of haunting that makes sense from a Māori perspective is the haunting effects of a colonial history whose descendants have been absolved of participation or concern' (239). Reflecting on Hester Joyce's assertion that Māori cinema can never be fully prised from the nation's colonial legacy (22), I suggest that the structural emphasis on the aftermath of death in *Waru* and *Māui's Hook* allows for a culturally specific mode of the uncanny to manifest, a form of haunting in which traumas of the past speak to a continued repression of Māori perspectives in the postcolonial present.

In contrast to earlier Pākehā works such as Peter Jackson's *Heavenly Creatures* (1994) and Christine Jeffs' *Rain* (2001), in which tension builds to a shocking climactic event, *Waru* and *Māui's Hook* are characterized by an upsetting event occurring *before* their diegetic narratives begin, resulting in simultaneously absent and haunted space in the aftermath of tragedy. This 'present/absent' (Kavka 231) role of the dead takes on a political function in which we are called to reflect on what could have been done to prevent these tragic events from occurring in the first place. The films therefore occupy an interesting position between the Gothic and Māori 'Fourth Cinema' (Martens 3–5). The term 'Fourth Cinema' was coined by renowned Māori filmmaker, Barry Barclay, to describe Māori films with 'a distinct politically engaged mode of filmmaking that has emerged from the shared Indigenous experience of exclusion in postcolonial settler states and allows for film practices and images that are controlled by – and do justice to – Indigenous peoples and their concerns and customs' (Martens 3).While on the one hand both *Waru* and *Māui's Hook* depict universal forms of tragedy and trauma that allow for them to be considered part of a 'Global Gothic' (Conrich, 'Māori Tales' 41), they are embedded in the Indigenous acknowledgment of a cultural framework in which Māori have been vilified and their connection to place and community has been fractured. Joyce describes Indigenous filmmaking as 'a manifold political and cultural activity', such that 'it is therefore impossible to talk about Māori film without acknowledging New Zealand's colonial legacy, racist past, and present-day postcolonialism. What identifies Māori storytelling in the cinema is its cultural particularity and historical specificity' (22). In *Waru*, uncanny space resulting from the aftermath of child death allows for the illumination of cultural disharmony between Māori and Pākehā. Such tension allows for the bursting through of what has been repressed and silenced within both the Māori community and the postcolonial nation. In *Māui's Hook*, the recurring gothic trope of ghostly space is transformed within the Māori cultural framework. While such space might initially be seen as sublime and threatening, the land becomes central to identity formation, communal restoration, and spiritual healing for Māori as *tangata whenua* (people of the land). The therapeutic *hikoi* (the geographic journey from grief and dislocation to communal and cultural restoration) allows the Māori figures in the film to reclaim their connection to the land and establish themselves as *tangata whenua*, a position that has always been challenged within postcolonial New Zealand society (Walker-Morrison 26).

Like earlier Pākehā narratives such as *Rain* and *In My Father's Den* (2004), *Waru* and *Māui's Hook* centre on youth death and present the home and its surrounding environment as a space of tension and violation. However, these Māori films differ from Pākehā works in their structural emphasis on aftermath that informs their cultural reconfiguring of the uncanny. Although *In My Father's Den* is non-linear, revealing that a body has been found at the beginning of the film, most examples of New Zealand Gothic cinema do not focus on the aftermath of violence or death. They instead build up, often quite gradually, to an abrupt moment of tragedy or graphic violence: the shocking drowning of little Jim in *Rain*, the abrupt murder of Celia in *In My Father's Den,* and the gruesome attack on a parent by the two troubled protagonists in *Heavenly Creatures,* to name a few. Aftermath, particularly of child death, however, has appeared in examples of Māori cinema, such as *The Strength Of Water* (2009) and *Kerosene Creek* (2004). In *The Strength Of Water*, directed by Pākehā Ballantyne and written by renowned Māori writer, Briar Grace-Smith, ten-year-old Kimi is confronted (and comforted) by the presence of his dead sister, Melody, after she has been killed by a junkyard dog. In *Kerosene Creek*, young Māori girl, Jayde, recalls her interaction with Wiremu, a boy she met at Rotorua's popular geothermally heated stream before he was killed in a car accident on the way home. The film begins at the *tangi* of Wiremu and his older brother Sonny Boy and transitions between flashbacks as Jayde recalls the final moments that she spent with the brothers. The idyllic stream is rendered uncanny, not only in its framing as a place of recalled trauma and the loss of childhood innocence, but also in the threat of the physical space itself. At the stream, Sonny Boy tells Wiremu not to put his head underwater or 'the amoebas will eat your brain', a warning that is also echoed on the visitor's guide webpage for Kerosene Creek. The final line of the safety guidelines reads: 'As with most geothermal pools, it's not safe to put your head underwater'. The warning alludes to an uncanny horror beneath the surface of New Zealand's recreational geographic spaces. The appearance of characters after their deaths in films such as *The Strength of Water*, *Waru* and *Māui's Hook* are not cases of conventional gothic haunting, but instead reflect the conjoining of the spiritual and physical world central to Māori culture. Haunting 'is not a Māori concept for the simple reason that spirits do not stand apart from the world, but rather move, and live, inside this world. Because Māori spirits never depart, there is no notion of spiritual trespass' and 'no possibility of anyone or anything being "out of place"' (Kavka 230). In *Waru* and *Māui's Hook*, however, the death of children – those who should be the furthest from it – is rendered uncanny when the inability of other characters to come to terms with their passing highlights the circumstances of death as unimaginable. This inability to process premature death informs the evocation of the films' uncanny spaces.

The construction of uncanny space in New Zealand film has its roots in national literature such as the works of Maurice Gee, Janet Frame, and Ronald Hugh Morrieson. Ian Conrich observes that even as 'a popular belief has [...] persisted that New Zealand is "a great place to bring up kids" and offers "a great way of life" [...] New Zealand fiction, its literature and film, has repeatedly portrayed spaces of isolation, loss, and despair, of a rugged, wild and treacherous land that can assail and entrap' ('New Zealand Gothic' 393). The New Zealand Gothic is rarely concerned with the explicitly paranormal or ghostly (Cameron 56) but rather, in line with definitions of the uncanny, lurks in ordinary and familiar places such as 'the farm shack [...]; the evacuated land stripped of native bush (and people); the suburban bungalow with the manicured front lawn, the Scarfie flat, the beach, the bach' (Lawn 13–14). The uncanniness of New Zealand Gothic arises from the displacement and disconnection from these familiar spaces that *should* be homely. In films such as *Heavenly Creatures*, *Rain*, *In My Father's Den*, *Crush* (1992), *Jack Be Nimble* (1993), and *Out of the Blue* (2006), spaces associated with leisure, comfort, security, and play are subverted, becoming frightening and unsettling. Whether it be the small communities and domestic spaces of *In My Father's Den* and *Out of the Blue*, the 'garden city' of Christchurch (Conrich, 'New Zealand Gothic' 400) in *Heavenly Creatures*, or the beachside holiday home in *Rain*, idyllic and iconic New Zealand spaces are rendered threatening through the fracturing of both family and community through violence, murder, estrangement, buried secrets, infidelity, alcoholism, and sexual competition. The relationship between uncanny space and the fracturing of self, family, and community in these films resonates with William Schafer's emphasis on the connection between the home and the body (142). Schafer declares that '[to] be "at home" is to feel comfortable inside one's body, one's house, one's country' (142). Despite the emphasis on displacement and not feeling 'at home' (142), most examples of uncanny space in New Zealand cinema steer away from representations of Māori as experiencing a sense of detachment and displacement from a place that both is and is not theirs within the context of colonial history and contemporary postcolonial tension.

Depictions of uncanny space as a means of portraying the detachment of Māori from their native land are rare. This highlights the fraught relationship between the Gothic and *Māoritanga*. Conversely, the tension between these two paradigms might also allow for an expression of colonial haunting and a reworking of the uncanny through a Māori framework. In observing the intertwining of Māori culture and the Gothic in Māori literature, specifically Keri Hulme's novel, *The Bone People* (1984), Mercer describes how '[t]he liminal nature of the Gothic mode means that depictions of a haunting past are intimately, often uncannily, connected with a recognisable depiction of modern social reality, clearly a valuable attribute for writers dealing with the continuing processes of decolonization' (113). In their depiction of tragic events grounded in real contemporary experience stemming from systemic oppression, *Waru* and *Māui's Hook* partake in this challenge of decolonization by offering a form of Indigenous storytelling, influenced by the Gothic, that comes from 'the perspective of the Indigenous storyteller rather than the silenced Indigene who borrows from the catalogue of European Gothic tropes in order to bypass the repression of colonial history' (Kavka 228). This 'inside' (228) response to loss and trauma is expressed through the films' aftermath structures, the reconfiguration of haunted space, and their emphasis on Māori voices.

Colonial Haunting and Indigenous Voices in *Waru*

Waru's 'present/absent' (Kavka 231) mode of haunting through the neglect of a child frames the present as continuously haunted by the past. This presence of the past within the Māori world becomes tied to the broader repetition of repression and systematic racism established during colonization. Comprised of eight segments, each of which depicts different Māori women on the morning of Waru's *tangi*, the film invites us to observe how they respond to Waru's death and to the broader issue of child abuse within the community. While the same timeframe is repeated in each segment, the film's political trajectory moves in a linear fashion from the repression and silencing of past atrocities to verbal expression and active intention to incite change. Repression of any vocalization of violence and the dismissal of the existence of child abuse within the community is the focus of the film's first half. In the first segment, directed by Grace-Smith, we follow the matriarchal figure of Aunty Charm as she orchestrates the preparation of food for the *tangi* taking place in a *wharenui* (meeting house) nearby. Although Aunty Charm attempts to remain steadfast in this domestic process, she is clearly troubled by the circumstances of Waru's death. Similarly, the second segment, directed by Casey Kaa, depicts the perspective of Waru's teacher, Anahera. It is implied that she was aware of the domestic violence but did not express this before Waru's death for fear of causing conflict. Waru's presence and absence is enfolded in the space of her classroom when one little girl enquires of Waru's whereabouts. Anahera is thus haunted by her own guilt as she contemplates whether to attend the *tangi*. This repression of the acknowledgment of neglect is subsequently foregrounded in a particularly disturbing segment by Katie Wolfe, where a young woman, Em, arrives home after a night out. Drunk and barely mobile, she discovers that she has been locked out of the house and that her baby, whom she had left in the hands of others, is alone on the kitchen floor. The barbeque is still smoking and the television is left blaring with an image of Waru flashing on the screen during a news report, his death uncannily haunting another space where a child has been neglected. This doubling is made more disturbing by our prior knowledge of Waru's death, an event that haunts the present but in this case dissolves into background noise.

While Pākehā presence is minimal in the film's first half, its selective placement in the narrative signals a pivotal transition from silence to active expression. In the segment directed by Chelsea Winstanley, Kiritapu, a Māori news presenter, calls out her Pākehā co-presenter for labelling child abuse as an Indigenous issue. This segment positions the film within a broader framework of postcolonial conflict. Its Māori characters are haunted not only by the tragic loss of a child in their community, but also through their continued vilification by Pākehā. Winstanley's segment makes clear that systemic racism, which contributes to 'the uncivil basis' of the nation's settler society (Turner 419), ensures that pressing social issues will never be properly resolved, while Winstanley herself describes the segment as capturing 'the perspective of a woman trying to survive within a system that breeds ignorance and apathy': '[t]here is an "Us and Them" mentality that still exists' and '[a]s long as we label one group more culpable than the other, we will never have the collective responsibility for this issue, we will never move forward. We must speak up' (qtd. in Croot). Kiritapu's vocalization instigates the film's remaining two segments where repression and anger transform into action. A young girl, Mere, holding out a *tokotoko* stick (a symbol of authority and expression), confronts a pair of abusers and addresses the community's silence by exclaiming: 'You all know what's going on. When is it going to stop? How many of us have to die before we say: enough! enough! ENOUGH!' The haunting of Waru's death augments Mere's moment of action, yet the conjoining of the spiritual world and the physical world through the ancestral *tokotoko* stick enables her to find strength in channelling her own familial history. The film ends with farmer sisters, Titty and Bash, stepping in to stop more violence being inflicted on children in the local community; Bash declares, 'I'm going to go in there and get those kids', as they pull up outside a run-down house that, like the gothic mansion, evokes a sense of that which is unknown and potentially threatening. The screen turns black as Titty and Bash exit their car and make their way towards the house, preventing us from witnessing their confrontation with the abusers. By barring the viewer from witnessing what takes place inside the house, this conclusion reinforces the repression of child abuse within the community, while also implicating the spectator in addressing it.

As the film's crucial turning point preceding both Mere's and Titty and Bash's stories, the structural placement of Kiritapu's retaliation in the newsroom, where Waru's death prompts historical oppression to haunt contemporary discourse while also transforming repression into action, positions the film as an example of both Māori 'Fourth Cinema' (Martens 3) and what Erin Mercer terms 'bicultural gothic' (111). Mercer describes how biculturalism 'entails the ability to function in more than one culture and to switch roles back and forth as the situation changes, meaning that identity is constantly modified by the interactions between self and society' (115). Focusing on *The Bone People*, Mercer observes 'a Gothic subtext suggesting bicultural identity remains haunted by trauma and contains the seeds of its own dissolution' (122). Such a subtext is also wholly applicable to *Waru*. Kiritapu's voice has been suppressed as a Māori woman in a Pākehā-dominated industry, yet she eventually stands strong in front of the newsroom monitor as her rebellion is broadcast to the nation, embodying the 'potential disharmony and disjuncture within a bicultural framework' (111). This moment in which the past haunts the present, in the form of both Waru's death and colonial oppression, is not so far removed from Fred Botting's perspective on the crossing of temporalities in the Gothic (3–4). Botting suggests that '[i]n seeing one time and its values cross into another, both periods are disturbed. The dispatching of unwanted ideas and attitudes into an imagined past does not guarantee they have been overcome' (3–4). This uncanny temporality characterizes the haunting that occurs within a Māori framework. This haunting does not arise from the spirits of the Māori world but from a colonial past where 'Māori are haunted, quite simply, by everything they cannot say in a way that is heard' (Kavka 239). This colonial haunting provides an impetus for the creation of Māori 'Fourth Cinema'. The haunting of the present by the past conveyed through the aftermath structure of *Waru* incites a subversive vocalization of communal trauma. This diegetic articulation of *wāhine* (women's) perspectives is mirrored in the film's production, with Māori women at the helm of the creative process.

Loss and the Land in *Māui's Hook*

The reconfiguration of the uncanny as a means of articulating Māori perspectives is also a crucial aspect of *Māui's Hook*, which depicts Paora Joseph's interaction with five grieving families who have lost family members to suicide as they partake in a healing *hikoi*, travelling by bus to several *marae* (Māori communal space) across the North Island from Parihaka to Cape Reinga. The route forms the shape of a hook, giving the film its name. The shape carries a powerful association with strength, perseverance, and a sense of home, referring to the legend in which, with a magical hook, the demi-god, Māui, pulled up a giant fish which became the North Island. This link between the hook and the film's aim of targeting the issue of youth suicide is evoked in a statement made by the film's producer, Karen Te O Kahurangi Waaka-Tibble, where she asserts that 'we want our young people to be like Māui – to push through life's challenges, using the Māui attitude' ('Māui's Hook'). Joseph's film blends this documentary component with a ghost story, in which the fictional character of Tama, who is suicidal, observes the grieving families as they come to terms with their loss. We are led to believe that Tama's suicide attempt in the film's opening was unsuccessful and that he has been encouraged to join the trip by Joseph to prevent him from trying again. It is revealed halfway through the film, through Tama's encounter with Hine-nui-te-pō, who takes the form of a young woman, that he was in fact successful and has been a ghost the entire trip. This jarring realization and subsequent regret inspires the film's tagline: 'There's no coming back'.

Throughout the film, the victims of suicide metaphorically haunt the families they have left behind through trauma and communal fracturing, and Tama haunts the spaces of the *hikoi* after his death. While this depiction of ghosts reflects the Gothic more directly than *Waru,* Tama's haunting of communal space from the *marae* to the *wharenui* and the *wharekai* (dining hall) to his own home, straddles the line between the uncanny and the unification of the spiritual and physical world in *Māoritanga* (Kavka 230–231). It is not until Tama's realization of his own demise that a 'disturbance of the familiar' occurs (Bennett and Royle 35). It is only *after* this recognition that space becomes uncanny to him, whereas prior to this shock he has continued to inhabit space just as he did when he was alive. This cohabitation between spirits and the living resonates with Māori belief where, as Kavka explains, '[i]n place of this central trope of horror-filled haunting, *Mātauranga Māori* (knowledge of the Māori world), embraces the spirits of the super/natural world as the basis of all knowledge of self, community, and land' (230). Kavka adds that gothic haunting therefore 'disappears, erased by the lack of a supernatural world that is hidden, repressed, or displaced by the world of the living' (230). The real haunting and repression in *Māui's Hook* is thus the traumatic loss which pervades the present through grief and guilt. This haunting is aptly expressed in an interview where the sister of an adolescent suicide victim reveals the times that she received phone calls from her brother telling her he was going to take his own life. She describes how she dissuaded him the first time but failed to help him on the second. She is haunted by guilt for not being able to save her brother and for keeping those details to herself, unable to articulate them to the rest of the family who are fractured in the aftermath of the boy's death.

Like *Waru*, the inability of the family, and by extension the Indigenous community, to vocalize the impact of trauma, echoes the broader fracturing of spiritual and communal identity in postcolonial New Zealand. Like other films that depict the crumbling and subsequent restoration of Māori identity, such as *Once Were Warriors* (1994) and *Whale Rider* (2002), *Māui's Hook* stresses the return to Indigenous roots through a reconnection with the land as integral to overcoming hardship and restoring identity. The dissolution of Māori culture in the urban space of *Once Were Warriors* is presented as symptomatic of contemporary hegemonic systems that stem from colonial oppression, highlighted more prominently in Alan Duff's novel than in Tamahori's filmic adaptation (Johnston 8; Columpar 467). Although *Māui's Hook* bears little explicit allusion to colonialism, the journey itself conjures the political significance of the *hikoi* in Aotearoa New Zealand's history where the attempt by Māori to reclaim their identity as *tangata whenua* through 'an ongoing process of redress of colonial injustices' such as 'widescale theft of land and other resources' has been met with resistance by Pākehā (Walker-Morrison 40). Like the politically resonant works of 'Fourth Cinema' from filmmakers such as Barclay and Merata Mita, *Māui's Hook* offers a subtextual process of decolonization by working through such injustices of land theft. The estrangement from the land through gothic tropes is reworked through the *hikoi* to evoke a reclamation of space as *turangawaewae* (a place to stand). Estrangement is articulated by the sublime framing of space where '[n]ature appears hostile, untamed, and threatening' and 'darkness, obscurity, and barely contained malevolent energy reinforce atmospheres of disorientation and fear' (Botting 4). This disorientation is further emphasized through Tama's intense shock when he discovers his own corpse submerged in water after following Hine-nui-te-pō into a lake. When he collapses at the water's edge, in the film's opening sequence, the scene is followed by the film's title appearing over a vast sweeping landscape of grassland and mountains. While the film emphasizes human vulnerability against the natural world, man-made spaces that should be full of life are also rendered desolate in the wake of grief and a dissolution of the community: a dark, flooded *wharenui* and a grey, overcast *marae*. Over the course of the *hikoi,* however, we see the land transform from being consumed by dark floodwater to being bathed in light when the group eventually reach Cape Reinga. The journey concludes with each family laying down a framed photograph of their lost loved one on the grassy hill, facing up towards the sky.

By turning an estrangement created through elements of the Gothic back on itself, *Māui's Hook* conveys a reclamation of the land as *turangawaewae,* (a place to stand one's feet) (Walker-Morrison 25). The thematic and aesthetic negotiation of space, in which the initially sublime landscape becomes a crucial site of healing and restoration, speaks to the continuously fraught negotiation of land ownership in the history of Aotearoa New Zealand. Walker-Morrison states that the 'history of colonization in this country, as elsewhere, has been largely a story of uprooting and dispossession' and that consequently 'issues of loss, conservation, regaining, and/or transformation of such a sense of place [is] central to Māori fiction film' (25–26). The grief and subsequent coming to terms with the loss of family though suicide in *Māui's Hook* is bound to the process of reconnecting with the land, exemplifying how '[i]ssues of central importance to the individual and community are always played out in relation to land and water as one's Place to Stand' (Walker-Morrison 30). This communal grounding is solidified in the final stage of the journey through the laying down of the victims' portraits at Cape Reinga. The *hikoi* itself reflects on postcolonial Māori history where *hikois* such as the Land March of 1975 stood as acts of reclamation and highlighted the 'colonial misappropriation of Māori lands' that 'ushered in an ongoing process of restitution' (Walker-Morrison 35). While not explicitly referencing colonial history, *Māui's Hook* nonetheless contributes to this restitution through its depiction of uncanny estrangement and the subsequent restoration of *turangawaewae,* where spiritual and physical loss is overcome through Indigenous expression and the foregrounding of *Māoritanga.*

In analysing the representation of uncanny space through the aftermath narratives of *Waru* and *Māui's Hook,* I have considered the extent to which the Gothic can operate within a cultural framework from which it is typically demarcated. Rather than colonizing these Indigenous texts by reading them through an exclusively gothic lens (Mercer 112), I have assessed how these works showcase the tension between the Gothic and *Māoritanga,* yet also foreground the potential for them to coexist. These modes of tension and coexistence are formed through the reworking of the uncanny through an Indigenous lens where colonialism manifests as the most unsettling form of haunting. By turning processes of estrangement and haunting back on themselves through *Māoritanga,* the thematic and aesthetic negotiation between gothic tropes and Māori culture in *Māui's Hook* and *Waru* allows for a politically resonant mode of cultural expression. Here repression becomes a mere ghost in the wake of Indigenous vocalization and activism.

Works Cited

Bennett, Andrew, and Nicholas Royle. *An Introduction to Literature, Criticism, and Theory.* 5th ed., Routledge, 2016.

Botting, Fred. *Gothic.* 2nd ed., Routledge, 2014.

Cameron, Allan. '*The Locals* and the Global: Transnational Currents in Contemporary New Zealand Horror'. *Studies in Australasian Cinema*, vol. 4, no. 1, 2010, pp. 56–72.

Columpar, Corinn. '"Taking Care of Her Green Stone Wall": The Experience of Space in *Once Were Warriors*'. *Quarterly Review of Film and Video*, vol. 24, no. 5, pp. 463–474.

Conrich, Ian. 'Māori Tales of the Unexpected: The New Zealand Television Series *Mataku* as Indigenous Gothic'. *Globalgothic,* edited by Glennis Byron, Manchester UP, 2013, pp. 36–49.

Conrich, Ian. 'New Zealand Gothic'. *A New Companion to the Gothic,* edited by David Punter, Blackwell Publishing, 2012, pp. 393–408.

Croot, James. 'Waru: The Nine female Māori Filmmakers United in their Passion to Start a Conversation'. *Stuff.Co.Nz,* 22 Oct. 2017. </www.stuff.co.nz/entertainment/film/98027844/waru-the-nine-female-maori-filmmakers-united-in-their-passion-to-start-a-conversation>.

Crush. Directed by Alison Maclean, produced by Trevor Haysom and Bridget Ikin, New Zealand Film Commission, 1992.

Derrida, Jacques. *Specters of Marx.* Routledge, 2006.

Duff, Alan. *Once Were Warriors.* Tandem, 1990.

Grace, Patricia. *Potiki.* Penguin, 1986.

Heavenly Creatures. Directed by Peter Jackson, produced by Jim Booth and Peter Jackson. WingNut Films, Fontana Productions, New Zealand Film Commission, 1994.

Hulme, Keri. *The Bone People.* Spiral, 1984.

In My Father's Den. Directed by Brad McGann, produced by Trevor Haysom and Dixie Linder, Warner Brothers, 2004.

Jack Be Nimble. Directed by Garth Maxwell, produced by John Barnett, Jonathon Dowling, Murray Newey, Kelly Rogers, Essential Films, New Zealand Film Commission, 1993.

Johnston, Emily R. 'Trauma Theory as Activist Pedagogy: Engaging Students as Reader-Witnesses of Colonial Trauma in *Once Were Warriors*'. *Antipodes*, vol. 28, no.1, 2014, pp. 5–17.

Joyce, Hester. 'Taonga (Cultural Treasures): Reflections on Māori Storytelling in the Cinema of Aotearoa/New Zealand'. *Storytelling in World Cinemas: Contexts,* edited by Lina Khatib, Columbia UP, 2013, pp. 21–34.

Kavka, Misha. 'Haunting and the (Im)possibility of Māori Gothic'. *The Gothic and the Everyday: Living Gothic,* edited by Lorna Piatti-Farnell and Maria Belville, Palgrave Macmillan, 2014, pp. 225–240.

Kerosene Creek. Directed by Michael Bennett, produced by Catherine Fitzgerald, New Zealand Film Commission, 2004.

'Kerosene Creek'. *100% Pure New Zealand.* New Zealand Tourism. <www.newzealand.com/us/feature/kerosene-creek/>.

Lawn, Jennifer. 'Warping the Familiar'. *Gothic NZ: The Darker Side of Kiwi Culture*, edited by Misha Kavka, Jennifer Lawn, and Mary Paul. Otago UP, 2006. pp. 10–24.

Martens, Emiel. 'Māori on the Silver Screen: The Evolution of Indigenous Feature Filmmaking in Aotearoa/New Zealand'. *International Journal of Critical Indigenous Studies,* vol. 5, no.1, 2012, pp. 2–30.

Māui's Hook. Directed by Paora Joseph, produced by Karen Te O Kahurangi Waaka-Tibble, New Zealand Film Commission, 2018.

'Māui's Hook'. *NZ On Screen/Iwi Whititiāhua.* <https://www.nzonscreen.com/title/mauis-hook-2018/quotes>.

Mercer, Erin. '"Frae Ghosties an Ghoulies Deliver Us": Keri Hulme's *The Bone People* and the Bicultural Gothic'. *Journal of New Zealand Literature*, vol. 27, 2009, pp. 111–130.

Miles, Geoffrey. 'Māori Gothic'. *A Made-Up Place: New Zealand in Young Adult Fiction*, edited by Anna Jackson, Geoffrey Miles, Harry Ricketts, Tatjana Schaefer, and Kathryn Walls. Victoria UP, 2011, pp. 194–218.

Once Were Warriors. Directed by Lee Tamahori, produced by Robin Scholes, Fine Line Features, 1994.

Out of the Blue. Directed by Robert Sarkies, produced by Steven O'Meagher and Timothy White. Condor Films, Dendy Films, Desert Road Films, New Zealand Film Commission, New Zealand On Air, Southern Light Films, TV3, 2006.

Rain. Directed by Christine Jeffs, produced by Philippa Campbell, New Zealand Film Commission, 2001.

Schafer, William John. *Mapping The Godzone: A Primer on New Zealand Literature and Culture.* U of Hawaii P, 1998.

Taylor, Apirana. 'In The Rubbish Tin'. *He Rau Aroha: A Hundred Leaves of Love*, Penguin, 1986.

The Strength of Water. Directed by Armagan Ballantyne, produced by Fiona Copland, New Zealand Film Commission, 2009.

Turner, Stephen. 'A Legacy of Colonialism: The Uncivil Society of Aotearoa/New Zealand'. *Cultural Studies*, vol. 13, no. 3, 1999, pp 408–422.

Walker-Morrison, Deborah. 'A Place to Stand: Land and Water in Māori Film'. *Imaginations,* vol. 5, no. 1, 2014, pp. 25–47.

Waru. Directed by Ainsley Gardiner, Briar Grace-Smith, Casey Kaa, Renae Maihi, Awanui Simich-Pene, Paula Whetu Jones, Chelsea Winstanley, Katie Wolfe, produced by Kiel McNaughton and Kerry Warkia, New Zealand Film Commission, 2017.

Whale Rider. Directed by Niki Caro, produced by John Barnett, Frank Hübner, Tim Sanders, South Pacific Pictures, ApolloMedia, Pandora Films, New Zealand Film Production Fund, New Zealand Film Commission, NZ On Air, Filmstiftung Nordrhein-Westfalen, 2002.

About the Author

Emily Holland is a PhD candidate in Media, Film, and Television at The University of Auckland, where she researches hauntology, nostalgia, and corporeality in British and North American horror media.

3.   *The Kettering Incident*: From Tasmanian Gothic to Antarctic Gothic

Billy Stevenson

Abstract

This chapter discusses the relationship between Tasmanian Gothic and post-continuity television through a sustained examination of how place operates in *The Kettering Incident* (2016). Just as post-continuity television works to undercut the unity of place typical of quality television, so Tasmanian Gothic challenges the rhetorics of place that are peculiar to Tasmania in Australian history and lore. Similarly, whereas post-continuity television challenges the fixation of quality television with regionalism, Tasmanian Gothic questions the way in which Tasmania, as a region, is received in the Australian popular imagination. Placing these two aesthetic orientations side by side reveals that Tasmanian Gothic is an inherently post-continuous aesthetic.

Keywords: Australian Gothic; Tasmanian literature; Australian television; Tasmanian television

When *The Kettering Incident* was released in 2016, the show prompted a common response from critics: this was Tasmanian Gothic, but it was something else as well. Set and shot almost entirely in Tasmania, the series follows Anna Macy, a doctor played by Elizabeth Debicki, who returns to her hometown of Kettering, after spending fifteen years in London. As the series unfolds, we learn that Anna left Kettering after her best friend, Gillian, disappeared while camping with her in the forest. Although Anna claimed that she saw strange lights and passed out before waking to find Gillian gone, many of the town's residents believe she had something to do with the disappearance. Across eight elliptical episodes, the series takes us

Gildersleeve, J. and K. Cantrell (eds.), *Screening the Gothic in Australia and New Zealand: Contemporary Antipodean Film and Television*. Taylor & Francis Group, 2022
DOI 10.5117/9789463721141_CH03

through a range of Tasmanian Gothic tropes that escalate so rapidly and converge so dramatically that they quickly seem to exhaust the genre itself.

In one of the foundational formulations of Tasmanian Gothic, Jim Davidson characterized this particular mode of the Gothic as peculiarly occupied with the double valency of presence. Tasmanian Gothic, Davidson argues, is above all concerned with a 'landscape containing presences [...] more correctly styled absences' (316). These negative presences – of the original Indigenous populations, of the particular cruelty of the Tasmanian colonies, of the endemic flora and fauna – were mobilized in the Tasmanian Gothic mode to articulate 'disjunctions between past and present' (Davidson 310). Davidson's comments suggest that Tasmanian Gothic is a structure of feeling as much as a discrete literary style or movement. In Australian history and culture, this structure of feeling is influenced by Tasmania's geographic and cultural isolation from the rest of the continent as much as its peculiar history of colonial brutality. More than any other state, Tasmania resembles Europe, making its differences all the more gothic to a European mindset. Ken Gelder identifies this 'isolation and uneasy sense of its own marginality' as critical to the Tasmanian Gothic outlook (388), while Briony Kidd suggests this marginality has only increased with greater mobility between Tasmania and the mainland, since 'the experience of going away, coming back, and trying to re-assimilate is quintessentially a Tasmanian one'.

In Kidd's terms, the relationship between Tasmania and mainland Australia recapitulates the relationship between Australia and Europe, and the colonial relation more generally. Precisely what makes this relation so uncanny, however, is that Tasmania is simultaneously the colonial homeland in its biophysical resemblances to Europe, and the colonized margin, due to its biophysical distinction from the Australian mainland. As both the Australian state that is closest to and furthest from Europe, Tasmania has bred a form of Gothic that focuses on spatial, temporal, and cultural disjunctions. These have only intensified over the past decade, leading Kidd to observe that 'the version of Tasmania most visible right now is heavily influenced by Tasmanian Gothic'. As a result, Tasmanian Gothic particularly thrives on historical disjunctions – moments where past and present collapse, or when the received account of the past dissolves and disperses. Alex Philp deploys the thylacine as an emblem of this process, arguing that it continues to haunt the Tasmanian and Australian consciousness as a series of unresolved contradictions, 'both a marsupial and a carnivore and therefore both maternal and killer, both domestic and wild, (at times) both female and male, and [...] therefore uncanny and liminal' (88). For Philp, the thylacine's extinction is resonant because it evokes our inability to properly extinguish or address the Tasmanian past. Like that gothic heritage, the thylacine is 'simultaneously extinct and not-extinct', allowing it to confound 'temporal boundaries between past and present' (88).

This motif of the 'not-extinct' corresponds to the gothic trope of the uncanny, or the undead, formulated by Sigmund Freud as 'something which is secretly familiar [*heimlich-heimisch*], which has undergone repression and then returned from it' (947). The uncanny operates when we recognize what has to be repressed in order to create the experience of 'homeliness', or *heimlich*. Since Tasmania occupies such an unusual position in the colonial attempt to establish both a homeland and homeliness on Indigenous soil, Tasmanian Gothic has tended to be especially emphatic in elaborating the role and return of the repressed in home-making. In fact, so complex are these discourses of home-making that it has not been sufficient for Tasmanian Gothic to simply 'recover' a repressed Indigenous substrate from the landscape. Gelder notes that recent instances of Tasmanian Gothic, such as the 2001 thriller *Van Diemen's Land*, have displaced Indigenous tropes into visions of European cannibalism, as if to evoke a finitude to the Gothic's capacity to articulate the intense uncanniness Tasmania holds in the Australian consciousness. Gelder also notes that Aboriginal Gothic, such as Tracey Moffatt's short film *Night Cries* (1989) and Sam Watson's novel *The Kadaitcha Sung* (1990), have tended to reject straightforward 'returns' of Indigenous presence. Instead, these texts simultaneously stage 'pre-colonial struggles' or refuse to sequester Indigenous stories by situating them alongside other forms of haunting, thereby displacing European 'arrival' as their orientating event (388).

Tasmanian Gothic, therefore, gestures towards the limitations of Gothic, as a European mode, in articulating questions of Eurocentric homeliness. As a limit case for the Gothic, Tasmanian Gothic has thus proven especially susceptible to hybridity with other modes – and this continues with *The Kettering Incident*. Not surprisingly, most of the commentary came from Australian publications, or from Australian branches of international publications, while most reviewers focused heavily on the Tasmanian backdrop, often presenting it as a key character. Chitra Ramaswamy, for example, identifies the landscape as the main source of emotion in the series, noting that 'fear, in *The Kettering Incident,* is so pervasive that it is virtually a character in its own right, as is Tasmania: remote, stunning, and perpetually and metaphorically misty'. Similarly, Clem Bastow reviews the series in part by describing her own tour of 'the series' locations, from Bruny Island to the sleepy town of Kettering', which 'intoxicated' her with their hypnotic beauty. Bastow also notes that the series deals with 'a typically Tasmanian conflict' in the 'desperate' battle between foresters and environmentalists.

Despite noting the clear elements of Tasmanian Gothic, however, critics are also united in their perception that the series included something more than Tasmanian Gothic. In the first instance, this involved drawing attention to the way in which the series' 'visual language plays with the – at times – bewildering nature of Tasmania's liminal spaces' (Bastow). Rather than simply featuring Tasmanian spaces, critics note, the series involves obscure, opaque, and liminal spaces. This liminal quality tended to be associated with the cliffs of the southern seaboard: an area that plays a significant role both in the series, and its critical reception. This focus on liminal spaces suggests that Tasmania, and Tasmanian Gothic, is inadequate to *The Kettering Incident*'s gothic aspirations. Conversely, it submits that the series simultaneously does something that is other than, or beyond, Tasmanian Gothic. Critics tended to note this difference by characterizing the series as an act of genre-splicing. Bastow, for example, refers to the series as '21st century Tasmanian gothic par excellence (read: Tasmanian Gothic with a shake of science fiction)' and describes Anna as 'tall and cool as a ghost gum', whose 'almost extraterrestrial presence' sets her apart from other characters.

Several critics also compare the series to the genre-splicing in David Lynch and Mark Frost's cult serial drama *Twin Peaks* (1990). Ramaswamy describes the landscape as 'bathed in the raw-blue light particular to small-town mysteries influenced by *Twin Peaks*', while Jake Wilson describes it as 'one of several recent Australian efforts to emulate American-style "prestige television", a genre that might be said to begin with [...] *Twin Peaks*, a reference point for every subsequent offbeat small-town mystery with hints of the supernatural' (Wilson). Wilson also references one of the key phrases of *Twin Peaks* when he describes the series as 'imagined by head writer Victoria Madden and her team as an insular community full of secrets', a phrase used to refer to protagonist Laura Palmer in *Twin Peaks*. Yet the comparison to *Twin Peaks* is complicated, and makes it difficult to posit a direct lineage of quality television. Where Wilson associates these *Twin Peaks* overtones with American-style 'prestige television', Bastow avers the series' 'pacing has more in common with "Scandi-noir" than the HBO model of golden age "event television"'. Several other viewers note parallels with Scandi-noir, while Wilson himself acknowledges the limitations of the *Twin Peaks* comparison, noting 'there is no equivalent here to Lynch's characteristic absurd humour. The sober tone is closer to Atom Egoyan's films about grief in a cold climate, such as *The Sweet Hereafter*' (Wilson).

Clearly, the series moves between cues familiar from the third age of quality television, and more contemporary televisual registers.

Between these critical commentaries, a rough consensus of the series emerges as an exercise in Tasmanian Gothic that splices genre in ways that defy the lineage of quality television. Figuratively, most critics linked this situation to the role that the green glow of the Aurora Australis plays in the series. This light was, in fact, the defining feature of the eponymous Kettering Incident, since Gillian's disappearance was accompanied by a series of bright green lights that condensed the Aurora into an event that Anna could not compute. The entire series follows Anna's efforts to 'read' this light following her return to the town.

In her review, Ramaswamy draws particular attention to 'the green glow of the Aurora Australis', which she links to the broader lighting scheme of the series 'bathed in the raw blue-tinged light peculiar to small-town mysteries influenced by *Twin Peaks*'. Ramaswamy also makes a connection between this green light and the 'greenies' in the narrative, suggesting that the Aurora Australis abstracts the series' environmental subject matter. Writing in *The Sydney Morning Herald,* Brad Newsome's experience of the series was driven by 'the Aurora Australis bathing everything in an unwholesome green glow', suggesting this green light was not entirely natural, and not entirely a product of the Tasmanian landscape. Rebecca Nicholson's review takes this characterization of the Aurora Australis one step further. Nicholson links the green light to 'the military-style goggles that made Dutch [a character] see green people in the forest'. She presents the green light of the Aurora as ushering in a different mode of perception that affects the relationship between humans and their ecology. Moreover, Nicholson connects the Aurora and the goggles to an emergent and unformulated perceptual possibility, averring that 'they're more than just army regulation night specs'. This convergence of the Aurora and extra-human perception, Nicholson ultimately suggests, is responsible for the open-ended nature of the series, which ensures that 'as the finale comes around, it's clear that almost nothing has been resolved'.

While all these reviews note the predominance of the Aurora Australis in the series, they refrain from mentioning one of the most distinctive features of this phenomenon – that the Aurora occurs between Australia and Antarctica. For this reason, the flagship Australian Antarctic vessel is also called the *Aurora Australis.* This connection is significant, since *The Kettering Incident* gradually gravitates towards Antarctica as it proceeds. Stylistically, the directors tend to focus on spaces with dramatic vantage points over the Southern Ocean. Similarly, Gillian's fate turns out be connected with a doomed Australian Antarctic expedition a decade earlier. However, while these critics might not have focused on this Tasmanian-Antarctic continuity, they do repeatedly come back to the main cipher for this continuity – the 'Kettering Incident' snow globe that is sold everywhere in Anna's hometown. That is, by the time that Anna returns to Kettering, Gillian's disappearance has become a media event, and has spawned different types of tourist texts. The most evocative of these is a mass-produced snow globe, in which the main features of Kettering, and the Tasmanian landscape, are set against an Antarctic vista.

This Tasmanian-Antarctic continuity suggests that the Antarctic Gothic may play a key role in articulating this 'extra' ingredient that critics noticed when describing the series' Tasmanian Gothic features. Only the tip of South America is more contiguous with Antarctica than Tasmania, but cultural and historical factors have precluded much crossover between Tasmanian and Antarctic Gothic before this point. Nevertheless, they share some striking similarities, which partly explains the oddity of how *The Kettering Incident* conceives of the Gothic. The seminal account of Antarctic Gothic comes from William Lenz, who coined the term in 1991 to account for a unique mode of Gothic that he saw operating in the maritime works of Edgar Allan Poe, Herman Melville, and H.P. Lovecraft. While Antarctica is geographically remote from the United States, exploration of the southern continent formed part of the same imperialist and nationalist patterns that led to the growth of American hegemony in the modern era. As a result, Lenz frames Antarctic Gothic as a reflection upon colonialism, in which 'the Antarctic is a new American frontier, an analogous and imaginative new world' (33).

However, as a frontier that resists colonization, Antarctica also reveals a Gothic essence to the project of colonialism itself. Lenz notes that Poe's vision of the Antarctic is pivotal in this respect, presenting the icy, endless landscape as defying human sensation and perception. This is evident in his novel *The Narrative of Arthur Gordon Pym of Nantucket* (1838), a fictional memoir of Antarctic exploration. In this novel, the protagonist Pym is overwhelmed by the icy frontier of Antarctica, and 'lose[s] consciousness and sensation, a response characteristic of a gothic world not bound by time and space, one in which identity itself is ambiguous'. In this venue, 'time, as represented by the watch [...] obey[s] no known laws' (Lenz 33–34). To some extent, this dissolution of time and space is characteristic of the gothic mode more generally. However, Lenz argues that the topographical peculiarities of Antarctica – especially the sheer scale and monotony of its whiteness – take this dissolution to its logical and gothic conclusion. Just as

Tasmania represents a particularly acute condensation of Australian Gothic, so Antarctica offers an especially eloquent culmination of the classical gothic lexicon. *The Kettering Incident* considers what happens when these two gothic endpoints are placed side by side – and how this might illuminate the media sphere in which its textuality unfolds.

While multiple textual lineages and progenies separate Poe from *The Kettering Incident,* Lenz's broad comments about the Antarctic Gothic speak to some of the reasons why this mode saw a resurgence in the 2010s. Expanding his argument out from Poe to a more general dissection of Antarctic Gothic, Lenz argues that this vision of the southern continent tends to confound living and non-living existence, along with sentience and sapience. In doing so, it suggests forms of being that are entirely discorrelated from, and disinterested in, human perception, 'literally beyond comprehension' (35). Poe, Lenz argues, achieves this by inverting the cliché that the Antarctic is barren or sterile: 'What is living may be dead, what appears dead may possess a bizarre form of life, and the laws of our normal universe do not hold' (35). In other words, the typical gothic focus on the undead and the uncanny is intensified by the Antarctic, which presents us with a sensory field so discorrelated from human perception that it defies our ability to distinguish meaningfully between entities that are alive or dead. For Lenz, the Antarctic 'remains a region from which there can be no verifiable report, a purely imaginative realm of symbol, supposition, and superstition [...] a journey into the metaphysical uncertainties of the Absolute Unknown' (35–36). This 'Absolute Unknown' is a function of the 'inhuman whiteness' of the Antarctic topos, 'a symbol of the limits to human perception' (37).

By collapsing the distinction between living and non-living entities, or between *meaningfully* living and non-living entities, Antarctic Gothic also displaces the hierarchies between white sentience and Indigenous sapience that have been used to justify the colonial project. Rather than functioning as a canvas for white projections, the 'inhuman whiteness' of the Antarctic landscape exceeds the white aspirations of its would-be colonizers, projecting their whiteness back onto them, and reifying that whiteness as both discorrelative effect and gothic trope. This foundational account of Antarctic Gothic sheds light on the peculiar opening and ending of *The Kettering Incident.* The narrative events are set in place by Anna flying from London to Tasmania. However, Anna has no memory of this flight, or her motivations for taking it. Instead, she abruptly shifts from London to a car perched on a precipitous road overlooking the Southern Ocean, and only gradually realizes that she has travelled halfway across the world. Rather than introducing Tasmania as a discrete place or mood, the writers and directors present Tasmania as a spatiotemporal dislocation born of its Antarctic-facing shores.

The final episodes of *The Kettering Incident* also converge living and non-living ontologies at the same time that they converge Tasmania and Antarctica. Before discussing these episodes in more detail, however, it is important to note that the series also reflects more recent developments in the Antarctic Gothic mode. In the early 2010s, there was a resurgence of critical discourse around Antarctic Gothic, which Douglas Fox attributes to the most significant exploratory venture into Antarctica since it was mapped – the excavation of its subglacial lakes, which are bodies of still water that lie, intact, deep beneath the icy surface. Fox situates this exploration of the subglacial lakes within a broader lineage of Antarctic Gothic imagery. He argues that this imagery has retreated as the continent has been progressively mapped. Initially, Antarctic Gothic tropes, like those found in the work of Poe and Melville, encompassed the entire Antarctic region, including the oceans and icebergs around the continent. Then, as these bodies of water were navigated, Antarctic Gothic tropes focused more on the interior of the continent, and the subterranean space beneath the continent, as occurs in the writing of H.P. Lovecraft, as well as the two film adaptations of John W. Campbell's novella, *Who Goes There?*: *The Thing from Another World* (1951) and *The Thing* (1982). Fox draws upon the work of microbiologist Brett Christner to suggest that 'even just a little new information from the lakes could fuel a new generation of science fiction'. Specifically, Fox speculates that the boring and drilling into the subglacial lakes will produce two new iterations of Antarctic Gothic, both of which are explored in *The Kettering Incident.* Both of these new forms of Antarctic Gothic, Fox argues, relate to the microbes that will likely occur within the lakes, which 'could turn out to be the ultimate monsters in this scenario'.

For Fox, even the possibility of these microbes has two distinct figurative implications for Antarctic Gothic. First, they reiterate the Antarctic Gothic dissolution of living and non-living entities, but on a planetary scale. If there are microbes beneath the surface of the Antarctic ice sheet, they will be among the oldest living creatures on Earth. However, they will simultaneously be adapted to some of the most adverse conditions on Earth – conditions that would normally preclude life as we are accustomed to conceptualize it. These creatures will thus reiterate the 'Paleozoic' nature of the Antarctic biome, 'an ecosystem like no other on Earth' and 'reveal plenty about life's limits', both figuratively and ecologically (Fox). At the same time, the release of these microbes might also reiterate the fundamental disinterest of the Antarctic continent, and the Earth itself, to human perception and colonization. In part, this is because the 'ability of ecosystems to survive in places with minimal nutrients and without sunlight [...] will provide clues to what life, if any, could survive in liquid oceans that lurk beneath many miles of ice in other parts of the solar system, on Jupiter's moon Europa or Saturn's moon Enceladus' (Fox). These microbes may also be methanogenic, meaning they will release significant quantities of methane into the atmosphere if disturbed, thereby contributing to global warming and climate catastrophe. While Fox's writing is speculative, it evokes a new Antarctic Gothic mode in which the southern continent operates as a figurative matrix between outer space and climate catastrophe. Both the universe and global warming form what Timothy Morton has described as hyperobjects, 'things that are massively distributed in time and space relative to humans' (1). The Antarctic also functions as a hyperobject in Antarctic Gothic, while clarifying that the hyperobject is itself inherently Gothic in nature, as Morton wonders if, 'when we think the hyperobject, are we in some sense thinking the conditions of the human mind?' (85)

The Kettering Incident treats the Antarctic as a hyperobject in this way. Rather than situating its narrative entirely or exclusively in Antarctica, the series treats the Antarctic as a figurative field that amplifies the effects of Tasmanian Gothic. In another recent treatment of Antarctic Gothic, Elizabeth Leane notes that it is quite distinct from depictions of the Arctic, which tends to be more domesticated in the history of exploration and representation. Leane argues that the remoteness and continental heft of the Antarctic landmass gives it a special status that distinguishes it from other icebound structures and landforms on Earth (60). However, *The Kettering Incident* challenges this conception of Antarctic Gothic, focusing on a series of Antarctic events that reiterate its status as narrative hyperobject. These events come into focus during the latter part of the series. For the first two-thirds of the narrative, Anna's investigation into Gillian's disappearance takes her down many avenues, all of which help unfold a sprawling portrait of the town of Kettering as a whole. These threads do not cohere as the series comes to a close; however, they do dissipate more pointedly around a series of Antarctic tropes that start to emerge. First, Anna discovers a link between the events taking place in town and an Antarctic expedition that ended in tragedy. Then, she finds out that the link resonates with other odd events that have occurred in icy regions of the world, such as the Dyatlov Pass Incident, which remains unsolved, or unresolved, to the present day.

The series therefore gravitates towards a series of Antarctic events that are divorced from the specific topography of Antarctica itself, but still partake of its gothic and hyperobjective status. For Lenz, this transplantation of the 'inhuman whiteness' of the Antarctic to the rest of the globe is the final stage of Antarctic Gothic – a stage that he sees as prefigured by Herman Melville's *Moby-Dick* (1851). Reading the white whale through the lens of Melville's Antarctic fixations, Lenz presents its 'hieroglyphic and blank-faced' whiteness as a fragment of Antarctic Gothic that has carved off from the continent to circle the globe (35). Just as Poe 'visualizes the Antarctic unknown in the reversal of conventional Gothic black', and discovers 'the symbolic meaning of the perfect whiteness of Antarctica', so Melville dissociates this whiteness from Antarctic topography and generalizes it to a broad Antarctic figurative field (35).

This Antarctic figurative field is also the subject matter of *The Kettering Incident,* which updates this field to reflect the human finitude in the face of climate change and anthropocentric decline that Fox's analysis suggests. By grafting this field back onto Tasmania, and effectively presenting Tasmania as another outpost of the Antarctic, the series takes the colonial contradictions that haunt Tasmania, and fuses them with the ultimate refusal of Antarctica, and the globe, to be colonized by human perception, especially in the midst of climate crisis. This is not to say, however, that *The Kettering Incident* is exactly 'about' colonization or climate crisis, but that it gestures towards a mode of being that bypasses the human as a category for understanding these traumas and uses the Antarctic figurative field as catalyst. This altered mode of being, along with the Antarctic Gothic that facilitates it, comprises the additional ingredient that early reviewers of the series discerned in their discussion of its Tasmanian Gothic features. Bastow identified this 'other' being with the life of plants. Similarly, Wilson alternates between describing vegetation as scenery – 'dolomite cliffs, forested hills, clouded skies' – and characterizing it as more assertive, as in his suggestion that 'moss climbs up walls and onto bodies, as if the land were an organism'.

Wilson's formulation positions vegetation – in this case, moss – in a paradoxical manner. On the one hand, he seems to grant moss an anthropomorphic or zoomorphic agency in its capacity to 'climb' up walls. At the same time, however, he presents moss as an interstitial space between 'bodies' and 'organisms' as conceived in human or at least animal terms. In this sense, moss is capable of drawing upon the motility of humans and animals, but it is not exactly human or animal itself, while still occupying a mode of being that is more than mere plant passivity. Wilson and Bastow's comments reflect the broader groundswell in vegetal ontology over the past decade. Matthew Hall, for example, has argued for an end to the 'human hyperseparation from the natural world' (1), and especially the plant world, since 'most places which consist of life are visibly *plantscapes*', such that 'being in the natural world first and foremost involves being amongst plants, not amongst animals, fungi or bacteria' (3). If this seems counter-intuitive, it is only because 'the phenomenon of plant blindness' (5) represses the fact that 'the bulk of the visible biomass on this planet is comprised of plants', the main sources of life and being (3). For Hall, there are several key reasons for a renewed interest in plant ontology. First, he argues, plants are intrinsically important on their own terms. Second, plants play a critical role in climate catastrophe, meaning that any proper account of climate catastrophe has to factor in the impact, utility, and significance of the plant kingdom. Finally, Hall suggests that discarding plant ontology is part of the reason for climate catastrophe in the first place, since 'conserving the natural environment is no longer sufficiently served by an anthropocentric nor a zoocentric account of moral consideration' (14). These dominate most ontologies, which have traditionally represented the presence of nature as 'amorphous and peripheral' due to the 'way that plants (synonymous with nature) are themselves perceived', or not perceived.

Michael Marder develops Hall's position further, arguing that 'vegetal being' represents an anti-hermeneutic orientation that performs much the same philosophical labour as Antarctic Gothic. Since vegetal activity 'encrypts itself in its mode of appearance by presenting itself in the guise of passivity', it ends up 'never presenting itself as such', consisting precisely of 'that which does not appear in the open' (20). In terms that anticipate Morton's hyperobject, plant ontology thus becomes 'an obscure non-object: obscure, because it ineluctably withdraws, flees from sight and from rigorous interpretation; non-object, because it works outside, before and beyond all [...] representations' (20). The convergence of vegetal and Antarctic Gothic motifs is especially clear in the way *The Kettering Incident* begins and ends. After a brief prologue depicting the 'incident' itself, the series opens in London, where Anna is working as a doctor. Since she works night shifts, there is very little demarcation of time and space, heightened through disorienting cuts, bleached close-ups, and a muted palette – an Antarctic visual scheme that further disorients Anna's body clock. In addition, the all-night rhythm of Anna's hospital is fused with the low-level hum of ambient climate crisis. At one point, Anna watches a broadcast stating that scientists will have to 'rethink London's flood protection by the middle of this century'.

Although these opening scenes are set in London, there is no clear sense of place – just a diffuse field of global anxiety that displaces Anna from her own sense of embodied autonomy. While we know that she is from Tasmania, there is no clear sense that going home will restore her with any clear sense of her own agency either. In an early scene, a young girl in the hospital asks

Anna, 'Will you miss me when I go home?', and Anna replies, 'I'll miss you very much', even though she has just heard that the girl is unlikely to go home in the near future, if at all. Such motifs of aborted and forestalled homecoming bleach Tasmania and England into a common Antarctic blankness and opacity. When Anna does 'return' to Kettering, her return does not occur as a conscious decision, or even as a conscious event, but as a further immersion in this Antarctic Gothic dissolution of time and space. This immersion is preceded by an unusual incident at the hospital in London. Anna's supervisor shows her footage that proves she has come into the hospital on multiple occasions, with no conscious memory of having done so. Before Anna can even process this information, she has another blackout and then wakes up in a car in Tasmania. This car is parked precariously on a bluff that overlooks the Southern Ocean and the Aurora Australis. At the very moment at which Anna is dissociated from her digitally mediated self, she is collapsed back into the Tasmanian-Antarctic continuum. As with Antarctic Gothic more generally, the Antarctic sheen that suffuses Woods's directorial style prevents Anna from being able to project a stable version of herself onto her adoptive homeland. Since she is a Tasmanian expatriate living in England, her adoptive homeland is both the colonizing and colonized space, turning her into an embodiment both of the paradoxes that drive Tasmanian Gothic, and of the figurative hinge at which Tasmanian Gothic segues into Antarctic Gothic.

The Antarctic Gothic is signalled in terms of the mise-en-scène and Anna herself. From the moment that Anna wakes up in Tasmania, the Southern Ocean, and the light of the Australis, are established as the driving force behind this Antarctic dissolution of time and space. The Australis becomes the medium linking Tasmania to Antarctica, and, later on, to other Antarctic events around the globe. Accordingly, the sky is foregrounded during these opening scenes – the first disturbances Anna sees are birds falling from the clouds, while she awakens to discover an origami bird on her car dashboard. Anna's awakening also starts a convergence of day and night that intensifies over the course of the series. When she emerges from the car, it is unclear whether the sun or the full moon is hanging over the water, partly because the Australis suffuses the entire sky with an uncanny sheen. As the series proceeds, we are not even offered the option of day or night, since the sun and moon start to appear next to each other in the sky. As Anna travels into Kettering, the iridescent sheen of the Australis starts to make its way into more quotidian objects and surfaces, including a bag containing drugs that sets several major plot points in motion.

In addition, the incursion of Antarctic Gothic is signalled by presenting Anna herself in a largely vegetal state. While she recovers from the shock of waking up in the car, and quickly situates herself in Tasmania, she never quite orients herself to the surrounding environment. Her presence is divested of any clear sense of motivation or intentionality, since she has no real sense of why she has returned, or what she is looking for. This is quite striking in that her return is eventful for the rest of the town. In this regard, the entire series traces Anna's efforts to articulate why she returned to Tasmania – and how Tasmania relates to the Antarctic sheen that continues to suffuse the series' cinematography. Although Gillian goes missing, and several other people have gone missing since Anna left Kettering, Anna is also missing, since she cannot recover the part of herself that travelled to Tasmania (or lived in Tasmania) to begin with. Caught halfway between investigating the missing, and missing herself, Anna's presence both conjures up and displaces Tasmanian Gothic as a point of reference, gesturing instead to a chillier Antarctic blankness. To that end, Anna is framed in a plant-like manner. Like a plant, Anna moves slowly and in a phototropic way, seeming to seek out the light, as she twists her limbs and head to the nearest window, door, or break in the clouds. Despite the incredible visual backdrops, she does not seem to use sight as her main sense – or, if she does use sight, she uses it in a non-human way, like the moths that flutter in and out of the narrative. Anna also feels an affinity with the forest around Kettering, albeit not a political or ideological affinity, since she is only provisionally associated with the party protesting the local timber mill. Instead, Anna's affinity is ontological – the first step in a gradual fusion of botanical and human physiognomy that disrupts the balance of life and non-life in the final two episodes.

The penultimate episode develops these concerns further. The episode starts with the revelation that the water supply of Kettering has been contaminated by a 'pathogen of unknown origin'. This pathogen causes cells to duplicate at an unprecedented rate, which is mirrored in the appearance of the moon during the day and the sun during the night. Doctors observe that the disease produces a vegetative state, but it is really more of a vegetal state, persisting even when the water supply to the town has been cut off. Much of the episode follows characters waiting in dreamlike torpor as their symptoms accumulate, resulting in a vegetal ambience that is enhanced by the pervasive atmosphere of quarantine and lockdown. The episode devotes significant attention to Barbara Holloway, a local artist. Barbara's art practice consists of turning tree trunks into abstract sculptures, appropriating vegetation, and then transforming it into something more alien – or revealing its inherently alien qualities. Shortly after, Officer Fergus McFadden punches a log in frustration, reiterating the materiality and opacity of vegetal being as expressed by Barbara's sculptures. These vegetal motifs coalesce around the first trip to Mother Sullivan's Ridge, a local landform that plays a prominent role in the landscape. As the site where Gillian went missing, and the epicentre of more recent happenings, Mother Sullivan's Ridge is both the quintessential Tasmanian Gothic space in the series, and the site where Tasmanian Gothic bleeds into its Antarctic counterpart. As the episode proceeds, we learn that the water supply has been contaminated by the dumping of unknown toxins at the ridge. These toxins have converged animal and plant physiologies, dooming anyone who ventures up there to become a plant themselves if they remain too long. In a grisly scene, a pair of locals travel up to the top of the ridge and discover another man who went missing, with leaves growing out of his dead body.

The depiction of Mother Sullivan's Ridge presages the depiction of the woods in *Twin Peaks: The Return*, released in the following year. Both *The Return* and *The Kettering Incident* present uncanniness as an electrical disruption of natural landscapes. As the action converges on the ridge, Kettering experiences a sonic boom, and then a local electrical storm that transmits energy from the ridge back to the town through elevated wires. Krawitz cuts from a montage sequence of electrical wires to Jens Jorgensson, the seer of the environmentalists, inscribing a cryptic symbol in a tall, pylon-like tree. This imagery suggests a transfusion, or interfusion, of blood, electricity, and plant life over the next part of the episode. This interfusion also produces a perceptual shift across the entire town. As Krawitz traces its process, we move from lights flickering in the local bar, to streetlamps bursting along the main street, to the perspective of a tawny frogmouth sitting in a tree. This shift from mechanical to animal perception is extended into the realm of plant perception, as the scene abruptly moves back to the forest, where we are presented with a disorienting combination of hand-held images and night vision images, both of which suggest an eerie botanical presence.

In the second half of the episode, these vegetal motifs are directly linked to Antarctica, as Anna discovers a mysterious figure in Kettering may be a scientist who was thought to have perished in a doomed Antarctic expedition a decade earlier. As she starts to investigate this Antarctic angle, the Aurora Australis dominates the episode's colour scheme, overlaying every scene with an iridescent hue that makes it difficult to distinguish between day and night. Soon after, Anna links the scientist to the Dyatlov Pass Incident, and other mysterious events in icebound regions of the world. This expansion of Antarctic Gothic is signaled by Krawitz's movement towards southern escarpments, suggesting a common gaze towards Antarctica.

Accordingly, this revelation about Antarctica gives way to a montage sequence of characters looking out on bodies of water. This draws together the dreamlike torpor and uncanny duration of the episode, evoking a collective communion between Tasmanian and Antarctic Gothic tropes. The communion corresponds to the Australis, which becomes the medium linking Tasmania to Antarctica, and Antarctica to the plethora of Antarctic Gothic spaces that the narrative posits around the globe. Rather than focusing exclusively on Antarctica, the episode presents Antarctica as a hyperobject, only conceivable in terms of Antarctic 'events' that are distributed across the globe and dispersed across the narrative. This connective tissue is also narrativized by the space beneath Mother Sullivan's Ridge, which two other characters discover through a trapdoor in a barn. In the later part of the episode, the two townsfolk explore this space, despite the fact that it is almost impossible to fully visualize or conceptualize. While we do not see any more of this space in this episode, it does introduce the most stylized Antarctic tableau yet – a local Antarctic scientist, camped on a precarious escarpment, gazing southwards over the ocean, lit by a double moon or double sun (it is unclear which). As the subterranean space below Mother Sullivan's Ridge converges with this sublime Antarctic tableau, Anna is institutionalized, and from here on displaced from the story – not in the sense that she is in it less, but that her agency becomes totally diffuse.

The final episode of *The Kettering Incident* converges these Tasmanian and Antarctic tropes on a vision of vegetal existence. As plants grow at an accelerated rate, they start to overtake houses and dwellings, while Anna learns about other Antarctic incidents that have occurred around the globe over the last fifty years. These motifs centre around a symbol found in both Antarctica and Kettering, but the meaning of this symbol dissolves into a series of patterns, allusions, and resonances that fuse human and vegetal existence. In doing so, they preclude any final account of Gillian's disappearance, or any stable reading of the landscape where it occurred. Instead, we are left with a radically accelerated Antarctic Gothic in which the very tools we might use to parse it are now destabilized by a field that exceeds human perception.

Works Cited

Bastow, Clem. 'The Kettering Incident Review – Tasmanian Gothic Thriller Par Excellence'. *The Guardian,* 10 June 2016. <www.theguardian.com/tv-and-radio/2016/jun/10/the-kettering-incident-review-tasmanian-gothic-thriller-par-excellence>.

Davidson, Jim. 'Tasmanian Gothic'. *Meanjin,* vol. 44, no. 2, 1989, pp. 307–324.

Fox, Douglas. 'Mountains of Madness: Scientists Poised to Drill Through Antarctic Ice and Into Gothic Horror'. *Wired,* 27 Dec. 2012. <www.wired.com/2012/12/antarctic-gothic-horror/>.

Freud, Sigmund. 'The Uncanny'. *The Norton Anthology of Theory and Criticism.* Translated by Alix Strachey, edited by Vincent B. Leitch, William E. Cain, Laurie A. Finke, Barbara E. Johnson, John McGowan, and Jeffrey J. Williams, Norton, 2001, pp. 929–952.

Gelder, Ken. 'Australian Gothic'. *A New Companion to the Gothic,* edited by David Punter, 2012, Wiley-Blackwell, pp. 379–392.

Hall, Matthew. *Plants as Persons: A Philosophical Botany.* SUNY P, 2011.

The Kettering Incident. Directed by Rowan Woods and Tony Krawitz, written by Victoria Madden, Louise Fox, Cate Shortland, and Andrew Knight, created by Victoria Madden and Vincent Sheehan, Showcase, 2016.

Kidd, Briony. 'How Tasmania became the Gothic Muse of Australian Film and TV'. *The Guardian,* 24 Nov. 2016. <www.theguardian.com/film/2016/nov/24/how-tasmania-became-the-gothic-muse-of-australian-film-and-tv>.

Leane, Elizabeth. *Antarctica in Fiction: Imaginative Narratives of the Far South.* Cambridge UP, 2012.

Lenz, William. 'Poe's "Arthur Gordon Pym" and the Narrative Techniques of Antarctic Gothic'. *CEA Critic,* vol. 53, no. 3, 1991, pp. 30–38.

Marder, Michael. *Plant-Thinking: A Philosophy of Vegetal Life.* Columbia UP, 2013.

Morton, Timothy. *Hyperobjects: Philosophy and Ecology after the End of the World.* U of Minnesota P, 2013.

Newsome, Brad. 'The Kettering Incident – Dark, Brooding, and Captivating'. *The Sydney Morning Herald,* 24 June 2016. <www.smh.com.au/entertainment/tv-and-radio/the-kettering-incident-reviewed-dark-brooding-and-captivating-20160624-gpqupu.html>.

Nicholson, Rebecca. 'The Kettering Incident – Do You Miss *Stranger Things*? This Will Tide You Over'. *The Guardian,* 2 Mar. 2017. <www.theguardian.com/tv-and-radio/2017/mar/02/the-kettering-incident-do-you-miss-stranger-things-elizabeth-debicki>.

Philp, Alex. 'Hunted, Now Haunting: The Thylacine as a Gothic Symbol in Julia Leigh's *The Hunter*'. *Gothic Animals: Uncanny Otherness and the Animal With-Out,* edited by Ruth Heholt and Melissa Edmundson, Palgrave, 2020, pp. 75–88.

Ramaswamy, Chitra. 'The Kettering Incident – Tasmania's Answer to *Twin Peaks*'. *The Guardian,* 16 Feb. 2017. <www.theguardian.com/tv-and-radio/2017/feb/16/kettering-incident-tasmania-answer-to-twin-peaks-real-marigold-hotel>.

Wilson, Jake. 'The Kettering Incident'. *Australian Book Review,* 5 Sep. 2016. <www.australianbookreview.com.au/arts-update/101-arts-update/3570-the-kettering-incident>.

About the Author

Billy Stevenson holds a PhD from the University of Sydney. He has published on post-cinematic media, changes in cinematic infrastructure, and the contemporary television landscape, and is at work on a book-length study of *Twin Peaks: The Return.*

4. 'Going Home is One Thing This Lot of Blockheads Can't Do': Unhomely Renovations on *The Block*

Ella Jeffery

Abstract

The Block (2003–2004; 2010–) exemplifies Australia's fixation on home renovation. Renovation programmes are a reality television sub-genre characterized by excess, artifice, and questions of property and possession – also key concerns of the Gothic. *The Block*'s renovations appear homely: the goal is to produce *more* comfortable, *more* stylish, *more* suitable homes. Following Sigmund Freud's assertion that homeliness inevitably gives rise to the unhomely, I argue that renovation on *The Block* is an unhomely process in which the unprepossessing suburban houses under renovation become labyrinthine counterfeits of the Australian dream of home ownership, where contestants encounter spectres of bankruptcy and housing insecurity, and undergo endlessly repeated cycles of claustrophobia and crisis that return to haunt them even after the programme has ended.

Keywords: *The Block*; renovation; Gothic; unhomely; Australia

Home renovation on Australian television is bright, energetic, upbeat – at first glance, not at all the stuff of the Gothic. Australia's longest-running reality renovation programme, *The Block* (2003–2004; 2010–), exemplifies many key themes of twenty-first-century Australia's obsession with renovation: aspiration (linked to class mobility and wealth accumulation), self-transformation, and excessive consumption. In each iteration of the hugely popular programme, now entering production of its seventeenth season, contestants compete in pairs to renovate rundown houses, hotels,

Gildersleeve, J. and K. Cantrell (eds.), *Screening the Gothic in Australia and New Zealand: Contemporary Antipodean Film and Television*. Taylor & Francis Group, 2022
DOI 10.5117/9789463721141_CH04

or other dwellings for a cash prize. *The Block* is a programme about property, aspiration, and improvement, and renovations on the show are, on the surface, inherently homely: the goal is to produce *more* comfortable, *more* stylish homes for an idealized Australian family. Space, architecture, and the home have long been key concerns of the Gothic (Aguirre 1), just as social anxieties surrounding property, ownership, wealth, and class have always supplied impetus for gothic narratives (Botting 4). Like the Gothic, *The Block* is a programme that dramatizes questions about and obsessions with property as a means of addressing broader Australian anxieties about housing access, insecurity, and the ongoing erosion of the Australian dream of home ownership in the twenty-first century.

The Block is not intended to be viewed as a gothic text, but nonetheless contains a great many elements that cleave to the traditions and tropes of the gothic mode. In reading this popular reality programme through the lens of the Gothic, this chapter unearths some of the programme's – and, more broadly, middle Australia's – most closely held anxieties about what it means to dwell in contemporary Australia. I explore gothic elements in *The Block*'s structure, format, and production, discuss the ways in which sensation and spectacle are common to both gothic and contemporary popular culture (Dolar 7), and consider in particular the *unheimlich* elements of *The Block*. The *unheimlich* is particularly central to this analysis, focusing as it does on a combination of that which is familiar and unfamiliar, and the discomfort or terror produced by this. First brought to prominence in Sigmund Freud's 1919 essay *Das Unheimlich*, the term is rendered in English as uncanny or unhomely – the latter is the term I apply in this chapter to emphasize its connection to the domestic space in particular. The unhomely is a subtler and more nebulous dimension of the Gothic, one that has to do with the permeable boundaries between that which is familiar and safe, and that which is unknown, repressed, or terrifying. The unhomely is, in Freud's sense, not the sensational terror of high Gothic, but a 'dread and creeping horror' (Freud et al. 545) or, as Anthony Vidler puts it, 'the perpetual exchange between the homely and the unhomely, the imperceptible sliding of cosiness into dread' (3), which are key dimensions of the dramatization of renovation on *The Block*.

On *The Block*, the process of dismantling the house transforms a space that was once familiar into a strange, unfamiliar, and often dangerous site, one where the reality TV contestants design and build an ever-expanding and increasingly luxurious house, dwelling in its half-completed guest rooms, moving through a space that, like the ruined piles of high gothic texts, becomes 'a labyrinth, a maze, a site of secrets' (Punter and Byron 261). I contend that renovation on *The Block* is a fundamentally unhomely process, in line with Freud's conception of homeliness as inevitably giving rise to the unhomely (in Freud et al. 623), and Nicholas Royle's assertion that the uncanny is inextricably bound up with thoughts of home and dispossession, the homely and unhomely, property, and alienation' (6).

As I have noted, *The Block*, like a great many gothic narratives, is a programme obsessed with property and possession. Contestants are terrorized not by patriarchal tyranny and disinheritance, as is the focus of many of the genre's classic texts, but by the spectres that menace twenty-first-century Australia: the capitalist fears of bankruptcy, bad taste, and housing insecurity. Like reality television as a genre, the Gothic, particularly its screen-based iterations, operate through 'the realm of spectacle' (Kavka 209): the deployment of common reality television tropes, such as frequent transgressions of private/public boundaries by camera crews, create claustrophobia, distress, and isolation for contestants, and a gothic sense of entrapment and paranoia (Botting 104) is heightened by the ever-expanding, maze-like houses in which the contestants eat, work, and sleep. Further, renovation on *The Block* is a compulsively repetitive practice that leads contestants through endless cycles of crisis and anxiety, an ongoing unhomely repetition in line with Royle's argument that the unhomely 'would appear to be indissociably bound up with a sense of repetition or "coming back" – the return of the repressed, the constant or eternal recurrence of the same thing, a compulsion to repeat' (1). Even after completing the show, contestants are caught in unending renovation projects long after they leave *The Block*, and are thus enclosed in an ongoing renovation that is impossible to complete, in the same way that upward class mobility and housing security is increasingly impossible to achieve for working class Australians.

There have been, at time of writing, a total of sixteen seasons of *The Block*, with a seventeenth season currently in production for 2021. The programme's premise involves five pairs of contestants, each allocated a rundown house or apartment to renovate one room at a time. The two-person teams comprise mostly heterosexual couples, or siblings, or friends, and each team arrives on *The Block* with an interest in renovation or in learning how to renovate. *The Block* compartmentalizes the renovation into smaller narrative arcs, so each week is devoted to the renovation of a particular room – e.g. 'Master Bedroom Week' and 'Kitchen Week'. Contestants renovate and style the assigned room, a process that involves major structural work as well as shopping for furniture, appliances, and other items. The show's hosts, Scott Cam and Shelley Craft, interact with the contestants throughout the week and Cam's voiceover guides the viewer through each episode. At the end of the week, a 'Room Reveal' takes place: the finished rooms are revealed to the programme's panel of three judges, each of whom score the rooms out of ten and deliver commentary on the design. The team with the highest score after each week's Room Reveal wins $10,000 (AUD) towards their renovation. In the season finale, the completed houses are auctioned to the public. All contestants win any amount of money that exceeds their property's reserve price (a price that is set by the programme's real estate consultants), and the team whose property fetches the highest price above their reserve also wins an additional $100,000.

In this chapter I focus on Season 13 of *The Block*, which aired from 30 July to 29 October 2017, as it is the most recent complete season to involve renovating houses (the 2020 and 2021 seasons were incomplete at the time of writing). The 2018 and 2019 seasons both involved renovating old hotels into high-end apartments, but I am particularly interested in exploring the unhomely resonances of *The Block*'s engagement with the twenty-first-century Australian obsession with houses: their attendant imagery of homeliness, security, and familiar comfort gives rise to the unhomely, which Freud describes as 'that class of the terrifying which leads back to something long known, to us, once very familiar' (in Freud et al. 620). *The Block*'s mix of high drama, interpersonal competition, property acquisition, and renovation speaks to Australian cultural fantasies of secure, stylish, upper-middle-class dwelling in a way that other programmes do not, but also to the Gothic's preoccupation with class and paranoia (Botting 4), and, in the staging of an Australian dream of home ownership that has always been suspect and exclusionary, 'the incursions and invasions of a semi-imaginary past into the present' (Kavka 211). Many other Australian-made renovation television programmes that have dominated free-to-air television in the last two decades, such as *Backyard Blitz* (2000–2007), *House Rules* (2013–), and *Reno Rumble* (2015–2016), have found success in Australia but have not been accepted by international audiences. Imported shows that enjoy a broad viewership in the United States and United Kingdom, such as *Extreme Makeover: Home Edition* (2003–2012), *Love It or List It* (2008–), *Fixer Upper* (2013–2018), and *Property Brothers* (2011–) have not achieved the same widespread recognition in Australia. *The Block* has widely been received as Australia's major contribution to the reality renovation genre, and in this analysis I examine the ways in which the sensationalized, property-obsessed mode of renovation reality and gothic interweave on screen.

The Gothic has always been a mode that dramatizes and explores cultural tensions and fears (Hogle 500), and the premise of *The Block* is also constructed to dramatize and symbolically resolve a set of cultural anxieties around the fraught reality of the Australian dream of home ownership and aspirational class mobility. The programme's room-by-room renovation and its series of weekly challenges are intended to stage the kinds of real-life situations that a homebuying, renovating couple might encounter: overspending, discovering structural flaws in the house, interpersonal conflict. Therefore, in addition to the unhomely resonances embedded in the process of renovation itself, it is unsurprising that the show itself also has a series of gothic themes, structures, and motifs since the show is, at its core, a programme grounded in contemporary Australia's anxieties about stable dwellings, and for this reason it continues to captivate audiences.

Botting notes that the 'Gothic remains an incredibly fertile and diverse cultural form. [...] [it] continually reinvents itself, and is reinvented' (196), but the gothic qualities of renovation programmes have rarely been the subject of scholarly investigation. Two scholars, Ruth McElroy and Catherine Spooner, have discussed links between the Gothic and acts of renovation on television: McElroy discusses UK renovation programmes in which 'the repressed returns to haunt the participants and the audience alike [...] as the presenters and experts reveal the bad taste that we endured but of which we may also be cured' (97), while Spooner examines lifestyle television and 'what happens when Gothic is brought into close proximity with conventional markers of taste' ('Gothic Lifestyle' 443). There has been little discussion, however, of the ways in which quintessentially gothic concerns such as 'social status and physical property' (Botting 4) or 'complex and conflicted cultural histories' (16) are invoked in renovation programmes. Similarly, *The Block*, despite its prominent position in Australian popular culture, has received minimal attention from scholars. Exceptions include Fiona Allon's book, *Renovation Nation* (2008), Andrew Gorman-Murray's exploration of representations of gay domesticities in *The Block*'s 2004 season (2011), and Buck Clifford Rosenberg's study of hegemonic masculinity as embodied by *The Block*'s host, Scott Cam, written in response to Cam's earlier roles on programmes like *Backyard Blitz* (2008).

Scholars have, however, extensively documented the rise of Australian obsessions with both renovation and renovation programmes, and have contended that the popularity of these programmes, which focus on the private, controllable domestic space, can be read as a response to viewer perceptions of national and global political instability, housing insecurity, terror, and risk (see Bonner 2003; Lewis 2008; Rosenberg 2011). Rosenberg ('Property and Home Make-Over' 507) examines the privileging, even fetishizing, of the space of the home and the symbolically self-governing position of the homeowner in Australian renovation culture, and suggests that Australia's cultural obsession with renovating can also be read as a response to personal and national insecurity:

> citizens live in a perpetual state of anxiety, driven by economic instability, the threat of nuclear war, terrorism, and environmental destruction. The risk society, however, is not restricted to nuclear, environmental, or terror threats. It resides more subtly in the advance of late capitalism, and the social retreat from the public sphere. [...] Through making over our homes we can symbolically erase or dislodge the build-up of risk from the very walls we hope will protect us. Risk then becomes managed through consumption and lifestyle. (507)

Australian anxieties about dwelling, possession, ownership, and property can be played out via the practice of home renovation on *The Block*, where symbolic resolution (via the completion of the renovation project) is always presented as an achievable goal; contemporary anxieties about bankruptcy and recession, the defence of Australia's borders, or the volatile housing market can be symbolically resolved in the hermetic, controllable space of the home. In Allon's view, the nation itself, and the home as microcosm of the nation, are implicated in complex questions about ownership, possession, displacement, and history (2), just as the Gothic has long been a mode through which social, cultural, and political upheavals have been negotiated (Punter and Byron 22). Acts of renovation on *The Block* become a vital tool through which Australian homeowners can confront and resolve larger fears, and can be read as a compulsion to readdress a long-buried insecurity, a 'dread and creeping horror' (Freud et al. 545) of the homeowner's lack of control in a housing market that is increasingly insecure, combined with enduring class-based anxieties linked to home ownership.

No scholars have yet noted that these are also key concerns of the Gothic: the secrets of the past, the question of inheritance, the haunting quality of personal and public history, as well as the unhomely 'sense of homeliness uprooted' (Royle 1). Frequently, the supernatural and sensational elements of the Gothic mask more practical concerns about property, power, wealth, and inheritance (Anolik 668). The castle, the ruin, the suburban house – all key loci of gothic narratives – are always bound up with concerns about ownership and possession: Anolik notes that a key concern of gothic plots is the question of 'who will be authorized to own, bequeath, and inherit the gothic property?' (667). This question lingers throughout much of Ann Radcliffe's *The Romance of the Forest* (1791) as La Motte makes minor renovations but, for fear of alerting his pursuers to his hiding place, will not go so far as to make the space fully liveable, while much of the plot of *The Castle of Otranto* (1764) is set in motion by the prophecy about the castle's real owner who will come to take it back. The classic texts of the genre deploy these concerns in service of addressing anxieties about industrialization, disinheritance, and power (Punter and Byron 20). *The Block*, by contrast, plays out contemporary anxieties about housing security, financial stability, border control, and the middle-class status quo. Eddie Robson argues that 'Gothic is a "safe" way of indulging and excising our fears' (242), and while *The Block* is certainly not constructed as a gothic programme, it frequently indulges, sensationalizes, and then resolves these anxieties in the same way texts that are more recognisably aligned to the Gothic seek to do.

In Season 13, for example, contestants renovate five run-down houses in the Melbourne suburb of Elsternwick. As noted earlier, contestants play as two-person 'teams': common pairings include the husband and wife team, of which Season 13 includes three (Ronnie and Georgia, Sarah and Jason, Clint and Hannah), the unmarried heterosexual couple, of which the second season has one (Elyse and Josh), and the friends – often staged as 'best mates' if the friends are both male, as is the case in Season 13, where the sole same-sex team consists of two friends (who go by their ocker nicknames, Sticks and Wombat). The houses under renovation on *The Block* are a far cry from the gothic piles of the genre's classic novels, and the contestants themselves are representative of Australia's upwardly mobile and aspirational working and lower-middle classes. Throughout the season, a series of 'experts' – real estate consultants, interior designers, lifestyle magazine editors – judge, discipline, and correct those contestants who commit transgressions against upper-middle-class notions of taste and refinement. Throughout each season, contestants acquire skills centred around appropriate consumption and middle-class domestic aesthetics. However, the spectres of incompletion, bankruptcy, or the failure to correctly spend money inevitably return to haunt them.

Season 13, like all seasons of *The Block*, begins with a particularly gothic form of displacement that recalls the trajectory of many gothic heroes or, more commonly, heroines who are removed or forced to flee from a secure home and arrive 'at a labyrinthine space [where] she is trapped or pursued' (Punter and Byron 279): where many renovation programmes are centred on the contestant or participant's own home, *The Block* displaces its contestants from their homes and families, and requires them to live full-time on the construction site, in the decaying, run-down house they are renovating. For the first weeks of the competition, the contestants dwell in a space that has no running water, a makeshift kitchen, and portable toilets and showers.

Until they renovate one of the bedrooms, contestants must sleep on the ground: Episode 2 shows Ronnie and Georgia sleeping on a small mattress on a cement floor ('48 Hour Challenge Reveal'). Putting contestants under physical and emotional strain is a tactic reality television frequently deploys, enabling producers to elicit a range of exaggerated emotional responses from the contestants. While it is conventional of the reality television genre, it can also be read as abrupt and shocking transition to an unhomely space in which contestants are disconnected from their homes and families, displaced into an unfamiliar, chaotic location, and divested of power (Punter and Byron 279). The results of this premise echo Royle's argument that 'the uncanny is a crisis of the proper: it entails a critical disturbance of what is proper (from the Latin *proprius*, "own"), a disturbance of the very idea of personal or private property' (1). Contestants are not simply separated from their families and homes; they are *prohibited*, for the most part, from spending time with them or returning to their homes, except for exceptional events like the birth or death of a loved one. This practice of enforced separation is a form of entrapment and containment common in many gothic texts: once they have arrived, there are very few opportunities for contestants to leave, which as Manuel Aguirre notes, is a common feature of gothic space – 'it is easy to enter the gothic castle, hard to come out' (4).

The paradox of the unhomely becomes more pronounced as contestants begin to renovate this unknown space, which results in them becoming more familiar with the house through the act of radically changing its structure, reflecting Freud's assertion that the uncanny moves in two directions, as '*heimlich* is a word the meaning of which develops towards an ambivalence, until it finally coincides with its opposite, *unheimlich*' (Freud et al. 624). As the season continues, this strange paradox heightens the contestants' feelings of ownership towards the space: the more time they spend renovating, the more the house becomes simultaneously theirs and not theirs. As early as Episode 2, after contestants have only spent 48 hours working on the first of their renovation projects, they are informed that the winner of the first renovation challenge will choose the house they will continue renovating, meaning that all contestants face being forced to swap houses. Elyse speculates that 'it would be hard to hand over a room that you've just renovated, and that you love' ('48 Hour Challenge Reveal'), which suggests that as contestants continue to renovate 'their' houses, they grow steadily more attached to the house even as it becomes increasingly unrecognizable – always already destined to be the property of a stranger.

The competition, crucially, requires contestants to design and construct luxury homes, fitted out with spaces, décor, and devices that befit a large upper-middle-class family – an aspirational, idealized Australian dream. Allon, discussing *The Block*'s first seasons, notes that 'in real life, none of these reality TV contestants could have afforded the apartments it was their task to renovate' (31). The restoration of a gothic site to its rightful owners is central to many gothic plots (Anolik 668) and is also central to *The Block*'s forward momentum. Ultimately, the contestants will never experience day-to-day life in these luxury houses after their completion and will only ever dwell in them as incomplete spaces undergoing renovation. The house's rightful owners are not the contestants who work furiously to renovate them; this is not a case of a peasant being revealed to have aristocratic origins, but a case of capitalist logic that rewards the wealthy – the rightful owners, in the end, are members of the upper-middle class.

The contestants, meanwhile, become trapped in the houses as their renovations progress. I noted earlier that the houses on *The Block* are, like many gothic spaces, easy to enter but always difficult to leave (Aguirre 6). This is also true for contestants on *The Block*, where time away from the house is time away from crucial work that needs to be completed, and any external task such as shopping is always done in panic and with the intention of speeding back to the house. The camera crews and the show's hosts regularly police this behaviour, questioning contestants who leave for too long and suggesting that it is a grave offense. In Episode 1 of Season 13, for example, Cam witnesses both Ronnie and Georgia leaving the construction site to go shopping. Cam chases the couple to their car and tells them, 'one person goes shopping, the other stays home!' ('48 Hour Challenge'), an injunction delivered jokingly but meant seriously. In this sense, the houses are gothic structures with the capacity to 'stretch beyond [their] own limits' (Aguirre 10) – even when shopping (one of the very few activities contestants are shown engaging in outside their houses), every item the contestants buy is for their house, so the act of purchasing more items always necessitates a return to the site, an uncanny circularity that entraps contestants.

The houses themselves, which begin as unprepossessing one-storey sub-urban homes, expand into enormous labyrinthine luxury homes throughout the season, which is in line with the programme's focus on upward class mobility as well as Aguirre's assertion that 'the Gothic space is anisotropic', a space in which proportions and dimensions frequently shift and distort (6). The houses of *The Block* undeniably conform to this logic, with dimensions and spaces that are in near-constant flux, so that some familiar areas quickly become unrecognizable, and the houses themselves literally expand both upwards and outwards. Each house is, of course, constantly changing over the course of the season as each room is renovated, but these changes go further than simple interior renovations to the existing structure of these small houses. As the season progresses, two significantly larger, two-storey structures are added on to each of the original houses, which cameras rarely show from the outside, but which dramatically expand the interior space. One annex sits flush against the back of each house, and accommodates large living and dining areas, while the other annex sits at the back of each house's yard, separated by what will later become the quintessential Australian space of a lawn, deck, and pool. The original house, then, becomes part of a much larger patchwork, a gothic pastiche of different and fragmented architectural forms and styles: 'excessive, discomforting, counterfeit' (Spooner, 'Gothic Lifestyle' 449). The 1940s weatherboard houses, with their stained glass windows and ornate moulding, lead on to the first annex, an angular, sleek contemporary architectural design for a modern family, which leads on to the traditional idealized Aussie backyard, which leads on to the final annex, a magnified and distorted version of the traditional Australian garage or backyard shed, in which a guest suite, media room, and garage are situated.

As the houses expand, the contestants' list of tasks, problems, and activities continue to multiply – as Aguirre puts it, 'in some obscure but perfectly predictable way the structure is endless or grows before them into unsuspected complexities, detours, obstacles', and the ultimate outcome is a gothic, palimpsestic space beyond control (13). The houses are also worksites, and this double function layers hazard over homeliness: the houses are where contestants rest and sleep, but they are simultaneously full of very practical risks and dangers: exposed wire, half-completed flooring, closed-off rooms, all of which make the interior space increasingly labyrinthine and dangerous as the cameras move through the space.

As Spooner notes, contemporary gothic texts have demonstrated that 'it need not be the barbarous past that imprisons us, but the mechanisms of Enlightenment itself, that expose us to constant surveillance and the total functioning of power' ('Twentieth Century' 44) and on *The Block*, the presence of the camera crews adds to these uncontrollable and distinctly uncomfortable domestic conditions. Cameras immediately place contestants under a form of panoptic surveillance, following contestants around their building sites, on shopping expeditions, and in their cars. The transgressive gaze of the cameras elides the boundaries between public and private space, directing the endless, intrusive gaze of the public, via the camera, onto the contestants at all times. As Gareth Palmer has established, 'reality television is a key precursor of modern lifestyle formats and has to a large extent been formed by surveillance culture' (7), while McElroy argues that 'television turns the house inside out so that what happens behind closed doors becomes available for public view' (97). McElroy's research highlights the transgressive role of the camera as it invites the voyeuristic gaze of the public into spaces that are usually kept private. Through this transgression of the public/private boundary, the viewer watches on as things that were once hidden or concealed are brought to light (Vidler 12), and the cameras on *The Block* collapse the hermetic sense of privacy commonly associated with houses – the private becomes inevitably public.

Contestants are also supplied with handheld cameras and encouraged to film themselves, which leads them to further internalize and normalize the procedures of self-surveillance. One contestant, Jason, replicates Cam's hammy dialogue when he speaks into the camera in Episode 5: 'You can all get a sneak preview, blockheads: there's our tiles down there, there's our shower screen, groovy gold taps' ('Bathroom Reveals'). Contestants also begin to focus a policing gaze on fellow contestants, to present themselves as surveilled subjects, and to believe themselves to be the object of the gaze of other contestants, as well as the cameras. In Season 13, one early sub-plot is Ronnie and Georgia's suspicion that other teams are copying their ideas, which leads to a general air of paranoia and uncertainty in the group as a whole. Scenes in Episode 14 of Ronnie scrawling 'TRUST NO ONE' on the bare walls of his house demonstrate the thin line between oppressive claustrophobia and the show's usual upbeat tone. In fact, the suspicion of copying is itself a fallacy: because uniform categories of taste and style are adopted by the judges, all of the teams replicate strikingly similar versions of the same house, and each house is distinguished from the others only by minor design elements and their colour palettes; in the end, the houses are all uncannily alike.

In line with this preoccupation with surveillance, each week the completed renovations are subject to other contestants' judgement as well as that of the judges. Room Reveals – the weekly event in which completed rooms are displayed to the judging panel – take place on Sunday night, and Monday's episode features the contestants touring each other's rooms and delivering their own assessments. This inscribes another level of collective surveillance into the renovation project and connects evidence of bad taste or failure to complete a renovation task to the potential for judgement and humiliation by their peers, as well as by the judges. At the end of the season, this weekly ritual of peer judgement is amplified into another judgement scenario involving a much larger intrusion of the public into the private space. In the final week, after the houses have been completed, the Australian public is invited to take part in house inspections. The viewer sees aerial shots of the Elsternwick street full of people waiting to tour the houses. This event is designed as a spectacle – Cam's voiceover tells us that 'around 20,000 fans have turned up to have a look' ('The Teams at Home'), and thousands of people tour the houses, delivering their opinions to camera, an act that literalizes the public's intrusive gaze.

The extravagant display recalls John Fiske et al.'s discussion of ideal Australian family homes and their relationship to social codes about community and privacy; the act of opening the houses for 'inspection' confirms

> the public's right to look, to share possession by looking, [which] is the corollary of the owner's responsibility to display a public front. Property that is hidden from public view fails to conform to the values of the suburban community: it is a message without a reader, an owner talking to himself (a sure sign of social deviance) or to his close friends (an equally sure one of elitism). (31)

The event transforms the houses into museum-like simulations, uncanny replicas of themselves, as well as bringing to life the previously implied presence of the public gaze.

Even more uncanny is the 'compulsive repetition' and endlessly deferred completion that underscores the programme's format and structure (Royle 84). Each week (e.g. 'Bathroom Week' or 'Kitchen Week'), contestants are assigned a room to work on and given six days – Tuesday to Sunday – to complete that room. Failure to complete each room is a source of extreme anxiety for contestants, a recurring weekly encounter with the spectres of social humiliation, bankruptcy, or bad taste. Contestants who produce a room renovation that is incomplete – revealed by the camera's close-ups on poorly finished architraves, sloppy painting, or unpainted elements, and hasty or unfinished styling such as an unmade bed – are judged harshly and given low scores. Contestants Sarah and Jason's failure to complete even a structural renovation of their master bedroom suite is described by the judges as an 'insult' to the show in Episode 25 ('Master Bedroom Judging').

Each week's winner receives an additional $10,000, so the scoring element of the format produces a competitive tension that reflects capitalist values of wealth accumulation. The fear of an incomplete renovation is connected in this way to the fear and social shame of bankruptcy. The horror of being broke is always held over the contestants, as those who succeed receive more cash and can subsequently buy more items, while those who fail are kept poor and returned to the endless repetition of being broke. Sarah and Jason place last in several consecutive weeks during Season 13 and subsequently encounter significant issues with their weekly renovation schedule. Contestants are able to hire a limited number of tradespeople to help, but with a massively reduced budget, Sarah and Jason simply have no money to hire such assistance, and therefore no way to resolve their situation. Their finances have effectively enclosed them in another gothic trap, one that is both difficult to escape and commits them to ongoing patterns of repetition in which they must relive the same fears and humiliations over and over as they are judged by their peers, the show's hosts, and finally the judges themselves.

The 'phenomena of the repetition' (Punter 219) is at the heart of both the Gothic and *The Block*: these repetitive cycles of crisis each week culminate – and are sometimes symbolically resolved – in the Sunday night Room Reveals. The three judges consider the room's positive and negative attributes, offering suggestions for how to continue developing both the room and the house as a whole. So, while the Room Reveals fetishize 'complete' spaces, the rooms remain under ongoing criticism and scrutiny. There is, to the contestants' ongoing horror, always more work to do and the completed renovation remains ultimately unachievable, always deferred. Contestants are caught in a repetitive cycle of performing the same acts and reliving the same extreme sense of urgency each week; like the gothic heroine, they experience 'anxiety with no possibility of escape' (Praz qtd. in Massé 684).

Room Reveals on *The Block* display spaces that are vacant, dreamy, and silent: they exist in a liminal state where the artifice of their completion is never disturbed. They are static spaces: once revealed, they are not returned to until the final week of the programme. The viewer almost never sees the completed rooms being dwelt in but, in another unhomely turn, can occasionally glimpse the 'finished' rooms being used for other purposes in later weeks. This is predominantly evident in the first rooms to be completed, the Guest Bedrooms, which is where the contestants sleep through the duration of the competition even the term for the bedroom reinforces their temporary role as the house's guests, and never the true owners, subject only to their spectral hospitality. While most of the time the contestants are depicted in action – talking to the camera as they work, shop, or survey the house – at times of high emotional intensity the camera transgresses the public/private boundary set up from the opening week and intrudes on contestants' bedrooms. These are particularly uncanny moments because of the stark contrast to the highly stylized images of other finished rooms in the house. The lived-in room is a clash of familiarity and unfamiliarity: while the viewer is used to being allowed the strange, transgressive pleasure of entering the contestants' houses (McElroy 97), these are usually limited to the room that is currently under construction. The bedrooms are often messy and disorganized, their stylish finishes and tasteful decorative items shoved aside immediately after the Room Reveal process is complete. In Episode 25, for example, we see footage of Jason snoring on the bedroom floor, and of his wife Sarah, in her dirty clothes and work boots, curled on a corner of the bed which is loaded with odd pieces of furniture and décor. She gets up, seemingly to get under the covers, but pulls a scarf from the top of a pile of clothes, returns to the same spot, and drapes the scarf over her legs. The contestants, then, seem never to be at home in these houses.

There are, however, brief instances in which the viewer is able to witness the rooms that have seemingly been finished, only to discover that these rooms have once again returned to disarray. For example in Episode 19, several weeks after Ronnie and Georgia's black-walled study with orange sofas was completed, the viewer glimpses it again as a cameraman follows Georgia through the house. For a moment, the viewer sees the room as it exists post-reveal: full of odd pieces of furniture, buckets of paint, lengths of wood, discarded clothes, and tools. In this moment, the secret of the apparently completed room's incompletion is revealed, and the viewer glimpses these rooms being put to use as storage spaces, or with pieces of furniture removed or altered, which demonstrates that they are in various stages of revision. Schelling argues that the *unheimlich* 'is the name for everything that ought to have remained [...] secret and hidden but has come to light' (Schelling qtd. in Freud et al. 623), and these images are repressed wherever possible in order for the fantasy of completion to remain intact. If the room needs to be reviewed, the slow-pan, soft-focus shots from the Room Reveal segments are recycled in order to present to viewers a counterfeit.

The final and most significant repetition in the programme becomes evident during the season finale, in which each house is put up for auction. The auctioning of the houses reenacts the original moment of displacement, removing contestants from their renovated houses, and, crucially, returning them to their previous homes where they will continue renovating their own or other properties. Renovation, then, in the logic of *The Block*, is a cycle of crisis that extends beyond even the limits of the programme itself. Episode 51, the penultimate episode of Season 13, shows each of the teams after they have completed their renovation on *The Block* and returned to their everyday lives to await auction day. Hannah and Clint are depicted in a café, discussing claw foot tubs with sketchbooks and magazines spread on the table. Clint tells the camera 'we've had this masterclass and this whirlwind adventure on *The Block* and it's probably amplified our desire to do this long-term' ('The Teams at Home'). Renovation, then, becomes a circular practice that leads renovators back through the same cycles of crisis and anxiety again and again. Clint qualifies his statement about his love of renovating by hinting that the experience of *The Block* is not what he hopes to replicate in his own renovations: 'If Scotty [Cam] rocks up at 9 a.m. on Sunday morning and yells out "tools down" I'm going to have nightmares I reckon' ('The Teams at Home'). The best example of the unhomely cycle of renovation is Sarah and Jason, who, despite being the underdogs, win over $500,000 in the finale of Season 13. Their winnings, however, simply lead them back to renovation: they return to the unfinished home they described in Episode 1 and use the winnings to begin the cycle of renovation all over again.

The gothic property is often destroyed as part of the narrative's resolution (Anolik 670); however, the capitalist and consumerist ideologies of twenty-first-century Australia require an ongoing process of profit and consumption – renovation must become work that never stops, and is instead bound up in endless repetition. All of the contestants win some amount of money and return home to continue renovating, indicating that they remain entrapped in the 'vortex of gothic space' (Lawn 134). No matter how much they desire to leave their maze-like houses, and even once those houses are completed and sold, contestants are never finished: they return, again, to their own homes which are simultaneously new and old, to begin a new renovation, to repeat the unfinishable renovations of the past and future.

The cash prize each contestant takes home thus encloses them in another renovation, which is, in many ways, the same renovation that they began. Episode 51 involves an interview with Sarah and Jason at their own house after returning from *The Block*, in which Cam's voiceover states that 'with a completed house behind them, Sarah and Jason were determined to finish their own home' ('The Teams at Home'). The camera pans the half-finished rooms and makeshift kitchen at Sarah and Jason's house, demonstrating that the fantasy of completion has been deferred indefinitely, and the couple's admission that the house has been in this state for ten years reveals the enduring unhomeliness of their experience. Asked about her relationship with Jason after *The Block*, Sarah's candid answer is, 'I don't think we've gotten closer; I think we're probably more frustrated with each other' ('The Teams at Home'). For this couple, 'the act of homecoming is not simply temporal regression: the return is also a beginning' (Brewster 145). Sarah's comments suggest that *The Block* has neither resolved the pair's housing problems nor repaired their relationship. In other words, although they have been relieved from the pressure of reality television's extreme emotional turmoil and constant surveillance, they are compelled to repeat the renovations and conflicts of the past.

Renovation culture presents itself as the opposite of unhomely: it is lively, dramatic, and exciting, and always results in revealing a new, beautiful space. While gothic concerns about property, inheritance, and possession are also key features of *The Block*, these are not supernatural or patriarchal, but fiscal and aesthetic: contestants are haunted by the fear and shame of bankruptcy, housing insecurity, and incompletion, as well as the less terrifying but more pervasive middle-class fear of having – or being thought to have – bad taste. On *The Block*, these unspeakable fears (of both contestants and viewers) can be superficially addressed and resolved through the programme's energetic, competitive, and dramatic depiction of renovation. Contestants overcome financial, personal, and social challenges as they renovate, but the process of renovation itself leads them through a series of gothic sites and experiences that render the process of renovation inherently unhomely. The contestants are effectively trapped in a cycle of renovation even after Season 13 has come to an end. Cam reminds viewers in Episode 5, 'going home is one thing this lot of Blockheads can't do!' ('Bathroom Reveals'), and his jokey commentary reveals the repetitious gothic logic of *The Block*: renovators are always compelled to continue renovating – each renovation project, no matter how successful or unsuccessful it is, leads inexorably to another.

Works Cited

'48 Hour Challenge' *The Block*, created by David Barbour and Julian Cress, Season 13, NineNetwork, 2017.

'48 Hour Challenge Reveal' *The Block*, created by David Barbour and Julian Cress, Season13, Nine Network, 2017.

Aguirre, Manuel. 'Geometries of Terror: Numinous Spaces in Gothic, Horror, and ScienceFiction'. *Gothic Studies*, vol. 10, no. 2, Manchester UP, 2008, pp. 1–17. doi:10.7227/GS.10.2.2

Allon, Fiona. *Renovation Nation*. U of New South Wales P, 2008.

Anolik, Ruth Bienstock. 'Horrors of Possession: The Gothic Struggle with the Law'. *LegalStudies Forum*, vol. 24, no. 4, 2000, pp. 667–686.

'Bathroom Reveals'. *The Block*, created by David Barbour and Julian Cress, Season 13, NineNetwork, 2017.

Bonner, Frances. *Ordinary Television*. SAGE, 2003.

Botting, Fred. *Gothic*. Routledge, 1996.

Brewster, Scott. 'Building, Dwelling, Moving'. *Our House: The Representation ofDomestic Space in Modern Culture*, edited by Gerry Smyth and Jo Croft, Rodopi,2006, pp. 141–159.

Cress, Julian and David Barbour, creators. 2017. *The Block: Season 13*. Cavalier Television,2017, *9now*. <www.9now.com.au/theblock>.

Dolar, Mladen. '"I Shall Be with You on Your Wedding-Night": Lacan and the Uncanny'.*October,* vol. 58, 1991, pp. 5–23.

Fiske, John, et al. *Myths of Oz: Reading Australian Popular Culture*. Routledge, 1987.

Freud, Sigmund, et al. 'Fiction and Its Phantoms: A Reading of Freud's Das Unheimliche(The "Uncanny")'. *New Literary History.* vol. 7, no. 3, 1976, pp. 525–645.

Gorman-Murray, Andrew. 2011. '"This is Disco-Wonderland!" Gender, Sexuality, and theLimits of Gay Domesticity on *The Block*'. *Social & Cultural Geography*, vol. 12, no. 5, pp. 435–453. doi:10.1080/14649365.2011.588801

Hogle, Jerold E. 'The Gothic Ghost of the Counterfeit and the Progress of Abjection'. *A NewCompanion to the Gothic*, edited by David Punter, Wiley-Blackwell, 2012, pp. 496–509.

Jeffery, Ella. '"I Find New Things I'd Forgotten I Needed": Consumption, Domesticity, and Home Renovation'. *Hecate*, vol. 42, no. 2, 2016, pp. 85–101.

Kavka, Misha. 'Gothic on Screen'. *The Cambridge Companion to Gothic Fiction*, edited by Jerrold E. Hogle, Cambridge UP, 2002, pp. 209–228.

Lawn, Jennifer. '*Scarfies*, Dunedin Gothic, and the Spirit of Capitalism'. *Journal of NewZealand Literature*, vol. 22, 2004, pp. 124–140.

Lewis, Tania. 'Changing Rooms, Biggest Losers, and Backyard Blitzes: A History of Makeover Television in the United Kingdom, United States, and Australia'. *Continuum:Journal of Media and Cultural Studies*, vol. 22, no. 4, 2008, pp. 447–458.

Massé, Michelle A. 'Gothic Repetition: Husbands, Horrors, and Things That Go Bump in theNight'. *Signs*, vol. 15, no. 4, 1990, pp. 679–709.

'Master Bedroom Judging' *The Block*, created by David Barbour and Julian Cress, Season 13,Nine Network, 2017.

McElroy, Ruth. 'Labouring at Leisure: Aspects of Lifestyle and the Rise of Home Improvement'. *Our House: The Representation of Domestic Space in Modern Culture*, edited by Gerry Smyth and Jo Croft, Rodopi, 2006, pp. 85–101.

McElroy, Ruth. 'Property TV: The (Re)making of Home on National Screens'. *European Journal of Cultural Studies*, vol. 11, no. 1, 2008, pp. 43–61. doi:10.1177/1367549407084963

Palmer, Gareth, editor. *Exposing Lifestyle Television: The Big Reveal*. Ashgate, 2008.

Punter, David. 'Gothic Poetry 1700–1900'. *The Gothic World*, edited by Glennis Byron andDale Townshend, Routledge, 2014, pp. 210–220.

Punter, David, and Glennis Byron. *The Gothic*. Blackwell, 2004.

Robson, Eddie. 'Gothic Television'. *The Routledge Companion to the Gothic*, edited byCatherine Spooner and Emma McEvoy, Routledge, 2007, pp. 242–250.

Rosenberg, Buck Clifford. 'Property and Home-Makeover Television: Risk, Thrift, and Taste'. *Continuum: Journal of Media and Cultural Studies* vol. 22, no. 4, 2008, pp. 505–513. doi:10.1080/10304310802189980

Rosenberg, Buck Clifford. 'The *Our House DIY Club*: Amateurs, Leisure Knowledge, and Lifestyle Media'. *International Journal of Cultural Studies*, vol. 14, no. 2, 2011, pp.173–190. doi:10.1177/1367877910382185

Royle, Nicholas. *The Uncanny*. Manchester UP, 2003.

Spooner, Catherine. 'Gothic in the Twentieth Century'. *The Routledge Companion to Gothic*, edited by Catherine Spooner and Emma McEvoy, Routledge, 2007, pp. 38–47.

Spooner, Catherine. 'Gothic Lifestyle'. *The Gothic World*, edited by Glennis Byron and Dale Townshend, Routledge, 2014, pp. 441–453.

'The Teams at Home'. *The Block*, created by David Barbour and Julian Cress, Season 13,Nine Network, 2017.

Vidler, Anthony. *The Architectural Uncanny*. The MIT P, 1992.

About the Author

Ella Jeffery is a Lecturer in Creative Writing at Queensland University of Technology. She researches intersections between contemporary literature, television, and renovation culture, and is particularly interested in conceptions and representations of unstable or insecure dwelling in twenty-first-century Australia.

Part II

Gothic Genres

5.   Glocalizing the Gothic in Twenty-First Century Australian Horror

Jessica Balanzategui

Abstract

The early twenty-first century saw the emergence of a transnational cycle of supernatural horror films with gothic themes and aesthetics, many of which featured uncanny child figures. Two Australian films that self-reflexively participated in this transnational cycle are *Lake Mungo* (2008) and *The Babadook* (2014). This chapter examines how these two Australian films contribute to this international Gothic horror cycle and related genre trends in ways that 'localize' globally resonant film genres. I argue that *Lake Mungo* and *The Babadook* integrate culturally specific media traditions and contexts with contemporary transnational film genre preoccupations in a self-consciously 'glocal' generic manoeuvre.

Keywords: glocalization; horror; Gothic; *Lake Mungo*; *The Babadook*

The turn of the twenty-first century saw the emergence of a transnational cycle of Gothic horror films preoccupied with uncanny child figures. As I have previously articulated (Balanzategui, *Uncanny Child*), this group of films includes now iconic Japanese horror films such as *Ringu* (Nakata, 1998) and *Ju-on: The Grudge* (Shimizu, 2002) as well as their Hollywood remakes, and Spanish films including the Spanish-produced English-language film *The Others* (Amenábar, 2001). As Keith McDonald and Wayne Johnson point out, transnational flows of cultural exchange underpin the genre mechanics of Gothic horror films in the twenty-first century, manifested as an 'oscillation between established discourse of genre and [...] counter discoursal responses' which continues to be 'invigorated by a heightened transnational ecology due to the increased effects of globalization in real world and artistic contexts' (3). Similarly, Glennis Byron points to 'increasing evidence of the emergence

Gildersleeve, J. and K. Cantrell (eds.), *Screening the Gothic in Australia and New Zealand: Contemporary Antipodean Film and Television*. Taylor & Francis Group, 2022

DOI 10.5117/9789463721141_CH05

of cross-cultural and transnational gothics that called out for attention and which suggested that, despite the emergence of so many national and regional forms, in the late twentieth and early twenty-first centuries gothic was actually progressing far beyond being fixed in terms of any one geographically circumscribed mode' (1). The transnational, transmillennial Gothic horror cycle I examine in *The Uncanny Child in Transnational Cinema* (2018) is one prominent example of these 'transnational gothics', and is a particularly self-aware example: this cycle of films deploys uncanny child characters to work through globally resonant *fin de siècle* anxieties about intersecting processes of cultural and technological change. In Australia, the films *Lake Mungo* (Anderson, 2008) and *The Babadook* (Kent, 2014) participate in this transnational cycle in self-aware ways, while imbuing the shared formal, stylistic, aesthetic, and thematic characteristics of this intercultural mode with a distinctively Australian inflection. This chapter examines how these two Australian films contribute to this international Gothic horror cycle and related genre trends in ways that 'localize' globally resonant film genres. I argue that while both *Lake Mungo* and *The Babadook* are part of the Australian Gothic tradition – a mode associated with prestige Australian film culture – they integrate elements of this culturally specific mode with contemporary transnational film genre preoccupations in a self-consciously 'glocal' generic manoeuvre.

As a result, *Lake Mungo* and *The Babadook* illustrate how the Gothic horror film genre of the twenty-first century combines locally rooted cultural specificity with globally accessible homogeneity. Xavier Aldana Reyes suggests that Gothic horror is an inherently 'interstitial' mode, which 'emphasizes the affective qualities of the horror genre' on the one hand, while 'on the other, it uses recognizable Gothic settings and conveys disturbing moods that aim to create the unease or destabilization often ascribed to the reading experience of the Gothic novel' (389). Like the other films that constitute the internationally successful Gothic horror mode of the twenty-first century, *Lake Mungo* and *The Babadook* deliver affectual resonances of horror underpinned by the moody psychological destabilization of the Gothic, a generic interstitially underscored by their global/local liminality. This global/local constellation troubles firmly established discourses of national versus global film cultures, a dichotomy that remains quite pervasive in scholarship on both popular film genres and Australian film. This chapter contributes to a recent turn away from such binary perspectives, which includes the work of Adrian Danks et al., who point out that Australia's 'national' cinema is 'part of a broader network of relations that have been in place since this cinema's inception and have greatly expanded under the accelerating processes of globalization' (12). In line with Danks et al.'s argument that Australia's 'national' cinema has always been distinctively transnational, *Lake Mungo* and *The Babadook* illustrate the potential of popular film genres to operate in productively culturally hybridized ways that both register the nuances and specificities of national contexts and media traditions, and participate in international genre trends from a diverse array of regions.

'Global' Film Genres and Cultural Hybridity

In Australian film culture and scholarship, there has been a tendency to craft dichotomies between commercially oriented but culturally homogenous (or deficient) 'genre' films, and culturally engaged art and drama cinema. In relation to the Australian film industry, this dichotomy has taken the specific form of Elizabeth Dermody and Susan Jacka's influential Industry 1 versus Industry 2 framework, with Industry 1 denoting 'socially concerned' films that aesthetically and ideologically convey a 'discourse of nationalism' (197), and Industry 2 referring to an 'industrialized, professionalized, streamlined, and undemocratic' (198) style of filmmaking that prioritizes commercial gain. The Industry 2 film, in the words of Dermody and Jacka, intends to be 'an international blockbuster or the formula genre piece' (198). A number of scholars have recently proposed interventions that complicate this binary opposition (Balanzategui, 'The Babadook'; Danks et al.), and notably, Deb Verhoeven contends that a third tier of the Australian film industry solidified from the end of the 1990s onwards, which 'comprises films and filmmakers happily embedded in *both* the local and global, where niche does not simply mean domestic or art-house and where global does not simply mean overseas or commercial' (162). Ben Goldsmith builds on Verhoeven's work, highlighting the 'material and discursive entailments' of this 'new international turn' in Australian cinema culture (201). Goldsmith describes this internationalization as 'outward-lookingness' that is both an 'indicator of and a response to the internationalization of the Australian cinema in recent decades' (201). Both *The Babadook* and *Lake Mungo* are examples of such 'outward-looking' or 'Industry 3' films, as they take part in internationally successful genre trends and transnationally resonant sociocultural concerns in ways that are regionally attuned and specific. However, this chapter avoids focusing solely on the national economic dynamics and international production agreements of 'outward-looking' Australian films: as Therese Davis points out in her work on transnational

Indigenous Australian filmmaking, such concerns have been a primary focus in scholarship on transnationalism and Australian cinema, 'with little attention paid to textual or social issues such as on-screen cultural representations' (595). In this chapter, the textual qualities of *Lake Mungo* and *The Babadook* are considered alongside their production contexts to examine how these films navigate the interplay between global and local via the transnational Gothic horror mode.

In doing so, these films challenge the genre/commercialism versus aesthetically meaningful/culturally engaged dichotomy that has long operated as a structural influence upon not only Australian film criticism and scholarship, but also genre and global cinema studies scholarship more generally. Tim Bergfelder contends that 'there remains a widespread assumption that popular film genres are synonymous with Hollywood, or at least that they originated in the American context before being exported and adapted across the world' (39). This tendency manifests in the key areas of focus of genre studies scholarship, which constellate around US genres to the point that 'popular genre film is tacitly understood to be Hollywood' (Bergfelder 40). Conversely, scholarship on global and transnational cinema often rests on oppositional discourse that addresses non-US cinema traditions as a means of counteracting genre studies' dominant focus on Hollywood. As Luisela Alvaray suggests, 'the national in cinema studies has been set against Hollywood's globalism' (68). Alternatively, foci on non-US cinema frequently adopt frameworks of cultural imperialism, 'which assumes a mere homogenization of local cinemas around the world according to the stipulation of dominant Hollywood productions' (Ritzer and Schulze 18). However, in an increasingly complex globalized film economy, such dichotomous approaches do not adequately capture the way genre functions as both a global force and a locally rooted system of production with culturally specific textual constellations. While attentiveness to complex and reciprocal global cultural flows has emerged as a key means of overcoming such limitations in recent analyses seeking to address the global/transnational dynamics of genres such as those previously cited, and in particular in studies of film industries and production settlements (Crane) and distributive logics (Lobato and Ryan), text-centric considerations of film genre still often turn to frameworks that contrast Hollywood/global with the local/national.

Yet even in a filmmaking culture like Australia's, where longstanding distinctions have been made between Industry 1 and Industry 2, genre has come to be a complex transnational framework addressing both global and local concerns and markets, as *Lake Mungo* and *The Babadook* highlight. Indeed, as Silvia Dibeltulo and Ciara Barrett point out, 'the generic approach presents itself as an effective critical tool for the analysis of contemporary global mediascapes that are increasingly characterized by transitional/transnational/transmedial practices in terms of production, distribution, exhibition, and consumption' (4). Both *Lake Mungo* and *The Babadook* were produced locally but are oriented towards global as well as local audiences. *Lake Mungo* was funded by the national government funding body Screen Australia, and distributed by Arclight films, a transnational company headquartered in both Sydney and California. *The Babadook* was funded by Screen Australia and the South Australian Film Corporation, and distributed by Australian company, Umbrella Entertainment, and major Canadian multinational, Entertainment One. Both films' stylistic and formal composition and thematic preoccupations contribute in specific ways to contemporary international Gothic horror film trends, while harnessing locally specific settings, characters, and cultural anxieties. Indeed, in her introduction to the 'globalgothic' mode of the early twenty-first century, Byron articulates an interplay whereby processes of globalization facilitate 'the cultural exchanges that were producing new forms of gothic' and also 'globalization itself was being represented in gothic terms, with traditional gothic tropes being reformulated to engage with the anxieties produced by the breakdown of national and cultural boundaries' (2). In their chapter in Byron's collection on this 'globalgothic' mode, Fred Botting and Justin D. Edwards theorize how this twenty-first century Gothic mode refracts transnational flows in revitalized but familiar tropes of spectres and the undead, noting that 'globalgothic registers the effects after the interpenetration of global and local has rendered the separation of both poles redundant, thus exploding the myth of a pure globality and shredding the nostalgic fantasy of a return to an untainted local culture' (18). Both *The Babadook* and *Lake Mungo* harness globally popular tropes of uncanny child characters and ghosts to convey such an interpenetration of global and local.

The Babadook depicts the story of a single mother, Amelia, who is still grieving the sudden death of her husband in a car accident on the day that her son, Samuel, was born. Amelia's grief manifests in the film as increasing resentment towards her son, who misbehaves to gain his mother's attention as her neglect escalates. The 'Babadook' of the film's title is a mysterious bogeyman-like figure who is featured in a seemingly homemade pop-up book that Samuel becomes fixated with after it appears on the family's doorstep. Samuel becomes increasingly terrified that the Babadook has escaped the pages of the book and has started to terrorize him in real life. Amelia initially dismisses these fears, but eventually succumbs to them herself. Throughout the film, the creature functions as an embodiment of the mother and son's shared resentment and emotional turmoil, and collectively they manage to banish the creature to the basement at the film's climax. *Lake Mungo* also depicts a narrative centred on the grief that invades the life of an ordinary suburban Australian family: in this film, family trauma stems from and circulates around the unexplained death of teenage girl, Alice, in a rural dam. The film is depicted in a documentary format, featuring interviews with Alice's parents, brother, and friends as they try to make sense of her death. The film also includes camcorder footage of Alice from before her death. Throughout the film, Alice seemingly comes back to haunt the family in ambiguous ways, her spectre manifested through mundane visual artefacts such as family photos and videos on Alice's old cell phone. Like *The Babadook*, the film draws on Gothic devices that position the supernatural haunting as a reflection on the family's inner torment and pain. Alice's ghost functions as an unsettling manifestation for the family of Alice's unknowable interior life, including a hidden sexual relationship with her adult neighbours, for whom she worked as a babysitter before her death.

Both of these films expose and self-consciously examine how genre can operate as a transnational phenomenon on multiple different levels, in line with Dibeltulo and Barrett's identification of the 'border-crossing capabilities of genre cinema as a cultural product/agent of cultural change' (10), and as a 'transitional, cross-cultural, and increasingly transnational, global paradigm of film-making in diverse contexts' (6). Furthermore, the transnational devices of *Lake Mungo* and *The Babadook* reveal how the concept of transnationalism in global cinema scholarship can be rethought to address how popular genre films have the potential to productively interrogate the relationships between nationally specific narratives and cultural identities, and diffuse and amorphously defined global communities. As Lesley Hawkes points out in her consideration of the work of globally successful Australian director Baz Luhrmann:

> It can be argued that transnational filmmaking is consciously incapable of making the ultimate version of any national story. This point is an important one because it exposes the multiplicity of these supposedly national stories. A nation's identity cannot be wrapped neatly into one story, and transnational filmmaking allows an unwrapping of the possibilities these stories offer. What is also revealed through transnational filmmaking is how these "national" stories were never monolithic or static in the first place but, rather, multifaceted and fluid. (305)

Analysis of *Lake Mungo* and *The Babadook* reveals the problematic dimensions of critical frameworks that prioritize Hollywood cultural imperialism.

Such frameworks often rest on an assumption that localized genre film-making is tantamount to conformity with US media traditions, and thus accentuates the 'homogenizing dynamic' of Hollywood cinema (Ezra and Rowden 2). The analysis of these two films in this chapter highlights the reciprocal and multilayered directions of transnational cultural flows underpinning globally popular film genres. This local/global plurality problematizes not only the notion that Hollywood is a homogenizing global force, but also the competing perspective in global cinema scholarship that national cinemas operate as 'defensive formations shaped in competition with and resistance to Hollywood products' (Hansen 67). As Alvaray asserts, cross-cultural exchanges underpinning generic hybridity can evidence how genre films 'inscribe local agency in transactions of differential economic and cultural power' (69). Yet, 'more work needs to be done to register and interpret the functions of genre in regional film industries' (69) in order to articulate the productive cultural, aesthetic, and industrial agency existent in transnational genre filmmaking.

Glocal Genres

Due to the sedimented binary oppositions charted in the previous section, the term 'transnational' in relation to genre film scholarship is often evacuated of specificity and precision, and thus can become limited in its critical usefulness. As Lindsey Decker points out in her analysis of the cultural and generic hybridity in British horror-comedy *Shaun of the Dead*, the term 'transnational is often defined prescriptively' (68), being used to problematically equate 'the transnational with the non-Western', to 'assume that transnational means Americanized', or to refer to an 'amorphous globalized culture' (78). The vague way in which the term 'transnational' can be used relates to the imprecision with which processes of globalization are sometimes articulated and understood. As globalization scholar, Roland Robertson, points out in an influential article, 'globalization is apparently widely thought of as involving cultural homogenization' ('Globalization' 192) and there is a tendency to 'cast the idea of globalization as inevitably in tension with the idea of localization' (205).

It is for this reason that Robertson advocates for the use of 'glocalization' to make more nuanced arguments about the multidirectional flows between global and local cultures (196). The term 'glocalization' – a hybrid of globalization and localization –allows for consideration of how local cultures and media traditions differentially interpret globally pervasive 'cultural messages' (Robertson, 'Globalization' 203), while at the same time addressing how locality shapes global processes. The term also transcends 'the tendency to cast the idea of globalization as inevitably in tension with the idea of localization' ('Globalization' 205). While the term 'glocalization' has mainly been deployed in association with marketing and branding practices rather than in film genre scholarship – and indeed, as Robertson points out, the term emerged in the 1980s as Japanese business jargon – 'glocalization' is a valuable critical tool for considering regionalized takes on international film genre trends. As Robertson contends in an earlier piece, 'homogenizing and heterogenizing tendencies are mutually implicative' ('Glocalization' 27) in the transnational flows underpinning globalization, and thus many instances can be identified of 'calculated attempts to combine homogeneity with heterogeneity and universalism with particularism' (27). *Lake Mungo* and *The Babadook* represent instances of such 'calculated attempts' to intertwine cultural specificity with global accessibility and resonance through film genre.

Lake Mungo and Global/Local Genres

From a production perspective, *Lake Mungo* is an example of Australian national cinema, being written, produced, funded, and performed entirely by Australians and Australian organizations. All the characters are Australian, and the film is set in Australia, being textually placed alongside national cinema traditions through its attentive focus on the contrasting environments of Australian suburbia and rurality, and the complex inner life of a suburban Australian family. Yet *Lake Mungo*'s 'glocal' generic status is evidenced through the various ways the film has been read in relation to both global and local screen genre trends. Some scholars have placed this Gothic horror film in relation to the 'found-footage' horror subgenre popular and successful in Hollywood in the first decade of the 2000s and into the early 2010s (Heller-Nicholas). The found-footage subgenre combines professional and amateur filmmaking techniques to construct the conceit that the film is not a fictional, polished production for the purposes of entertainment, but is a 'found' amateur audio-visual artefact documenting horrifying events (often from a first-person perspective). Found-footage horror films are thus often produced – or are constructed to *appear* like they have been produced – using amateur equipment such as camcorders, mobile phones, and security cameras. This subgenre can thus 'accommodate large and small budgets alike' (Heller-Nicholas 68) and is geared towards enhancing the aura of authenticity and verisimilitude around the unnerving events of horror films. The subgenre is typically understood to be a North American cultural phenomenon – with popular films including *The Blair Witch Project* (Myrick and Sanchez, 1999), *Cloverfield* (Reeves, 2008), and *Paranormal Activity* (Peli, 2007) – even though influential found-footage films have been produced outside of the US, such as Jaume Balagueró and Paco Plaza's Spanish [*REC*] series (2007–2014). This is because the formal, aesthetic, and thematic tendencies of found-footage horror tend to be aligned with the socio-political context of the US in the early 2000s, in particular the 9/11 terrorist attacks on the World Trade Center in 2001. As Kevin Wetmore asserts, 9/11 was mediated for US and global citizens via a 'variety of camera shots, shaky footage from mobile, handheld cameras, and footage from a variety of sources' that were 'combined together to frame a single narrative' of the event, and 'the experience of viewing these [...] shaped the "found-footage" horror film' ('Post 9/11 Horror' 20).

Lake Mungo has been understood as a distinctively nationally specific contribution to this globally pervasive, 'Hollywood' film genre. Alexandra Heller-Nicholas suggests that while found-footage horror is 'another in a long line of the [horror] genre's zeitgeist-defining popular fads' (70), *Lake Mungo* illuminates how this Hollywood genre can be deployed for 'national self-reflection' with a 'surprising cultural potency' (70). Heller-Nicholas's contention that *Lake Mungo* represents a local inflection of US screen trends and traditions also relates to her identification of David Lynch's cult US television series, *Twin Peaks* (1990–1991), as another key influence on the film. US film scholar, Aviva Briefel, also relates *Lake Mungo* to the found-footage subgenre, noting that it 'makes a singular intervention into this cinematic tradition' (133). Her essay opens by highlighting the film's reception context in the US, describing the film as a 'mere detail in the horror canon, released as part of the After Dark HorrorFest in 2010' (Briefel 132), an annual film festival in the US for independent horror films. Thus, Briefel approaches *Lake Mungo* through the lens of US genre festivals and generic 'canons'.[1] In Australia and the UK, the film's limited festival release aligned it with national cinema rather than global, US-centric genre traditions, as it was released as part of the Travelling Film Festival in Australia, and the Barbican London Australian Film Festival in the UK.

Notably, Briefel's reading of the film in relation to 'two key cinematic predecessors' (133) implicitly addresses the film's liminal position between Hollywood genre trends and local cinema traditions: she identifies the two

---

1   Notably the film also screened a year earlier at the popular South by Southwest Film Festival in Austin, Texas, another US festival with a strong horror and cult genre tradition.

key influences upon the film as *The Blair Witch Project* – the film often credited with kickstarting the early 2000s found-footage horror subgenre in the US – and iconic Australian Gothic drama film, *Picnic at Hanging Rock* (Weir, 1975). *Picnic at Hanging Rock* is typically regarded as the pinnacle of 'Industry 1' – films Dermody and Jacka associate with a culturally engaged discourse of nationalism. The film is metonymic of the Australian 'New Wave' of 'quality' cinematic output in the 1970s and early 1980s, and is widely known and understood in relation to this context outside of Australia. That Briefel contextualizes *Lake Mungo* in relation to these two films thus positions it as a contribution to a Hollywood-centric, global subgenre with roots in a regional film history that is internationally recognized.

While *Lake Mungo* has primarily been understood as a localized inflection of or offshoot to the global found-footage horror subgenre, Tyson Wils aptly reads the film in relation to acutely localized media contexts and influences. In particular, Wils links *Lake Mungo* to the Australian Broadcasting Corporation's *Australian Story* series, a documentary television show that has appeared weekly on Australian screens since 1996. As the name suggests, *Australian Story* is thoroughly engaged with communicating and imagining Australia's national narrative and identity through 'a human-issues television documentary' format, with each episode crafting 'a narrative based on a personal story that contains inspiring and/or fascinating characters' (Wils 121). Indeed, Australian viewers are likely to read *Lake Mungo*'s faux-documentary format in relation to this popular series. Like the series, the film relies on attentively focused interviews to craft a human-interest story around the grieving family of the teenage Alice. These interviews with the family – Alice's parents and her brother Matthew – are used to foment mystery around Alice's identity and disappearance, in combination with fly on-the-wall cinematography of the family's mundane existence and camcorder home movie footage.

As Wils points out, this structure aligns with the dramatic documentary format of *Australian Story*, which 'pays attention to characterization, emplotment, and thematic development' (121) to convey storylines based on personal stories with 'twists and turns that are designed not only to give audiences unexpected moments, which can draw them into the intrigue of the story, but also to advance certain themes' (121). This combination of documentary styles is common to both found-footage horror films and to *Australian Story*, and the result of drawing both together is that *Lake Mungo* self-reflexively contorts found-footage horror conventions to Australian screen traditions by amending – or, more precisely, by 'localizing' – their overarching conceit and thus formal approach. Notably, the footage that constitutes the film is presented as not simply a 'found' audio-visual document of horrific events, as is typical of North American found-footage horror films like *The Blair Witch Project*, *Paranormal Activity*, and *Cloverfield*. Instead, the main conceit underpinning the film's documentary format is that the audience is watching an *Australian Story*-style journalistic investigation into Alice's death and the aftermath for her grieving family.

The Babadook and Global/Local Genres

Like *Lake Mungo*, as was detailed above, *The Babadook* was produced by Australian funding and production organizations, and created and performed by an almost entirely Australian team. The film is set in Australia, and, like *Lake Mungo* and many culturally engaged Industry 1 Australian films before it, has a close focus on the minutia of a suburban Australian family's mundane existence and inner turmoil. Like *Lake Mungo*, *The Babadook* has been read in relation to both Australian national cinema traditions and Hollywood horror genre trends. Both myself and Stephen Gaunson position the film in relation to Australian Gothic literary and cinematic tropes, highlighting intertextual connections to Weir's *Picnic at Hanging Rock*; the literary trope of the child lost to the Australian bush; and the Australian bush mythology of the bunyip, which, as Gaunson, citing Gelder, points out, is 'the one respectable flesh-curdling horror of which Australia can boast' (Gelder qtd. in Gaunson 362–363). Similarly, while Amanda Howell designates the film 'recognizably Australian' (194) in its suburban Australian setting, characters, and tone, she also points out that the film avoids 'some of the most familiar cinematic markers of Australianness' (185), and clearly bears the influence of subversive New Hollywood productions of the 1970s and 1980s, including *The Shining* (Kubrick, 1980) and *Rosemary's Baby* (Polanski, 1968).

Indeed, this kind of 'glocal' reception was the intention of director Jennifer Kent: she has stated that her aim was to 'create a myth in a domestic setting. And even though it happened to be in some strange suburb in Australia somewhere, it could have been anywhere. I guess part of that is creating a world that wasn't particularly Australian [...] I'm very happy, actually, that [the film] doesn't feel particularly Australian' (Kent qtd. in Lambie). This glocalization strategy proved necessary for Kent, because while the Australian setting, characters, and commentary on Australian suburban life helped her to acquire Screen Australia funding, it did not necessarily contribute to a successful Australian release: after an international premiere at The Sundance Film Festival, the film was initially released on only thirteen cinema screens in Australia, faring much better on international screens across the US, the UK, and France (Hardie). Receiving global critical acclaim, overseas the film was understood in relation to influential Hollywood and international horror films. For instance, William Friedkin, director of *The Exorcist*, stated on his Twitter profile that he 'had never seen a more terrifying film', relating it to '*Psycho, Alien*, and *Diabolique*'. Los Angeles-based film critic, Dan Schindel, compares *The Babadook* to British horror film, *Attack the Block*, via its quality 'genre creature creation'. Furthermore, while both Gaunson and myself have previously highlighted the local influences on the film's style, form, and themes, we also link the film to international genre trends, such as the transnational uncanny child trend of the early 2000s (Balanzategui, 'The Babadook' 29) and European art-horror films including the early work of Roman Polanski (Gaunson 359).

The Babadook's local specificities were thus calibrated in a way that was tailored to international as well as domestic markets. Yet the film does not neatly fit within the categories Mark David Ryan outlines in his exploration of how Australian horror film has tended to function as 'largely an internationally oriented sector' (164). Ryan outlines three primary genre-based internationalization strategies: attempts to 'trade on the "Australianness"' of films as a means of differentiation in an international market; attempts to 'pass off' films as 'faux-American'; and the creation of 'placeless films that efface their national origins' (164). He concludes that 'so long as the commercial potential of the domestic market remains limited' for Australian horror filmmakers, 'such tendencies may remain unfortunate but unavoidable' (177). However, the glocally attuned generic composition of *Lake Mungo* and *The Babadook* suggests a productive alternative approach to the three strategies outlined by Ryan, one that has garnered international critical acclaim for both films, and in the case of *The Babadook*, international financial success after a limited initial domestic release, and subsequent belated box office success in Australia.[2] Further, the international influences upon both *Lake Mungo* and *The Babadook* extend beyond Hollywood-centric genres, which troubles Ryan's claim that Australian horror films often seek commercial viability by tailoring films specifically for US markets and thus according to US genre conventions. The multilayered integration of various global with local genre trends also highlights the transcultural polyphony and reciprocity of the twenty-first century Gothic horror film mode.

2   Notably, the rights for a Hollywood remake of *Lake Mungo,* produced by Paramount Vantage, were acquired in 2009, indicating the film's global success, but this remake never materialized (Barton).

Glocalizing Gothic Genres in *The Babadook*

In addition to those influences already outlined, *The Babadook*'s approach to Gothic horror screen storytelling and aesthetics bear the influence of genre trends spawning from diverse regions and time periods. The cultural diversity of the film's influences are built into its audio-visual landscape through explicit references to the silent films of pioneering French film-maker, Georges Méliès, whose penchant for visual magic tricks with physical props influences the 'lo fi' (to use Kent's terms) design of the central bogeyman of the film's title, who was animated using stop-motion effects (O'Hara). As Gaunson points out, the first time that single mother Amelia sees the creature is when she is watching Méliès's *The Magic Book* (1900) on television: in this short film, a monster emerges from a giant pop-up book, just as he does in *The Babadook*'s diegesis. This explicit reference to Méliès's work reveals how Kent intentionally stitches specific national influences on global screen genre trends into *The Babadook*: Méliès's films stand as historical documents of how filmmaking innovations outside of Hollywood shaped screen storytelling practices, and in particular horror, Gothic, sci-fi, and fantasy screen storytelling techniques and styles. Notably, Méliès is credited with making the first horror film in history with *The House of the Devil* (1896) (Jones 23). Kent has also cited the silent French film *The Fall of the House of Usher* (Epstein, 1928) – another non-US influence on the Gothic horror film's style and form – as inspiration for her visual style (Kent qtd. in O'Hara).

In addition, as well as being influenced by the aforementioned New Hollywood films, *The Babadook* contributes in direct ways to the transnational body of uncanny child films in the early 2000s, which includes Japanese films such as *Ringu* (Nakata, 1998) and its American remake *The Ring* (Verbinski, 2001), US film *The Sixth Sense* (Shayamlan, 1999), Spanish film *The Orphanage* (Bayona, 2007), the Spanish-produced, English language film *The Others* (Amenábar, 2001), and US film *Insidious* (written and directed by Australian team James Wan and Leigh Whannel, 2010). As I have previously articulated, this assemblage of films communicates cross-culturally through aesthetics, themes, and direct remakes or transnational coproductions (Balanzategui, 'The Uncanny Child'). This body of films pivots on a particularly tragic, Gothic incarnation of the uncanny child, subverting the pervasive possessed or evil child trope to articulate how the central child figure is both eerie and threatening, yet also a victim of personal trauma. *The Babadook* follows a similar trajectory, as the 'haunting' in the film is gradually revealed to 'stem not from Amelia and Samuel's house, but from the mother and son's fraught relationship and shared grief' (Balanzategui, 'The Babadook' 29). Significantly, 'through their self-conscious transnationality', this early twenty-first century body of uncanny child films 'tend to engage in meta-textual encounters with the shifting ways in which cinema is produced and consumed in globalized, postmodern media culture' (Balanzategui, 'The Uncanny Child' 226). By participating in this transnational assemblage of globally popular and influential films, *The Babadook* wears its transnationality on its sleeve, rather than aligning in straightforward ways with national cinema traditions.

Yet this does not mean that the film is 'placeless' or that it attempts to 'pass off' as 'faux-American' in line with Ryan's previously outlined arguments. Instead, the film integrates global genre trends into its locally rooted setting. The suburban Adelaide setting in the film resists, as Howell points out, depictions of suburbia and domesticity common to American horror films. As Howell outlines, Amelia and Samuel's bluestone terrace house aligns with the Victorian-era architecture of both Sydney and Adelaide. Howell thus connects the suburban setting to specific histories of suburban development in Australia, including both 'the nineteenth-century origins of Australia's inner suburbs as well as the reform movements of the 1930s–1960s that re-categorized such inner suburban terraces as slums' (194). This culturally specific setting works together with the combination of international genre influences and the local tropes and aesthetics of the Australian Gothic to shape a distinctively 'glocal' take on the Gothic horror genre.

Lake Mungo and Generic Glocalization

Like *The Babadook*, *Lake Mungo* is firmly rooted in the local, yet self-reflexively aligns this locally positioned narrative in relation to international traditions and trends in Gothic horror aesthetics, form, and style. The opening montage features examples of Victorian era 'spirit photography', as the voice of a teenage girl with a broad Australian accent (which we later learn is the voice of the central character, Alice), says, 'I feel like something bad is going to happen to me. I feel like something bad has happened. It hasn't happened yet, but it's on its way'. We then hear the voices of other characters speaking about ghosts, grief, and secrets, their words disembodied and uncontextualized like Alice's. All of these statements are replayed later in the film, and thus are given bodies and contexts at various junctures throughout the film's narrative. Most notably, the words we hear spoken by Alice in this opening montage represent a significant narrative reveal in the film when we hear them in context: Alice speaks these words in videotaped consultations with a local psychic, Ray, to suggest that she has had dreams and visions about her own death, soon before she dies.

It is significant that this film, which is set in the small Australian town of Ararat in the twenty-first century, opens with Victorian-era spirit photography. This opening montage places *Lake Mungo* in relation to some of the most significant international influences on Gothic horror media's visual forms from the outset. Spirit photography is a tradition rooted in the spiritualist movement of the late nineteenth century, stemming from France, North America, and England. As Tom Gunning points out, the spirit photography tradition influenced the earliest Gothic and uncanny films, such as Méliès's *The Spiritualist Photograph* (1903), which plays upon spirit photography's visual tricks, a feature directly addressed through the film's title and intertitles. Spirit photography and other occult practices of the spiritualism movement, including seances and post-mortem photography – which was particularly popular in Victorian England – have become pervasive in the international visual language of the ghost film. For instance, influential ghost films including British film *The Innocents* (Clayton, 1961), Canadian film *The Changeling* (Medak, 1980), and aforementioned English-language Spanish film *The Others*, all draw heavily on the style and practices of the spiritualist movement. In *The Others*, for example, a 'Book of the Dead' – an album of Victorian-era post-mortem photographs – is key to the film's climactic narrative reveal that the lead characters are in fact ghosts. By opening with a montage of spirit photography, *Lake Mungo* is aligned in self-aware ways with such long-standing international ghost movie traditions that are recognisable and accessible to diffuse global audiences. Once this opening montage concludes, *Lake Mungo* abruptly transitions to a mundane photograph of the Australian family at the centre of the film, and then camcorder footage of the family, and finally footage on *WIN News* of a dam being dredged for a body. WIN is a national television network that covers regional Australia, and *WIN News* is a longstanding daily news programme on the network that would be familiar to many Australians. The framing of the murder mystery at the heart of the film via an excerpt from *WIN News* thus conjures regionally specific media histories and cultures. This opening montage serves to emplace the longstanding international Gothic genre tropes associated with spirit photography and occult traditions within a precise cultural landscape. The montage's transition from Victorian spirit photography to photographs and home video footage of a suburban Australian family and a local news broadcast emphasizes *Lake Mungo*'s localized adoption and translation of internationally legible Gothic aesthetics from the opening moments of the film.

Throughout *Lake Mungo*, this culturally hybridized approach to film genre is maintained through an engagement with local cultural and audio-visual traditions that intersect in complex ways with internationally resonant Gothic horror characteristics and influences. As I pointed to earlier, the film unfolds in the style of an *Australian Story* documentary series episode, a format recognisable to most Australian audiences, and one that constitutes a locally rooted spin on the global found-footage horror trend. While it has been received in relation to found-footage horror, *Lake Mungo*'s regional inflection of found-footage aesthetics defies the subgenre's structuring conceit that the documentary- or amateur-style video that the audience experiences in the course of the film was 'found' after the horrifying events depicted, and is subsequently being exhibited for audiences in an unadorned, unedited state. *Lake Mungo* instead aligns more closely with the culturally polyphonic *generic heritage* of found-footage horror: cinema verité. As Barry Keith Grant suggests, this mode relies heavily on observational documentary formats, a style which ensures 'the spectator's identification' is aligned 'more with the camera itself than with any particular character' (154). Keith Grant argues that found-footage horror is closely related to and extends cinema verité styles, because the documentary format is used to 'present horror in the most realistic manner possible' (155). He points out that amongst the antecedents of verité horror is spirit photography, in which 'charlatan' spiritualists attempted to convince sceptics of the existence of spectres by 'showing supposed documentary evidence in support of their claims regarding visitations by the dearly departed' (155). *Lake Mungo*'s format and audio-visual allusions to the spiritualist tradition accentuate the cinema verité roots of the twenty-first-century found-footage horror trend. Keith Grant points to the fact that cinema verité was, from its beginnings, a distinctively 'international style' (158), with influential works in this mode appearing 'roughly simultaneously in such countries as France, Canada, and the US' (158). Thus, *Lake Mungo*'s 'glocalization' of film genres through its documentary format resonates on multiple different levels because it combines the influences of Victorian-era spirit photography; Australian documentary and news series; twenty-first century found-footage horror; and the international cinema verité mode popular since the 1960s.

Illuminating this combined interaction with cinema verité, found-footage horror, and Australian documentary formats, the mysteries surrounding Alice's life and death are gradually unfurled through realistic and mundane imagery as *Lake Mungo*'s narrative develops. For example, we learn that after Alice's mysterious death, her 'ghost' seemingly started to appear in the photographs of her younger brother, Matthew. Matthew explains via a direct-to-camera interview that he has long had a photography project in which he takes a photograph of his suburban backyard, something that he has done every three months for the last four years. It is in these mundane photos that Alice's spectre first seems to appear. Matthew explains his intention to capture the family's backyard in a way that looks out to the hills that border his small country town, and examples of his photography accompany his narration. These photos capture a juxtaposition between Australian suburbia and rurality in a microcosm of the film's larger plot, in which suburban teenager Alice's life is threatened and then taken by the expansive rural spaces that surround her mundane, small-town existence: before Alice mysteriously drowns in a rural dam, her spirit already seems to haunt Lake Mungo, an ancient dry lake with a complex history of Indigenous inhabitation and ritual. Thus, despite *Lake Mungo*'s engagement with international genre trends, the film adopts the kind of 'discourse of nationalism' common to Industry 1 Australian filmmaking traditions, in particular celebrated Australian Gothic films *Picnic at Hanging Rock, Wake in Fright* (Kotcheff, 1971), and *Walkabout* (Roeg, 1971), all of which dwell on the eerie power of the Australian rural landscape and its threatening juxtaposition with the mundane suburban life of white characters. In tandem with evoking these localized film histories, Matthew's photos simultaneously function as an updated incarnation of the 'spirit photography' tradition that lingers within the generic DNA of both cinema verité and twenty-first-century found-footage horror.

The film engages with these generic influences in self-reflexive ways, as it is subsequently revealed that Matthew was in fact a contemporary 'charlatan' spiritualist, faking the appearances of Alice's ghost in his photographs and camcorder footage. Yet, after we learn that Matthew's spirit photography is fraudulent, we later encounter Alice's 'real' ghost in her own cell phone footage. At this climactic moment, Alice's family and the audience discover that Alice was seemingly haunted by her own spectre in the weeks leading up to her death: the ghost manifests in footage that Alice captured on her own cell phone, appearing just as Alice's corpse did when her father identified the body after it was recovered from the dam in which she drowned. The dreadful, bloated, and water-logged 'death mask' that haunts Alice through her cell phone footage thus recalls Victorian post-mortem photography and its narrative and visual centrality to ghost films like *The Others*. Furthermore, at the end of the film, Alice's spectre seems to appear in family photographs of her family's home as they prepare to move house, something that is not acknowledged by the family's direct-to-camera monologues accompanying these images, suggesting that the film's characters have not noticed the spectre's appearance in their photographs. These images are thus presented as though they are authentic, unfiltered spirit photographs, unlike Matthew's earlier faked photographs. In this way, *Lake Mungo* presents a mise en abyme of first-person camera and documentary-style footage that seeks to unveil the 'truth' of Alice's death and return as a revenant. This technique aligns with both cinema verité attempts to use observational camera techniques to 'reveal deeper truths about the world' through direct observation (Keith Grant 158), and with the more recent found-footage horror technique in which seemingly amateur, first-person cinematography is used to present realistic depictions of supernatural occurrences, in defiance of the codes and conventions of professional cinematography.

Lake Mungo's multilayered glocal generic composition is also illuminated through its intersections with the tropes and trends of Asian technohorror films from the turn of the millennium and 2000s. This regionalized genre is primarily associated with the globally popular Japanese horror films of this period, including *Ringu* (Nakata, 1998), *Dark Water* (Nakata, 2002), *Ju-on: The Grudge* (Shimizu, 2002), and *Pulse* (Kurosawa, 2001), all of which received Hollywood remakes. This movement came to be known as 'J-horror', which, as Mitsuyo Wada-Marciano points out, is a term that denotes both a regionally rooted genre but also a globally recognisable brand, 'thoroughly connected with the media distributor's strategy of marketing their product both inside and outside Japan' (29). Furthermore, the global success of J-horror came to be conflated with the popularity of East Asian supernatural horror films during the early twenty-first century, as films from Thailand, for instance *Shutter* (Pisanthanakun and Wongpoom 2004); Singapore, such as the Hong Kong-Singaporean film *The Eye* (The Pang Brothers, 2002); and South Korea, such as *A Tale of Two Sisters* (Jee-woon, 2003), also achieved international critical acclaim and were remade in Hollywood. As Leon Hunt and Wing-Fai Leung suggest, during this period 'East Asian cinemas' came to function as a 'mutating network of film practices at the intra- and inter-regional levels' (5). These Japanese and East Asian supernatural horror films influenced the shape and form of the global horror genre in the early twenty-first century, including via both direct Anglophonic remakes and original films like *Lake Mungo* which participate in this trend in localized ways.

In particular, *Lake Mungo* adopts the 'technohorror' devices common to the early twenty-first century East Asian supernatural horror movement, in which technology becomes the conduit for disquiet spirits, and these spectres manifest as uncanny technological glitches or viruses. Wetmore calls these spirits 'technoghosts', because they 'display the physical properties of electronic or technical media' and thus they appear staticky and blurry, their physical appearance 'featuring interference, as if they are being broadcast, rather than haunting', underscoring that their 'manifestation is both made possible by technology and mediated through it' ('Technoghosts', 72). Alice's spirit manifests in this distinctively technologically mediated way throughout *Lake Mungo*, particularly at the film's frightening climactic moment in which Alice's spectre lurches towards Alice on her pixelated cell phone recording. At this moment, the visage of the ghost is rendered deeply uncanny not just through its bloated, waterlogged disfigurement, but because of the pixelated, jerky nature of the cell phone footage. In camcorder footage captured by her friend, Alice is later seen burying her phone after capturing this dreadful footage, as if the phone itself is the vehicle for her own ghost. This aligns with the conceit that electronic media has the potential to be spectrally contagious, a trope pervasive in J-horror films of the 2000s. This narrative conceit in particular mirrors Takashi Miike's s popular *One Missed Call* film franchise (2003–2006) – remade in the US in 2008 – in which teenagers are haunted by their own future deaths through their cell phones.

Alice's waterlogged spectre also recalls the aesthetics and identities of the ghostly figures common to J-horror, which David Kalat has described as 'dead wet girls': in some of the most iconic J-horror films, the ghosts are young women who, like Alice, meet their ends in watery graves, such as wells (*Ringu*) and water tanks (*Dark Water*), and their spectres thus appear soggy and wet. *Lake Mungo*'s connections to the Thai horror film, *Shutter,* are also notable: in this film, the ghost of a young woman haunts those who tormented and raped her while alive through spectral appearances in their photographs. In the like-named US remake of the film, which was released a year before *Lake Mungo,* this photographic haunting is related explicitly to historical spirit photography traditions.

The strange technological logic of Alice's ghost also parallels the acclaimed Kiyohsi Kurosawa J-horror film, *Pulse* (2001; remade in the US in 2006). In this film, ghosts are associated with the Internet, and their uncanny visual poetics embody technological anxieties: as Kit Hughes rightly suggests, in *Pulse* the 'ghostly moments and ghostly figures provoke fear not because they disrupt distinctions between life and death' (23), but more for the way they 'destabilize viewers' ability to decode screens or understand technically recorded images' (29). Alice's spectre functions in a similar way, its uncanniness manifested through its liminal and difficult to pinpoint appearances, and its slippages between a mise en abyme of frames and naturalistic images. Thus, the mysterious hauntings of *Lake Mungo* resonate in polyphonic ways with global Gothic ghost traditions, including adopting narrative, aesthetic, and thematic characteristics specific to East Asian technohorror films of the early twenty-first century. The film is a 'glocal' contribution to the Gothic horror genre, revealing the problems involved in casting 'the idea of globalization' – and the idea of popular film genre – as 'inevitably in tension with the idea of localization' (Robertson, 'Gobalization' 205).

Conclusion

Lake Mungo and *The Babadook* illuminate the extent to which film genres can operate in the culturally heterogenous and reciprocal manner Robertson associates with 'glocalization'. In both films, the settings, aesthetics, themes, and formulae of national film traditions are aligned in self-aware ways with popular global genre trends, and as a result these films precisely and directly address local audiences while at the same time being accessible and engaging to international audiences. These films, therefore, do not accord with the binary oppositions of national specificity versus global homogeneity and commercialism which often underpin scholarship on Australian cinema, popular film genres, and national and transnational cinema. Instead, the films demonstrate how Gothic hauntings can occupy the liminal space not only between interior and exterior lives, but between specific national and diffuse global cultures.

Works Cited

A Tale of Two Sisters. Directed by Kim Jee-woon, BOM Film Productions, 2003.

Aldana Reyes, Xavier. 'Gothic Horror Film, 1960 – Present'. *The Gothic World*, edited by Glennis Byron and Dale Townshend, Routledge, 2014, pp. 389–398.

Alvaray, Luisela. 'Hybridity and Genre in Latin American Cinemas'. *Transnational Cinemas*, vol. 4, no. 1, 2014, pp. 67–87.

Australian Story. Presented by Caroline Jones, ABC, 1996–.

The Babadook. Directed by Jennifer Kent, Screen Australia, 2014.

Balanzategui, Jessica. '*The Babadook* and the Haunted Space Between High and Low Genres in the Australian Horror Tradition'. *Studies in Australasian Cinema*, vol. 11, no.1, 2017, pp. 18–32.

Balanzategui, Jessica. *The Uncanny Child in Transnational Cinema: Ghosts of Futurity at the Turn of the Twenty-First Century.* Amsterdam University Press, 2018.

Barton, Steve. '*Lake Mungo* Remake on the Way'. *Dread Central*, 2009. <www.dreadcentral.com/news/12174/lake-mungo-remake-on-the-way/>.

Bergfelder, Tim. 'Transnational Genre Hybridity: Between Vernacular Modernism and Postmodern Parody'. *Genre Hybridization: Global Cinematic Flow*, edited by Ivo Ritzer and Peter W. Schulze, Schüren, 2013, pp. 39–55.

The Blair Witch Project. Directed by Daniel Myrick and Eduardo Sanchez, Haxan Films, 1999.

Botting, Fred and Edwards, Justin D. 'Theorizing Globalgothic'. *Globalgothic*, edited by Glennis Byron, Manchester University Press, 2015, pp. 11–24.

Briefel, Aviva. 'Rules of Digital Attraction: The Lure of the Ghost in Joel Anderson's *Lake Mungo*'. *Quarterly Review of Film and Video*, vol. 34, no. 2, 2017, pp. 130–147.

Byron, Glennis. 'Introduction'. *Globalgothic*, edited by Byron. Manchester University Press, 2015, pp. 1–10.

The Changeling. Directed by Peter Medak, Chessman Peak Productions, 1980.

Cloverfield. Directed by Matt Reeves, Bad Robot Productions, 2008.

Crane, Diana. 'Cultural Flows and the Global Film Industry: A Comparison of Asia and Europe as Regional Cultures'. *Asian Cultural Flows: Cultural Policies, Creative Industries, and Media Consumers*, edited by Nobuka Kawashima and Hye-Kung Lee, Springer, 2018, pp. 113–127.

Danks, Adrian, et al., editors. *American-Australian Cinema: Transnational Connections.* Palgrave Macmillan, 2018.

Dark Water. Directed by Hideo Nakata, Oz Films, 2002.

Davis, Therese. 'Locating *The Sapphires*: Transnational and Cross-Cultural Dimensions of an Australian Indigenous Musical Film'. *Continuum: Journal of Media and Cultural Studies*, vol. 28, no. 5, 2014, pp. 294–304.

Decker, Lindsey. 'British Cinema is Undead: American Horror, British Comedy, and Generic Hybridity in *Shaun of the Dead*'. *Transnational Cinemas*, vol. 7, no. 1, 2016, pp. 67–81.

Dermody, Elizabeth and Susan Jacka. *The Screening of Australia: Anatomy of a Film Industry*, vol. 1, Currency P, 1987.

Dibeltulo, Silvia and Ciara Barrett. 'Introduction: Genres in Transition'. *Rethinking Genre in Contemporary Global Cinema*, edited by Silvia Dibeltulo and Ciara Barrett, Palgrave Macmillan, 2018, pp. 1–11.

Epstein, Jean. *The Fall of the House of Usher*, Films Jean Epstein, 1928.

The Exorcist. Directed by William Friedkin, Hoya Productions, 1973.

The Eye. Directed by the Pang Brothers, Applause Pictures, 2002.

Ezra, Elizabeth and Terry Rowden. *Transnational Cinema: The Film Reader.* Routledge, 2006.

Friedkin, William. '*Psycho*, *Alien*, *Diabolique*, and now THE BABADOOK'. *Twitter.* 1 Dec. 2014. < https://twitter.com/williamfriedkin/status/539244895236390912?lang=en>.

Gaunson, Stephen. 'Spirits Do Come Back: Bunyips and the European Gothic in *The Babadook*'. *A Companion to Australian Cinema*, edited by Felicity Collins, Jane Landman, and Susan Bye, Wiley Blackwell, 2019, pp. 355–372.

Goldsmith, Ben. 'Outward-Looking Australian Cinema'. *Studies in Australasian Cinema*, vol. 4, no. 3, 2010, pp. 199–214.

Gunning, Tom. 'Phantom Images and Modern Manifestations: Spirit Photography, Magic Theatre, Trick Films, and Photography's Uncanny'. *Cinematic Ghosts: Haunting and Spectrality from Silent Cinema to the Digital Era*, edited by Murray Leeder, Bloomsbury Academic, 2015, pp. 17–38.

Hansen, Miriam Bratu. 'The Mass Production of the Senses: Classical Cinema as Vernacular Modernism'. *Modernism/Modernity*, vol. 6, no. 2, 1999, pp. 59–72.

Hardie, Giles. 'Why was *The Babadook* Kept from Australian Audiences?' *The New Daily*, 3 Dec. 2014. <www.thenewdaily.com.au/entertainment/movies/2014/12/03/babadook/>.

Hawkes, Lesley. 'Baz Lurhmann's *The Great Gatsby*: Telling a National Iconic Story Through a Transnational Lens'. *American-Australian Cinema: Transnational Connections*, edited by Adrian Danks, Stephen Gaunson, and Peter C. Kunze, Palgrave Macmillan, 2018, pp. 295–313.

Heller-Nicholas, Alexandra. 'Finders Keepers: Australian Found-Footage Horror Film'. *Metro Magazine*, no. 176, 2013, pp. 66–70.

The House of the Devil, Directed by Georges Méliès, Star Film Company, 1896.

Howell, Amanda. 'The Terrible Terrace: Australian Gothic Reimagined and the (Inner) Suburban Horror of *The Babadook*'. *American-Australian Cinema: Transnational Connections*, edited by Adrian Danks, Stephen Gaunson, and Peter C. Kunze, Palgrave Macmillan, 2018, pp. 183–201.

Hughes, Kit. 'Ailing Screens Viral Video: Cinema's Digital Ghosts in Kiyoshi Kurosawa's *Pulse*'. *Film Criticism*, vol. 36, no. 2, pp. 22–42.

Hunt, Leon, and Leung Wing-Fai, ed. *East Asian Cinemas: Exploring Transnational Connections on Film*. I.B. Tauris, 2008.

The Innocents. Directed by Jack Clayton, Achilles Film Productions, 1961.

Jones, David Annwen. *Re-envisaging the First Age of Cinematic Horror, 1896–1934: Quanta of Fear*. University of Wales Press, 2018.

Ju-on: The Grudge. Directed by Takashi Shimizu, Pioneer LDC, 2002.

Kalat, David. *J-Horror: The Definitive Guide to The Ring, The Grudge, and Beyond*. Random House, 2007.

Keith Grant, Barry. 'Digital Anxiety and the New Verité Horror and SF Film'. *Science Fiction Film and Television*, vol. 6, no. 2, 2013, pp. 153–175.

Lake Mungo. Directed by Joel Anderson, Arclight Films, 2008.

Lambie, Ryan. 'Jennifer Kent Interview: Directing *The Babadook*'. *Den of Geek*, 10 Oct. 2014. <www.denofgeek.com/movies/jennifer-kent-interview-directing-the-babadook/>.

Lobato, Ramon, and Mark David Ryan. 'Rethinking Genre Studies Through Distribution Analysis: Issues in International Horror Movie Circuits'. *New Review of Film and Television Studies*, vol. 9, no. 2, 2011, pp. 188–203.

The Magic Book. Directed by Georges Méliès, Star Film Company, 1900.

McDonald, Keith, and Wayne Johnson. 'Introduction'. *Contemporary Gothic and Horror Film: Transnational Perspectives*, edited by McDonald and Johnson, Anthem Press, 2021.

O'Hara, Helen. 'The Scariest Film of the Year? Jennifer Kent on *The Babadook*'. *Empire*, 21 Nov. 2014. <www.empireonline.com/interviews/interview.asp?IID=1950>.

The Omen. Directed by Richard Donner, Mace Neufeld Productions, 1976.

One Missed Call. Directed by Takashi Miike, Kadokawa-Daiei Eiga, 2003.

The Others. Directed by Alejandro Amenábar, Warner Sogefilms, 2001.

Paranormal Activity. Directed by Oren Peli, Blumhouse Productions, 2007.

Picnic at Hanging Rock. Directed by Peter Weir, British Empire Films, 1975.

Pulse. Directed by Kiyoshi Kurosawa, Daiei, 2001.

[*REC*]. Directed by Jaume Balagueró and Paco Plaza, Filmax International, 2007.

Ringu. Directed by Hideo Nakata, Toho, 1998.

Ritzer, Ivo and Peter W. Schulze, editors. *Genre Hybridization: Global Cinematic Flows*. Schüren, 2013.

Robertson, Roland. 'Globalization or Glocalization?' *Journal of International Communication,* vol. 18, no. 2, 2012, pp. 191–208.

Robertson, Roland. 'Glocalization: Time-Space and Homogeneity-Heterogeneity'. *Global Modernities*, edited by Mike Featherstone, Scott Lash, and Roland Robertson, Thousand Oaks, 1995, pp. 25–44.

Rosemary's Baby. Directed by Roman Polanski, William Castle Enterprises, 1968.

Ryan, Mark David. 'Australian Horror Films and the American Market'. *American-Australian Cinema: Transnational Connections*, edited by Adrian Danks, Stephen Gaunson, and Peter C. Kunze, Palgrave Macmillan, 2018, pp. 163–182.

Schindel, Dan. '*The Babadook* Review'. *Movie Mezzanine*, 24 Nov. 2014. <http://moviemezzanine.com/sundance-review-the-babadook/>.

Shaun of the Dead. Directed by Edgar Wright, StudioCanal, 2004.

The Shining. Directed by Stanley Kubrick, The Producer Circle Company, 1980.

Shutter. Directed by Banjong Pisanthanakun and Parkpoom Wongpoom, GMM Grammy, 2004.

Shutter. Directed by Masakyuki Ochiai, Regency Enterprises, 2008.

The Spiritualist Photograph. Directed by Georges Méliès, Star Film Company, 1903.

Twin Peaks. Created by David Lynch and Mark Frost, CBS Television Distribution, 1990–1991.

Verhoeven, Deb. 'Film, Video, DVD, and Online Delivery'. *The Media and Communications in Australia*, edited by Stuart Cunningham and Sue Turnbull, Allen & Unwin, 2014, pp. 151–172.

Wada-Marciano, Mitsuyo. *Japanese Cinema of the Digital Age*. U of Hawai'i P, 2012.

Wake in Fright. Directed by Ted Kotcheff, NLT Productions, 1971.

Walkabout. Directed by Nicolas Roeg, Max L. Raab-Si Litvinoff Films, 1971.

Wetmore, Kevin. *Post 9/11 Horror in American Cinema*. Continuum, 2012.

Wetmore, Kevin. 'Technoghosts and Culture Shocks: Sociocultural Shifts in American Remakes of J-Horror'. *Post Script*, vol. 28, no. 2, 2009, pp. 72–81.

Wils, Tyson. 'Conjuring the Real: Ghosts, Technology, and Landscape in *Lake Mungo*'. *Screen Education*, no. 82, 2016, pp. 120–127.

About the Author

Jessica Balanzategui is a Senior Lecturer in Cinema and Screen Studies at Swinburne University of Technology where she is also the Deputy Director of the Centre for Transformative Media Technologies. She is the author of *The Uncanny Child in Transnational Cinema* (Amsterdam UP 2018) and the founding editor of Amsterdam University Press's new book series, 'Horror and Gothic Media Cultures'.

6.   *Terra Somnambulism*: Sleepwalking, Nightdreams, and Nocturnal Wanderings in the Televisual Australian Gothic

Kate Cantrell

Abstract

Sleep disturbance has a rich textual history, one that predates the Australian Gothic. However, in the Antipodean context, episodes of deranged and disordered sleep – from daymares and nightdreams to somnambulistic trances – cannot be read as simple restagings of early gothic concerns such as demonic activity or possession. Rather, sleep disturbance in the Australian Gothic brings to light more ordinary horror: the horror of embodied automaticity, the horror of blind complacency, and the horror of discovering the mechanical processes that hide behind the self. The televisual texts examined in this chapter can be linked thematically as a way of working through this horror, a necessity that demands female vigilance but which often culminates problematically in monstrous behaviour or monstrous transformation.

Keywords: Australian Gothic; gothic television; sleepwalking; nocturnal wandering; *The Cry*; white vanishing

Since the global outbreak of COVID-19 – 'the most crucial health calamity of the century and the greatest challenge that humankind has faced since the Second World War' (Chakraborty and Maity 1) – a number of sleep neurologists have reported an increase in sleep disorders associated with the pandemic. From insomnia and hypersomnia to recurrent nightmares and abnormal dreams, this surge in sleep disturbance has been coined 'COVID-somnia' (Geffern qtd. in Goldfarb), a new epidemic of sleep pathologies that,

Gildersleeve, J. and K. Cantrell (eds.), *Screening the Gothic in Australia and New Zealand: Contemporary Antipodean Film and Television*. Taylor & Francis Group, 2022
DOI 10.5117/9789463721141_CH06

according to one study, 'could be short-lived [...] abating once the pandemic subsides, or it could become, in some cases, a chronic condition' (Taylor et al. 713). Initially linked to a fear of infection, including a fear of infecting others, reported declines in sleep quality have been reconceptualized through the development of multi-factorial measures of pandemic-related distress. For example, a recent study of COVID Stress Syndrome identified five correlated facets of the syndrome's severity: (1) fear of the danger of COVID-19, including a fear of coming into contact with contaminated objects and surfaces; (2) concern about socioeconomic impacts, such as stress on finances; (3) xenophobic fears that foreigners are spreading the virus; (4) traumatic stress symptoms associated with direct or vicarious exposure to the virus, such as nightmares and intrusive thoughts or images; and (5) compulsive news checking and reassurance seeking from family and friends (Taylor et al. 707). In an unintentional nod to the Gothic, a number of studies also identify as exacerbating factors excessive daytime napping, increased social isolation and confinement, and a reduced exposure to natural light, as well as over-exposure to artificial light at night.

While the pandemic, then, has prompted new research into sleep disturbance, the significant upturn in sleep-deprivation studies pre-COVID suggests that pandemic-related sleep distress has only intensified the incompatibility of an irreducible human need with the unremitting demands of the 24/7 neoliberal economy. The institutionalization of sleep science, combined with the subjugation of sleep to pharmacological control, coincides with the increasing commodification of sleep through sleep-optimizing products and services, from sleep-regulating apps and wearable trackers to portable napping pods, sleep-boosting pyjamas, anti-snoring pillows, and spooning robots. The booming sleep economy represents a gothic excess of pseudo-necessities, biotechnologies, and so-called 'smart' devices – a fascinating if not morbid phenomenon when read in light of Edgar Huntly's conjecture that 'the incapacity of sound sleep denotes a mind sorely wounded [...] the possession of some dreadful secret' (Brown, 'Edgar Huntly' 12). Certainly, the erosion of sleep and its pathological excess or absence pervades the Gothic, while at the same time defying straightforward representation. Nathaniel Wallace's observation that there is 'a fundamental antagonism between sleep and narrative' (236) suggests that the usually dull and uneventful nature of slumber does not lend itself to the building of narrative tension; however, 'the story of sleep', as Michael Greaney points out, 'is not just the story of its storylessness, but the story of the friction between its storylessness and the imperatives of a story-driven and story-shaped world' (11). In other words, the very tension that sleep evokes – especially when it malfunctions – is the tension between narrative representation and its alleged failure, between what it means *to be* and *not be* in the world.

Thus, this chapter takes, as a point of departure, representations of sleep disorders and other nocturnal disturbances in recent examples of the televisual Australian Gothic, all of which were produced pre-COVID, but all of which gesture towards a new model of normativity in which disruptions to sleep-wake cycles are expected, and the 'natural' oscillations between light and darkness, activity and rest, and work and regeneration are reconfigured if not eradicated completely. As Jonathan Crary writes, 'it should be no surprise that there is an erosion of sleep now everywhere [...] Sleep is now an experience cut loose from notions of necessity or nature' (11, 13). In Crary's polemic against the dehumanizing effects of neoliberalism (also penned pre-pandemic), sleep is the final barrier to the full realization of late capitalism, an affront to both the permanent illumination and non-stop operation of global consumption and exchange. As 'one of the unvanquishable remnants of the everyday' (127), sleep cannot be eliminated, but it can be deferred, disrupted, or diminished. As Crary, speaking of the phenomenon of 'sleep-mode', explains, 'the notion of an apparatus in a state of low-power readiness remakes the larger sense of sleep into simply a deferred or diminished condition of operationality and access. It supersedes an off/on logic, so that nothing is ever fundamentally "off" and there is never an actual state of rest' (13). For Crary, sleep represents both 'a human need and an interval of time that cannot be colonized' or harnessed for profitability (11) – the denial of sleep not only represents a form of violent dispossession but a lack of sleep becomes analogous with, and inextricable from, the dismantling of other social protections. In other words, sleep, 'as the most private, most vulnerable state common to all [...] is crucially dependent on society in order to be sustained' (25).

In the Australian television drama, *The Cry* (2018), the corrosion of sleep gradually leads to a personal 'awakening' or epiphanic disturbance for the female protagonist. Joanna Lindsay is trapped in what we might call a waking nightmare – a *terra somnambulism* (or sleepwalking land). In this liminal space, the borders between sleep and wakefulness are fertile grounds for exploring the permeability between self and Other, and conscious reality and unconscious dream. Through these breaches, the spectral manifests not only through the past's haunting of the present but through the invisible threat of complacency, which demands vigilance or 'wakefulness'. In this way, disrupted or deranged sleep, which is typically linked to reduced cognitive and psychological functioning, ironically leads to heightened perceptual ability, which culminates in individual action and self-determination. As a result, the moment of awakening, though often ambiguous (since we do not always know if the subject is awake or asleep), is connected to both physical and metaphorical expressions of vision and sight. As Crary explains, 'awakenings are usually articulated in perceptual terms as a newfound ability to see through a veil to a true state of things, to discriminate an inverted world from one right-side up, or to recover a lost truth that becomes the negation of whatever one has awoken from' (23). This reality is complicated by 24/7 temporality since time without the pause of sleep not only blurs the distinctions between day and night, action and repose, and agency and passivity, but masks what is essentially a non-social model of mechanistic performance – one designed to eliminate sleep completely and to ensure, therefore, that 'no potentially disturbing awakening is ever necessary' (24). In this context, the diagnosis of Shakespeare's famous sleepwalker, Lady Macbeth, takes on a different meaning: unnatural deeds do indeed breed unnatural troubles.

Sleep/lessness and the Contemporary Australian Gothic

In the contemporary Australian Gothic, the injuring of sleep is inextricable from questions of good citizenship, good moral virtue, and good mothering. For this reason, sleeplessness or sleep dysfunction is often experienced by irrational and unregulated female bodies. In *The Babadook* (2014), for example, 'the true monster of the film is Amelia's sense of her own failed motherhood. The horror she has faced daily since [her son] Samuel's birth is the horror of being [...] a shadow of a mother' (Gildersleeve 100). As Amelia, a harried single parent, becomes emotionally trapped in her suburban home, her attempt to perform the role of the 'good' mother is undermined by the unseen forces that conspire against her: her untreated postnatal depression, the resurfacing of unresolved familial trauma, the increasingly destructive effects of mother and son's social isolation, and of course, the supernatural powers wielded by Mister Babadook, the imaginary monster who lurks within the pages of Samuel's bedtime book. 'You look tired', remarks a concerned neighbour, and a weary Amelia responds, 'Nothing five years of sleep wouldn't fix', in a conspicuous reference to her five years of motherhood. Indeed, as the narrative builds, it is sleep (and its lack) that provides the film's psychological texture. Amelia's escalating irrationality and aggressiveness towards her son reflects her disorderly sleep habits: alternating periods of sleep deprivation and hypersomnia, punctuated by somnambulistic trances in which the sleep-wake cycle is inverted. This reversal of the 'natural' rhythms of sleep, combined with Amelia's 'unnatural' lack of maternal instinct, sets the stage for her monstrous transformation into a frightening automaton; the ease with which she routinely medicates Samuel for sleep is a confronting example of her maternal ambivalence and indifference (Buerger; Gildersleeve). By the film's resolution, the original threat that is issued by Mister Babadook – 'and you won't sleep a wink' – is fulfilled.

Similarly, in *The Kettering Incident* (2016), the waking self and the sleeping self are disassociated when Anna Macy, a consultant in London, returns home to her native Tasmania after suffering from a series of unexplained blackouts, nosebleeds, and insomniac trances, all of which point to the uncanny return of the psychologically repressed but also to 'the unbearable automaticity of being' (Bargh and Chartrand 462). In the opening episode, Anna is firmly positioned in the uncanny realm of automaticity when security footage at the city hospital where she works captures her tap-dancing in a somnambulistic daze. With no memory of her nocturnal wanderings, Anna blacks out in her supervisor's London office and wakes in her hometown of Kettering, a small Tasmanian coastal town now embroiled in an ideological rift between old logging interests and renewed environmental concerns. Gradually, we learn that Anna's mysterious fugue states are embodied automations that are connected to the disappearance of her best friend, Gillian, from Kettering forest some fifteen years earlier. Anna's inability to remember not only how she has come to be in Tasmania but also the circumstances of Gillian's disappearance is a pointed reminder of the personal and cultural amnesia that manifests in the ancestral ghosts that greet Anna upon her return: the environmental destruction caused by old-growth logging, the persistent small-town suspicion of perceived 'outsiders', and the long-standing denial of the island state's brutal history of massacre, involuntary exile, and mass dispossession of Indigenous Australians from their land (Gelder). In this way, the uncanny automatism of the CCTV footage in which the sleepwalking Anna performs a tap dance is a gothic rendering of the horror of blind mechanicity; it is not the haunted house or landscape that stands in for the haunted nation but the act of sleepwalking itself.

Equally, in the televisual reincarnation of *Picnic at Hanging Rock* (2018), the girls' trance-like state as they ascend the eponymous rock is conceived as a deliberate response to the horror of automaticity, a gothic fever dream in which the girls, who are oppressed subjects, become unrestrained from the constraints of daily life. From the outset, Mrs Appleyard's cautionary warning that 'maladies flourish in the dark' establishes the need for female vigilance, or what Crary describes as 'an ethic of watchfulness' (19). Certainly, the remedy prescribed to Irma upon her return from the rock – 'a nice big spoon of sleep' – combined with the relentless monitoring of her sleeping body, is a gothic rendering of sleep as a 'rest cure' for female hysteria. However, now, the returned girls feign sleep, always aware they are being watched. In this sense, the revival of *Picnic* for a contemporary audience prompts a significant shift in meaning; where popular readings of both Joan Lindsay's novel and Peter Weir's melancholy dream suggest that the girls have either succumbed to the supernatural, or been punished for their transgression of a sacred Indigenous site, the televisual reimagining implies that the girls are deliberately lost. That is, the now-empowered girls, who are likened to 'horses that won't be tamed', curate their disappearance in order to escape the patriarchal trappings of marriage and reproduction. The 'secret vow' that the girls make to their 'sacred selves', pledged during nightfall and executed in daylight, is the result of their heightened perceptual ability or intensified clarity and awareness. In this way, the girls are positioned not as innocent victims but as proto-feminist heroines who effectively transform their situation; indeed, 'they seem more vengeful than doomed' and 'more reminiscent of St Trinian's than the Appleyard College of old' (Craven 57, 58). This positive inflection, described by Allison Craven as the 'post-millennial Gothic' (46), is an optimistic retelling that parodies both the trope of the lost child and the fantasy of the perpetual picnic, while at the same time paying tribute to the earlier adaptations. Indeed, in the television series, as in both the film and the novel, the language of sleep is used to measure time and to figure transitions between different ontological states. The Aboriginal Dreaming, as it features in *Picnic*, debunks the myth of *terra nullius* and exposes the landscape as a *terra somnambulism*, drawing attention to the precariousness of the colonial enterprise and disrupting the enduring mystique that surrounds white Australia's morbid fascination with white vanishing.

Naturally, then, sleeping, like dreaming, is a universal experience with a long and complex social, cultural, and representational history. Sleepwalking and other nocturnal transgressions frequently call into question distinctions between functional and dysfunctional bodies, conscious and non-conscious states of mind, and voluntary and non-voluntary acts. Yet despite the universality of sleep, or perhaps because of it, sleep is a blind spot in Australian screen studies: its narrative representation is naturally complicated by its general banality and prolonged duration. Sleep disturbance, on the other hand, has a rich textual history, one that predates the Australian Gothic to long-standing preoccupations with somnambulistic bodies and their nocturnal wanderings; from Emily's midnight explorations of the gloomy labyrinths of Udolpho, to Lucy's compulsive sleepwalking in *Dracula* (1897), to the grisly crimes of Dr Caligari's murderous somnambulist, nocturnal transgressions abound in the early Gothic. Sleepwalking, especially, figures significantly in the writings of seventeenth-century French philosophers like Pierre Gassendi and Descartes, and in the medical writings of eighteenth-century physicians like Polidori, Bertrand, and Wienholt. In fact, in Polidori's 1815 dissertation on sleepwalking, he links the disorder to a number of predisposing causes: 'intoxication, overeating, ingesting foods that produce gas, using too much bedding, and using opium' (Umanath et al. 259).

Regardless, when Shakespeare penned *Macbeth* 200 years earlier, he could not have known that the paradoxical nature of Lady Macbeth's 'slumbery agitations' – that is, her ability to simultaneously *see* and *not see* – would later reverberate through the medical literature of the seventeenth and eighteenth centuries. As the German physician Johann August Unzer wrote some time between 1759 and 1799, 'the most extraordinary circumstance in the case of somnambulism is that the secret power of the soul supplies our perceptive faculties at a time when the external senses are oppressed [...] such sleepers see without eyes, hear without ears, and accurately perform all functions, otherwise requiring sensibility, without the assistance of the special organs of sense' (qtd. in Wienholt 149). While Lady Macbeth's nocturnal wanderings are often read as either a manifestation of her unconfessed sins or as an outward expression of her internal anguish, sleepwalking's peculiar pathology, as a disorder that disrupts both conscious thought and memory, complicates the problem of moral accountability since the latter relies on the retention of both conscious choice (or intention) and rational reflection (Handley, 'Deformities of Nature' 407). This problem is not only central to a number of gothic fictions – Charles Brockden Brown's *Edgar Huntly* (1799) is an early example, as is Brown's short story 'Somnambulism: A Fragment' (1805) – but this tension also underpins a number of Australian Gothic dramas in which sleep disturbance and, by extension, spatiotemporal disruption, abnormalizes what has been lost, what compulsively returns, and what continues to defy resolution.

For this reason, the gothic texts examined in this chapter can be linked thematically as a way of working through the horror of automaticity – what Dawn Keetley calls 'the horrifying revelation of the mechanical at the heart of the human' (1018) – the unconscious, uncontrollable, and unintentional operations that 'not only undermine the notion of a "unitary" self but also the idea of the self as autonomous' (1018). However, unlike Keetley's reading of embodied automation as 'inevitably tainted with the demonic' (1026), I want to suggest that female vigilance, when combined with the shock of the mechanical corporeal, actually makes visible 'everything that was meant to remain secret and hidden', or denied (Freud 132). This 'coming to light' is achieved paradoxically, not in the high-intensity glare of a permanently illuminated 24/7 world, but rather in the liminal space between darkness and light, between oblivious sleep and 'true' wakefulness. In this malleable state, episodes of disrupted or deranged sleep ironically lead to heightened perceptual ability. For women trapped in 'terror cycles' (Wheatley 12), 'coming to light' is synonymous with 'coming to realization', which often culminates problematically in monstrous behaviour or a monstrous transformation.

Indeed, in the female Gothic, the association of female awakening with vigilante justice is problematic because self-realization that culminates in violence, regardless of whether said violence is morally or aesthetically justified, not only appropriates masculine agency but also risks retraumatizing the already traumatized self (see Gildersleeve, Sulway, and Howell in the present volume). In other words, acts of violent revenge or retribution may perpetuate cycles of violence, which can exacerbate the emotional and psychological suffering of the individual and diminish the potential for social reconciliation and healing. In fact, David Mendeloff suggests that even the affective power of truth-telling is dubious because debriefing interventions 'can lead to increased traumatic responses (or even spark PTSD where it might not have otherwise developed), even when people report that they feel better after the fact' (613). Certainly, in *The Cry*, there is a sense that Joanna's quest for retributive justice is both a harmful exercise, since the violent punishment that she dispenses serves to isolate her further, and a morally questionable one, since it continues 'the spiral of violence' by framing violent interventions as the only viable means for overcoming other violent acts. In this way, the female vigilante can only defeat the gothic monster by adopting a deviant subjectivity that is itself monstrous, an embodied identity that is expressed as a monstrous alterity.

Daymares, Nightdreams, and Somnambulistic Trances: *The Cry*

Released as a four-part miniseries in 2018, *The Cry* (directed by Glendyn Ivin) is a British-Australian coproduction that was sold to domestic and international audiences as an example of 'Scaussie Noir' – a Scottish-Australian crossover, filmed in Glasgow and Melbourne, and starring an international cast (Mundell qtd. in Miller). Based on the 2013 novel of the same name by Australian author Helen FitzGerald, *The Cry* takes as its premise 'every parent's worst nightmare' – the disappearance of one's child – but obscures the subject through its patterning as a gothic drama that casts the failure of the family as a metaphor for the degeneration of the nation as a whole. This gothic rendering of the collapsed domestic space, as presented through the domestic medium of the television, is not only characteristic of the British and American televisual Gothic but is also typical of the Australian presentation of the genre. In fact, *The Cry*'s configuration as a gothic story that is primarily concerned with familial trauma is fixed, before viewing, in the series' logline: 'The abduction of a baby from a small Australian coastal town is the catalyst for a journey into the disintegrating psychology of a young woman, Joanna, as she and her husband, Alistair, deal with an unthinkable tragedy under both the white light of public scrutiny and behind closed doors' (Screen Australia). The series' convoluted plotting and complex non-linear arrangement is also characteristic of the televisual Australian Gothic, as is the 'frequent deployment of horror and/or disgust, and an obsession with motifs of the uncanny' (Wheatley 2). As evident in *The Cry*, *Picnic at Hanging Rock*, and *The Kettering Incident*, the long-established trope of white vanishing, as a paradigm that incorporates narratives about lost (white) children, persists in the Antipodean Gothic (Pierce; Tilley; Gildersleeve). Indeed, the figure of the lost child, originally a symbol of the growing nation, still haunts the Australian imagination, recalling 'the old colonial nightmare that usually has to wait for daylight for its terrible or joyful conclusion' (Pierce 54).

In *The Cry*, Joanna Lindsay (Jenna Coleman) is a primary school teacher in Glasgow who falls in love with media spin doctor and Australian ex-pat Alistair Robertson. Cast from the outset as 'the other woman', Joanna soon discovers that Alistair (Ewen Leslie) is married to Alexandra Grenville (Asher Keddie), with whom he has a young daughter, Chloe (Markella Kavenagh). When Alexandra learns of her husband's infidelity, she and Chloe flee Scotland for Australia, leaving Alistair seemingly distressed by the loss of his only child. Meanwhile, Alistair and Joanna remain in Glasgow and have a baby of their own, Noah (Noah and Oliver Rennie). When Noah is four months old, Alistair plans a family 'holiday' to Australia, insisting the trip will be a welcome respite for Joanna, but returning home with a more malevolent intention: once home, Alistair plans to prove Alexandra an ineffectual mother in order to obtain full custody of Chloe. A diffident and sleep-deprived Joanna, struggling to adjust to motherhood, reluctantly agrees to the overseas trip, and on the drive from Melbourne airport to the coastal town of Wilde Bay, Noah disappears. As Joanna becomes increasingly distressed, she begins to experience different types of sleep disturbance, including recurring daymares in which she sees a young boy, presumably lost or abandoned, in a bushfire-ravaged field. As Joanna's sleep habits deteriorate, Alistair worries that Joanna's erratic behaviour will turn public opinion against them and jeopardize his custody appeal. Thus, Alistair begins coaching Joanna to placate the media, goading her to cry on cue and assuring her that 'the world wants to see a good mother crushed, not a bad mother in hiding'.

The situation comes to a head when, at the end of episode two, a flash-back reveals that Noah was not with his parents on the night of his alleged disappearance. Instead, we learn – again through flashback – that on the family's drive from Melbourne airport to Wilde Bay, Noah has died in his capsule in a suspected case of Sudden Infant Death Syndrome (SIDS). With Alistair's prompting, however, Joanna recalls that on the flight to Australia, she accidentally medicated Noah with her pain killers, resulting in a fatal overdose. Alistair, certain that Joanna will be convicted of manslaughter, persuades Joanna to let him bury Noah's body by the sea, and together the pair conspire to cover up the truth of their child's death. Meanwhile, media interest in the case persists, with Alistair becoming increasingly manipulative in his effort to control the family's public image, and Joanna questioning her decision to conceal the truth. Running alongside the central narrative, which is set in the recent past, we learn that in the present day Joanna is on trial in Scotland – not for the death of Noah, as we are initially positioned to believe, but for the murder of Alistair. In a turn of events, it is revealed that Alistair has beguiled Joanna into believing that she killed Noah when, in fact, it was Alistair who accidentally administered the wrong medication. When Joanna realizes the full extent of Alistair's deception, she invites him on an afternoon drive through the highlands where she proceeds to release Alistair's seatbelt and deliberately drive off the cliffside road. Joanna survives the collision; however, Alistair is killed on impact. In the final scene, Joanna returns to Australia to be close to Noah. She purchases a display home in a new residential estate, and the series closes with a pan of Joanna, with her head pressed to the floorboards, the implication being that she has escaped literal prison but realized that her dead son is buried – not by the sea, as Alistair claimed – but in the earth beneath her home.

In *The Cry*, sleeplessness is initially associated with sensory impoverish-ment and the deleterious effects of cognitive impairment; for Joanna, the absence of sleep is literally the absence of mind. In the opening scene, the new mother, overcome with fatigue, fails to hear baby Noah's cries; in her semi-comatose state, she is unable to soothe her crying son, and on the verge of breakdown, she recklessly co-sleeps with Noah due to exhaustion. From the outset, Joanna's inability to mother, at least from Alistair's perspective, is closely aligned with her perceived failure to manage a regular sleep-wake cycle for both herself and her son. Indeed, Joanna's chronic sleeplessness is later established (though erroneously) as the cause of Noah's death, and Noah himself dies while asleep on account of Alistair's accidental dosing. However, as Joanna crosses the threshold between waking and dreaming – her everyday life now 'every parent's worst nightmare' – she comes to inhabit a zone where artificial lights and shadowy presences project a phantasmal double that renders her unfamiliar to herself. In other words, it is the violent denial of sleep – 'the only enduring "natural condition" that capitalism cannot eliminate' (Crary 74) – which becomes the epiphanic disturbance that shatters Joanna's illusion of a unitary self, thereby revealing her uncanny double. The 'awakened' Joanna explains: 'That's when this began. Two faces. Two Joannas'.

This doubling continues through the gradual revelation of the family's destabilizing secret. When Alistair accepts a new job at Broken Circle, an international organization for parents who have lost their children to violent crime, the thin veneer of Joanna's complacency finally cracks. Alistair's decision to sign a book deal – effectively capitalizing on his son's death – only heightens Joanna's profound sense of estrangement, again ushering in the uncanny. 'I'm sorry', Joanna says to Alistair and also to Noah's spectre, 'suddenly everything has just become very strange to me [...] what we've become'. While the focal point for secrecy is still the nuclear family, the public staging and restaging of the family's trauma, which includes the public memorialization and sacralization of Noah, collapses the boundaries between private and public, between 'the darkness of sheltered experience' and 'the harsher light of the public realm' (Arendt 51). However, the transmission of trauma, from the private sphere of the family to the broader community, is bidirectional, since the domestic space is enmeshed with digital space, and subject to the penetration of social media and technologies of surveillance. As a result, there is, in Crary's words, 'no possibility of nurturing the singularity of the self' (21) because the impossibility of privacy means that 'one accumulates a patchwork of surrogate identities that subsist 24/7, sleeplessly, continuously, as inanimate impersonations rather than extensions of the self' (104). Thus, *The Cry* reimagines an old colonial nightmare – the disappearance of a child in the bush – however, it is the mass media, as one of the preeminent agents of modernity, that transports this nightmare from the rural setting to the urban space.

In Noah's case, as in many real-life cases of missing children, the prolonged trial by media, coupled with the relentless and often global intermediation of both the child and the child's parent/s, results in saturation coverage that is fuelled by both moral outrage and punitive sentiment (Greer and McLaughlin 400). Sleep disorders and other nocturnal transgressions have historically been rooted within a moral framework; sleeplessness, for example, has long-established social, cultural, and religious associations with madness and the externalization of anxiety, guilt, and shame (Handley, 'Sleepwalking'; Umanath et al.; Riva et al.). To be sure, Joanna's inability to sleep is presented, on one level, as a signifier of her complicity in the deceitful operation that Alistair has orchestrated. However, more than a marker of culpability, Joanna's sleep deprivation represents the dispossession of her volitional self; her mechanistic nocturnal life is the result of her inability to 'unplug' from the television, from her iPhone, from the rolling news coverage of Noah's disappearance. In this way, the violent subjugation that Joanna experiences, both at the hands of Alistair and in the hands of the media, is enacted against her digital body as much as it is her physical one. For example, at a press conference designed to raise awareness of Noah's disappearance, Alistair insists that Joanna cries on camera to emotionalize the unfolding drama and garner public sympathy. When Joanna reviews the footage and watches her digital self play along with the deception, the uncanny autonomy of the moving image confounds the real with the artificial, and again ruptures the idea of a stable self, calling to mind Guy Debord's suspicion that 'the spectacle is the bad dream of a modern society in chains, expressing nothing more than its wish for sleep' (18).

Certainly, for Keetley, the notion of automaticity as it manifests both in person and on screen is central to contemporary manifestations of the uncanny. American horror, Keetley observes, reveals how the uncanniness of sleep negates human agency in order to assert the agency of the demonic and the agency of the body (1019). Human monsters 'are not purposefully malevolent characters [...] but versions of ourselves wrenched free from reason and volition' (1017). Since monstrous mothers are often depicted as childless, whether involuntarily or by choice, the locus of Joanna's monstrosity is not only the violent revenge that she exacts on Alistair but the abject horror of her faulty body, which continues to produce milk after Noah's death. Thus, as Joanna's sleep is routinely interrupted by a mechanistic operation that she cannot control, her maternal body is rendered defective, which again draws attention to the fragility of the self and its mortal materiality. Further, the body's expulsion, not of waste, but of nutritive contents and immunological substances, compounds Joanna's sense of maternal failure because her embodied leakage or 'seepage' (Grosz 203) provides sustenance for an absent body that she can no longer nourish. As Joanna's lactating body, then, is both the site and source of the abject, her ability to express milk is ironically contrasted with her inability to express the inexpressible: the truth of Noah's death. In this way, the automatized body that leaks instead of sleeps is not associated with demonic activity or supernatural possession but with the abject horror of the involuntary self, of the body that is bereft of mind. The fact that Joanna's production of milk is technologized by a breast pump only reinforces this idea, as does the discourse of breastfeeding itself, which tends to discursively reduce the female body to a machine through industrial metaphors of 'supply' and 'demand' and through mechanistic terms such as 'output', 'frequency', and 'duration' (Dykes 2288). Similarly, the eponymous cry of the series' title foreshadows the collision of the abject and the maternal as Joanna's guttural cry on discovering Noah's lifeless body is imperceptible in the empty expanse of rural Victoria; the loss of a white child in the natural environment is a familiar recasting of the Australian landscape as a biological black hole.

Indeed, Joanna's failure to heed the warning issued by the land, by Alexandra, and by Alistair's past can be read as emblematic of a national psychosis in which white Australia's repression of colonial history and continuing failure to accept moral responsibility for the past ultimately leads to, if not self-annihilation, then irreparable loss: the loss of the child (the promise of futurity), the loss of participatory democracy (the promise of the national project), and the loss of coherent order and rationality (the promise of modernity). While these different types of loss attest to the complex entanglements of identity, power, and place, all arise from the same formulation: 'the classic colonial triangle' between white settler, Other, and the land (Hulme 159). Since the legacy of white presence in Australia is fraught with narratives of violence and trauma, crimes that involve children, especially the physical or metaphorical loss of white children, are always framed as morality tales (Innes 52). In other words, stories of white vanishing are not merely nostalgic or inexplicably compelling; rather, they are cautionary tales with moral messages at their core.

Certainly, Joanna's initial failure to 'see through' Alistair's façade – to recognize signs of gaslighting and to awaken from the nightmare of his psychological abuse – is connected not only to her out-of-placeness as a white British woman in a foreign land but also to her short-sightedness as a woman who is sleepwalking, with eyes wide open, through life. In the end, Joanna is a fallen mother not because she has failed to care for her son but because she has failed to remain vigilant of her child's father, the ruthless and destructive Alistair whose power is dependent on violent authoritarian subjugation and control – the same power wielded under colonial rule. This narrative is allegorized through the latent menace of the land and the danger posed by naïve or willful ignorance of its sublime power, as well as the danger posed by white Australia's physical possession and imaginative and symbolic appropriation of Indigenous land. For example, as Alistair and Joanna make their way to their holiday house, unaware that Noah is dead, there is a bushfire warning on the radio: 'If you are in this area, you are in danger. You must act immediately [...] Do not leave or enter the area'. The warning, though issued anonymously, is clear. However, when Joanna questions if the couple should proceed, a smug Alistair dismisses her concern, and they continue nonchalantly into the unseen (but not unforewarned) danger ahead. Here, Joanna's complacency is symbolic of the sleepwalking nation as a whole, since sleepwalking, after all, is a condition in which sense and motion malfunction, in which memory is erased or interrupted, and in which the perpetrators themselves bear no legal responsibility for the acts they commit while asleep.

Eventually, however, Joanna's frightening automaticity breaks down; her newfound ability to see through the smoke and mirrors to the 'true' state of things represents the end of her childlike naivety and automatic responsiveness to the world. Indeed, when the court-appointed psychologist who is tasked with assessing whether Joanna is fit for trial asks what has changed for Joanna, she simply responds, 'I woke up'. This declaration of self-epiphany is juxtaposed against one of the most frightening lines in the series – a simple caption on a drawing by a child in Joanna's class: 'The monster was only pretending to be asleep'. The description of the furtive monster who is only pretending to be dormant is a subtextual reference that is deliberately ambiguous. Is Alistair the sleeping monster who lures Joanna with his false charms and calm façade? Or is Joanna the dormant monster who feigns sleep, who pretends to be silent and motionless, to ensnare Alistair in her plot for revenge and perhaps even to absolve herself of any responsibility for Noah's death? In the closing scene, there is a sense that Joanna's vigilantism is, if not morally justified, then at least a necessary and emotionally satisfying response to the gendered violence that she has endured as both a woman and a mother, an idea made evident when Joanna addresses Alistair's ghost in the courtroom. 'Whoever took my son from me', Joanna says, 'made me believe that I had failed to protect him, made me think I was a bad mother [...] You can judge me how you see fit [...] I've already been to hell'. The stage directions provided in the post-production script also imply that Joanna's vigilantism is the necessary means of ensuring not only her survival but her freedom; in the final episode, her 'awakening' is again framed through metaphors of light and darkness, and presented as a self-transforming encounter that is the direct result of her newfound perception: 'The courthouse doors are open and Joanna's lawyer leads her out [...] Joanna blinks slowly as the light of day hits her face and she is free. The sound of the world disappears as Joanna walks out of the courthouse [...] She stumbles for a moment on her heels, then sweeps past them into the light' (BBC 39). The fact that the greater part of Joanna's final testimony is a fabrication suggests continued deception, sealing her monstrous transformation. However, the dramatic irony is that Joanna is performing for the camera, just as Alistair has trained her. In the end, the heavy burden of Joanna's secret, combined with her ongoing subjection to public scrutiny and surveillance, undermines the notion that she will ever be free. Even as Joanna evades prosecution, she cannot evade the past; the retributive justice that she enacts is incapable of reversing her loss. As Paul Doro, speaking of the female vigilante in mainstream cinema, explains, 'She will continue to be haunted by her actions. She will not go to prison, but that does not mean she is free' (242).

In her collection of essays, *On Not Being Able to Sleep*, Jacqueline Rose writes that 'it is not easy to think about sleep' (105). Indeed, it is difficult to think about sleep – the timeless void in which 'we relinquish our thinking selves' (105) – but it is necessary if we are to wake up not only to the trauma of the past but to the lived experience of that trauma in the present. The televisual Australian Gothic, as *The Cry* makes clear, is a hybridized and increasingly transnational genre, marked as it is by the irruption of the horrific within the mundane; the gradual revelation of destabilizing secrets, usually established and exposed within the claustrophobia of the home; the presence of a ruthless and often destructive patriarchal figure whose control is dependent upon physical and/or emotional violence; the configuration of the landscape as a biological black hole; and white Australia's failure to recognize, or make reparations for, the abuses of the past. For this reason, in the Antipodean context, episodes of deranged and disordered sleep – from daymares and nightdreams to somnambulistic trances – cannot be read as simple restagings of early gothic concerns such as demonic activity or possession. Rather, sleep disturbance in the Australian Gothic brings to light more ordinary horror: the horror of embodied automaticity, the horror of blind complacency, and the horror of discovering the mechanical processes that hide behind the self. Indeed, for Jentsch, it is the artificial mockeries of humanity that summon the uncanny, the 'dark knowledge' (14) that paradoxically threatens to blind us should we decide to close our eyes or look the other way.

Works Cited

Arendt, Hannah. *The Human Condition*. U of Chicago, 1998.

The Babadook. Directed by Jennifer Kent, Screen Australia, 2014.

Bargh, John A., and Tanya L. Chartrand. 'The Unbearable Automaticity of Being'. *American Psychologist*, vol. 54, no. 7, 1999, pp. 462–479.

BBC. 'Episode 4: Post-Production Script, *The Cry*'. *Synchronicity Films*, Oct. 2018. <www.downloads.bbc.co.uk/writersroom/scripts/The-Cry-Ep4-UK-TX-Script.pdf>.

Brown, Charles Brockden. *Edgar Huntly; or, Memoirs of a Sleep-Walker*. M. Polock, 1857.

Brown, Charles Brockden. 'Somnambulism: A Fragment'. *Literary Magazine and American Register*, vol. 3, no. 20, 1805, pp. 335–347.

Buerger, Shelley. 'The Beak that Grips: Maternal Indifference, Ambivalence, and the Abject in *The Babadook*'. *Studies in Australasian Cinema*, vol. 11, no. 1, 2017, pp. 33–44.

Chakraborty, Indranil, and Prasenjit Maity. 'COVID-19 Outbreak: Migration, Effects on Society, Global Environment, and Prevention'. *Science of the Total Environment*, vol. 728, 2020, pp. 1–7.

Crary, Jonathan. *24/7: Late Capitalism and the Ends of Sleep*. Verso, 2013.

Craven, Allison. 'A Happy and Instructive Haunting: Revising the Child, the Gothic, and the Australian Cinema Revival in *Storm Boy* (2019) and *Picnic at Hanging Rock* (2018)'. *Journal of Australian Studies*, vol. 45, no. 1, 2021, pp. 46–60.

The Cry. Directed by Glendyn Ivin, written by Jacquelin Perske, produced by Claire Mundell and Brian Kaczynski, Synchronicity Films, 2018.

Debord, Guy. *The Society of the Spectacle*. Translated by Donald Nicholson-Smith, Zone Books, 1994.

Doro, Paul. 'Vengeance is Mine: Gender and Vigilante Justice in Mainstream Cinema'. *American Revenge Narratives*, edited by Kyle Wiggins, Palgrave Macmillan, 2018, pp. 227–244.

Dykes, Fiona. '"Supply" and "Demand": Breastfeeding as Labour'. *Social Science and Medicine*, vol. 60, no. 10, 2005, pp. 2283–2293.

Freud, Sigmund. *The Uncanny*. Translated by David McLintock, Penguin, 2003.

Gelder, Ken. 'Australian Gothic'. *A New Companion to the Gothic*, edited by David Punter, Wiley-Blackwell, 2012, pp. 379–392.

Gildersleeve, Jessica. 'Contemporary Australian Trauma'. *The Palgrave Handbook of Contemporary Gothic*, edited by Clive Bloom, Palgrave Macmillan, 2020, pp. 91–104.

Goldfarb, Anna. 'Considering Melatonin for Sleep? Here's a Guide to Help'. *The New York Times*, 24 Apr. 2020. <www.nytimes.com/2020/04/24/well/melatonin-sleep-aid-coronavirus.html>.

Greaney, Michael. *Sleep and the Novel: Fictions of Somnolence, from Jane Austen to the Present*. Palgrave Macmillan, 2018.

Greer, Chris, and Eugene McLaughlin. 'Media Justice: Madeleine McCann, Intermediatization, and "Trial by Media" in the British Press'. *Theoretical Criminology*, vol. 16, no. 4, 2012, pp. 395–416.

Grosz, Elizabeth. *Volatile Bodies: Toward a Corporeal Feminism*. Indiana UP, 1994.

Handley, Sasha. 'Deformities of Nature: Sleepwalking and Non-Conscious States of Mind in Late Eighteenth-Century Britain'. *Journal of the History of Ideas*, vol. 78, no. 3, 2017, pp. 401–425.

Handley, Sasha. 'Sleepwalking, Subjectivity, and the Nervous Body in Eighteenth-Century Britain'. *Journal for Eighteenth-Century Studies*, vol. 35, no. 3, 2012, pp. 305–323.

Hulme, Peter. *Colonial Encounters: Europe and the Native Caribbean, 1492–1797*. Methuen, 1986.

Innes, Martin. 'Signal Crimes: Detective Work, Mass Media, and Constructing Collective Memory'. *Criminal Visions: Media Representations of Crime and Justice*, edited by Paul Mason, Willan, 2003, pp. 51–69.

Jentsch, Ernst. 'On the Psychology of the Uncanny'. *Angelaki: Journal of Theoretical Humanities*, vol. 2, no. 1, 1997, pp. 7–16.

Keetley, Dawn. 'Sleep and the Reign of the Uncanny in Postrecession Horror Film'. *The Journal of Popular Culture*, vol. 52, no. 5, 2019, pp. 1017–1035.

The Kettering Incident. Created by Victoria Madden and Vincent Sheehan, directed by Rowan Woods and Tony Krawitz, Showcase, 2016.

Mendeloff, David. 'Trauma and Vengeance: Assessing the Psychological and Emotional Effects of Post-Conflict Justice'. *Human Rights Quarterly*, vol. 31, no. 3, 2009, pp. 592–623.

Miller, Phil. 'Can Glasgow-made *The Cry* Echo the Feats of *Bodyguard?*' *The Herald*, 28 Sep. 2018. <www.heraldscotland.com/arts_ents/16908384. can-glasgow-made-cry echo-feats-bodyguard/>.

Picnic at Hanging Rock. Directed by Michael Rymer, Larysa Kondracki, and Amanda Brotchie, written by Beatrix Christian and Alice Addison, Showcase, 2018.

Pierce, Peter. *The Country of Lost Children: An Australian Anxiety*. Cambridge UP, 1999.

Riva, Michele Augusto, et al. 'Sleepwalking in Italian Operas: A Window on Popular and Scientific Knowledge on Sleep Disorders in the 19th Century'. *European Neurology*, vol. 63, no. 2, 2010, pp. 116–121.

Rose, Jacqueline. *On Not Being Able to Sleep: Psychoanalysis and the Modern World*. Princeton UP, 2003.

Screen Australia. *The Screen Guide: The Cry*. <www.screenaustralia.gov.au/ the-screen-guide/t/the-cry-2018/36425/>.

Taylor, Steven, et al. 'COVID Stress Syndrome: Concept, Structure, and Correlates'. *Depression and Anxiety*, vol. 37, no. 8, 2020, pp. 706–714.

Tilley, Elspeth. *White Vanishing: Rethinking Australia's Lost-in-the-Bush Myth*. Rodopi, 2012.

Umanath, Sharda, et al. 'Sleepwalking through History: Medicine, Arts, and Courts of Law'. *Journal of the History of the Neurosciences*, vol. 20, no. 4, 2011, pp. 253–276.

Wallace, Nathaniel. 'Vertical Slumber, the Hypnoglyph, and the Outs and Ins of the Postmodern'. *Comparative Literature*, vol. 53, no. 3, 2001, pp. 233–261.

Wheatley, Helen. *Gothic Television*. Manchester UP, 2006.

Wienholt, Arnold. *Seven Lectures on Somnambulism*. Translated by John Campbell Colquhoun, Adam and Charles Black, 1845.

About the Author

Kate Cantrell is a Lecturer in Writing, Editing, and Publishing at the University of Southern Queensland. Her research interests include narrative accounts of illness, immobility, and displacement. Her short stories, essays, and poems have appeared in *Overland*, *Meanjin*, and *Westerly*, and she writes regularly for *Times Higher Education*.

7. Gothic Explorations of Landscapes, Spaces, and Bodies in Jane Campion's *Top of the Lake* and *Top of the Lake: China Girl*

Liz Shek-Noble

Abstract

Jane Campion's work has been described as sympathetic towards the Gothic in its aesthetic and thematic explorations. This chapter offers a comparative analysis of Campion's television miniseries, *Top of the Lake* (2013), and its sequel, *Top of the Lake: China Girl* (2017), in order to consider how landscapes, spaces, and bodies are 'gothicized' in the series to explore established themes of the genre including sexual violence, epistemological uncertainty, and contested family histories. It compares the geographies of the first and second seasons to consider the significance of regional particularities in contributing to the formation of a national understanding of the Gothic.

Keywords: New Zealand Gothic; Australian Gothic; genre; gender; commercial surrogacy; transnationalism

The New Zealand director, Jane Campion, has enjoyed an illustrious directorial and screenwriting career, in which her cinematic works have drawn on feminist gothic conventions to explore women's struggle within interlocking structures of masculine oppression. In particular, *The Piano* (1993) is notable in using 'neo-Gothic aesthetics' (Rueschmann) to challenge the sexualization of the 'male imperial master' (Hendershot 97) in Antipodean settings. This chapter takes up Campion's gothic explorations of bodies, spaces, and landscapes in her television miniseries, *Top of the*

Gildersleeve, J. and K. Cantrell (eds.), *Screening the Gothic in Australia and New Zealand: Contemporary Antipodean Film and Television*. Taylor & Francis Group, 2022

DOI 10.5117/9789463721141_CH07

Lake (2013), and its sequel, *Top of the Lake: China Girl* (2017, hereafter *China Girl*). Campion collaborated on these miniseries with writer Gerard Lee, and directors Garth Davis and Ariel Kleiman for the first and second seasons respectively. The series was initially set in the fictional town of Laketop near Queenstown, New Zealand, and later relocated to Sydney, Australia, for its second season. As suggested by scholars such as Deb Verhoeven, Annabel Cooper, and Tessa Dwyer, Australia and New Zealand are key geographical and biographical reference points in Campion's career. Cooper notes that Campion's time spent outside of New Zealand has resulted in the cultivation of a 'cinematic eye' that views New Zealand from the perspective of an expatriate seduced by its 'pastness' (280), while Campion's representations of Australia are often 'modern, dystopic, and urbanized' (293). This chapter will investigate Campion's recent exploration of Antipodean geographies in *Top of the Lake* and *China Girl* to argue that their distinct treatments articulate Gothic themes of bodily autonomy and sexual violence, familial association, and epistemological uncertainty in contrasting ways. Although scholars have observed that *Top of the Lake* marks Campion's return to New Zealand after many years of living and working in Australia (Mayer), little has been made of the parallel narrative of 'homecoming' apparent in the series, in which the protagonist, Sydney-based detective, Robin Griffin, travels back to Queenstown in order to care for her terminally ill mother. Likewise, scholars have not recognized the geographical back-and-forth within the series that sees Robin – like Campion – returning to Australia following the conclusion of the first season. As a result, this work departs from earlier scholarship that analyzes the seasons in isolation. Instead, as with Campion's binational career, I argue that it is crucial to compare their representation of landscapes and interior spaces in order to make sense of how regional particularities result in different aesthetic and thematic articulations of the Gothic.

Changing Landscapes in *Top of the Lake* and *China Girl*

Landscapes in Gothic fiction are typically exploited for affective purposes, both as a means to stir strong emotions amongst the audience and as a symbolic complement to a character's psychological and emotional condition. Yet as Sharon Rose Yang and Kathleen Healey note, landscapes in Gothic texts are also a central means 'by which political, psychological, social, and cultural ideals are laid bare, transmitted, and often critiqued'

(1). *Top of the Lake* and *China Girl* are no different in their employment of landscapes for these purposes. In the first season, the stark tranquillity of Laketop and its surrounding environs contrasts with the metaphoric ugliness of its townsfolk and social culture. *China Girl* incorporates both sweeping views of the sunny coastline of Bondi Beach and claustral interior shots to present modern-day Sydney as a city both excessive in its beauty and vice. A comparison of *Top of the Lake* and *China Girl* shows that each season uses natural and interior landscapes to communicate different Gothic themes and moreover, speak to regional variants of the genre across national borders. The landscapes of *Top of the Lake* play on the tendency for New Zealand Gothic to 'emphasize the remoteness of provincial, rural or farm living, with the immensity of the land overpowering individuals who can appear eccentric, disturbed, or disadvantaged' (Conrich, 'New Zealand Gothic' 397). Establishing and wide-angle shots of natural landscapes in *Top of the Lake*, including those that sweep over the expansive property of 'Paradise' and GJ's commune, are commonly used in the miniseries as a metaphor for the social isolation of characters and their often-aberrant behaviour towards one another and themselves. Alternatively, physical spaces in *China Girl* are used to symbolize the powerlessness and vulnerability of its female characters in both familial and commercial exchanges. Notably, visual and spatial differences emerge when comparing the immaculate coastline of Sydney's Bondi Beach and the squalid and dark interiors of the Silk 41 brothel and Puss's apartment. The contrast that is established in *China Girl* between the expansiveness of nature and 'the claustrophobia of confinement' (Gelder 380) in such moments brings attention to a common feature of Australian gothic texts, which is to exploit the colonial history of its nation in order to dramatize anxieties about belonging and nationhood. Viewers might be prompted to understand Robin's wistful gaze towards the ocean as not only hinting at her own migration from New Zealand to Australia, but also the sea as the medium through which British colonizers and convicts first made their way to the country. Christina Tondorf remarks that the earliest convict novels used the coastline as a geographical limit/barrier that separated settlers irrevocably from their British homeland. For Tondorf, 'the coast was a gaol wall' (95). *China Girl* uses the dialectic of expansion and containment signified by the coastline in order to highlight the sexual, bodily, and economic movements that are made across transnational borders. This is in contrast to *Top of the Lake* in which the delimited surroundings of Laketop suggest the horror of sexual exploitation as a 'homegrown' and insulated pathology.

Landscapes at the Edge of the World: Laketop and Paradise

Katie Moylan's analysis of *Top of the Lake* examines how its 'pronounced visual style' (270) produces a sense of the uncanny that is most apparent in foregrounding its natural landscape as 'an entity which surrounds and dwarfs the small built community depicted' (271). Laketop is the primary setting by which *Top of the Lake* explores the dialectical movements between the strange and familiar, and the known and unknown, which characterize the notion of epistemological unsettledness in Gothic texts. It is also the area that dominates the psychological and social relations of the adjacent Queenstown community, viewed as a source of recreation, death, and proprietary conflict. Laketop is first introduced as the scene of Tui's attempted suicide and disappearance. Scenery as viewed from Robin's perspective, in which she scans the lake in search of the missing girl, Tui, introduces various mysteries of the season: the mythic origins of the lake, its history of misfortune, and Robin's inability to make progress in her case. Like the mist that wafts over the lake, Robin's attempts to understand herself and the inhabitants of Laketop are thwarted by subterfuge and silence. Wide-angle shots of Laketop and aerial views of the surrounding mountain terrain compound the viewer's sense of awe at the area's unspoiled and primordial beauty. Yet such vastness also contributes paradoxically to a sense of optic limitation. The visual qualities directly fold into obfuscations in Robin's case. Robin's boss, Al Parker, deliberately misdirects her while she investigates Tui's disappearance, suggesting her belief that Tui was raped by multiple perpetrators is a product of her own inability to come to terms with her sexual assault when she was a teenager. Workers for Matt Mitcham refuse to testify against him until one of their children falls victim to his violence. Robin's mother goes to her deathbed, hiding the knowledge that Mitcham is, in fact, Robin's biological father. Such revelations go hand-in-hand with the cinematic prominence afforded to the titular lake of the series. Often shot at crepuscular moments and devoid of human and animal life, the lake functions to conjure secrets from a forgotten past that has both personal and collective implications.

As Jennifer Lawn, in her introduction to a co-edited collection on the New Zealand Gothic, states, there is 'no critical consensus' among scholars on what the genre is and more importantly, 'whether it even exists' (11). Timothy Jones corroborates this sentiment when he writes that 'the most distinct feature of the New Zealand Gothic' might, in fact, be its generic slipperiness, in which a difficulty exists in how to define it and in addition how to identify 'which texts belong within it'.[1] While the absence of a Gothic tradition in New Zealand is said to connect with 'the task of creating a national literature distinctive from Britain' (Mercer 8),[2] Erin Mercer nonetheless finds that writers have a tendency 'to represent the landscape in terms of a Gothicized threat' (8). Affects of darkness, unease, uncertainty, and foreboding are pervasive in New Zealand fictional landscapes, and this is apparent in both the cinematography of *Top of the Lake* and the myths surrounding its origins. The sense of affective instability that is created in *Top of the Lake* by filming its landscapes at either crepuscular moments, or when shrouded in a mysterious fog, relates to Campion's own understanding of New Zealand's natural environment as 'unsettling, claustrophobic, and mythic all at the same time' (qtd. in Cooper 296). Thus, such camerawork goes beyond simply a narrative investigation into Tui's disappearance (Radstone 92) and functions instead 'as another brooding character' (Blundell qtd. in Lane) that demonstrates the capacity for landscapes to be enlivened through mythmaking and the personal narratives which people invest in them. Johnno's reference to the Māori legend of the lake's origins, in which the rise and fall of the lake is the still-beating heart of the now-vanquished demon, recalls the Māori belief 'in the land as a living thing' (Lane). Yet it also demonstrates how landscapes are touched and haunted by the emotional and physical traces of those who have traversed them in the past. Indeed, the eponymous lake is the site of not only Tui's disappearance but the drowning of Robin's father, and the murder of Bob Platt, a real-estate agent who sells the land of 'Paradise' off to an outsider. Moreover, the interweaving of Robin's personal history with her current work as a detective is evident in the visual mirroring of her movements across the lake with the two young characters caught up in Queenstown's paedophile ring: Tui and Jamie. In one memorable scene, Robin enters into the freezing waters of the lake as a way to experience, through osmosis, Tui's fear at the moment she attempts suicide. The doubling of the characters' actions through split scenes demonstrates their emotional connection with each other in more ways than one: it is later revealed that Robin is not only the detective in charge of finding Tui, but also her half-sister.

---

1   David Punter makes a similar claim about the Gothic genre as a whole, in that it is 'a contested term, a revival of a revival' (3).
2   Timothy Jones also makes reference to the lack of antiquity in New Zealand that made it difficult to transplant architectural tropes from early Gothic fiction in England into this foreign context: 'These early [New Zealand] narratives encountered the pragmatic problems of authoring Gothics in a newly minted nation devoid of the elaborate stock in trade of the European genre' (469).

Māori Myth in *Top of the Lake*

The transplantation of the gothic genre into an Antipodean context can introduce conflict between European-Western and Indigenous notions of myth, spiritual beings, and the non-material world. Jones's paper on 'New Zealand Gothic' references the ambiguous relationship that this body of fiction holds with Māori history and folklore. For Jones, Gothic texts of the colonial era appropriate Māori spirits as a way to heighten the spectrality and darkness of the landscape for Pākehā ('white-settler colonialists'). In *Top of the Lake*, the eeriness of the titular landscape is not only communicated through the haunting presences of individuals who have died in its waters, but through the superimposition of a Māori origin myth. During the episode 'Paradise Sold', Johnno tells Robin about the lake after they discover Bob Platt's body floating in its waters:

> There's a Māori legend [...] There's a demon's heart at the bottom of it [the lake]. It beats, [and] makes the lake rise and fall every five minutes. [...] There's a warrior who rescued a maiden from a giant demon called Tipua. He set fire to the demon's body while it slept. He burnt everything but its heart. And the fat melting from the body formed a trough. And the snow from the mountains ran down to fill it to form a lake.

Sophie Mayer's paper on the feminist utopian possibilities inherent in the exploration of Robin and Tui's parallel narratives regards the lake as having a one-to-one correspondence with the real Lake Wakatipu on New Zealand's South Island (103). Mayer's conflation of real and imagined spaces points to the increasing importance that on-location shooting plays in stimulating audience interaction through a sense of authenticity (Dwyer). Contrastingly, Tessa Dwyer's essay focuses on the transnational entanglements of cultural specificity, location, and vocal (in)authenticity in *Top of the Lake* to generate a strong affective response from viewers. She goes further to argue that the affective response generated by the series' emphasis on on-location shooting is one akin to the touristic gaze; for Dwyer, a 'self-reflexive mediation on New Zealand's brand as tourism mecca is forcefully brought to the fore' (21). Yet affective and emotional connections to landscapes in *Top of the Lake* are also reinforced through cultural and individual memories. Mayer observes that Johnno's storytelling bears a striking resemblance to a Māori tale involving a *taniwha* ('ogre') who abducts a young woman called Manata. Manata is eventually saved by a young warrior named Matakauri, who dispatches with the *taniwha* in a similar fashion to what is explained in

Johnno's version of the myth (Mayer 103). While Mayer deploys this Māori legend in order to argue that the show mobilizes a feminist and decolonial critique of the heteropatriarchal gaze resulting in the sexual exploitation of minors and women (104), Johnno's adaptation of the legend is also prescient when examining the tensile relationship that Māori fiction shares with both the Gothic genre and Pākehā literature in general. Ian Conrich has written about the disparity between the use of Gothic tropes by Pākehā and Māori writers based on a fundamental difference in their understanding of the relationship between the real and mythic worlds ('New Zealand Gothic'). According to Conrich, it is incongruous to speak of a 'Māori Gothic'[3] since its literature is already replete with tales of *mauri* ('life force'), *wairua* ('spirituality'), and *taniwha* ('monsters'): forces that are not considered an unwelcome or forbidding incursion into the physical world. That these otherworldly denizens constitute an absent presence in the physical world sets Māori fiction apart from Pākehā literary treatments of ghosts within and outside of the Gothic genre. While the myth in 'Paradise Sold' could be treated as a postcolonial critique of Pākehā claims to property, most notable in Matt Mitcham's pronouncement that Paradise is *his* land, Campion's *oeuvre* has been criticized for reducing Māori characters and their history to decorative set pieces in narratives that primarily revolve around white protagonists. According to Rueschmann on *The Piano*, its Māori characters 'are reduced to secondary chorus players who merely serve to undermine the main conflict between Ada and the patriarchal settler society' (13). This criticism would appear to extend to *Top of the Lake*, given that the myth to which Johnno refers is largely divorced from historical context and there is little reference elsewhere in the series to Māori culture. Therefore, it would be better to interpolate the myth in the context of the contemporary 'demon' that terrorizes the Laketop community. Coupled with the biblical nomenclature of Paradise and Matt's own self-styling as the 'serpent' in the Garden of Eden, it could be argued that he is the insidious agent that triggers the proverbial 'fall' of Laketop and its descent into sexual depravity. However, the poison that infects Laketop goes far beyond one man, as we are

3   The question of the transferability of the Gothic genre outside of a Western thematic, cultural, and conceptual framework is taken up in the penultimate section of Punter's *A New Companion to the Gothic*, which includes not only Conrich's contribution about New Zealand Gothic but also chapters on 'Asian Gothic' and 'Canadian Gothic'. Punter identifies a central problematic that these chapters pose: 'Has Gothic become, in the contemporary marketplace, a means of expression for local ghosts, or a means of imposition of Western conceptions which have no idea of, to take but one example of ignorance, the enduring cultural and communal power of the ancestors?' (6).

first led to discover in the double meaning of Tui's 'NO ONE' and later when Robin uncovers the paedophile ring that finds its home in Al's basement.

Buried Secrets in Paradise

Paradise is another landscape that holds great symbolic relevance in *Top of the Lake*. The naming of this unspoiled property deliberately recalls the paradox in how New Zealand is represented and imagined by outsiders and Kiwi writers respectively. This disjunction is exploited to its fullest extent in New Zealand Gothic texts that depict the country's tranquil, peaceful landscapes as concealing the deadening social experiences of rurality or concealing unspeakable collective horrors. Conrich writes, 'if New Zealand, the pastoral paradise, can be observed as an Eden, then there needs to be a recognition that alongside splendour, excess and disorder can [also] exist within this overgrown garden' ('Kiwi Gothic' 114). The viewer first learns of the property in the first episode when it is revealed that Bob Platt, a real estate agent, has recently sold Paradise to Bunny. Bunny has subsequently turned Paradise into a women's commune headed by the androgynous spiritual leader, GJ, much to the amusement of the townsfolk and the chagrin of Matt. The selling of Paradise establishes an immediate conflict in the series over the issue of land ownership and its connection with familial history and promises. Matt is furious upon finding out that Paradise has been sold, leading him to be complicit in Bob's murder and to court one of its inhabitants to obtain information about Bunny's property arrangement. Matt's anger lies in the fact that Paradise is the burial site for his mother, and as such, is marked as a sacred space at risk of becoming literally and spiritually tainted by its new tenants. Matt's belief that their inhabitation of Paradise is tantamount to a physical *and* spiritual violation of the land is communicated in his misogynist outburst in 'The Edge of the Universe': 'Your fucking menstrual waste, your fucking scum, is going right in there [the ground]'.

The question of what is interred in the land, and how its re-emergence may destabilize established hierarchies, is further explored in *Top of the Lake* through the burial site of Matt's mother. Mercer observes that 'the trope of the body buried in a Gothic landscape [...] rais[es] questions relating to criminality and social order' (11). After Matt and his romantic interest, Anita, take ecstasy and frolic in 'the arse end of Paradise', he takes her to his mother's burial plot. Fully naked, he flagellates himself with a belt he keeps draped over his mother's tombstone while uttering the words, 'I promise you. You will rest in my land'. Anita watches on in horror at Matt's self-inflicted violence. The scene is presented in stark contrast to the preceding moments in which Matt and Anita joyfully laugh, play, and bask in the natural wonders of Paradise while on an ecstasy-induced trip. The sounds of birdcalls, rushing water, and of wind rustling through an open landscape offer a fitting aural backdrop to Matt and Anita's heightened sensorial experience. Viewers witness Matt and Anita as they gaze upwards towards a mountain range and a waterfall, where a reaction shot communicates their astonishment at their enormity and vitality. The cumulative effect of sound and visuals in the scene creates an impression of Paradise as a landscape outside of contemporary space and time, and indeed as somewhere that approximates the unspoiled beauty of Eden. Yet what remains most jarring in the scene is Matt's childlike innocence, since viewers have come to regard his character as sinister and volatile. Subsequently, Matt returns to his former self when he lashes out at Anita for accidentally stepping on his mother's grave: 'Get the fuck off her! Get off her'. Such traits are also foregrounded when Matt ominously refers to the Adamic fall in an earlier dinner date with Anita: '[Paradise] has quite a history, you know: Adam and Eve, the Garden of Eden, the coming of the serpent'. Such sentiments demonstrate that the fantasy of Paradise for Matt – as an unmediated link to his ancestors – cannot be sustained, and that ultimately it is a place whose history is permeated with familial violence. As Matt explains to Anita over dinner, the first inhabitants of Paradise were a family that came to a brutal end when the father killed his wife and children, and then himself. The next family was driven to madness because they 'thought they could hear the kids wailing through the walls'. The cycle of crimes committed against one's kin continues to the present moment, when Matt is discovered as both Tui's rapist and the father of her child.

Knowing and Unknowing through the Coastal Landscapes of *China Girl*

China Girl has often been compared unfavourably to *Top of the Lake* for the seemingly implausible way that Robin's personal storyline intersects with her criminal investigation into the illegal surrogates at the Silk 41 brothel. Critics of the second season have also taken issue with the geographical relocation of the narrative from the 'bleak, otherworldly landscape' (Gilbert) of Laketop to the suburban sprawl of Sydney. Sophie Gilbert regards the lack of a unifying and singular location for *China Girl* to be its fundamental flaw. In her review, Gilbert argues that the topographical changes inherent in migrating the series from New Zealand to Australia have 'neutered the narrative potential' of the drama's 'characteristic obsessions [with] [...] motherhood, misogyny, [and] self-actualization'. Gilbert's comments suggest that a large part of the first season's success is the allegorical connection between landscape and theme, wherein the characterization of Laketop as a remote and isolated locale 'enables primal notions and emotions to be challenged and explored' (Dillon 34). Nevertheless, Gilbert's review of *China Girl* overlooks the centrality of the Sydney coastline in the second season of the series. Furthermore, the transnational migration of the series from Queenstown to Sydney sets up important considerations on how differing landscapes may articulate national modes of the Gothic.

The most significant and obvious topographical difference between *Top of the Lake* and *China Girl* is the foregrounding of mountainscapes in the former and littoral spaces in the latter. Indeed, *China Girl* deploys the coastal landscape of Sydney's Bondi Beach for plotting and atmospheric purposes. The shoreline becomes the place upon which the suitcase containing the eponymous 'China Girl' washes up, subsequently leading to Robin's investigation of an illegal surrogacy ring in Sydney. The coastal landscape of *China Girl*, however, is also used to dramatize the theme of transgression within Gothic texts. As Coral Ann Howells writes, 'Gothic occupies borderline territory where there is always the possibility of transgression (both in the sense of crossing borders and of trespass)' (vii). A coastline is arguably ideal ecological terrain upon which to examine the threshold separating self and other, reality and fantasy, and conscious and unconscious psychological states. Jimmy Packham, one of a few Gothic scholars who has considered the Gothic's convergence with coastal works, argues that coastal landscapes are an appropriate visual metaphor for representing the epistemological uncertainty that suffuses the worldview of Gothic fiction, where 'knowing and processes of perception and memory become almost tidal in this world' (206). Like Packham, Tondorf views the rise and fall of the sea as a seductive metaphor by which (Australian) gothic writers can explore the psychological and emotional variegations of the self (97). In this way, *China Girl* employs Sydney's coastline to heighten atmospheric tension surrounding the case of China Girl as well as mirror Robin's psychological vacillation between clarity and obscurity with respect to the entanglement of her personal life with her work as a detective.

Landscapes and transitions in *China Girl* are used to estrange the viewer and present a place that is both visually and affectively dissimilar to *Top of the Lake*. While aerial shots of Bondi Beach are a visual analogue for the panoramic views of mountains and forests in *Top of the Lake*, the optical and thematic devices of expansiveness differ in these seasons. *China Girl*'s vision of the sea stretching out towards the horizon paradoxically shows Robin's own epistemological limitations in both her professional and personal lives; Robin belatedly learns that Miranda, her partner on the force, is an intended parent, and is unaware of the extent to which Puss, Mary's boyfriend, is involved in illegal surrogacy arrangements. Thus, extended sequences portraying the rhythmic ebb and flow of the ocean are appropriately used as a metaphor for the interplay of knowing and unknowing within the series. In the first episode, the suitcase in which China Girl's body is stuffed is viewed both above and under the ocean's surface. The gruesome nature in which her body is contorted to fit into the suitcase, and the haunting images of her hair floating in the water like seagrass, point to an enduring theme in the feminist Gothic of using women's imprisonment within physical spaces as a symbol of their entrapment by patriarchal forces (Wallace and Smith 2). Images of the suitcase underwater are accompanied by a melody that ascends and descends in a manner similar to the movement of the waves. The melody is delivered in a minor key and at a slow tempo which, when coupled with the non-verbal humming of the singer, lends a soporific and haunting quality to these scenes. The melody is repeated at transitional moments in the narrative. This motif thus acts as a chilling aural provocation for both Robin and the viewer not to forget how China Girl's treatment is enmeshed in patriarchal institutions that exploit and then dispatch with women's bodies. Further, images of China Girl's body contained in the suitcase point to the persistent silencing of women's voices in both seasons of *Top of the Lake*. Upon discovering China Girl's body in the first episode, Robin asks, 'Want to tell me what you saw?'. Robin's quasi-interrogation of the lifeless China Girl recalls the selective silence of both Tui and Jamie in the first season. Tui's inability to tell Robin her rapist's name, instead writing down the apposite, 'NO ONE', is a resounding statement on the collective silence that surrounds and in turn enables the paedophile ring in the first season. Additionally, the silencing of women in *China Girl* is apparent in the erasure of the identity of the Silk 41 workers, evidenced in the naming of Padma as 'China Girl' and in the women's instrumental use as commercial surrogates.

The Blurring of Intimate, Commercial, and Bodily Spaces in *China Girl*

As noted in the previous section, the recurring motifs of the coastline and ocean in *China Girl* are used to enhance the sense of uncertainty over

Robin's investigation into Padma's death. The ocean is also significant in marking the different transnational journeys that occur in the season. Packham observes that the shoreline operates in Gothic fiction as 'a means of investigating nation formation and the understanding of the nation state itself' (207). It would therefore be remiss to neglect the 'conception of the coastline as a national border' (Packham 207) when considering both Australia's colonial history and its impact on the development of a Gothic tradition in the Antipodes. Australia was 'Gothic *par excellence*' for British colonialists, claims Gerry Turcotte, as a land designated to become a penal colony ('the dungeon of the world') and which had already been imagined as 'a land peopled by monsters' (10). The fear of entrapment evoked by the carceral image of a 'dungeon' suggests that the coastline signifies both threshold *and* boundary. *China Girl* exploits this notion to powerful effect. As with season one, Robin's personal life is entangled with her job as a police detective. Her investigation into Tui's disappearance and sexual assault in season one brought Robin into painful focus with the traumas of her own past,[4] in which she was not only gang raped as a teenager but forced to give up her baby for adoption. In *China Girl*, Robin's return to Australia leads to establishing contact with Mary, her biological daughter adopted by Pyke and Julia. Through Robin's storyline, the series suggests the porous emotional and geographical borders between the Antipodean nations of New Zealand and Australia, and moreover, how familial association is complicated by transnationalism. This complication is further explored in the major plot point of *China Girl* concerning illegal surrogates. The surrogates and sex workers of Silk 41 are subject to transnational networks of bodily and sexual exchange, which are facilitated by the porous borders of nation states. Yet their seamless entry (and later exit) from the country contrasts with their literal and psychological entrapment within the interior space of Silk 41. In the miniseries, Bondi Beach is typically shown in daylight hours and with wide-angle shots. It is also represented as a lively space in which large numbers of people congregate, relax, and play with one another. On the other hand, due to its association with sex work, scenes involving Silk 41 often occur at night. Its workers and visitors are invariably shot at close range and in a darkened mode, as if to emphasize the deviant nature of prostitution and the claustral qualities of this environment. Moreover, CCTV images

---

4   Punter writes that in spite of its generic elasticity (or ambiguity), the Gothic is consistently fixated on psychoanalytic notions of the suppression and invocation of traumatic histories: 'And Gothic speaks, incessantly, of bodily harm and the wound: the wound signifies trauma' (2).

of the Silk 41 workers, in which they are often huddled together in a single room, reveal that they are by no means consensual players in their use as surrogates. This slippage between intimate and commercial modes of bodily exchange, typified in the Silk 41 space, highlights an enduring Gothic theme that is explored in both seasons. *Top of the Lake* first introduces how women's right to bodily agency is violated as a result of the interconnecting heteropatriarchal networks of family and law. Tui's pregnancy and the revelation that she was raped by 'NO ONE' exposes the pervasive rape culture of Laketop as the actual *taniwha* or demon that terrorizes the community. The ultrasound to which Tui is subjected in episode one marks her body as one in which both 'non-agential sexuality and sexual activity [are] forcibly inscribed upon it' (Mayer 110). On the other hand, *China Girl* transplants the issues of familial association and bodily ownership into the domain of commercial surrogacy. The series raises competing claims to the children who are the products of surrogacy arrangements by representing the viewpoints of the intended parents and surrogates. One of the surrogates, Caramel, tells Mary about her difficulty in disassociating her emotional bond from her baby, since it is destined to be the child of another couple: 'I won't do that [love], even if I feel it'. The way that Caramel addresses the unborn child differs starkly from the 'market rhetoric' (Williams-Jones 7) that the intended couples employ when referring to 'their' babies and the surrogates. In the final episode ('No Goodbyes, Thanks'), the intended parents, along with Robin and Adrian, go to the safehouse where they believe Puss has been keeping the surrogates. When they discover that the surrogates have in fact left Australia indefinitely, one parent bursts out, 'This is theft. These are our babies'. Such language construes the surrogacy arrangement as a purely commercial enterprise, where the babies are considered the 'rightful' property of the commissioning parents. The disregard that the intended parents display towards the surrogates is perhaps best demonstrated in a scene involving Robin and the couple who are connected with China Girl. The couple request to bury 'their' child; the certainty with which they claim the unborn baby as their own, and their attending lack of concern for China Girl's fate, indicate their perception of the surrogacy arrangement as a purely commercial transaction. China Girl is a means to an end, pejoratively figured as a 'womb for rent' (Williams-Jones 1), since her value extends only to her labour in carrying the child.

  China Girl further utilizes the blurring of domestic and commercial spaces to play out the ethical dilemmas inherent in transnational surrogacy relations, in which affluent individuals from the Global North can utilize the reproductive labour of those in the Global South. In so doing, Johanna Gondouin et al. believe that the season highlights 'the global division of reproductive work across axes of gender, race, nationality, migration status, and class' (118). Indeed, Silk 41 operates as both a brothel and the location in which commissioning parents can make contact with their surrogates. This is made apparent in a scene where Adrian visits Silk 41 to gift Caramel (his and Miranda's surrogate) with an oversized teddy bear. Silk 41 is also used as the shooting location for Puss's bizarre video for the commissioning couples, which he sets in an Asian country reminiscent of Thailand to highlight the economic disparities and exploitation of the surrogates by the intended couples. In 'No Goodbyes, Thanks', the devastated couples watch the video as Puss tells them their 'babies have flown away'. Puss's video is periodically interrupted by reaction shots of the parents as they begin to absorb the horrifying news that they will never get to meet 'their' babies. Clustered in a small room as the sun begins to set, the intended parents continue to watch as Puss chastises the West for its decadence and exploitation of women in the Global South:

> For too long the West has exploited the poor and impoverished women of Asia. Girls as young as 12 years old are sold as virgins to gratify the appetites of the wealthy. But what sort of life is that, huh? Fucked to feed? And now, you all want to grow your vile DNAs, your precious little babies, inside the slave wombs of enslaved women too poor to choose. [...] But now the shoe is on the other foot. The tide has turned. Your babies have flown away and now it's your turn to cry.

Although Puss is perhaps the most ethically and ideologically tainted of all characters in *China Girl*,[5] his video nonetheless raises legitimate concerns about the economic imbalances between the Global North and Global South that commodify some bodies while protecting the value of others. Puss's video is a damning indictment of wealthy Western couples who believe they may use the reproductive labour of women from developing nations with impunity. Critics of commercial surrogacy, including Jennifer A. Parks,

---

5   It is difficult for viewers to take Puss's character and ideologies seriously. *China Girl* reveals the depth of his hypocrisy in self-declaring as a feminist, while continuing to exploit and abuse women around him. Perhaps the most obvious example is his manipulation of Mary; for her eighteenth birthday, he forces her to prostitute herself as a sign of 'solidarity' with her friends at Silk 41.

find that commissioning couples often fail to 'think relationally about their actions' (335) and how the employment of a surrogate can inadvertently perpetuate harms against the surrogate and child-to-be. The disregard that Puss believes the parents show towards the surrogates, and their attendant disbelief in what the surrogates have done, draw a clear picture of the power imbalances between the Global North and Global South when it comes to reproductive autonomy. Certain advocates of commercial surrogacy highlight the fact that such arrangements provide economic relief for women from impoverished backgrounds and underline the inherent choice involved in becoming a surrogate. However, Puss's words cast into doubt whether the women were free agents in becoming surrogates, in the same way that they and other women from the Global South are forced to use their bodies for the sexual gratification of others: 'fucked to feed?'. In this rhetorical question, Puss identifies one of the common objections made against commercial surrogacy – that it 'ensures the exploitation of poor families for the benefit of rich ones' (Standing Committee of Attorneys-General Joint Working Group qtd. in Millbank 477). Here, however, Puss upends the normative script by depriving the intended couples of their ultimate prize: 'your babies have flown away'.

Conclusion

In this chapter, I have compared the aesthetic and thematic aspects of *Top of the Lake* and *Top of the Lake: China Girl* in order to consider how both seasons of this miniseries illuminate differences in the Gothic mode as they are drawn along national lines. Set in the fictional Laketop town, *Top of the Lake* utilizes the vast wilderness of the South Island of New Zealand to comment paradoxically upon the insularity of regional communities that facilitate indescribable violence against minors. However, the coastal aesthetics of *China Girl* invite consideration of how transnationalism can facilitate the sexual exploitation of women from disadvantaged socio-economic backgrounds. While speculation persists on whether New Zealand Gothic in fact exists – as opposed to the Australian Gothic, which has conventions that Gelder confidently proclaims 'go right back to the colonial period' (379) – *Top of the Lake* nevertheless demonstrates how natural landscapes in New Zealand fiction often take on aesthetic features that mark them out as sympathetic towards affects of uncertainty and mystery, cornerstones of the genre irrespective of national categorization.

Works Cited

Conrich, Ian. 'Kiwi Gothic: New Zealand's Cinema of a Perilous Paradise'. *Horror International*, edited by Steven Schneider and Tony Williams, Wayne State UP, 2005, pp. 114–127.

Conrich, Ian. 'New Zealand Gothic'. *A New Companion to the Gothic*, edited by David Punter, Wiley Blackwell, 2012, pp. 394–408.

Cooper, Annabel. 'On Viewing Jane Campion as an Antipodean'. *Jane Campion: Cinema, Nation, Identity*, edited by Hilary Radner, Alistair Fox, and Irène Bessière, Wayne State UP, 2009, pp. 279–304.

Dillon, Jo. '*Top of the Lake*: Expanding the Small Screen'. *Metro Magazine*, vol. 176, 2013, pp. 30–35.

Dwyer, Tessa. 'Changing Accents: Place, Voice, and *Top of the Lake*'. *Studies in Australasian Cinema*, vol. 12, no. 1, 2018, pp. 14–28.

'The Edge of the Universe'. *Top of the Lake*, written by Jane Campion and Gerard Lee, directed by Garth Davis, See-Saw Films, 2013.

Gelder, Ken. 'Australian Gothic'. *A New Companion to the Gothic*, edited by David Punter, Wiley Blackwell, 2012, pp. 379–392.

Gilbert, Sophie. 'The Strange Confusion of *Top of the Lake: China Girl*'. *The Atlantic*, 12 Sep. 2017. <www.theatlantic.com/entertainment/archive/2017/09/top-of-the-lake-china-girl-review/539367/>.

Gondouin, Johanna, Suruchi Thapar-Björkert, and Ingrid Ryberg. 'White Vulnerability and the Politics of Reproduction in *Top of the Lake: China Girl*. *The Power of Vulnerability: Mobilizing Affect in Feminist, Queer, and Anti-racist Media Cultures*, edited by Anu Koivunen, Katariina Kyrölä, and Ingrid Ryberg, Manchester UP, 2018, pp. 116–132.

Hendershot, Cyndy. '(Re)Visioning the Gothic: Jane Campion's *The Piano*'. *Literature/Film Quarterly*, vol. 26, no. 2, 1998, pp. 97–108.

Howells, Coral Ann. *Love, Mystery, and Misery: Feeling in Gothic Fiction*. Bloomsbury, 2013.

Jones, Timothy. 'New Zealand Gothic'. *Wiley-Blackwell Encyclopedia of Literature: The Encyclopedia of the Gothic*, edited by William Hughes, David Punter, and Andrew Smith, Wiley, 2012, pp. 468–471.

Lane, Megan. '*Top of the Lake*: Is New Zealand's Greatest Actor New Zealand Itself?' *BBC Magazine*, 17 Aug. 2013. <www.bbc.com/news/magazine-23686419>.

Lawn, Jennifer. 'Introduction: Warping the Familiar'. *Gothic NZ*, edited by Misha Kavka, Jennifer Lawn, and Mary Paul, Otago UP, 2006, pp. 11–21.

Mayer, Sophie. 'Paradise, Built in Hell: Decolonizing Feminist Utopias in *Top of the Lake* (2013)'. *Feminist Review*, vol. 116, 2017, pp. 102–117.

Mercer, Erin. '"A Deluge of Shrieking Unreason": Supernaturalism and Settlement in New Zealand Gothic Fiction'. *M/C Journal* 17, no. 4. doi:10.5204/mcj.846

Millbank, Jenni. 'Rethinking Commercial "Surrogacy" in Australia'. *Journal of Bioethical*

Inquiry, vol. 12, no. 3, 2015, pp. 477–490.

Moylan, Katie. 'Uncanny TV: Estranged Space and Subjectivity in *Les Revenants* and *Top of the Lake*'. *Television & New Media*, vol. 18, no. 3, 2015, pp. 269–282.

'No Goodbyes, Thanks'. *Top of the Lake: China Girl*, written by Jane Campion and Gerard

Lee, directed by Jane Campion, See-Saw Films, 2017.

Packham, Jimmy. 'The Gothic Coast: Boundaries, Belonging, and Coastal Community in Contemporary British Fiction'. *Critique: Studies in Contemporary Fiction*, vol. 60, no. 2, 2019, pp. 205–221.

'Paradise Sold'. *Top of the Lake*, written by Jane Campion and Gerard Lee, directed by Jane Campion, See-Saw Films, 2013.

Parks, Jennifer A. 'Care Ethics and the Global Practice of Commercial Surrogacy'. *Bioethics*, vol. 24, no. 7, 2010, pp. 333–340.

The Piano. Directed by Jane Campion, Jan Chapman Productions and CiBy 2000, 1993.

Punter, David. 'Introduction: The Ghost of a History'. *A New Companion to the Gothic*, edited by David Punter, Wiley-Blackwell, 2012, pp. 1–9.

Radstone, Susannah. '*Top of the Lake*'s Emotional Landscape: Reparation at the Edge of the

World'. *Critical Arts*, vol. 31, no. 5, 2017, pp. 87–94.

Rueschmann, Eva. 'Out of Place: Reading (Post)colonial Landscapes as Gothic Space in Jane

Campion's Films'. *Post Script*, vol. 24, nos. 2–3, 2005, pp. 8–21.

Tondorf, Christina. *Lure and Does the Coast Have a Place in the Australian Gothic Landscape*. 2016. Southern Cross U, Masters thesis.

Top of the Lake. Created by Jane Campion and Gerard Lee, See-Saw Films, 2013.

Top of the Lake: China Girl. Created by Jane Campion and Gerard Lee, See-Saw Films, 2017.

Turcotte, Gerry. 'Australian Gothic'. *The Handbook to Gothic Literature*, edited by Mulvey Roberts, Macmillan, 1998, pp. 10–19.

Verhoeven, Deb. *Jane Campion*. Routledge, 2009.

Wallace, Diana, and Andrew Smith. 'Introduction: Defining the Female Gothic'. *The Female Gothic*, edited by Andrew Smith and Diana Wallace, Palgrave Macmillan, 2009, pp. 1–12.

Williams-Jones, Bryn. 'Commercial Surrogacy and the Redefinition of Motherhood'. *The Journal of Philosophy, Science and Law*, vol. 2, no. 2, 2002, pp. 1–16.

Yang, Sharon Rose, and Kathleen Healey. 'Introduction: Haunted Landscapes and Fearful Spaces – Expanding Views on the Geography of the Gothic'. In *Gothic Landscapes: Changing Eras: Changing Cultures, Changing Anxieties*, edited by Sharon Rose Yang and Kathleen Healey, Palgrave Macmillan, 2016, pp. 1–18.

About the Author

Liz Shek-Noble is a Project Assistant Professor at the University of Tokyo. Her research has appeared in *Disability & Society, Journal of the Association for the Study of Australian Literature,* and *Journal of Literary & Cultural Disability Studies.* She is currently working on a project funded by the Japan Society for the Promotion of Science on cultural representations of disability in Australian literature and society.

8. At the End of the World: Animals, Extinction, and Death in Australian Twenty-First-Century Ecogothic Cinema

Patrick West and Luke C. Jackson

Abstract

Australian twenty-first-century Ecogothic cinema often explores ecocritical concerns of animal and human extinction within global hypercapitalism. *The Hunter* (2011) and *The Rover* (2014) offer different perspectives on these concerns through their representations of animals, death, space, and place. *The Hunter* relates the story of a man sent to hunt the only remaining Thylacine, or Tasmanian Tiger, on behalf of a nefarious multinational corporation. In more allegorical mode, *The Rover* is structured around the protagonist's recovery of his car from a highway gang in order to bury his pet dog. The Ecogothic has, to date, largely been approached through literary rather than cinematic examples, and this chapter redresses this imbalance.

Keywords: Ecogothic; ecocriticism; animals; extinction; Australian Gothic cinema; hypercapitalism

Ecogothic cinema might be approached in many ways. One could pay attention, for example, to changes of place, like deforestation or beach erosion caused by rising sea levels, or to weather extremes resulting from climate change, such as heatwaves or torrential rainfall. This chapter traces an ecogothic pathway through two contemporary Australian films, *The Hunter* (2011) and *The Rover* (2014), through a consideration of the representation of animals in both films. Given that Catherine Simpson has lamented that 'despite the preponderance of animals in Australian cinema, little work

Gildersleeve, J. and K. Cantrell (eds.), *Screening the Gothic in Australia and New Zealand: Contemporary Antipodean Film and Television*. Taylor & Francis Group, 2022

DOI 10.5117/9789463721141_CH08

has been done on their role or function' (44), this chapter attends to the representations of animals in *The Hunter* and *The Rover* to enable a broader engagement with death and extinction in Australian twenty-first-century ecogothic cinema.

Animals as a Portent of Death and Extinction in *The Hunter* and *The Rover*

The current increase in global awareness of 'green' concerns, such as climate change, environmental catastrophe, and urban and non-urban habitability is likely to raise the profile of animals in cinema studies. *The Hunter* and *The Rover* tender different perspectives on animals themselves and on the always already troubled distinction between 'non-human animals' and 'human animals' in the face of environmental and social collapse. Rather than offering an exhaustive textual analysis, this chapter engages with *The Hunter* and *The Rover* through a number of thematic lenses in order to contribute to the scholarship around Australian ecogothic cinema. Our approach proceeds from the definition of gothic cinema proposed by Jonathan Rayner, specifically the thematic concerns of 'a questioning of established authority' and 'a disillusionment with the social reality that that authority maintains' (25). We build upon this definition by exploring four themes that we suggest are specific to *The Hunter* and *The Rover*: the global-local relationship and space and place; hypercapitalism; the extinction-death (and human-animal) relationship; and resources, energy, and place-based technologies.

Rayner proposes that 'instead of a genre, Australian Gothic represents a mode, a stance and an atmosphere, after the fashion of American film noir, with the appellation suggesting the inclusion of horrific and fantastic materials comparable to those of gothic literature' (25). Rayner's emphasis on 'a mode, a stance and an atmosphere' rings true more than two decades on with respect to *The Hunter* and *The Rover*. Although quite different films at the level of form – especially in their treatment of each protagonist's alienation – the two films intermingle as examples of gothic filmmaking on the nebulous terms evoked by Rayner and elaborated in his assertion that gothic cinema is permeated by three central themes: 'a questioning of established authority; a disillusionment with the social reality that that authority maintains; and the protagonist's search for a valid and tenable identity once the true nature of the human environment has been revealed' (25). Thus, *The Hunter* tells the story of a mercenary hired to travel to

Tasmania by Red Leaf, a military biotech company, in search of the last remaining Thylacine, or Tasmanian Tiger. Staying at the home of a scientist named Jarrah Armstrong, who recently disappeared while searching the same mountain on what was ostensibly a scientific mission, the hunter finds himself drawn into the role of protector of Jarrah's wife and children. In an unmapped pocket of Tasmania the hunter uncovers simmering tensions between the local community of loggers and environmentalists. *The Rover* is also set in Australia, in a desert region of the mainland. We enter the narrative ten years after a so-called 'collapse', a cataclysmic event that appears to have badly impacted the country's (and, we must assume, the world's) infrastructure. The collapse has left those who remain to eke out an existence within a parched and desolate landscape. With shades of the dystopian *Mad Max* films, the unnamed protagonist, played by Guy Pearce, is paused at a rest stop when three men steal his car. He sets off in pursuit of them, on the face of it only to retrieve his vehicle, killing anybody who gets in his way. In his search, he stumbles across the badly injured brother of one of the thieves, Reynolds (known as Rey), who leads the rover in his quest south in pursuit of the men who wronged him.

Both films use animals as a vehicle to explore human empathy and respect for both other people and other species. While the protagonist in *The Hunter* begins the film intent on killing his prey, his exposure to two children and their mother allows him to see himself differently, as a protector rather than a destroyer. In the process of embracing this alternate identity, he eschews the financial rewards associated with collecting samples of the Thylacine and kills the creature only to stop its relentless pursuit by Red Leaf and other companies of its ilk. At the film's conclusion, he burns the creature's body and scatters its ashes in a final act of respect. This motif of ceremonial burning illuminates a stark contrast between the depiction of human-to-human relations in *The Hunter* and *The Rover*. The latter begins with the theft of the rover's most treasured possession: the body of an animal (a dog), which is stored in the boot of the rover's car. The chase ultimately ends in the massacre of the thieves, many of whom are killed in cold blood. In the film's concluding scenes, the rover prepares a funeral pyre composed of the bodies of his enemies, and even that of his companion, Rey. In contrast, and similarly to the protagonist of *The Hunter*, the rover shows respect for his dog, which he buries rather than burns. Respect for animals by humans does not then necessarily connote respectful relations with other humans.

Across the two films, the spectacle and impact of the animal's death recalls the premise of the Ecogothic: a fundamental (even murderous) antagonism between nature and culture. Rayner's thematic concerns of 'a questioning of established authority' and 'a disillusionment with the social reality that that authority maintains', are thus always already in a heightened state (25). In working with Rayner's description of Australian Gothic cinema this chapter signals the continuity and discontinuity in the movement from the Gothic to the Ecogothic in Australian filmmaking in the twenty-first century. Unsurprisingly, however, given their plot and character variations, *The Hunter* and *The Rover* approach Rayner's thematic concerns in very different ways.

The Gothic, the Ecogothic, and Australian Ecogothic Cinema

Scholarly attention to the Ecogothic is a twenty-first-century phenomenon. Indeed, Ecogothic itself, at least under that name, is also of relatively recent origin. Writing in 2013, Andrew Smith and William Hughes suggest that their volume is the 'first to explore the Gothic through theories of eco-criticism' (1). Reviewer Suzanne Roberts agrees (131), while acknowledging her own dissertation on the topic, produced in 2008. The emergence of the Ecogothic as a distinct branch of the Gothic can be traced to a growing environmental awareness that Ecogothic is both contemporary with Romanticism and, in accelerated and diverse forms, comes long after it. As Smith and Hughes note, 'debates about climate change and environmental damage have been key issues on most industrialized countries' political agendas for some time' (5). Such debates, however, occur within different national contexts: Smith and Hughes foreground British, Canadian, and American ecogothic formations, while *The Rover* and *The Hunter* are both Australian films set in Australia. As already noted, the latter film is set in Tasmania, the only *island* state of the Australian Commonwealth, which thereby complicates its national and geographical status. Furthermore, when compared with *The Rover*, *The Hunter* sits within a more nuanced and complicated, post- and transnational ecogothic context. Smith and Hughes thus refer to the need for 'a global geopolitical context for an eco-critical engagement with the Gothic and images of the ecological' (4).

Reflecting, perhaps, its roots in the literature of the Gothic and Romanticism, the Ecogothic has largely been approached through literary examples. While film is certainly not entirely neglected in Smith and Hughes's volume, its clear focus is on novels, short stories, and other works of literature. Relatedly, film criticism on the Gothic, such as Rayner's study, has not yet assertively segued into consideration of the specifically cinematic Ecogothic. Even Simpson's promisingly titled article, 'Australian

Eco-Horror and Gaia's Revenge: Animals, Eco-Nationalism and the "New Nature"', only mentions the Gothic once (50). Indeed, *The Hunter* as an adaptation of Julia Leigh's novel of the same name (1999), takes a detour via literature in its journey to the screen, indicating perhaps the relative immaturity of the production apparatus for specifically ecogothic cinema – some hesitation at the point where an original script, rather than an adapted one, might be brought into existence. If ecogothic cinema is itself relatively immature as an artform, this prompts the question of the maturity or otherwise of Australian ecogothic cinema. What is specifically *Australian* about Australian ecogothic cinema in the twenty-first century? What continuities and discontinuities are there in the movement from Australian gothic to ecogothic cinema related to their (in)stability as genres?

Rayner's hesitancy in calling Australian gothic cinema a genre might be linked to Tom O'Regan's earlier, and broader, suggestion that

> Australian cinema is a cinema without a strong identity and market presence. It does not have a market and aesthetic niche in some evident cinematic domain, like say the French cinema or Hong Kong's action cinema. Instead, it grafts itself on to other cinemas – including other national cinemas – producing an Australian version of them. (161)

O'Regan's influence may also be discerned in Stuart Richards's allusion to the 'nebulous quality of the Australian gothic' (222), his comment that it is 'difficult to classify' (223), and his summative statement that 'the Australian gothic film does not have a universal, distinctive aesthetic' (224). Richards entertains the idea that the Australian postcolonial context sharpens the notion of a distinct national gothic cinema. However, we suggest that the (related) notion of place is what defines Australian ecogothic cinema. Nevertheless, it is still a matter of 'grafting' these films, to use O'Regan's expression (161), onto the broader international trend evident in films such as *On the Beach* (1959) and *Until the End of the World* (1991) to present Australia as a final resort or outpost: a place of sanctuary and safety.

Although place and environment must be important in all examples of ecogothic cinema, be they international or Australian, it is the concept of an 'end place' which is the most distinctive element of Australian ecogothic cinema in the twenty-first century. Australia is a comparative place of sanctuary and safety in both *The Hunter* and *The Rover*, presented as the final or end place in which global concerns may be examined, tested, and worked through. At the end of the world, Australian ecogothic cinema stakes its claim as both a unique mode of cinema and as an eschatological cinema of ecological hope or redemption.

The Global-Local Relationship, Space and Place

Historically and conceptually ecocriticism has always been liable to the cleft stick of the global and the local. Ursula Heise observes that 'the challenge for environmentalist thinking [...] is to shift the core of its cultural imagination from a sense of place to a less territorial and more systemic sense of planet' (56). Similarly Andrew Bennett and Nicholas Royle argue that ecocriticism 'involves a change of scale and vision: rather than an obsession with human-sized objects, it attends both to the miniature realm of a blade of grass, an ant, amoeba, or pathogen, and to the mega scale of the ocean, the mountain, or even to the earth itself (as well as everything in between)' (141). John Charles Ryan credits Heise with the paradigm shift captured in the proposition that 'the exigencies of the Anthropocene [...] demand new forms of translocalism, transregionalism, and transnationalism that situate the local and global in dialogical interchange with each other' (164). This suggests a moral obligation on the part of ecocritical cinema scholars to attend to the presence or otherwise of such 'dialogical interchange' in films (Ryan 164). At the historical juncture of the twenty-first-century Anthropocene, new and old work on (global) space and (local) place converges. Yi-Fu Tuan's classic study *Space and Place: The Perspective of Experience* (1977) anticipates, and in some ways proleptically overtakes, these developments in ecocriticism. Tuan's basic proposition that 'place is security, space is freedom' founds, to a certain extent, the prevailing and enabling tension within ecocriticism between local (place) and global (space) (3). *The Hunter* is in some ways an exploration of the risks attendant on cleaving too tightly either to place, as bed-ridden Lucy does, or to space, as exemplified in the hunter's blank identity in the global 'anywhere and everywhere' of his Paris airport hotel room. Similarly, Tuan's assertions that 'in a narrow sense, spatial skill is what we can accomplish with our body' (75) and that 'at one extreme a favourite armchair is a place, at the other extreme the whole earth' (149) suggest that Ryan's idea of 'dialogical interchange' (164) is too limited. Theoretically at least, the global might be thought of or experienced as entirely local, and the local as entirely global. At times, each film pushes towards these extreme positions at the limits of the place-space spectrum.

   The Rover provides very little, if any, sense of local place, while elevating space to an all-encompassing presence. Australia as a setting interlocks with the imperatives of the plot because it is an island and may therefore be one of the final places to fall in the event of a worldwide catastrophe. This is not, however, the Australia of a more hopeful film, which might offer the striated and water-focused space of a coastal city. Instead, it is outback Australia, where towns are dropped, seemingly at random – very much unplaced – over the flat, dry landscape. Characters' sweat-soaked clothes and constant search for water adds to the impression that they are traversing an endless desert in search of an oasis, one that appears to be embodied by a town named Kowloon. But this town is just another featureless settlement, slowly being reabsorbed into the landscape. More generally, the Chinese presence in the film, from the name Kowloon, to the language some characters speak, to the hieroglyphics on train carriages, does not operate to create the intersection of different places within one space, and still less to create a full sense of localness. Rather, it seems to make all signifiers of the local, of place, meaningless. In fact, as Cher Coad points out, with reference to the train's hieroglyphics, 瓦元 or 'wa yuan' is essentially meaningless, translating as something like 'element of tiles' or 'tile unit'. These symbols are 'junk signifiers' of 'junk place'.

Relatedly, in *The Rover*, any familiarity of the landscape is drained away. What dominates instead are roads, cars, trains. The detached anonymity of endless movement becomes the principle of the space that might otherwise be said to surround the circumstances of such movement. Interestingly, the cinematography of *The Rover* also insists upon the lack of connection between the rover and the surrounding space, in which he cannot find or occupy a place. The frame is expansive when it captures the outside world, and restrictive when it frames the rover, appearing to box him in. Sound, too, works to highlight this contrast, as diegetic sounds – for example, a sand-filled wind, or a dog barking in the distance – contrast with non-diegetic, dirge-like synthesizers. These very different parallel soundtracks hint at a fundamental rift in the film's world, heightening the disjuncture between space and place. In *The Rover*, the entirely global characteristics of the local (attenuated by the free-floating references to America and China) recall Tuan's point concerning 'the whole earth' as a place (149). At this scale, the very notion of place nearly dissolves into space. But this absence of place almost makes the film, not so much replete with space as 'space-less' to the extent that place and space depend upon each other.

In stark contrast, *The Hunter* reflects Ryan's call for 'new forms of translocalism, transregionalism, and transnationalism' (164). In *The Rover*, interiors often contain more depth, and are richer with detail (albeit murky and shadowy detail) than exteriors. Roughly speaking, the opposite applies in

The Hunter. The images of the hunter's airport hotel room in Paris are flat, depthless and relatively undetailed, showing up the contrast with the richly depicted wilderness – remote from cars, roads, and trains – of what is (from Paris's perspective at least) the end of the world. When the hunter, Martin David, first reaches the top of the mountain, the immediately preceding sombre mood lifts: suddenly, the trees part, and the hunter's face is bathed in sunlight. He walks towards the cliff's edge and the valley is revealed, shot in classical style, with the horizon line at the halfway point of the frame. He is staggered by the beauty of the view, exclaiming, 'Good Lord!' In a film that makes no other overt references to God or religion the line is striking and seems to highlight the sublime nature of the Tasmanian world in which our protagonist finds himself. Shots gliding above the landscape, framing him as a mere speck, are accompanied by a vaulting score, and appear to reflect his reverence for this natural world. The shift from interior to exterior is also a shift the length of the planet, emphasizing how some places close in upon themselves or empty themselves out (Paris), while others unfurl into space (the Tasmanian wilderness), in rich 'dialogical interchange' (Ryan 164). By contrast, in *The Rover*, the detail and depth of the interiors – their 'still life' quality – only serves to widen the gap between (absent) place and space.

The transition in *The Hunter* from one end of the world to the other also juxtaposes an animal that is ancient and untamed with one that is bred for its usefulness to human beings. The former is represented in the file footage of the last Thylacine in captivity; significantly, the hunter views this animal on his computer in his Paris hotel room. The latter is represented by a brief sighting of a sniffer or detection dog on duty at the Hobart airport in far-off Tasmania. The final crosscut shot of the Thylacine, in this prologue to the film's major action, shows its mouth open almost impossibly wide, eyes staring at the camera, before this crossfades with an extreme longshot of a Tasmanian mountain. In these images, the animal takes us to place, while place (Tasmania) takes us to the animal. This underscores the ecocritical position that the wellbeing of the planet and its animals is intimately braided through a necessary double vision of the global and the local: that is, of space and place. Meanwhile, burrowing away beneath this relationship, the suturing of the sniffer dog to human needs, even as it remains an animal like the Thylacine, effectively places the human up close to the Thylacine.

Even as Paris crossfades with Tasmania, however, the global isolation of the Tasmanian setting is made clear to the hunter by the man who hires him: 'There's a lot of ground to cover [...] difficult terrain [...] remote'. The first time the hunter climbs the mountain it is with Jack Mendy as his guide. Once the pair enter the bush, eye-level shots are replaced by a varied assortment of angles, some high, some low, with the trees appearing to form a frame, almost as if the trees themselves are observing the hunter and his guide. Place here is watchful and present. As they cross a large creek strewn with fallen trees, Jack's voice can be heard off-screen. He explains that much of the area has never been mapped (not by colonizers, anyhow), hinting at the seclusion and mystery of the region. The dangers of the isolated bush setting are highlighted by Jack as he speculates about what could have happened to Jarrah Armstrong: 'Slipped, fell, broke a leg, froze, starved, then the devils got him. Eat you alive, you give 'em a chance'. To say that Paris and the Tasmanian highlands are in some ways intimately connected is not at all to suggest that they are merged indistinguishably. The movements of the hunter in the wilderness are dictated by his location, and one aspect of his 'located-ness' is that he is not now in Paris, with its cosmopolitan ways of comporting oneself (waiting at a hotel airport bar, for example, or leaning forward in an armchair to emphasize a point). In the Tasmanian wilderness, when the hunter walks, takes notes, marks his map, sets traps, shoots, kills, he never wastes a movement. He holds his clothing above the smoke of his fire to mask his scent. The longer he remains in the bush, the more at home he appears. In Tuan's sense, this is place as security (3). Indeed, as the film approaches its climax, and the hunter's path approaches that of the Tasmanian Tiger he seeks, he gives up more of the trappings of his humanity, discarding anything non-essential, and covering himself with mud. This 'place-ness' in the Tasmanian wilderness is what finally enables the hunter to discover the Thylacine. However, it is only after the female members of the hunter's host family have died and he is forcibly separated from that home that the hunter finds the animal for which he has been searching. In this way, *The Hunter* foregrounds place (security and home) as a key element of its political and ethical engagement with (animal) extinction in the context of the hypercapitalist and globalized imperatives and motives represented by Red Leaf.

Hypercapitalism

In the age of the Anthropocene, the global-local relationship is entwined with capitalism and neoliberalism. This largely involves the erasure of the local by the global. As Marina Vujnovic argues, capitalism's latest and most egregious incarnation as hypercapitalism is fundamentally characterized 'by the speed and intensity of global flows', even as globalization itself, in some sort of historical sleight of hand, operates as a 'mask' for hypercapitalism. While underscoring the phrase 'hypercapitalist global economy', Vujnovic reiterates Jeffrey S. Juris's point 'that globalization and hypercapitalism are intrinsically related and bound together'. Citing Gaile S. Cannella, Vujnovic also notes that 'neoliberalism as a term has taken over the term hypercapitalism to denote processes such as privatization, competition, profiteering and corporate value structures that prioritize profit over any other kind of life'. Anonymity might be added to this list of neoliberalism's characteristics, for George Monbiot observes that the 'anonymity [of neoliberalism] is both a symptom and cause of its power'.

Anonymity is a central trait of the eponymous protagonists of *The Hunter* and *The Rover*. The use of the definite article makes both characters a type rather than a personality – men defined by a specific role within their world, but simultaneously anonymous men. It is never clear whether Martin David is the hunter's real name, but it is hard to believe that it is, while the rover's name (Eric) is never mentioned in the film's diegesis, only appearing in the non-diegetic credits. The hunter's anonymity is further highlighted when his employer, in one of the film's opening scenes, tells him that it must be nice not to need anybody. The hunter seems most at home when he is picking his way across the landscape in near silence, while the rover is most at home on the open road, propelled through space by grief. Neither is given a detailed back story, with the viewer forced to infer most of the events that have brought each man to this point. For the hunter and the rover, as for the viewer, the only important moment – wedged between unknown past and unknown future – is now.

Further, both the hunter and the rover represent neoliberalism in their hypercapitalist, single-minded, and anonymous pursuit of a goal at the expense of human connection. The representative of Red Leaf tells the hunter that '[he is] looking for something most believe is extinct, the rarest, most elusive creature on the planet'. Red Leaf wants exclusive access to this creature's DNA; the extreme rarity of this material indexes the extremes of neoliberalist profit to be made from it. The desire for profit can thus be seen not only in the faceless multinational Red Leaf, but in the exploitation of the bush itself. When Martin enters the local pub tensions between those within the small logging community and those from outside are made clear. The bartender refuses to rent Martin a room, no doubt unwilling to offend his best customers, and obliges him to order a beer before he can use the bathroom. Here the camera lingers on a towel dispenser, where a bumper sticker that reads 'SAVE OUR NATIVE FORESTS' has been defaced, and now reads 'SAVE OUR JOBS'. At every level the desire for profit takes precedence over the wellbeing of the native forests and their human and non-human inhabitants.

By contrast with what is for the most part the smoothly realized naturalism of *The Hunter*, *The Rover* provides a more allegorical presentation of hypercapitalism. The dissolute marketplace the rover enters early in the film provides several such examples. Capitalism invades and transforms the traditional family structure in this scene. An elderly woman offers to hire out a young boy for sex. She describes the boy as 'smooth, like the inside of your arm', while a fly buzzes somewhere offscreen, suggesting decay. The kitchen-cum-dining room, usually symbolizing the heart of the family home, has been transformed into a gambling den, where two young men sit whispering conspiratorially, while a third man – a gunrunner, it turns out – threatens to kill them if they do not stop. When the rover asks to buy a weapon, the gunrunner leads him to a cache and offers to sell him three guns for $300 each. Reluctant to pay for his purchase, the rover simply turns one on the man himself. Thus, in short order, the film segues from a presentation of the capitalist concept of exchange involving money and bargaining to the abrupt and rupturing murder of the seller by the prospective purchaser. The life of the seller becomes the currency of the exchange. The hypercapitalist desire for profit (the guns) not only trumps morality, it also destroys the very notion of exchange familiar from (traditional) capitalism. Such a reading also allows us to make sense of the otherwise nonsensical line of dialogue spoken by the rover at a petrol station later in the film, when the store owner refuses his request for $50 of fuel. When the store owner tells the rover that he will only take American (rather than Australian) dollars, the rover explodes: 'It's a piece of fucking paper! It's worthless'. The capitalist exchange of money goes on, but it is simultaneously presented as a sort of farce or allegorical dumb play. Although of course cash as paper is always worthless, the difference here is that its symbolic value is also drained, as if capitalism has hereby mutated into a form in which even money is inadequate to calculate profit. If it is true, then, that 'globalization and hypercapitalism are intrinsically related and bound together' (Juris qtd in Vujnovic), then *The Rover* represents a still-more-extreme form of hypercapitalism equivalent to the globalization the film depicts.

The Extinction-Death (and Human-Animal) Relationship

While several types of animals are depicted in *The Hunter* and *The Rover*, they are represented only marginally or incidentally in most cases. That said, each film brings one species of animal – or rather, in the case of *The Hunter*, a single representative of one species of animal – to the centre of attention. The Tasmanian Tiger, or Thylacine, manifests early on as the driving force behind the plot of *The Hunter*. We see, in fact, two Tasmanian Tigers in the film, but because each of these individual animals is figured, in different contexts and at different depths of the story, as the 'last of their kind', they merge into a single creature at the level of the film's diegetic logic. In *The Rover*, the plot is driven all along by a dog, the last of a number of dogs portrayed in the film, only realized in the final scene. Significantly, *The Hunter* and *The Rover* foreground animals from opposite ends of the spectrum between those animals either extinct or at 'extinction minus one' (as the Tasmanian Tiger is for most of *The Hunter*) and those animals so very far from extinction that humans have no qualms about suturing them to themselves, in this case as 'man's best friend' (the dog). Such antithetical alignments with animals in *The Hunter* and *The Rover* produce very different perspectives on the core concerns of Australian twenty-first-century ecogothic cinema. Taken together, the films cast wide the net of animal representation.

The title of *The Rover* can be interpreted through the layered meanings it carries. 'Rover' is a common name for a dog and a word for a wandering human. Incidentally, the first film to star a dog was the short film *Rescued by Rover* (1905), which was an immediate hit. *The Rover*, therefore, may not refer exclusively to the human protagonist, but may be attributed to both the human protagonist and the dog that drives his quest. If the rover is actually named Eric, then the dog we only see at the end of the film, never named, has a greater claim to being called Rover. Pursuing this line of thought, if the dog is the rover then the protagonist's dog is not just any dog, but the final dog of its type, akin to the long-sought-after Thylacine. Its burial in the desert takes on the quality of burial rites for a species pushed past the brink of extinction, past the point at which a final individual animal was the last living example of an entire type or species. The ambiguity of the title of *The Rover* troubles the human-animal distinction and, by extension, shifts death into the territory of extinction.

A similar ambiguity of title-as-name also infuses *The Hunter*. The hunter may be as much the hunted animal, the Thylacine, as the human hunting the Thylacine. Certainly, the human hunter's name, Martin David, sounds artificial. Oddly, it is two consecutive Anglo-Saxon first names, which are just as plausible (or implausible) when reversed. There is also an odd resonance of this name with the structure of animal names, for animals only ever have one name: a first name and no surname. Still, without the play of diegetic absence and non-diegetic presence of the name Eric evident in *The Rover*, the title ambiguity of *The Hunter* has less impact. This may be because *The Rover*, despite the adverted strangeness of a world after 'the collapse', sustains a much more familiar version of the human-animal relationship than *The Hunter*. In this way, the ambiguity in *The Rover* around the title/name is more explicit. The central animal of *The Rover* is a familiar breed of dog, possibly a Labrador or Golden Retriever. Feeling sad at the death of a dog, and burying it with due solemnity, is a familiar cultural and personal experience. In fact, the burial site for the rover's dog is manifestly the most 'placed' of places in the entire film, even if it is also merely convenient to the road and located atop anonymous gibber stones and dirt. A similar notion of a familiar human-animal relationship applies to the makeshift boarding kennel run by *The Rover*'s veterinarian/doctor: 'These guys came to me – people would just drop them off and ask me to look after them while they went away somewhere or because they had to go somewhere or do something, and none of them ever came back. I guess they've gone looking for money'. In contrast to the more allegorical representations of hypercapitalism elsewhere in *The Rover*, this dialogue adumbrates the incorporation of everyday matters, such as pet ownership, within capitalism.

It would appear that animals are more likely to survive the hinted-at Anthropocenic disaster of 'the collapse' than their human owners. The ecopolitics of *The Rover* as ecogothic cinema are curiously reactionary at just those moments in its narrative where animals and humans come into relationship. Mitigating this state of affairs is the fact that *native* Australian animals are almost entirely absent from the film. Despite the appearance of what appears to be a native wedge-tailed eagle early in the film, the absence of familiar, even stereotypical, Australian animals, such as kangaroos, koalas or black swans, in combination with the survival of introduced dogs, suggests a strong ecocritical stance. By contrast with *The Rover*, *The Hunter* sidelines the death of animals in favour of a more direct and more sophisticated engagement with notions of extinction. Remarkably, the viewer is positioned to sympathize with the hunter in his quest, not so much to save the Thylacine, but rather to save it from capitalism, or rather hypercapitalism, through killing the individual and driving the species to extinction in the one move. In a telephone message to Red Leaf's representative, the hunter says: 'What you want is gone forever'. In the previous scene, he has scattered the ashes of the Thylacine from Jarrah Armstrong's water bottle into the mountaintop air of a gloriously and vibrantly present landscape. Where the rover burnt human bodies immediately before burying his dog beneath the lifeless gibber stones of the desert, the hunter burns the body of the Thylacine in order to scatter its ashes in the Tasmanian highlands. Alongside the Romantic aesthetic at work in the destruction of the Thylacine, then, is an element of 'potlatch', wherein the hunter destroys the Thylacine as a way of disrupting the hypercapitalist enterprise that would seek to exploit it at the intersection of culture and nature-on-the-brink. In the culmination of the hunt, the film thus works within two traditions of nature studies – one an artistic movement and one a critical stance – that broadly inform the Ecogothic. The Romantic celebration of nature in the image of God is married to ecocriticism in its concern with the despoiling of nature by hypercapitalism. Where an animal (the Thylacine) carries the major burden of *The Hunter's* critique of hypercapitalism through its death, *The Rover* employs animals with much greater nostalgia for a world in which the distinction between culture and nature was clearer and more comfortable, and animals were not at threat of disappearing due to humans grasping after profit. That said, as two examples of Australian twenty-first-century ecogothic cinema, *The Hunter* and *The Rover* trouble and complicate the intersecting relationships of both death and extinction, and of human and animal.

Resources, Energy, and Place-Based Technologies

Ecocritical concerns with the resource and energy circumstances of the planet find representation in *The Hunter* and *The Rover*. In the public consciousness, as in more scholarly forms of ecocriticism, 'green' politics is often associated with anxieties about the dwindling availability of fossil fuels and the embrace of alternative energy sources, such as solar and wind power. *The Rover*, once again, is relatively reactionary in its representation of natural resources and energy sources. There is little indication that, for example, petrol is actually running out. The greater concern, it appears, is which national currency (Australian or American) to use to pay for the fuel. As it happens, this is a key difference between *The Rover* and the *Mad Max* franchise, in which characters kill for fuel itself. While *The Hunter* does not engage directly with the depletion of legacy industrial energy sources such as oil and coal, in one of the most affecting scenes in the film, one that is almost (and unusually for this film) allegorical, the mute boy, Jamie, adds the magic touch to the petrol-driven generator that allows the hunter to finally get it started. Suddenly, all the lights come on in the house, and in the trees surrounding the house, just as the record player resumes playing Bruce Springsteen's 'I'm on Fire'. The children's mother wakes to the sound and, apparently thinking it signals the return of her (deceased) husband, Jarrah, embraces the hunter from behind as he dances joyfully with her children in the yard. While her joy soon turns to pain as she recognizes that the hunter is not her husband, for a brief moment some sort of new community of family has been created in association with the restarting of the generator. Lucy's misapprehension of the hunter as her missing husband is a central element in the series of (mis)correspondences integral to the film's allegory. This group of people allegorizes (and by that very movement, transforms) the previous, more conventional family unit, while the successful operation of the generator, and the subsequent bursting into life of household appliances, allegorizes the usually unexceptional provision to households of electrical power and the use made thereof. In a way, the far-fetched technologies of energy extraction in some of the *Mad Max* films find an equivalent in the intensely localized, place-based technology (combining adult, child, and inanimate forces) that restarts the generator in *The Hunter*. By adopting allegory in this scene, *The Hunter* tentatively suggests the existence of, and a way past, energy shortages that are largely ignored in *The Rover*. In fact, the dominant discursive thread of *The Rover* is the notion that there are plenty of things to buy, plenty of resources to go around, but no longer the people (willing) to buy them. In some ways, strangely, the world of *The Rover* is a world of abundance and plenitude.

Conclusion

Set in two worlds blighted by hypercapitalism, where the populace must make the most of dwindling (or at least peculiarly inaccessible) resources, these films offer an eschatological meditation on society in the grip of ecological ruin. These are the 'end times' in the 'end place', where death and extinction are ever-present. This returns us to Rayner's third thematic concern: that is, 'the protagonist's search for a valid and tenable identity once the true nature of the human environment has been revealed' (25). Needless to say, the term 'human' in Rayner's final theme is entirely what is at stake in both these films. It is not just a matter of a possibly distressed but tenaciously '*human* environment' that is at stake here, but of the contested place of the human in relationship to the animal and to nature.

Yet both films offer hope, and some reason to hope. In the case of *The Hunter,* after Lucy and her daughter Sass are killed in a house fire, the boy, Jamie, is sent far away. The hunter – using his tracking skills for good – tracks him down. In a reassuringly Hollywood-style ending, Martin David appears at Jamie's new school, offering him a hug and sanctuary within a newly formed family unit of two. In *The Rover*, on the other hand, a qualified hope is conveyed by the suggestion that humanity may prevail despite societal collapse and associated ecological destruction. After all, even a decade on from 'the collapse', these are living, breathing humans there on the screen. Hypercapitalism may be the root cause of the ecocritical ills diagnosed, in different ways and to different extents, by both films. Still, the variations worked on capitalism, such as potlatch in *The Hunter* and the allegorizing of currency in *The Rover*, suggest that the key to humanity's survival – our reason for hope – may lie in understanding and exploiting the absurdities, and what Marxists might call the contradictions, of capitalism itself. The originality of contemporary Australian ecogothic cinema lies in the related notions of 'end place' and 'end times', as well as in its economic knowingness; perhaps surprisingly for works of the Gothic, these also become a reason for hope.

Works Cited

Bennett, Andrew and Nicholas Royle. *An Introduction to Literature, Criticism and Theory*. 4th ed. Pearson Education, 2009.

Bullock, Emily. *The Cultural Poetics of Tasmanian Gothic*. Unpublished PhD diss. Macquarie University, 2009.

Coad, Cher. Personal communication. 8 Aug. 2021.

Heise, Ursula K. *Sense of Place and Sense of Planet: The Environmental Imagination of the Global*. Oxford UP, 2008.

Hepworth, Cecil, and Lewin Fitzhamon, dir. *Rescued by Rover*. American Mutoscope and Biograph Co., 1905.

Kramer, Stanley, dir. *On the Beach*. United Artists, 1959.

Leigh, Julia. *The Hunter*. Penguin, 1999.

Michôd, David, dir. *The Rover*. Roadshow, 2014.

Miller, George, dir. *Mad Max*. Warner Bros, 1979.

Miller, George, dir. *Mad Max 2: The Road Warrior*. Warner Bros, 1981.

Miller, George, dir. *Mad Max: Fury Road*. Warner Bros, 2015.

Miller, George, and George Ogilvie, dir. *Mad Max Beyond Thunderdome*. Warner Bros, 1985.

Monbiot, George. 'Neoliberalism – the Ideology at the Root of All Our Problems'. *Guardian*, 15 Apr. 2016.

Nettheim, Daniel, dir. *The Hunter*. Magnolia, 2011.

O'Regan, Tom. *Australian National Cinema*. Routledge, 2005.

Rayner, Jonathan. *Contemporary Australian Cinema: An Introduction*. Manchester UP, 2000.

Richards, Stuart. 'Reawakening in Yoorana: *Glitch* and the Australian Gothic Film'. *New Review of Film and Television Studies* 16, no. 3, 2018, pp. 221–237.

Roberts, Suzanne. *The EcoGothic: Pastoral Ideologies in the Gendered Gothic Landscape*. Unpublished PhD diss. University of Nevada, Reno, 2008.

Roberts, Suzanne. Rev. *Ecogothic* by Andrew Smith and William Hughes. *Pacific Coast Philology* 50, no. 1, 2015, pp. 131–134.

Ryan, John Charles. 'Foreword: Ecocriticism in the Age of Dislocation?' *Dix-Neuf* 23, no. 3–4, 2019, pp. 163–170.

Simpson, Catherine. 'Australian Eco-Horror and Gaia's Revenge: Animals, Eco-Nationalism and the "New Nature"'. *Studies in Australasian Cinema* 4, no. 1, 2010, pp. 43–54.

Smith, Andrew, and William Hughes. *Ecogothic*. Manchester UP, 2013.

Tuan, Yi-Fu. *Space and Place: The Perspective of Experience*. U of Minnesota P, 1977.

Vujnovic, Marina. 'Hypercapitalism'. *Wiley-Blackwell Encyclopedia of Globalization*. Wiley-Blackwell, 2012.

Wenders, Wim, dir. *Until the End of the World*. Warner Bros, 1991.

About the Authors

Patrick West is Associate Professor of Writing and Literature in the School of Communication and Creative Arts at Deakin University. His work on the Australian Gothic, 'Towards a Politics and Art of the Land: Gothic Cinema of the Australian New Wave and Its Reception by American Film Critics', was published in *M/C Journal* in 2014.

Luke C. Jackson is an author and teacher based in Melbourne. He has written novels, graphic novels, films, and games, and has a PhD in Education. He is currently enrolled in a PhD in the School of Communication and Creative Arts, Deakin University, focusing on the literary sense of place in comics.

Part III

Gothic Monsters

9. Dead, and Into the World: Localness, Culture, and Domesticity in New Zealand's *What We Do in the Shadows*

Lorna Piatti-Farnell

Abstract

This chapter investigates how the film *What We Do in the Shadows* (2014) provides a distinctly New Zealand take on the traditional vampire narrative. Presented as a mockumentary, the film exploits the limits of the Gothic horror imagination and tells the tale of four Old World vampires who have 'emigrated' to New Zealand. Their secluded existence is continuously challenged as they become acquainted with contemporary gadgets, technologies, and customs. In response to this, the chapter explores the 'domestication' of the vampire in *What We Do in the Shadows* as connected to notions of localness and culture. The vampiric creature ceases to be relegated to layers of supernatural mystique, and instead becomes part of the Gothicized narrative of our twenty-first-century everyday.

Keywords: social and cultural identity; approaches to the everyday; folklore and fiction; regionality

In recent years, the vampire has returned to the popular media scene as a creature deeply entangled with the cultural preoccupations of our contemporary moment. As the fanged creature of myth finds renewed popular status in different, and at times discordant, manifestations, it is not surprising to see that a variety of regional reinterpretations of the vampire have now flourished. *What We Do in the Shadows* (2014), a New Zealand-based film directed by Taika Waititi and Jemaine Clement, is an example of this revitalization. Presented as a mockumentary, with often parodic tones, the film exploits the limits of the gothic horror imagination, and tells the tale of four Old World vampires

Gildersleeve, J. and K. Cantrell (eds.), *Screening the Gothic in Australia and New Zealand: Contemporary Antipodean Film and Television*. Taylor & Francis Group, 2022

DOI 10.5117/9789463721141_CH09

– Viago, Deacon, Vladislav, and Petyr – who have 'emigrated' to New Zealand, and unexpectedly share a house in the city of Wellington. The vampires recall – in look, names, and mannerisms – a number of 'famous' literary, folkloristic, and cinematic vampires, from Vlad the Impaler to Nosferatu, and the aristocratic vampires from Anne Rice's *Vampire Chronicles* (1976–). But while there is 'quite a bit of blood' in the film, this is not the 'average horror flick' (Ramji 1). *What We Do in the Shadows* often gestures towards well-known vampire tropes and stereotypes – from not having a reflection to being sexually irresistible – while also mixing the old with the new, and forcefully including centuries-old vampires, with all their historical quirks, in the technologically advanced bounds of our twenty-first century.

Taking the popularized and regionalized status of the vampire as a point of departure, this chapter investigates how *What We Do in the Shadows* provides a distinctly New Zealand take on well-known vampire narratives. The film presents a particular blend of folkloristic, literary, and popular imagery, and attunes the vampire to local sensibilities and ways of life. As a result, a cultural and figurative reinterpretation of the vampire takes place, and the creature is moulded into a seemingly approachable and familiar entity. Through a good dose of humour, the vampires in the film are portrayed as part of the cultural fabric of Wellington and emerge as increasingly 'human' in their habits and routines. The implied feeling of 'localness' pervades the geo-political and geo-social representation of the vampires' surroundings. The identification of the vampire, as both a creature and an individual, happens distinctly through the survey of its 'location' as a primary element (Weinstock 59). Ultimately, this chapter explores the domestication of the vampire in *What We Do in the Shadows*, as the creature ceases to be relegated to layers of supernatural mystique, and instead becomes part of the gothicized narrative of the twenty-first-century everyday.

A Feeling of Localness

The setting of *What We Do in the Shadows* is peppered with a variety of clearly recognizable landmarks that seamlessly identify the location of the narrative as the city of Wellington. From the shops to the local bus system, from the bars and clubs to visible and iconic fountains, the look of Wellington – at least to those familiar with the city – is virtually impossible to miss. Even for those unfamiliar with Wellington, the clear markers paint an identifiable picture of the location; this serves the narrative well in portraying the vampires as operating in a seemingly common urban setting. Identifying the city of

Wellington aids the construction of a sense of everyday commonness. The location markers work instrumentally in conjunction with each other to clarify the idea that, while these vampires originate from different parts of the world, they have also become 'Kiwi' in their lifestyles. In this, the comic potential is specifically opened up in the film 'by a particular convergence of the spectacular and the mundane' (Wright 137). There is a certain and undeniable local feeling to the vampires' New Zealand existence. The term 'local', of course, comes with a number of problematic associations. Even defining the very notion of 'localness' brings its own set of problems. Trisha Dunleavy and Hester Joyce suggest that 'localness' involves 'a raft of assumptions, questions, and problems concerned with cultural identity' (25). The identification of localness relies heavily on the individual view recognizing the idiosyncratic characteristics of a certain place as specifically connected to a pre-established weave of conventions, looks, and associations. Therefore, there is a certain subjectivity involved in the classification of something as 'local', and this is inevitably based on pre-existing knowledge. Because of its inherently individualistic characteristics, 'localness' is often difficult to pin down and a matter of opinion.

Nonetheless, because of its connections to a broader sense of belonging and identity, the notion of localness is also inevitably linked to an assumed community that will recognize both people and place as belonging to a certain environment and cultural microcosm. National identity, as Benedict Anderson has suggested, is often a matter of 'imagined community' (15). As such, it is intangible and open to shifts and (re)appropriation. Within this, the idea of localness also relies on an imagined sense of both locality and behaviour, which mix and merge in constructing a vision of the everyday, making it accessible and familiar to those who encounter it. In spite of the difficulties with both defining and explaining the very nature of localness, one would be hard-pressed not to want to term the milieu of *What We Do in the Shadows* as having a distinct local flavour. While localness may be hard to measure, what is not so hard to pinpoint is the seemingly conscious desire of the film to establish the vampire lifestyle of the characters as marked by standards of localness. All the same, this localness openly interacts with broader elements of cultural collectivity. Although something may feel 'local', this does not mean that it is solely reliant on the representations of a particular context and negates intangible notions of national belonging. John Tomlinson suggests that although any narrative, especially a cinematic one, is produced in a certain place, its status as a local product exists as a blended notion. Any 'instance of local production', Tomlinson argues, is 'never purely "local produce", but always contains the traces of previous cultural borrowing or influence' (91). The vampires in *What We Do in the Shadows* emerge as the result of a clear representational intermingling that relies on both localization and universality. The latter is particularly connected to representations of a vampire that have long been part of our cultural imagination, borrowing from literature, film, and television, as well as many aspects of European folklore.

The identification of localness in relation to the vampires in *What We Do in the Shadows* is also complicated by the idea of managing viewers' expectations. The latter encompass the perception of a New Zealand as including a set of iconographies and conventions, which instrumentally combine here to identify the context of the undead as belonging to a specific geo-political and cultural framework. 'Judgments about localness', to borrow Dunleavy and Joyce's words, lie at the centre of the question of how both New Zealand audiences and international audiences will react and process a regionalized version of the vampire icon (Dunleavy and Joyce 25). A way to unpack the difficulty of identifying the vampires in *What We Do in the Shadows*, particularly in regard to a sense of localness, would be to look at their interactions – with each other, as well as with the world outside of their home – as part of a system that collectively proposes their context as unavoidably Kiwi. The most significant part of the vampires' localness could be considered in terms of how they appear to be providing a social commentary about 'New Zealand society and experience' (25). Certain aspects of the vampires' lifestyles – and the general ways of interacting within the broader undead community of Wellington – would be easily identifiable as part of the wider system of New Zealand life. For instance, one should only think of the context of the famed and long-awaited annual ball, 'The Unholy Masquerade', which takes place in what is termed 'The Cathedral of Despair'. The name of the event is appropriately menacing and makes reference to well-known Gothic horror narratives in the broader popular media landscape, such as the game *Vampire: The Masquerade* (1991).

Indeed, the name of the location for the Unholy Masquerade is chilling and appropriately gothic-sounding. The notion of the 'cathedral' immediately communicates the idea of an organized community, a pseudo-religious set of affiliations that are ritualistic in nature. However, once the 'Cathedral of Despair' finally appears in the film, it is revealed that it is, in fact, a rented space, and the actual physical location is shown as the Victoria Bowling Club. The inside of this village sports hall is neither sombre nor particularly gothic, and it is cheaply decorated with everyday party supplies. The Unholy Masquerade could be any other function organized by any members of the (very much alive) community – especially milestone birthday parties – and fails to live up to the name that the undead insist on bestowing upon it. The revelation is intended to be humorous, and it is undoubtedly so. Hiring the space in a village hall or sports club for a function is, of course, not a prerogative of New Zealand alone, but viewers familiar with the New Zealand context will not struggle to identify this as a characteristic – albeit a rather traditional one – of the wider Kiwi community lifestyle. Here, one can see here how the vampire metaphor becomes entangled with the larger network of the 'national imaginary' (Longinović 3). Even for those unfamiliar with the practice of hiring the local sports club for family events, being presented with such an unthreatening place as the location for the ostentatiously named Unholy Masquerade is certainly cause for an amusing reaction.

The expectations made intrinsic to the appellative of the 'Cathedral of Despair' are quickly shattered by its localization as part of the everyday community within the broader Wellington region. One may wish to argue that the idea of hosting a party in the grounds of a local sports club is part of the wider system of tacit connotations that collectively comprise a sense of national identity. Localness, in this sense, is a highly politicized notion. Hosting the undead Ball in the local sports hall speaks to a system of implicit yet carefully constructed realism, which channels both the dominant language of vampire cinema and the regional qualities associated with the 'local' Kiwi context. The vampires' localness is rendered via the interaction and exploitation of characteristics that communicate verisimilitude, and work together in comprising an identifiable sense of the cultural everyday. In addition, we are told that the event is hosted by the Wellington Vampire Association, in conjunction with the Lower Hutt Vampire/Witch Club and the Karori Zombie Society. The evocation of the 'undead' clubs also intensifies the humour tacitly associated with the presentation of the event, and presents the undead themselves as living a rather integrated existence, even organizing themselves into groups that promote different social activities and engagements. The undead do not find anything humorous in their club activities, but the film's viewers are clearly intended to gain amusement. The specific naming of Wellington, Lower Hutt, and Karori also leaves no doubt as to the localized nature of the event itself.

In addition, there is a specific sense of regionality added to this particular interaction, one that perhaps complicates the idea of 'localness' even further. By clearly calling out the names of locations within the Wellington region, *What We Do in the Shadows* plays with both New Zealand and international sensibilities. To the international viewer, the explicit naming of Wellington locations implies the idea of 'New Zealandness', as nebulous a concept as this might be. To a New Zealand viewer, however, the identification of such definite localities – especially the Wellington suburb of Karori – specifically plays with the notion of regionality. The idea of the 'region', of course, is another difficult notion to define, being as complex a concept as 'localness'. But while 'localness' implies a broader national recognition, 'regionality' engages with an interplay of ideas and conventions that is even more connected to individual contexts within a broader national context. Although there is a geographical set of qualities that is naturally associated with the idea of a region, the understanding of regionality as part of identity systems is, for the most part, a constructed one. In approaching regionality, a number of elements come into play that go beyond simply placing a particular area on the map. 'Region' stands for the unspoken fusion of both people's ways of life and the topographical layout of the area, which can be ideally articulated via an engagement with community establishments such as social clubs and groups. This particular cultural fusion is clearly identifiable in *What We Do in the Shadows*: elements that create the very idea of 'region' are skillfully blended in order to provide a very localized notion of the vampires, and the greater undead and cultural communities that surround them. Barbara Johnstone argues that regions 'are meaningful places that are constructed, as well as selected, as reference points by the individual' (73). Regionality is, in the broader sense, a distinctly human characteristic that is constructed by the interactions of ecologies, landscapes, habits, practices, and customs. But in *What We Do in the Shadows*, regionality also becomes a definitive characteristic of the vampires' existence. By engaging specifically with the undead societies in the Wellington region, the vampires of the film also construct specific identities for themselves as members of a very specific regional group.

There is no doubt that the vampires in the film invest significant time and emotional attachment in their various societies and clubs. This is made clear by Vladislav's (Jemaine Clement) excitement at the prospect of being elected as the guest of honour at the Unholy Masquerade, followed by his crushing disappointment when the coveted title is bestowed upon someone else. Regionality, in this case, brings with it a whole set of recognizable activities and customs which are 'chosen' and performed within the bounds of a previously constructed context. Being a recognized and highly valued member of the Wellington vampire community is very important to Vladislav, as this becomes synonymous with the reestablishment of his identity as a vampire. As Johnstone argues, 'the process by which individuals ground their identities in socially constructed regions is analogous [to] the process by which people construct, claim, and use ethnic identities' (73).

The vampire community is treated as its own ethnic group, bringing with it a variety of associations and inevitable stereotypes that often come with ethnic identifications. Although not human, the characters' categorization as 'vampire' also gives them specific social and cultural characteristics that carry a sense of both universality and selected regionality. Therefore, the vampires' attachment to the undead clubs of the Wellington region is not simply a matter of geographical location; it is also a matter of choice. The very idea of 'being a vampire' becomes inextricably attached to the sense of regionality that identifies the undead as an unexpected part of the sociocultural frameworks of Wellington, in turn constructing identities and communities over time and space. Being part of the vampire community, and taking part in its events and interactions, adds to the sense of what it means to be a vampire in twenty-first-century Wellington. It is not difficult to see the vampire icon being used here as a metaphor for identity discourses attached to the regional New Zealand context, providing commentary on social choices, interactions, lifestyles, and ways of being.

Domestic Vampires

In conjunction with the survey of local Wellington landmarks, a particular emphasis is placed on the home of the vampires in *What We Do in the Shadows*. The house they share provides the setting for most events and interactions. This focus is important and evocative. As Mihaly Csikszentmihalyi and Eugene Rochberg-Halton suggest, the home should be considered a 'symbolic environment' (121). The very term 'home' is a powerfully charged one, bringing with it many associations that are both implicitly and explicitly connected to notions of family, childhood, and 'the security of a private enclave where one can be free and in control of one's life' (121). In the human context, there is a certain universality to the idea of home as a place of safety – even if, in truth, this is not always the case. Also widespread is the idea of interpreting home as a reflection of people's identities, sense of belonging, and sense of self. The home 'fulfills many needs', as a 'place of self-expression', and as a 'refuge from the outside world' (Cooper Marcus 7). Having a home is, of course, a privilege, but when that privilege is granted, the multifaceted significances of the concept are difficult to miss.

Although it might seem initially strange to see such a focus placed on the vampires' home, it is important to remember that this is not a new occurrence. Even the famous Count Dracula himself, in Bram Stoker's eponymous novel (1897), holds a strong connection to the idea of home, since the castle in Transylvania that serves as his abode carries with it a variety of metaphorical meanings in terms of representation and identity. For example, when the Count leaves his castle to travel to England, the connection to 'home' is maintained, as it is clearly stated that the vampire transports crates of 'freshly dug earth' (Stoker 54), with him, because of his need to rest in his native soil. This long-standing connection to the vampire and the home is firmly cemented in the twenty-first-century bounds of the vampire's mystique. Multiple literary, cinematic, and popular media interpretations have recently made a virtue of highlighting the importance of the vampire's home. The latter is usually said to be a lavish affair, and a reflection of the vampire's perceived wealth and different ways of being. From the *Twilight* saga (2008–2012) to Charlaine Harris's *Southern Vampire Mysteries* book series (2001–2013), and even to cult films such as *Let the Right One In* (2008), the vampire's home is at the centre of the creature's characterization. Even when little attention is given to the aesthetics of the building as an actual abode, it is made clear that the vampire's home is a place of extreme importance: a place of safety, separation, and independence.

The vampires' house in *What We Do in the Shadows* is not a particularly lavish one, but its meaning as 'home' remains unchallenged. The building is an old one, belonging to a different era and noticeably in need of attention as it sits in various stages of disrepair. While it is not made clear whether the vampires in *What We Do in the Shadows* actually own the building, the clear environment of the 'flatting situation' – as Viago (Taika Waititi) puts it – indicates that it is probably a rental. The architecture of the house, with its high ceilings and long, imposing corridors, suggests that it was built in the early years of the twentieth century, preserving an aesthetic that is not uncommon for New Zealand houses from that era. The size of the building, with its many rooms and bedrooms, implies that the house must have been, in its youth, a rather grand home, but its aesthetic heyday and appeal are clearly long gone. Objects of luxury – a common presence in the vampires' homes of contemporary fiction and media – are nowhere to be seen. Instead, the house is filled with old knickknacks from the vampires' pasts, including aged, blood-splattered clothes, timeworn furniture, and decaying curtains. These objects strangely and unexpectedly familiarize the vampire even further, making it a more relatable creature as far as the human context is concerned (Piatti-Farnell 183).

One must wonder here if the house itself actually acts as a metaphorical reflection for the vampires themselves. It is often implied that all four vampires – especially Vladislav – were once extremely powerful and irresistible creatures. Yet, it is also made clear that they all belong to a different era, and their great powers are mostly gone: they live in the past, and they have failed to fully adapt to the changing world. Petyr (Ben Fransham), in particular, lives exclusively in the basement of the house and does not travel beyond the confines of the property's garden. We are also told that being '8000 years old', Petyr is uninterested in the seeming banality of the everyday. Although the vampires do regularly venture out into Wellington city in search of human prey, their outings are difficult, and their behaviour is often awkward and out of place. They struggle, for example, to assimilate with the humans, and they are often denied entry into public establishments, such as the ultra-trendy Lotus bar. They are abused in the streets for being 'different', and they do not have friendly interactions with anyone, except other vampires. Their house, as decaying and inhospitable as it is, is clearly their safe space. Fearful that their nature will be exposed, Viago, Deacon, and Vladislav are reluctant to engage with human contexts, and even when they aspire to, they are incapable of doing so. Although curious about modern ways – including the appeal of dance clubs and bars – the vampires crave the safety of their own home. Their home is 'their base', a place 'so tied up' with their selves that it is 'almost inseparable from their being' (Heathcote 1).

Although the vampires of *What We Do in the Shadows* are keen to mingle with the human world whenever they need to hunt and feed, they are also very concerned to protect their home from outside scrutiny and unwanted human attention. For instance, Deacon (Jonathan Brugh) shows his disapproval of newly made vampire Nick's (Cori Conzalez-Macuer) flying activities, claiming that his behaviour will cause the neighbours to notice and that he will therefore bring 'attention to [the] house'. The 'house' in this context, should not simply be understood as a building, but as a metonymic rendition of the vampires' activities and their lifestyle. Although the term 'house' commonly denotes a physical structure in the English language, its metaphorical meaning in the vampires' context also indicates an emotional space. There is a psychological significance to the safeguarding of 'the house', implying its meaning as 'home', and therefore its conceptual connotations as a place of safety. The lexicological difference here could simply be perceived as a play on the vampires' patronage of the English language, which is at least a second language for most of them. This explanation, however, would not be fully satisfying. The choice of 'house' as a term, and its related connotations of 'home', also suggests the importance of physically delineating the vampire as an entity that is kept physically distant from the outside world. The conceptual meaning of the house as a home also brings with it notions of much-needed vampiric privacy. Here, the vampires can be comfortable in their own spaces: Vladislav even has his own sex-torture chamber in his bedroom. Furthermore, it is reiterated throughout the film that maintaining secrecy is an essential part of ensuring the vampires' safety. As Vladislav puts it: 'If the human discovered what we were, they would destroy us'. The focus on protecting the home, as a result, should not come as a surprise. The use of the house/home metaphor quickly renders the representational importance of the vampire as a domestic figure, one that is closely connected to the value and importance of its own surroundings. The idea of home has shared meaning for the vampires, highlighting the importance of collective experience in 'everyday life' (Csikszentmihalyi and Rochberg-Halton 121).

In spite of its representational significance, the vampires' home is also a place of extreme mundanity, carrying with it the mark of human existence. For instance, one of the first scenes in the film sees Viago, Deacon, and Vladislav holding a 'flat meeting', and discussing the need to do chores and allocate home duties such as washing the dishes. It is in equal parts humorous and surprising to see vampires – creatures who are usually surrounded by layers of gothic horror mystique – being made so accessible and common. Viago is particularly vocal in his instructions and demands that his flatmates do their part in keeping the house tidy: he claims to dislike untidiness, and to be 'embarrassed when people come over'. His fellow vampires are enraged by the suggestion, responding that it does not matter if the house is untidy, as people are only brought over to be killed. As an argument ensues over the need to do chores, the exchange becomes more and more comical. The humour springs precisely from the apparent incongruity of seeing vampires discussing household chores; this is openly addressed by Vladislav when he declares that 'vampires don't do dishes'. It is made clear by Viago, however, that some vampires do. These are fully domesticated vampires. Although still feeding on blood, and possessing other supernatural qualities, the vampires are extremely human in their interactions. The 'comic turn' (Horner and Zlosnik 3) presents itself in the narrative precisely because of the vampires' representation as petty, grounded, and conflicted. In addition, the vampires have very common, and very 'human' hobbies and pastimes. They do pottery and knitting, for example, and collect small shovels. Generally speaking, they seem to hold an everyday lifestyle belonging to centuries long gone. Their overall secluded existence is challenged, to some extent, when the new vampire, Nick, and his still-alive human friend Stu (Stuart Rutherford), are thrown into the undead mix, and the old vampires are forced to become acquainted with contemporary gadgets, technologies, and customs. In the latter part of the film, when the vampires are introduced to the Internet, they also become adept at online shopping. Here, humour for the viewers continues to stem from witnessing undead creatures – whose tales traditionally belong to the horrors of literature and folklore – engaging in such commonplace activities.

The vampires' home in *What We Do in the Shadows* is also a place of contradictions, as much as it is a conduit for safety and group identification. The house regularly serves as the location for the vampires' killings, as they invite prospective human victims to enter their abode and meet their untimely death. The commonality of the vampires' everyday activities – from their hobbies to their squabbles over chores – is juxtaposed with images of killing and suffering. This coexistence is reiterated on multiple occasions, so there is very little chance of missing the vampires' deadliness. The staging of the killings, however, still carries a distinct layer of humour, which is often presented as simultaneously jarring and disarmingly normal. The binary between 'serious' and 'comic' is challenged, as the killings provide an appropriate context for the humour to eventuate, mixing 'comic hysteria' with the 'Gothic's propensity' to elicit a response of fear, horror, and anxiety' in the viewer (Horner and Zlosnik 4). The play between humour, disgust, and the everyday is particularly of note. In this respect, the mockumentary nature of *What We Do in the Shadows* aptly places the film in the category of 'comic Gothic', containing its own class of 'sophisticated humour', and relying on seemingly unsophisticated 'gross' integrations (Cross 58). On one particular occasion, we witness Viago interacting with his next victim, a young woman. While he engages in light conversation as they sit on his antique sofa, Viago is seen putting down towels and newspapers on the floor, in preparation for his kill. As he proceeds to bite his victim, it is obvious that – in spite of his multiple centuries of existence as a vampire – Viago is not particularly adept at the practice. As the victim's artery is nipped, blood begins to gush everywhere, covering both the sofa and the surrounding surfaces as Viago desperately attempts to catch a sip. The whole scene is as comedic as it is grotesque. Indeed, the film makes a virtue of merging the framework of Gothic horror with the clearly delineated conventions of humour, echoing the narrative proposed in other filmic examples, including those by a number of Kiwi directors such as Peter Jackson's *Braindead* (1992).

In spite of the extremely graphic nature of the killing scenes in *What We Do in the Shadows*, examples of this nature are also presented as extremely common, even normal. As the protagonists are vampires, there is a sense of acceptance that surrounds their killing activities, merged as they are with seemingly very human habits and practices. Although noticeable and inescapable, the killing scenes, while filled with violence and blood, are seamlessly integrated into the plot, and only occasional hints at fear are put forward. While it would be unwise to generalize as to the effects that the scenes might have on the viewers, there is a certain self-conscious quality to the use of blood in the film. The film exposes how gothic humour 'exists in a characteristic state of tension' (Round 626), carefully balancing the interaction between parody and terror. The vampires are funny, but they are presented more as tragicomic figures. So much so, in fact, that the gothic humour is seen as an intrinsic part of the ridicule that comes of encountering creatures that should rightfully belong in the fictional pages of a novel. Yet, the vampires are there to be seen, openly going about their day-to-day lives. Instead of being suave and aloof, they are awkward and often incapable of even making a decent killing. We see here a conceptual conflict that seems to be inherent to the ways in which the vampires are portrayed in the film: as everyday yet unavoidably undead creatures. Maintaining the narrative trajectory of gothic humour, *What We Do in the Shadows* relies on the dynamic interplay of laughter and horror, where the jokes do not necessarily trivialize but certainly familiarize the murderous actions. The gothic humour is successful precisely because it engages 'critically with aspects of the contemporary world', but also because it offers 'a measure of detachment from scenes of pain and suffering' (Zlosnik and Horner 124–125). Indeed, one might even be tempted to suggest that it is precisely the incongruity of the context that creates the humour, where elements of both parody and irony intersect and blend. The perceptive clash between expectations and reality forms the basis for the film's gothic humour and its ability to provide a subtle commentary on our visions of both the everyday and the exceptional within social, cultural, and textual contexts.

The break in vampire conventions here may seem unordinary, but close inspection of twenty-first-century films, novels, and other popular media forms would reveal that vampires have fully adapted to contemporary human life, from driving cars to using phones, and purchasing expensive human commodities, often showing a penchant for particular brands. Examples such as *The Vampire Diaries* (2009–2017), *The Originals* (2013–2018), and the *Blade* franchise (1998–2006) show vampires leading ordinary lives in the midst of their unordinary blood-drinking existence. 'Ordinary', of course, is a complex term, but in this case, it can be used to signal that which is recognizable, and which suits the conventions of our broader conceptions of the everyday. The representational shift in rendering the vampires' geo-social background is openly addressed in *What We Do in the Shadows*. As Viago puts it: 'Vampires have had a pretty bad rap. We're not these mopey old creatures who live in castles. And while [...] most of us are, a lot are [...] there are also those of us who like to flat together in really small countries like New Zealand'. Viago's admission is undoubtedly amusing, as truly, one can probably think of very few other instances – if any – of vampires wanting to flat together in New Zealand. What is made clear, however, is that these vampires prefer forms of interaction rather than complete solitude, and aim to integrate both with each other and with society at large. This is not a prerogative of this particular film alone, as many literary and cinematic vampires in the late twentieth and twenty-first centuries have moved away from stereotypically gothic castles and gloomy locations, preferring instead either the hustle and bustle of the city, or the safety and quietness of suburban living. In *What We Do in the Shadows*, the move to New Zealand is identified for most of the vampires as a matter of necessity rather than choice. For instance, Viago travelled to New Zealand to follow his long-lost human love, Catherine, while Deacon moved there in order to escape the fate that would likely await him as a Nazi-collaborator at the end of the Second World War. The background stories paint a picture of these European vampires as emigrating to New Zealand in search of a 'better life'.

With this idea in mind, it is not surprising to see such a focus on the vampires' domestic space in *What We Do in the Shadows*. The reliance on the domestic space aids the construction of *unheimlich* situations, where the culturally inscribed safety of the home is twisted and subverted by gothic occurrences – from killing to drinking blood, to all manners of supernatural encounters. This reinterpretation of the domestic space becomes even more important if one considers the place occupied by homes in the broader New Zealand psyche. Discussing the importance of domestic spaces in New Zealand horror, Ian Conrich suggests that socially and culturally 'the home [...] carries an immense value in New Zealand and is central to the virtues of local and national citizenry' (123). Historically, the home has been at the centre of the construction of a cultural imaginary identifying New Zealand as an isolated and somewhat idyllic place. The home was – and to some extent still is – representative of the 'good way of life' that is often synonymous with the Kiwi lifestyle (123). The traditional Kiwi home, with its large section and curated garden, is an important part of the vision of 'Kiwi domesticity' (124). Family lies at the centre of the Kiwi understanding of home; this is true for the domestic realities of Māori groups, the cultural contexts generated by decades of colonialism, and subsequently immigration within Pākehā ('white New Zealander') communities. This idea remains in the foreground in *What We Do in the Shadows* and is mirrored in the vampires' desire to live communally, aiding their sense of family and belonging.

The home where the vampires live, however, is a monstrified version of the tranquil Kiwi home. As the home hides horrific secrets, it becomes uncanny and enhances the 'feeling of vulnerability' that acts as a counterpart to the 'sense of place' associated with the notion of home (Conrich 124). In exposing the home as the site of horrors, the film also proposes a critical counterpart to the understanding of the New Zealand domestic space as peaceful and desirable. The vampires live primarily in isolation and fail to successfully interact with the outside world. It is not difficult to see how this narrative framing functions as a veiled critique of the claims that often surround visions of New Zealand as a secluded and alienated place, especially by observers outside of New Zealand itself. This is certainly the view put forward in Sam Neill's 1995 documentary *Cinema of Unease*, which was acclaimed internationally but widely criticized in New Zealand for its 'dark portrayal of local culture' (125). Neill's documentary reinforced – arguably unfairly – the understanding of New Zealand as an inevitably dark and gothic place, where people do not simply possess a home but are also 'possessed by it' (125). This interplay of isolation and the everyday, of the ordinary and the Gothic, lies at the centre of the portrayal of home in *What We Do in the Shadows*. The vampire, as a gothic icon, merges with the conventions of the home as a 'Kiwi icon', and in so doing exposes the fear of both isolation and separation that tacitly still lives in the folds of New Zealand life.

Concluding Remarks

The vampires of *What We Do in the Shadows* belong to the material realities that construct our human world. Although existing within their own 'spatiality and temporality' (Weiss 119) – as the vampires, for example, are generally unaffected by the physical tolls of ageing and dying – they provide a clear reflection of our human interactions, emerging as belonging to a network of cultural significance where our practices, customs, and activities are an intrinsic part of identity. The space the vampires occupy in the film – both physically and conceptually – is filled with objects that form an 'indispensable background' in the projection of the gothic everyday, as well as its (un)natural and blurred limits as part of 'lived existence' (99). It is not difficult to see how the vampires act as a metaphor for the difficulties encountered in the human world, whenever interpersonal interactions take place. The domestic environment of the vampires' home serves perfectly as an illustration of individual-society relations and the all-too-real 'human dramas of life' (Cooper Marcus 8). As the undead creatures become normalized, localized, and strangely approachable, they transform into representational and cultural hybrids, rendering the difficulties of the human everyday. The vampires of *What We Do in the Shadows* are tangible and relatable, and in exploring the intricacies of the domestic New Zealand setting, they also propose universal considerations on the broader impact of the human condition in our twenty-first-century social and cultural context.

Works Cited

Anderson, Benedict. *Imagined Communities: Reflection on the Origin and Spread of Nationalism*. Verso, 1991.

Conrich, Ian. 'Kiwi Gothic: New Zealand's Cinema of a Perilous Paradise'. *Horror International*, edited by Steven Jay Schneider and Tony Williams, Wayne State UP, 2005, pp. 114–127.

Cooper Marcus, Clare. *House as a Mirror of Self: Exploring the Deeper Meaning of Home*. Nicholas Hays, 2006.

Cross, Julie. 'Frightening and Funny: Humour in Children's Gothic Fiction'. *The Gothic in Children's Literature: Haunting the Borders*, edited by Anna Jackson, Roderick McGillis, and Karen Coats, Routledge, 2008, pp. 57–76.

Csikszentmihalyi, Mihaly, and Eugene Rochberg-Halton. *The Meaning of Things*. Cambridge UP, 1981.

Dunleavy, Trisha. 'Narratives of Identity: TV Drama Production in New Zealand'. *Performing Aotearoa: New Zealand Theatre and Drama in an Age of Transition*, edited by Marc Maufort and David O'Donnell, Peter Lang, 2007, pp. 431–454.

Dunleavy, Trisha, and Hester Joyce. *New Zealand Film and Television: Institution, Industry, and Cultural Change*. Intellect, 2011.

Heathcote, Edwyn. *The Meaning of Home*. Frances Lincoln, 2012.

Horner, Avril, and Sue Zlosnik. *Gothic and the Comic Turn*. Palgrave Macmillan, 2005.

Johnstone, Barbara. 'Place, Globalization, and Linguistic Variation'. *Sociolinguistic Variation: Critical Reflections*, edited by Carmen Fought. Oxford UP, 2004, pp. 65–83.

Longinović, Tomislav Z. *Vampire Nation: Violence as Cultural Imaginary*. Duke UP, 2011.

Piatti-Farnell, Lorna. *The Vampire in Contemporary Popular Literature*. Routledge, 2014.

Ramji, Rubina. '*What We Do in the Shadows*'. *Journal of Religion and Film*, vol. 18, no.1, pp. 1–2.

Round, Julia. 'Horror Hosts in British Girls' Comics'. *The Palgrave Handbook to Contemporary Gothic*, edited by Clive Bloom. Palgrave Macmillan, 2020, pp. 623–642.

Stoker, Bram. *Dracula*. 1897. Oxford UP, 2011.

Tomlinson, John. *Cultural Imperialism*. Johns Hopkins U, 1991.

Weinstock, Jeffrey. *The Vampire Film: Undead Cinema*. Wallflower, 2012.

Weiss, Gail. *Refiguring the Ordinary*. Indiana UP, 2008.

What We Do in the Shadows, directed by Jemaine Clement and Taika Waititi. Funny
    or Die/New Zealand Film Commission, 2014.

Wright, Andrea. "'Vampires Don't Do Dishes": Old Myths, the Modern World, Horror
    and the Mundane in *What We Do in the Shadows*'. *Journal of New Zealand and
    Pacific Studies*, vol. 6, no. 2, pp. 137–149.

Zlosnik, Sue, and Avril Horner. 'Comic Gothic'. *Encyclopaedia of the Gothic*, edited by
    William Hughes, David Punter, and Andrew Smith. Blackwell, 2013, pp. 122–125.

About the Author

Lorna Piatti-Farnell is Professor of Film, Media, and Popular Culture at
Auckland University of Technology, where she is also the Director of the
Popular Culture Research Centre. She is the President of the Gothic Association of New Zealand and Australia (GANZA). Her research interests
lie at the intersection of film, popular media, and cultural history, with an
emphasis on Gothic and horror studies.

10. Mapping Settler Gothic: Noir and the Shameful Histories of the Pākehā Middle Class in *The Bad Seed*

Jennifer Lawn

Abstract

This chapter addresses the ways in which the New Zealand television series *The Bad Seed* (2019) narrates intersections between settler-colonial identity and social class. It makes the case that *The Bad Seed* sits within a line of storytelling in New Zealand settler Gothic which serves to secure innocence by presenting the relatively privileged Pākehā family as 'middling', vulnerable and at risk. The chapter progresses through an analysis of traumatogenic spaces, culminating at the isolated farmstead locale that is so generative to the settler Gothic imaginary. Ultimately, *The Bad Seed* employs mixed and hybrid genres to tell a story of Pākehā middle-class self-exculpation.

Keywords: New Zealand; social class; settler colonialism; settler Gothic; Pākehā identity; noir

Timothy Jones opens his entry on New Zealand Gothic for the Wiley-Blackwell *Encyclopedia of the Gothic* with the rather alarming statement that 'the most distinct feature of the New Zealand Gothic might be the critical and popular difficulty in defining what the category describes, and which texts belong within it' (468). Some of this diffidence can be attributed to New Zealand's relatively small and, at times, insular body of cultural theory. There is, as yet, no agreed canon of Gothic texts, no authoritative monograph on the subject, and some hesitation as to whether it is even a valuable way to frame the kinds of work that are produced in Aotearoa. During an influential period of New Zealand's settler cultural history in the mid

Gildersleeve, J. and K. Cantrell (eds.), *Screening the Gothic in Australia and New Zealand: Contemporary Antipodean Film and Television*. Taylor & Francis Group, 2022

DOI 10.5117/9789463721141_CH10

twentieth century, Gothic romance and the supernatural were specifically discounted as remnants of Victorian and Edwardian sensibilities. As Jones points out, creative artists of the time were swayed by international trends which disparaged popular genres and promoted pared-down realism as a favoured form (469). A properly New Zealand idiom would portray reality as disenchanted, confined to a single, flat, materialist plane of existence.

Far from stamping out the Gothic, depictions of stagnant settler life across towns and rural areas only served to emphasize the ways in which psycho-familial disturbances are embedded in the structures of settler colonialism. As Lorenzo Veracini establishes in his book *The Settler Colonial Present* (2015), settler identity relies on a series of assertions of negative differentiation: settlers are not Indigenous, not violent and usurping colonizers, not more recently arrived migrants, not bound by social class in the manner of the older, less adaptive societies that settlers left behind. The effort to bracket off a benighted colonial history from a just and moderate settler present – and the psychological contortions and rationalizations involved in this effort – have generated a line of gothic representations across New Zealand narrative cinema and literature. In the discussion that follows, I place the cross-genre television series *The Bad Seed* (2019) broadly within this gothic tradition of settler self-justification, as an instructive, hybrid, and ideologically layered text.

Genre Mutations: Splicing Noir and Settler Gothic

As Craig Sisterson notes in his survey of Antipodean crime dramas, *Southern Cross Crime* (2020), New Zealand (along with Australia) arrived relatively late to the global neo-noir screen phenomenon. Over the last decade, New Zealand creators have made up for the delay with a run of quality, locally produced productions that Sisterson, playing on a Kiwi idiom, terms 'yeah noir'.[1] Along similar lines, *The Bad Seed* started out with considerable promise. The opening sequence is arresting: a woman comes home alone in the evening with her shopping, notices her golden retriever is whining, and is knifed to death by a masked intruder. The following day, a contractor who is netting leaves out of the backyard pool sees the dog scrabbling bloody paws

---

1   Recent crime series set and produced in New Zealand include *Harry* (2013), *Top of the Lake* (2013), *Brokenwood Mysteries* (2014–), *The Gulf* (2019–), *The Sounds* (2020), and the paranormal police procedural *One Lane Bridge* (2020–). Sisterson's neologism 'yeah noir' plays on the Australian and New Zealand colloquialism 'yeah nah' which, confusingly, can mean either 'yes' or 'no' depending on the context.

on the ranch slider. The camera pans the length of an immaculate corpse, expensively dressed, her white face and staring eyes mirrored in a thick, glossy pool of blood. Detective Marie Da Silva (Madeleine Sami) arrives on the scene, her grim face flared red by flashing police sirens. The victim's neighbour and obstetrician, Dr Simon Lampton (Matt Minto), is quickly implicated in the investigation. Never mind the slightly ropey continuity – an autumn leaf in the pool in the New Zealand spring, still-uncongealed blood, the tardy arrival of the police – the first episode promised a quick-paced, visually lush thriller.

By the second episode of *The Bad Seed,* the genre conventions begin to mutate. A 'whydunit' develops as the killer is revealed to be Simon's brother Ford Lampton (Dean O'Gorman), later unmasked during a non-fatal attack on the woman with whom Simon is having an affair, Mereana (Keporah Torrance). Despite some knowing comments and intent glares, Detective Da Silva turns out to be a relatively ordinary 'paint-by-numbers' cop (Murray) who carries none of the tormented backstory and hardboiled grit that we expect from more conventional noir. The third and fourth episodes turn into 'sinister soap opera' (Hopwood). The brothers return to the scene of their childhood trauma at an isolated farmhouse, and Simon and his wife Karen (Jodie Hillock) confront the predatory birth mother of their adopted daughter Elke – who also happens to be the wife of David Hallwright (Xavier Horan) who is very soon to become New Zealand's Prime Minister. The series finale returns to the psychological thriller format as the killer, struggling to control his own emotional disturbances, kidnaps the Lamptons' daughter and lures the central characters back to the dilapidated farm, where the antagonists mete out their own justice before being rounded up by the police.

Clearly, the series involves some rather convoluted plotting in its genre travels from noir to police procedural to melodrama to Gothic. To be fair to the creative team behind *The Bad Seed,* working with the source material was never going to be straightforward. The series is a loose adaptation of works by Pākehā writer Charlotte Grimshaw, spanning her short story collection *Singularity* (2009) (where the characters of Ford and Simon are first introduced) to novels *The Night Book* (2010) and *Soon* (2012), which centrally concern the Lamptons' interaction with wealthy business family, the Hallwrights.[2] Criminality suffuses Grimshaw's fictional universe,

---

2   'Pākehā' is a contested Māori term referring to New Zealanders descended from British or Western European settlers. Many New Zealanders who fit this group do not use it as a self-designation. The term is commonly used in cultural and demographic analysis, and may carry a particular association with the intellectual middle class. For a detailed discussion on the usage of term and the question as to whether Pākehā constitute a distinct ethnic group, see Matthewman (2017).

yet her novels do not fit within any standard formulation of the crime genre. Grimshaw's social milieu is the Pākehā middle class and the central Auckland suburb of Remuera where she grew up and now lives with her own family. Tonally, Grimshaw's novels are a slow burn: at first her style seems plain, setting out quietly enough in the mode of domestic realism. Then, almost imperceptibly, psychological pressures begin to build. The central characters' habits of mind tilt toward obsession, addiction, or paranoia; with a kind of self-gnawing energy, they spiral toward personal breakdown, finding it increasingly difficult to rationalize their own actions. Presented with a genre mix that is difficult to translate into the most readily recognizable narrative formulas of commercial television drama, the creators of *The Bad Seed* opted to ramp up the criminal elements into a full-blown murder investigation, while also intensifying the relationship between Simon and Ford into a gothic-inflected dynamic of psychological doubling and traumatic dissociation.

Downplaying the line of criminal investigation in the series, I will suggest that it carries more narrative cohesion, and more purchase as social commentary, when viewed through a gothic lens. At a stylistic level, *The Bad Seed* conveys the trait of 'conflicted un-naturalness' which Jerrold E. Hogle argues is 'basic to the Gothic itself' (75). More evidently, by siting the originary trauma for the Lamptons on a ruinous farm, the scriptwriters make a conscious allusion to a set piece of settler Gothic imagery. As in so many New Zealand 'farmstead Gothic' narratives (Jones), the ultimate trajectory of *The Bad Seed* is the reunification and consolidation of the Pākehā nuclear family. The series moves beyond this trope, however, by linking the gothic farmstead to multiple other levels and sites of social tension. Much of the plot is driven by ambitions of class mobility and usurpation, associated with psychological pathologies of identification, disidentification, doubling, and traumatic dissociation. The social world of *The Bad Seed* spans a four-tier hierarchy of social stratification: a financial élite, represented by the Hallwrights; a comfortably wealthy middle class, represented by Simon's family; a lower socio-economic tier, constitutive of Ford as the resentful bludger and Mereana as the honourable worker; and a degenerate underclass, represented by the brothers' father, Frank. This element of social allegory is framed by a political context, as the series opens on the weekend of the campaign launch for Hallwright's conservative political party and ends on the weekend of his election triumph. Whatever its weaknesses in narrative coherence, *The Bad Seed* certainly aims a wide scope at New Zealand's social geographies, extending well beyond the tendency in contemporary noir to focus intensely on a single locale.

What, then, are the lines of traversal from gothicized family drama to the depictions of social stratification and criminality? In the discussion that follows, I will relate *The Bad Seed* back to a social function that stems from the earliest Gothic: the narrative trajectory of endorsing a 'middling', implicitly middle-class, self-definition. The appeal to the cultural politics of class as an analytical tool has some limitations in a contemporary New Zealand context, where considerations of ethnicity, gender, and sexual orientation have taken priority, where Western conceptions of class are incompatible with traditional Māori social organization, and where ethnicity and socioeconomic status have tended to be closely aligned within settler colonial conditions (Brickell et al.; Crothers 115–118). With these caveats in mind, my specific and limited concern is the ways in which settler self-representations as 'middling' in popular cultural narratives can mask social privilege (Borrell et al.; Bell, 'Reverberating Historical Privilege'). Contrary to material reality in contemporary New Zealand, Kiwi Gothic tends to represent the settler middle-class family as vulnerable and at risk, beset by its own temptations and (in the case of *The Bad Seed*) by corrupting forces from both lower and higher social tiers. In making this case, I will survey the the main locations in the series, mindful of the ways in which Gothic presents a highly charged example of the 'spatial forms and fantasies through which a culture declares its presence' (Carter qtd in Noyes 12). I will refer to Grimshaw's fiction along the way, not to position the original source as authoritative but rather to set the fiction in counterpoint to the series, where each text amplifies certain aspects of the other. Ultimately, I will argue that both Grimshaw's fiction and *The Bad Seed* employ hybrid genres to tell a story of Pākehā middle-class self-exculpation.

Remuera: Simon and Ford

The Lampton household first appears when Simon and Ford race in through the family's double garage. The pair have been running hard through suburban streets at night, and it seems to matter very much who wins. As the brothers enter Simon's home in their jogging gear, we see the trophies of Simon's professional success as an obstetrician. The Lamptons' home is spacious, comfortable, and well-lit. There is a generously sized backyard pool – in line with the gothic visual trope of distorting and reflecting surfaces seen throughout the series – with views over the Waitematā Harbour. Simon's wife Karen is preparing dinner while watching the news on television; she is a stay-at-home mum who does the rounds of neighbourhood book clubs, pilates, kids' sports, and school pick-ups. Karen is just about to leave for a fundraising event for Hallwright's conservative party. She does not vote for the party, but she joins the charity event because, in her words, 'David Hallwright's going to be the next Prime Minister. Don't you want to be a part of that?' The Lamptons' charity extends to their younger daughter, Elke, who was originally a foster child. In *The Night Book,* it is made clear that the Lamptons eventually learned to love Elke as Karen's 'charity case, her whim' (16). The couple finally adopt her so that they can travel to London for Simon's sabbatical – a gesture that might imply a full embrace of Elke within the family or, more cynically, a shift to avoid inconvenience at international borders. For the Lamptons, charity is certainly not its own reward; rather, it is tied into a circuit of professional and personal self-advancement.

The most irritating charity case in the household is Ford himself. In Grimshaw's fiction, Simon's older brother is a more marginal character in terms of plot progression, but as a leftist academic he is a goad to Simon's complicity with his wife's social-climbing ambitions. In *The Bad Seed,* Ford represents the detritus, the grime, the degeneration that Simon believes he has left behind. Ford lives with the family in a spare room near the laundry. As Karen later explains to Detective Da Silva, he is 'in between girlfriends, houses, you know. He seems to quite like it here'. As an 'old leftie', Ford embraces gestures associated with a Pākehā working-class style. He smokes rollies, sports a beard, and wears gym shoes, baggy jeans, singlet, and a checkered flannel shirt. When Ford pays for his own beer, which appears to be as infrequently as possible, he drinks from a generic can, not a craft beer bottle. His accent and use of idiom is middle New Zealand, the kind of language one would hear at a sports bar. Karen's bare tolerance of Ford's presence is reflected in the fact that she chooses not to mention him to her friend and neighbour, Tish. If Karen is the vector to the one per cent in the form of the Hallwrights, Ford is a vector in the inverse social direction: a visible and insistent reminder of the brothers' impoverished childhoods.

Indeed, the first intimations of the brothers' childhood are glimpsed through flashback during their nighttime runs. It seems that they are living a double moment, and that their physical exertion is some kind of somatic working through of an earlier body memory. In episode one, the camera zooms into Simon's face, and through his consciousness we see, in flashback, a boy with brown floppy hair and a checkered flannel shirt running through the bush. In a parallel flashback, reflecting Ford's consciousness, another boy is running: an older boy with dark short-cropped hair and a dark grey shirt with a roughly cut neck. As Simon edges ahead in the race through the streets, so does the younger boy slip ahead of his brother in the flashback sequence. This is a memory that the present-day brothers hold in common but do not share, in the sense that they are blocked from being able to offer each other recognition or consolation. They remember separately, via a psychic binding that is transferred into movement, not words.

As police and media attention start to circle around Simon after the death of his neighbour, the flashback sequences become longer and more evidently distressing as Simon struggles to ward off multiple sources of shame. When Simon accompanies Mereana to a South Auckland pub, his memory is triggered by a man swigging from a bottle. Simon recalls a similar movement by a shadowed man in an indistinct, dark interior space. In a further flashback, a man with a strap in hand chases two boys through trees, silhouetted along a ridge. At the end of the sequence, the disturbed extradiegetic music crescendos into the sound of a slap. In a second flashback, while the brothers are jogging, Simon's childhood trauma draws close to reflexive consciousness as the soundtrack bridges past and present: a boy's voice, then a man's, calls 'Simon', and the slap of the strap, almost like a shot, merges with the sound of the brothers' shoes slapping on the wet footpath. If Simon is trying to outrun his past, the very action of trying to do so hysterically somatizes and repeats the traumatic origin. It nearly brings him to destruction: Ford yells out to his brother to avoid being run over by a car.

Fugue, in general, characterizes Simon's way of being and engaging with others. He is constantly on the move, between home and office in central Auckland and Mereana's place in South Auckland. His physical elusiveness is reinforced by a visual signature that suggests duality and equivocation. Relative to other characters, Simon is more likely to be mirrored in reflective surfaces or positioned in a frame-within-the-frame within the shot, often through a glass film such as an office or car window. When Karen discovers that Simon has been having an affair, she throws a framed graduation photograph of him out of an upstairs window into the pool, and we watch it sinking underwater. Since Simon is plunging headlong into trouble while being framed by his brother, the visual metaphor is apropos in all respects. More generally, Simon is not transparent, at least not in any straightforward way. He is psychically splintered, and his blundering and self-preoccupation bring danger to others around him. Ford, by contrast, watches, listens, and waits. Iago-like, he inveigles himself into Karen's confidence. His intentions become clear in a scene that takes place when the family are out for the evening. Here, Ford helps himself to one of the expensive beers from the fridge, turns up the stereo, walks down the hallway trailed by the camera, and flops onto Simon and Karen's bed. In contradistinction to his apparent working-class pride, it transpires that the ultimate point of Ford's psychotic campaign is to get into Simon's salubrious home, bed, and wife. It is by following Simon's movements in episode one that Ford discovers Simon's greatest vulnerability, his affair with Mereana, providing Ford with his next victim.

South Auckland: Mereana

The Bad Seed departs markedly from its source material in the depiction of South Auckland, and the location and psychological contours of the brothers' family trauma. It is useful to compare these representations, not necessarily to judge *The Bad Seed* as an adaptation, but rather to grasp alternate forms of stock representation and traumatogenic zones in a gothicized Pākehā middle-class imaginary. In *The Night Book,* Mereana and Simon have a backstory. They first meet when Simon attends Mereana's delivery of her baby while she is a prisoner. Some years later, they meet again by chance at Auckland Airport, when Simon offers Mereana a ride home and subsequently learns that Mereana has lost her baby to meningitis. The affair that develops is to some extent mutually exploitative, though both know that Simon is overstepping professional boundaries. There are transactional elements: Simon offers Mereana cash and, as he is about to leave, she reminds him of her offer. While there are overtones of prostitution, this moment makes most sense when it is linked to Simon's attempt to hand $20 to a child on the street as he drives away from a later encounter. Simon is acting out of a mix of misplaced charity and abjection associated with the compensatory psychology of middle-class guilt.

Underlying Simon's actions is a traumatic kernel: the fact that he and Ford were raised in South Auckland by his alcoholic father Aaron Harris. Later, they opt to take the name of their mother's second husband, emphasizing their efforts to obliterate the psychological stain of the past. Implicitly, the negative gravitational pull of Simon's traumatic childhood experience helps to explain how he ends up with Mereana. Simon is unconsciously drawn back to this world, with little thought for his own motivations or the consequences his actions might have on Mereana. South Auckland drags him closer to the real of trauma, both in terms of his personal family history and in a sense of his uncomfortable awareness of his own social privilege, and he starts to experience intrusive visions of Mereana's death. These involuntary images seem in keeping with earlier suggestions of misogyny in Simon's approach to his profession, where he usurps the power of women to give birth and shows a distracted or even aggressive manner with his clients. Simon's fantasies are brought to realization in *The Bad Seed,* when Ford, drawing on the evil twin archetype, acts out the physical violence that Simon first imagines in his professional dealings with his female patients.

Evidently, this depiction of South Auckland is fraught with the risk of 'poverty porn', and there are multiple reasons why the elaborate ironies and self-exposure of the middle class that characterize Grimshaw's fiction would play out very differently in the politics of representation on screen. Demographically, South Auckland has high numbers of Pacifica and Māori residents. There is a comprehensive body of research showing that this population has been stigmatized through disproportionate emphasis on crime and lack of community safety in both news media ('Ofa Kolo) and reality television (Macdonald). For example, in their analysis of 388 news articles published both in print and online, Jean M. Allen and Toni Bruce find that South Auckland exists in mainstream representation as an imagined community (228); that South Aucklanders are subject to stereotypes and negative labelling; and that media stories are fundamentally 'antidialogical' in the way in which 'the people and community of South Auckland are *represented by* the mainstream media, rather than *dialogued with*' (225; original emphasis). As evidence of efforts to recognize and provide partial redress for this structural racism, in November 2020 New Zealand media company Stuff offered a comprehensive, front page apology for the contemporary and historical portrayal of Māori in their media outlets. This landmark action is indicative of a palpable shift in the effectiveness of Māori in seizing more authority over representational power, and in the awareness of liberal Pākehā that ostensibly neutral reporting of crime rates can couch heavily racialized fears and biases.

The Bad Seed seems to manage the complexities of representing ethnicized place in a mixed way. On the one hand, South Auckland is represented as a place of imprisonment and social eccentricity. Trains rattle past Mereana's home and planes regularly roar overhead, indicating that she lives near the flight path for Auckland's airport at Mangere. Throughways are closed off by chicken-wire fences and barrier arms. In Mereana's yard, there is an abandoned car inhabited by a savant named Nalf, who provides crucial though cryptic clues to the unfolding police investigation. The relationship between Mereana and Simon is sanitized to the extent that we do not know how they first met or how she lost her baby, even though Simon reassures her in episode two that she is 'a good mother'. Yet unlike her independent-spirited fictional counterpart, the televised Mereana is also needy. She follows Simon home and confronts him in his front yard, breaching the serenity of

Simon's Remuera existence and alerting Karen to his double life. In terms of the ethics of representing political and gendered minorities on screen, this reduction of Mereana's role to a mere plot device does not seem to be much of a step forward. In the final episode, Mereana literally exculpates Simon by furnishing his alibi when Da Silva eventually locates her. In fact, the whole investigative chain seems to have been premised on Simon's unwillingness to acknowledge his affair with Mereana, as he chooses to lie to the police about his whereabouts on the night of the murder, leading Ford to glean a vulnerability in Simon that he can further exploit. While this plot point is a weakness in the construction of the police procedural elements of the series, in terms of Simon's class-based consciousness it suggests that a mix of shame, vanity, and an ingrained habit of deception is a potent motivating force.

The Mansion: The Hallwrights

The competition for maternal 'ownership' of Elke is the least evidently gothic element of the series. Nonetheless, I register it here for the ways in which this plot thread intensifies the toxic interweaving of shame and personal ambition that motivates Simon and Ford's actions and is symptomatic of a broader national malaise in Grimshaw's world. By episode three, domestic tensions are rising in the Hallwrights' suburban mansion. David's election campaign is reaching a critical point. His beautiful, petulant wife is caus-ing headaches for the campaign public relations team with her tasteless behaviour. Roza Hallwright's (Chelsie Preston Crayford) resistant character is shown, rather blatantly, by the colour design of her costume. For much of the series she wears relentless pink, suggesting not only an act of sartorial rebellion against publicity advisors, but also a sense that she is stuck in an arrested stage of girlishness. Roza also becomes increasingly predatory through the series. A former prostitute and drug addict, Roza gives Elke up for adoption at the age of 19 (16 in Grimshaw's fiction). Now Roza has hired a private investigator to shadow Elke. Under pressure from David to have a baby to complement his two children from a former marriage, she confesses her teenaged secret to him: 'You have your people, your politics, your bloody election. What say I want something of my own? Now the Lamptons have [Elke]. And I want her back'. Teaming up together, the Hallwrights set their sights on the Lamptons' guardianship of their teenage daughter.

To New Zealand audiences, the fictionalized election bears strong resem-blances to the 2008 general election, which was won by the conservative

National Party on an 'aspirational' economic platform under the leadership of former financial trader, John Key. Although Grimshaw has denied basing Hallwright on Key, the similarities are too strong to avoid comparison.[3] Like Key, Hallwright was fast-tracked through the committee selection process. In Grimshaw's fiction, the spur to Hallwright's drive for personal wealth and ambition is (again like Key) to exceed and disavow his own impoverished childhood. In *Soon,* Claire says of Hallwright: 'For him the "gap between rich and poor" means more distance from his childhood' (262). As Key's political rivals, Labour Party campaigners dubbed him 'trader-in-chief', insinuating that there would be no national asset, social benefit or public good that he would not put on the table to be traded in corporate deals.

Key's tactics, like Hallwright's, worked. In the 2008 election, the New Zealand electorate took a swing to the right. Significantly, Key won an increased proportion of votes in South Auckland, suggesting upwardly mobile identification both in lower socioeconomic areas and among Māori and Pacifica voters (Crothers 118–119). The Māori Party was also drawn to the politics of aspiration and entered into a coalition government with the National Party. During the campaign, Key had staged a media walkabout in the deprived area of McGehan Close, located in the electorate of Labour leader Helen Clark, and described at the time by Key as a place where 'helplessness is ingrained, a dead end, a place where rungs on the social ladder have been removed' (qtd in Collins). Once in office, however, Key presided over welfare reforms in his second term, moving away from wider social provision to targeted and authoritarian approaches to welfare beneficiaries. Picking up on this political licence, stigmatizing discourse raising the spectres of 'feral families' and the 'underclass' became more prevalent in New Zealand media representations (Beddoe).

The Bad Seed blunts Grimshaw's political satire to some extent by presenting Roza, rather than David, as the character who is most haunted by a shameful past. The televised rendition of Hallwright is generally less ruthless than his literary counterpart. However, he loves his wife, and he wants to win the election. Sensing the public's eagerness to consume redemption narratives, Hallwright decides to take a gamble with the media. He appeals to the mode of political communication that Slavoj Žižek has termed 'false self-transparency', in which the only matter considered scandalous for

---

3   In an interview in the *New Zealand Listener,* Grimshaw (12) suggests that John Key grew into her fiction, rather than the other way around: 'John Key has come along later and imitated my art, which has been an interesting move on his part, and very useful. Maybe I should send him a Christmas card'.

members of an elite class is the mismanagement of information, rather than any specifically damaging quality of the material (246). With the help of a compliant television journalist (possibly based on right-wing New Zealand media personality Mike Hosking), Hallwright ensures that Simon's identity is leaked to the media, with the headline 'Suspected high society killer unmasked'. Later, he makes a call to Auckland Central police station and requests that Simon be let off all charges. When Simon is picked up from the police station by Hallwright's public relations manager, he understands the implicit blackmail that Hallwright holds over him.

That evening, the Hallwrights call a meeting with the Lamptons to advise their wish to publicly announce that Roza is Elke's birth mother. In keeping with the melodramatic trope of maternal sacrifice and struggle, the 'good' mother and the 'bad' mother square up. Karen is defiant: 'Over my dead body will you turn her into an election issue'. However, the Lamptons know they have been outplayed. When Karen jabs, 'Would your adoring public still love you if they knew about the drugs?' Roza parries: 'Would Simon send Elke postcards from prison?' Simon and Karen have built their middle-class nest around accumulation in affective as well as material terms. The Hallwrights take this dynamic one step further: they belong to a class where no relationship, no matter how intimate, can be exempted from the logics of instrumentalism and exchange. Karen's final rhetorical appeal for her daughter – 'Do you have any idea what it takes to be a mother?' – is met with deadpan serenity by Roza: 'Thank you, Karen. I'm about to find out'.

The Farmstead: Frank Lampton

I have left discussion of Frank Lampton's farm until last because it is not only the location where the struggle between Simon and Ford reaches its climax, but also the most iconic setting in a nation state where the appropriation and agricultural transformation of land was, and continues to be, a primary tool of colonization. As a radical departure from Grimshaw's fiction, it seems that the scriptwriters of *The Bad Seed* were deliberately keying into the representational history of a subgenre that is variously termed 'farmstead Gothic' (Jones), 'rural Gothic' (Conrich) or 'settler Gothic' (Kavka). The setting is an isolated farmhouse or shack, inhabited by a broken or destabilized nuclear family beaten down by the harsh work of breaking in the new land, where acts of crazed and unpredictable behaviour are viewed from a point of innocence, most typically through the observation of a child or teen.[4] The psychic logic of the gothic farmhouse is mimetic: as animals are chained, trapped, abused, and slaughtered to service an agricultural economy, so too are children treated like animals in these stories. Although Kiwi Gothic is often highly regionalized (as 'Dunedin Gothic', 'Wellington Gothic', 'Taranaki Gothic', for example), this rural variant of Kiwi Gothic is very rarely set in an identifiable geographic location. Instead, farmstead Gothic appears to exist in a mythical imaginary space, perhaps attesting to its profundity and longevity as a self-founding narrative for an emergent national consciousness.

In this respect, *The Bad Seed* potentially serves as a reminder that *all* Pākehā cultural production stems from this specifically settler-colonial history and its ongoing consequences. As Bell has noted, 'structurally, present-day white New Zealanders […] occupy the positions in our societies that were created by the labour of the early settlers. We still constitute the dominant culture of our societies, and our political and economic institutions are largely governed by people like us' (*Relating Indigenous and Settler Identities* 6). Yet the cultural work that New Zealand settler Gothic performs is complex. The most common narrative outcome of farmstead Gothic involves the settlers' departure from the land. In most cases, the narrative closure is achieved when the protagonist, and usually his or her family, exit from the farm to seek a life in a more civilized social and geographical zone. In doing so, they exit the mythic time of the settler and enter the mundane, compromised, *middling* time-space of the suburb or the city. While this repeated narrative may seem to speak of failure through withdrawal from the land, it is more accurately described as a narrative of disavowal, where the historical reality of settler domination is downplayed in the project of securing settler innocence (Hardy; Lawn, 'Domesticating Settler Gothic').

---

4   Kavka nominates Vincent Ward's *Vigil* (1984) as the 'ur-text' of settler Gothic in New Zealand cinema, and traces a line of descent through Jane Campion's *The Piano* (1993), Brad McGann's short film *Possum* (1997), and McGann's feature-length adaptation of the novel by Maurice Gee, *In My Father's Den* (2004). Farmstead Gothic appears again, more recently, in the first episode of the television series *The Gulf* (2019), where a mute boy escapes after years of abuse from a farmer who has kidnapped the boy and locked him in a pigpen, along with his own daughter. In literary fiction, Jones traces farmstead Gothic to Katherine Mansfield's short story 'The Woman at the Store' (1912). Novels by Mike Johnson (*Dumb Show*, 1995) and Carl Nixon (*The Tally Stick*, 2020) most harrowingly inhabit similar terrain. Māori author Becky Manawatū includes violent farmstead scenes in *Auē* (2019), with a specifically Pākehā perpetrator. In comic mode, Rachel King's novel *Magpie Hall* (2010) blends New Zealand farmstead Gothic with a spoof of Emily Brontë's *Wuthering Heights* (1847). While acknowledging the prevalence of the farmstead Gothic trope, Erin Mercer (2017) argues that the related genre of 'slaughterhouse Gothic' is more specifically unique to New Zealand.

Kavka even asserts that 'no grasp of the New Zealand Gothic is possible without an awareness of the struggle between the young nation and the longer, indigenous history of the place that is repressed in the process of building it over' (68).[5] Paradoxically, in this representational regime, settlers show that they have earned the right to inhabit the country by leaving the land.

The Bad Seed shows farmstead Gothic in reverse, so to speak: it opens with a privileged, seemingly happy Pākehā family, descends into family disintegration, and reaches its narrative climax through regression to the originary site of both personal and cultural trauma. Ford and Simon first visit the Lampton farm in episode three. As details of Simon's connections with the attacks spread in the news media, journalists start sniffing around the brothers' father with offers of cash in exchange for unsavoury details of Simon's past. At Ford's suggestion, the brothers drive overnight to their childhood home – taking Ford's ute rather than Simon's Lexus to avoid Frank's derision – in order to buy their father off by 'giv[ing] him a better offer'. In keeping with stock representations, the farm itself seems to have little economic value; it is atavistic and cruel without rationale. Dogs strain at their chains, there are flies and trash everywhere, and the carcasses of rabbits and possums swing in the breeze. Frank himself is busy skinning a rabbit; as he stabs his knife into the cutting table, it is easy to see where Ford's own handiwork with a blade comes from. As Simon might have feared, given his father's capacity for belligerence, Frank is enraged by his sons' offer of money. It seems that the farm is a zone that is exempt from the rule of exchange (both financial and social) on which Simon bases his intimate relationships as well as his work. Frank treats his sons to a dose of their childhood discipline by locking them in a shed. Ford watches Simon's frantic attempts to get out with some satisfaction; he seems to have appointed himself as baroque justice bearer whose mission is to make Simon feel guilt, shame, and panic.

In the final episode, the original act of usurpation perpetrated by Ford is revealed through flashbacks located, unusually, in the recap sequence at the beginning of the episode. For years, Simon has been carrying the guilt

---

5   Kavka is writing in the context of McGann's *Possum*. A Pākehā family lives in isolated, dense bush, where they eke a living trapping possums, deemed an ecological pest in New Zealand. In the climax of the film, one of the family's children, a non-verbal, half-wild girl, herself becomes fatally caught in a possum trap. The ecological threat rebounds metaphorically on the family: like possums, they too are out of place and destructive of the local habitat. Kavka derives the broader point that much of New Zealand's settler Gothic cinematic tradition revolves around the psychic pathologies of forging habitation in a colonized land.

of being sent to a youth detention centre for striking a girl at a party. As becomes evident, however, this is not his guilt to bear. In fact, Ford hit the girl, and blamed Simon – though it remains unclear whether Ford took this action to protect Simon from their violent father, or simply to avoid taking responsibility. 'I smacked that girl', Ford says at the point of villainous confession, 'I got you sent away. You got the free pass, mate. You got the good life'. Frank has certainly made up his mind; he shoots and incapacitates Ford, who, almost radiant in his psychopathy by his stage, seems to have incited this moment of self-purgation. As the shot recalls and repeats the slap of Frank's strap when the brothers were young, Simon is released from his traumatic memories, and from the thrall of Ford as his shadow self.

Conclusion: Off the Hook

Simon's character arc sees him finally go through a series of exculpations; he never was the murderer, he never hit any girl in the past, he merely thought about harming his clients, he led Ford to Mereana but she survived Ford's attack. Simon has one last exculpation to receive in the form of Karen's forgiveness for his affair with Mereana. It is implied that he receives Karen's absolution when she accompanies him to the farm to rescue Claire from her kidnapper, Ford. As their car arrives at the farm, Karen gives Simon a 'now I understand everything' look. Now that she has seen where her husband grew up, Karen's pity and charity will prevail. The final shot of *The Bad Seed* shows Karen, Simon, and Claire picking up Elke from the Hallwrights. The Lamptons walk arm-in-arm away from the camera, and away from Roza, who pouts and turns from her doorstep back into her house. The Lamptons have fought off the various threats to Simon's role as father and husband, and Karen's role as mother. The Lamptons are not corrupt and dangerous: they have simply been beset by temptations from which they can now recover with better mutual understanding. In the end, they do not even seem so rich. They have learned humility; they are simply middling.

Could this self-consolidating and conventional form of closure have been otherwise? What if *The Bad Seed* had stayed closer to the noir-infused vision of Grimshaw's fictional world, rather than offering a self-serving moral clarity? Grimshaw's vision dwells within a cynical, pervasive malignity of the Pākehā élite as the social stratum that works hard, in terms of its self-representation, to secure its own innocence and deny social reality. In the character of Simon, Grimshaw provides us with a male protagonist whose emotional suffering stems from his own choices, but which he attributes wholly to victimization at the hands of his father – thereby rationalizing his own infidelities and crimes, not least of which is his alliance with a power politician whose dismissal of the lives of the poor is founded on avoiding personal emotions of social discomfort (Lawn, *Neoliberalism and Cultural Transition* 118). *The Bad Seed,* by contrast, offers a cautionary tale of social mobility. The introduction of a clearer line of criminal intent and investigation serves a redemptive purpose which expunges class domination, arguably buys into a conservative narrative of degeneracy, and quarantines then purges the origins and zones of criminality. Hogle has ascribed this closing over of guilty knowledge as part of a pattern of 'ideological suggesting-and-obscuring' of a traumatic kernel that underlies the Gothic itself (73). Remuera's toxic rounds of social climbing and political complacency may stink, but all that matters to Simon – to quote his first words of dialogue in the series – is that it is a *winning* stink.

Works Cited

Allen, Jean M., and Toni Bruce. 'Constructing the Other: News Media Representations of a Predominantly "Brown" Community in New Zealand'. *Pacific Journalism Review,* vol. 23, no. 1, 2017, pp. 225–244.

The Bad Seed. Directed by Mike Smith and Helena Brooks. Written by Michael Beran, Joss King, and Sarah-Kate Lynch. South Pacific Pictures with Jump Film and Television, 2019.

Beddoe, Liz. 'Feral Families, Troubled Families: The Spectre of the Underclass in New Zealand'. *New Zealand Sociology* vol. 29, no. 3, 2014, pp. 51–68.

Bell, Avril. *Relating Indigenous and Settler Identities: Beyond Domination.* Palgrave Macmillan, 2014.

Bell, Avril. 'Reverberating Historical Privilege of a "Middling" Sort of Settler Family'. *Genealogy,* vol. 4, no. 2, 2020. doi:10.3390/genealogy4020046

Borell, Belinda A.E., Amanda S. Gregory, and Tim N. McCreanor. '"It's Hard at the Top but It's a Whole Lot Easier Than Being at the Bottom": The Role of Privilege in Understanding Disparities in Aotearoa/New Zealand'. *Race/Ethnicity: Multidisciplinary Global Contexts,* vol. 3, no. 1, 2009, pp. 29–50.

Brickell, Chris, et al. 'Stratification and Class'. *Exploring Society: Sociology for New Zealand Students.* 4th ed., Auckland UP, 2019, pp. 116–134.

Collins, Simon. 'Residents Share Tales of Terror from Youth Gangs in "Dead-End" Street'. *New Zealand Herald,* 31 January 2007. <https://www.nzherald.co.nz/nz/residents-share-tales-of-terror-from-youth-gangs-in-dead-end-street/7U7FL4ADS552JGRMDY4ZGSQU4M/>.

Conrich, Ian. 'New Zealand Gothic'. *A New Companion to the Gothic,* edited by David Punter, Blackwell, 2012, pp. 393–408.

Crothers, Charles. 'Social Class in New Zealand: A Review Based on Survey Evidence'. *New Zealand Sociology,* vol. 29, no. 3, 2014, pp. 90–127.

Grimshaw, Charlotte. *The Night Book.* Vintage, 2010.

Grimshaw, Charlotte. *Singularity.* Vintage, 2009.

Grimshaw, Charlotte. *Soon.* Vintage, 2012.

Grimshaw, Charlotte. 'Two Minutes with Charlotte Grimshaw'. Interview. *New Zealand Listener,* 6 Oct. 2012, p. 12.

Hardy, Linda. 'Natural Occupancy'. *Meridian,* vol. 14, no. 2, 1995, pp. 213–227.

Hogle, Jerrold E. 'History, Trauma, and the Gothic in Contemporary Western Fictions'. *The Gothic World,* edited by Jerrold E. Hogle, Routledge, 2013, pp. 72–81.

Hopwood, Malcolm. '*The Bad Seed* a Seismic Shift in Quality of Kiwi Drama'. stuff. co.nz, 5 Apr. 2019. <https://www.stuff.co.nz/entertainment/tv-radio/112138932/the-bad-seed-a-seismic-shift-in-quality-of-kiwi-drama>.

Jones, Timothy. 'New Zealand Gothic'. *The Encyclopedia of The Gothic, Volume 1: L–Z,* edited by William Hughes, David Punter, and Andrew Smith, Wiley-Blackwell, 2013, pp. 468–471.

Kavka, Misha. 'The Settlement Trap'. *Short Film Studies,* vol. 6, no. 1, 2016, pp. 67–70.

Lawn, Jennifer. 'Domesticating Settler Gothic in New Zealand Literature'. *New Literatures Review,* vol. 38, 2002, pp. 46–62.

Lawn, Jennifer. *Neoliberalism and Cultural Transition in New Zealand Literature, 1984–2008: Market Fictions.* Lexington, 2016.

Macdonald, Finlay. 'Struggle Street: How the "Scum Zoo" of Struggle Street Became a Ratings Smash'. *The Spinoff,* 21 May 2015. <https://thespinoff.co.nz/featured/21-05-2015/struggle-street-how-a-low-budget-australian-poverty-porn-series-became-a-smash/>.

Matthewman, Steve. 'Pākehā Ethnicity: The Politics of White Privilege'. *A Land of Milk and Honey? Making Sense of Aotearoa New Zealand,* edited by Avril Bell et al., Auckland UP, 2017.

Murray, Anna. 'Why *The Bad Seed* Isn't So Bad'. 17 Apr. 2019. <https://www.nzherald.co.nz/entertainment/why-the-bad-seed-isnt-so-bad/CELOCAZNNK75GLK-6JOIT6VOPII/>.

Mercer, Erin. '"Shot at and Slashed at and Whacked": The Gothic Slaughterhouse in New Zealand Fiction'. *JNZL: Journal of New Zealand Literature,* vol. 35, no. 2, 2017, pp. 51–71.

Noyes, J.K. *Colonial Space: Spatiality in the Discourse of German South West Africa 1884–1915.* Harwood, 1992.

'Ofa Kolo, F. 'An Incident in Otara: The Media and Pacific Island Communities'.
    Between the Lines: Racism and the New Zealand Media, edited by Paul Spoonley
    and Wally Hirsch, Heinemann Reed, 1990, pp. 120–122.
Sisterson, Craig. *Southern Cross Crime.* Oldcastle, 2020.
Veracini, Lorenzo. *The Settler Colonial Present.* Palgrave Macmillan, 2015.
Žižiek, Slavoj. *Did Somebody Say Totalitarianism?* Verso, 2001.

About the Author

Jennifer Lawn is Associate Professor in English at Massey University. Her research interests focus on narrative genres studied within social contexts, including Gothic studies, crime fiction, and literatures of Aotearoa/New Zealand. She is the author of *Neoliberalism and Cultural Transition in New Zealand Literature, 1984–2008: Market Fictions* (Lexington 2016). Jennifer identifies as a Pākehā New Zealander.

11. Monstrous Victims: Women, Trauma, and Gothic Violence in Jennifer Kent's *The Babadook* and *The Nightingale*

Jessica Gildersleeve, Nike Sulway, and Amanda Howell

Abstract

This chapter compares Jennifer Kent's *The Babadook* (2014) and *The Nightingale* (2019) in terms of their explicit construction of violence conducted by and against women. Both films draw on the gothic trope of women suffering trauma and the more recent conversion of that suffering to the perpetuation of violent revenge. However, this chapter shows that rather than constituting a kind of bravery, or a subversion of that victimization along the lines of the figure of Carol Clover's 'Final Girl', the acts of violence committed by the women in these films compound their traumatization by severing them both from others and from themselves.

Keywords: Australian Gothic cinema; Jennifer Kent; trauma; revenge

Jennifer Kent's *The Babadook* (2014) has received a great deal of critical attention, primarily for its depiction of monstrous motherhood. This essay seeks to extend that discussion through a comparison to Kent's second film, *The Nightingale* (2019), and its even more explicit construction of violence conducted by and against women. In this way we show that both films draw on the gothic trope of women suffering trauma and the more recent conversion of that suffering to the perpetuation of violent revenge. However, we argue that rather than constituting bravery, a restoration of justice, or a subversion of that victimization along the lines of the figure of Carol J. Clover's 'Final Girl', the acts of violence committed by the women in these films compound their traumatization by severing them from both others and themselves. The adoption of behaviours rendered masculine

Gildersleeve, J. and K. Cantrell (eds.), *Screening the Gothic in Australia and New Zealand: Contemporary Antipodean Film and Television*. Taylor & Francis Group, 2022

DOI 10.5117/9789463721141_CH11

in the Gothic through the invasion of the home and the colonization of the bush thus confirms these women as monstrous rather than heroic. As in other recent Australian horror films, such as Julia Leigh's *Sleeping Beauty* (2011) and Sean Byrne's *The Loved Ones* (2010), women's monstrosity is bound up with their enactment of a masculine agency, such that there is no opportunity for them within the Australian Gothic to move beyond this traditional binary construct.

The Babadook and *The Nightingale* share many thematic and narrative concerns, but centrally, both depict a young woman struggling to deal with her traumatic loss: each film functions as a commentary on the impacts of gender on the experience of violence and mourning in the aftermath of horror, in the particular context of Australian colonial and contemporary history. Indeed, both films exemplify the way in which women's 'oppression by patriarchal controls, embodied in the domestic, economic, legal and financial structures of society and allegorized in the varied physical and spiritual perils of gothic narratives, persists in the Australian Gothic's exploration of iniquitous authority and its repeated depiction of brutal and uncompromising masculinity' (Rayner 92). It is true that, as Nathanael O'Reilly and Jean-François Vernay note, 'Australian history [...] is crammed with a vast array of fears and anxieties [...]. From the first contact between the European settler/invaders and the Indigenous inhabitants of the continent through to contemporary concerns regarding domestic terrorism, fear and anxiety have been part of life in Australia' (5). To be sure, anxiety and (in)security are central points of concern throughout Australian history, and Kent's films especially underscore the way in which this is true for women in both the contemporary and colonial periods. The 'horror tropes' in both films can be seen as 'always in service to a deeper thing', Kent has said (qtd. in Howell 120) – the horror of 'traumatic bereavement' (Ingham 269), but also 'a thematic concern with women's lives, familial relations, and the workings of grief and its suppression' (Kent qtd. in Howell 120). In both films the women protagonists suffer the horror of violence and loss, ultimately enacting similar behaviour themselves. However, Amelia in *The Babadook*, and Clare in *The Nightingale*, are not simply the passive victims of that anxiety and insecurity – rather, both women internalize the monstrosity of invasion, although to different effect.

Women – and particularly young women – as both victims and perpetrators of violence have been the subject of a range of recent Australian gothic and horror films. Such films can be seen as part of an international tradition of female vengeance films, from early examples such as *I Spit on Your Grave* (1978, remade in 2010 and followed by several sequels) and

Carrie (1976, remade in 2013), to more recent examples including *Hard Candy* (2005), *Elle* (2016), *MFA* (2017), and *Revenge* (2017). In each of these films, the links between women's experiences as the subjects or objects of violence are made explicit, so that in each case the woman's apparent monstrosity is portrayed as erupting from her experience of living within sexist and patriarchal cultures, and particularly cultures in which female victims of sexual assault are denied closure, catharsis, or justice. Some texts combine a critique of men's violence against women with a critique of the ineffective processes through which such violence should be, but is not, addressed. In this sense, the failures of workplaces, families, police, and the courts to prevent, prosecute and/or punish violence against women provokes or creates the need for women to seek their own, private forms of justice. Women's monstrous violence, then, is most commonly framed in female vengeance films as a last resort: an enactment of justice (as violent punishment) in an unjust patriarchal culture. Importantly, in this context, the female vigilante does 'not take sadistic pleasure in murdering people nor does committing homicide serve as a restorative balm that alleviates the suffering they experienced following the death of a loved one' (Doro 228). Rather, the act of justice is portrayed as necessary, but simultaneously incapable of restoring the order or salvation the vigilante craves.

Byrne's film *The Loved Ones* is unusual in its muddying of this somewhat comforting or 'traditional' depiction of female vengeance as always already provoked by gendered violence and systemic failures. In Byrne's film, Lola Stone abducts and tortures Brent Mitchell on the night of their senior school dance. There is no suggestion that Lola has been the subject of sexual assault or harassment by Brent (or any of her previous victims). Rather, Brent is shown as emotionally vulnerable and sensitive; he is unwilling to engage in carpark sex with his girlfriend Holly, guilt-ridden over his role in his father's death, and subject to suicidal ideation. When Lola invites him to the dance, he does not tease her, but turns her down gently and sensitively, twice apologising ('Sorry, Lola, I'm going with Holly. Sorry'). Instead, Lola's abduction of and various acts of violence against Brent are depicted not as vengeance for his wrongdoing, except in the most comical and exaggerated terms, but rather as part of a family tradition of torture and murder linked to the incestuous desire Lola expresses for her father. Thus, while many female vengeance films depict women's experience of enacting violence as something of a grim necessity in which they are tasked as something like judge and executioner, Lola is unusual in taking pleasure in her skills as a torturer.

Leigh's *Sleeping Beauty* also marks a departure from the narrative tropes of female vengeance films, focusing less on the logic or motives for women's violence or vengeance, and more on the structural and physical suppression of Lucy's resistance to the various ways in which her body is penetrated, arranged, and used. Part of Lucy's strength and uncanniness – her monstrosity – is the extraordinary passivity, or lack of affect, she maintains in the face of the various indignities she suffers. There is a quiet and creeping continuity between her willingness to participate in work that requires things to be done to her without expressing distaste, revulsion, or discomfort, and the insistence that she be increasingly incurious and unaware of the things enacted on or with her body (or the bodies of other girls she sees at her workplace). Though markedly less violent than the drilling, hammering, and cannibalism of Byrne's Lola, Lucy's vengeance is more subtle and ambiguous. In secretly filming herself and a client, Lucy knowingly breaks the terms of her contract and, as her employer explicitly states, places both her client and her employer at risk of exposure, blackmail, and prosecution. Unlike many other heroines of female vengeance films, her final resistance not only enacts justice for past wrongs committed against her as an individual, but also exposes, and thereby destroys, the institution within which she and other young women were exploited, silenced, drugged, and violated. The consequences of her quiet vengeance, which seeks to prevent the exploitation of other women, are underscored in the ambiguous final images of the film, in which we are either watching Lucy (and her client) sleep, or observing their dead bodies lying, deathly still, in a shared bed.

By engaging with the challenges of motherhood in ways that more conventional dramas cannot, and by blurring the lines between the supernatural and psychological, haunting, possession, and madness, monster and victim, *The Babadook* uses Amelia's haunted house as a stage for performances of repressed emotion that alternately horrify and engage our sympathy. Puppet-like Mister Babadook, released from the mysterious pop-up book, is the source of jump-scares, a goblin for Halloween. His spooky effects are effectively upstaged when Amelia's strained efforts to cope give way to a towering rage where the all-too-familiar vernacular of domestic abuse – verbal taunts, physical threats – appear horrifically heightened and theatrically transformed. In Amelia's operatic performances, monstrosity overtakes victimhood, and horror trumps our sympathy. By contrast, we are simultaneously afraid both of and for Amelia in those scenes where, through the homely, happy, child-focused medium of the pop-up book, with its aesthetic of pleasurable surprise and tactile engagement, she is confronted with a prognosticatory image of her rage realized in bloodshed and the murder of the vulnerable. As an allegorical tale of maternal rage and the dangers of repression, *The Babadook* ultimately provides catharsis in the expressionist style of body horror – black gouts of what we understand to be Amelia's anger, grief, and resentment physically expelled under her son Samuel's loving and watchful eye after he captures and restrains her, Gulliver-like, in the basement. Yet there is also a cautionary note in the film's fairy-tale happy ending where mother and son are reunited in the garden, a reminder that monstrous Mister Babadook, the top-hatted, shark-toothed avatar of Amelia's maternal rage, is not gone, only kennelled.

Barbara Creed has argued that 'when the woman is represented as monstrous it is almost always in relation to her mothering and reproductive functions' (qtd. in Middleton and Bak 14). Indeed, one of the primary points of discussion provoked by *The Babadook* is its representation of Amelia's monstrous motherhood, the failures and disappointments of her maternal behaviour towards her young son, Samuel: she resents and suffers his caresses, makes regular snide remarks to him about his fears and beliefs, requests unnecessary medication to make him sleep, refuses to celebrate his birthday (the anniversary of his father Oskar's violent death), and meets only his most basic needs of food, warmth, and shelter. Indeed, she can at best be said to merely perform the tasks of motherhood, these gestures only ever made on the surface, 'dutiful but mechanical', such that her 'refusal of her maternity [is] the locus of her monstrosity and abjection' (Buerger 39, 34). Thus, Amelia's behaviour has been variously described as the product of trauma (Mitchell), postnatal psychosis (Alter), an enactment of 'antiquated ideas of femininity and motherhood' (Aranjuez 126), precarious maternal authority (Briefel 3), and as a demonstration of her simultaneous roles as a '[m]onstrous mother' and a 'heroically self-sacrificing one' (Howell 131). The construct of the gothic maternal, the monstrous mother in this film, is concerned with the blame for the death of Samuel's father placed on the child by his mother and thus, as an ultimate consequence, not only his effective responsibility for Oskar's death, but in a corruption of Sigmund Freud's Oedipal model of the growth of the boy-child, Samuel's destruction and replacement of his father (Buerger 38, 40). That he repeatedly insinuates himself, unwanted, into Amelia's bed, entwining her in his arms as she turns away, and that he interrupts her attempt at a moment of sexual pleasure, are just two examples of this strategy of replacement. The figure of Mister Babadook might in this way be read as a counter to the boy's invasion, a symbol of paternal punishment for his social and psychic disruption.

On the other hand, Clare in *The Nightingale* enacts her monstrosity towards those who committed profound violence against her and destroyed her husband *and* child; her rage is directed outside rather than within the family. As such, her monstrosity is more clearly aligned with the quest for justice inherent to female revenge narratives rather than rage against the disruptions to familial order. Importantly, however, *The Nightingale* employs several parallels with *The Babadook* which invite a comparison of their twin depictions of monstrous motherhood and ultimately the reparative possibilities of each woman's actions. Both are, of course, not only bereaved, but directly witness the moment of the violent death of their husbands and, for Clare, her child. Both Amelia and Clare are employed in roles that involve what Aviva Briefel calls 'relentless caretaking' (5), the former as a nurse in an aged care facility, the latter as a servant in an army barracks. While Amelia is exhausted by this work and barely able to care for her child, Clare's love and care for her infant daughter provides a site of solace from the physical demands of her labour. Indeed, the films offer parallel scenes of these mother-child relationships to clarify the distinctions between the two women: while Amelia reads bedtime stories to Samuel without much care or interest and which only result in the boy's fears, such that she must medicate him to sleep, Clare softly narrates stories from memories of her own childhood in Ireland, lulling the baby to sleep. In a more extreme comparison, while Amelia threatens Samuel, 'Sometimes I just want to smash your head against a brick wall until your fucking brains pop out!', Clare is forced to watch with helpless horror as this very thing happens to her own baby. The parallels and critical distinctions between the two films thus work to construct and implicitly question our ideologies of ideal motherhood, for while Amelia is in this way shown to be psychologically unstable, terrifying even to the viewer, Clare is made heroic for her pursuit of attempted justice. For instance, where *The Babadook* uses focalization to depict Amelia's experiences of trauma and depression, *The Nightingale* instead returns the viewer to extreme close-ups of Clare's face in order to hone in on the abject horror and misery she experiences: the effect is that we see Amelia as unlikeable and unstable, while Clare is pitied and understood.

While *The Babadook* eventually garnered praise, prizes and significant box office success worldwide, *The Nightingale* could not be more different, despite the common interest of Kent's two films in female anger, revenge, and maternal monstrosity as worked through familiar but transformed generic materials. After a lacklustre six-week theatrical release in Australia, where it opened on only thirteen screens, *The Babadook* went on to be heralded as a 'breakout success' at the Sundance Film Festival in January 2014 (Gibbs). Garnering consistently positive word-of-mouth reviews abroad during its 39 international screenings, the film subsequently gained significant box office success in Europe, and after its Halloween 2015 release became the most profitable film to date for American indie film distributor IFC Midnight. Since then, *The Babadook* has become something of a benchmark for critically acclaimed horror, routinely grouped with or compared to titles like Robert Egger's *The VVitch* (2015), Babak Anvari's *Under the Shadow* (2016), and Ari Aster's *Hereditary* (2018) (see Dowd, '*Under the Shadow*'; Smith; Sharf; Zinoman; Wilkinson), all of which are family and female-focused gothic horrors that use generic materials as the basis for cinematic art.

The Nightingale, as Kent's highly anticipated second film, offers a sharp contrast, in spite of its early win of a Special Jury Prize at the Venice Film Festival in September 2018, ahead of its opening on 33 screens in Australia in mid-2019. Despite a much longer theatrical run in Australia (32 weeks), as well as critical responses that are generally positive (in respect of star and numerical ratings), the film garnered less than half the domestic box office realized by *The Babadook* in its initial thirteen-week run (Box Office Mojo). Whereas festival walkouts can often generate curiosity as well as controversy and thus boost attendance (as in the case of Julia Ducournau's 2016 cannibal horror film, *Raw*), this did not appear to be the case for *The Nightingale*. In setting up its tale of revenge in the claustrophobic world of colonial Tasmania, three rape scenes in the first 20 minutes went beyond audience endurance at its Sydney Film Festival screenings as a number of festival-goers walked out, with one attendee even directing criticism at Kent, who sat among the audience: 'She's already been raped twice, we don't need to see it again!' (Graham).

Even the most positive reviews of *The Nightingale* tend to serve as warnings for potential viewers, calling it a 'tough watch' (Sims), with many critics describing the viewing experience filmgoers could expect as 'harrowing' (see Dowd, '*Babadook* Director Returns'; Hughes; Ide; Scott; Sims; York). As *Guardian* critic Wendy Ide summed it up, '[l]ike the world she depicts, Kent's storytelling shows no mercy'. Indeed, when one of the authors of this chapter arrived, heavily pregnant, at a showing of *The Nightingale*, the well-meaning cinema proprietor attempted to dissuade her from purchasing a ticket to the film, concerned by the stress she might experience. Using the language of torture to describe the viewing experience, critics link Kent's film with hardcore horror or extreme cinema that aims to push the boundaries of what audiences can bear. What these critics share with prospective viewers appears to be their own lingering affective response to the film, of the sort Matt Hills characterizes as an 'objectless anxiety' that can spill beyond the actual 'experiential time of reading/viewing' (27). In this way, critical reviews of *The Nightingale*, despite being largely laudatory for its treatment of a difficult historical subject, nevertheless identify Kent's film as 'ordeal cinema', where the 'viewer commits to watching a film that will take them through a horrendous experience' (Kuhn and Westwell 152).

Like *The Babadook*, *The Nightingale* is a film about female rage, with a protagonist who is rendered as simultaneously victim, mother, and monster. But the stakes are higher; the scope is epic; and there is no cathartic release available in the claustrophobic environs of colonial Tasmania during the so-called Black Wars (1824–1831), despite the violent satisfactions that the rape-revenge genre might seem to promise. Clare is a young Irish convict whose family is murdered before her eyes while she is restrained and raped; afterwards, she pursues in a righteous fury the British officer responsible for her family's destruction. That officer, Lieutenant Hawkins, is determined to reach Launceston to secure the promotion denied him by his superior officer. In both Clare's and Hawkins's stories, then, we witness monstrous abuses of power among soldiers and prisoners and Indigenous populations, performances of domination and resistance that repeatedly point us back to the material conditions of colonialism.

In this way it is clear that the victims and victimizers of *The Nightingale* proliferate beyond the familiar binary logic of rape-revenge and its avenging victims. Indeed, Kent herself has observed that while '[s]ome people categorize this as a rape revenge film [...]. I don't think it fits in that canon at all. Most of those films play out in a very masculine way, and relentless and brutal violence is often the end game [...]. I wanted to talk about what happens *after* someone is given the opportunity to exact revenge [...]. It's about love and compassion and kindness' (qtd. in Fuller 26). Clare's urgent need for violent retribution is reframed when Billy, Clare's tracker, a Letteremairrener man, identifies the footprints of Private Jago and leads the young woman to her baby's murderer. The callow young soldier, injured and left behind by Hawkins's group, is caught and downed. Jago is wide-eyed with fear as Clare stabs him repeatedly in the chest; enraged, she obliterates his face with her rifle butt. Here, Jago's youth and vulnerability, highlighted by his uncomprehending final plea, 'Mother', transform the scene, as well as Clare herself. Her obliteration of his childlike response thus echoes the other acts of extreme violence against children performed throughout the film: the murder of her baby daughter, the kidnapping of the toddler Koa, and the shooting of young Eddie. Her act of retributive justice, a mother's vengeance born out of grief and loss, appears at this moment not as triumphant, but as just another abuse of the vulnerable, her own experience mirrored in his face at the moment of death. Afterwards, framed in an extreme low angle shot against the trees, her face and torso covered in the young man's blood, she stands unsteadily in the canted frame, confused, breathing hard, her shaking hands held out – the stance of some newly created or arisen monstrous thing. This monstrous maternal rage, in contrast to Amelia's in *The Babadook*, is not something that can be cathartically released or domesticated. Made strange to herself by violence and terrified to be alone, Clare pursues the tracker who has retreated from this blank, bloodied woman, begging Billy to stay with her.

To be sure, *The Nightingale* is a bold and confronting work of historical horror. According to the film's production notes, the film is intended 'to show an authentic and honest representation of Tasmanian history during colonization' (Transmission Films 4). The focus of this authenticity is most clearly on the repeated violence against women (particularly convict women, or Irish indentured servants), and against Indigenous peoples, perpetrated by White/English colonial culture. In aiming to 'authentically' represent the violent history of colonial Tasmania, *The Nightingale* invites viewers to recognize that this violence is both historical and ongoing: that it is a part of Australian history that bleeds uncannily, uneasily, and persistently into the present, such that these acts of nation-building violence become unhealed wounds in the Australian imaginary. Horror films that deal with historical trauma and violence, Adam Lowenstein argues, are particularly well placed to negotiate a 'complex process of embodiment, where film, spectator, and history compete and collaborate', because it is in this way that we might 'produce forms of knowing not easily described by conventional delineations of bodily space and historical time' (2–3). In part these 'forms of knowing' involve ways of accessing the traumatic and shameful colonial past. Julia B. Köhne, Michael Elm, and Kobi Kabalek, for instance, describe the way in which such histories are transformed by narrative film 'into even more complex cultural material. It gives them a new, altered shape, a symbolic, more readable form that might arouse less of a society's fear than the historical event itself' (10). This sentiment is echoed in Kent's assertion that 'by placing something in the past, you can give people a distance from it, so they can see it without feeling like they're being attacked' (qtd. in Transmission Films 7). Critically, however, that distance from attack or discomfort is only offered to white and/or male audiences, the perpetrators of violence in the film: the discomfort experienced by Aboriginal peoples or women viewing the film lies in the intense unease provoked by visions of bodies like theirs being repeatedly raped, beaten, humiliated, enslaved, mutilated, and murdered.

In responding to the controversy, Kent asserts that 'ultimately for me, this film isn't about violence, it's about the love between two very unlikely people' (qtd. in Handler). Twinned through their bird imagery (the nightingale and the blackbird), the Irish convict Clare and Indigenous man Billy gradually overcome their suspicion of one another in order to forge a relationship based on their shared experiences of trauma, loss, and cultural hatred for the English settlers and lawmakers. Billy continues to serve as her guide – and ours – even after the murder of Jago, despite, or perhaps because of, his warning that Hawkins and his crew are 'mad devils': 'If I saw those white ones, the ones that killed my family', Billy says, 'I would have done what you did'. Yet Billy is more than just Clare's guide: he hunts, forages, feeds and protects her, reminds her to wash the blood from her clothing, wakes her from her nightmares, performs a smoke ceremony to ease her mind, even shares his auntie's recipe for drying her milk and soothing the pain in her engorged breasts. One might wonder how Billy would know such details of women's business, but Kent is clear on the rigour of research behind his character, as well as its approval by elders at the Tasmanian Aboriginal Centre (Zuckerman).

Nevertheless, a comment made by *Hollywood News* critic, Kat Hughes, that the relationship between Clare and Billy 'feels like [...] *Driving Miss Daisy*', gives one pause. Meant as praise for the 'rather lovely dynamic between' Franciosi and Ganambarr, it is an observation that nevertheless points us back to a tradition of mainstream fantasies of blackness made for white audiences. Layered over familiar tropes of colonial Australian literature – 'the sadistic redcoat, the Aboriginal tracker, and more troubling, the convict as victim rather than agent of colonization' (Arrow and Findlay 1) – is another more recent cinematic trope, associated especially with mainstream Hollywood, where black characters are attributed with special powers used largely to benefit white characters. Like chauffeur Hoke (Morgan Freeman) in *Driving Miss Daisy*, Billy acquires greater personal power in the course of the film, but it is Clare who, by virtue of her white skin, has greater social power despite her gender and convict status. Indeed, as the Launceston sequence confirms, Clare has a certain freedom of movement that Billy does not, since she can 'pass' as a free woman. In his caring yet subservient role to Clare and the wealth of knowledge, skills, and insight he puts at her disposal for the price of a shilling, Billy recalls the 'Magic Negro' of contemporary American film, who is 'articulate, asexual, and self-sacrificing with supernatural powers used to help a film's white protagonist' (Lloyd 188). The 'Magic Negro' is descended from the 'good negro' characters that made Sidney Poitier a box-office star in Civil Rights-era America, each willing to sacrifice his freedom (*The Defiant Ones* [1958]) or even his life (*The Edge of the City* [1957]) for a white character. Contemporary 'Magic Negro' characters are, like Poitier, typically likeable, helpful, and attractive, and are easily assimilated into white-focused narratives because they have 'no history or future and no community' (Lloyd 188). It is true that Billy is prompted to join Clare's cause of revenge against Hawkins by the murder of his Uncle Charlie. Nevertheless, the motivations for Billy's final, suicidal rampage remain somewhat obscure, since Hawkins is only one of his several victims. Billy's implied death as a consequence of this desperate action thus recalls a cinematic tradition where black lives are sacrificed for white and, what's more, where Billy is made monstrous by association with Clare.

The risks inherent in *The Nightingale* are clear: a film that re-presents trauma in ways that merely reinscribe that trauma for its viewers may be 'authentic', but it is unlikely to provoke or invite the viewer to embrace Lowenstein's negotiated 'forms of knowing'. Instead, viewers may feel affronted, confronted, appalled, and uneasy in ways that provoke them to reject the film (as demonstrated by the actions of those who walked out of the film's screenings). This risk of provoking new trauma in both survivors and other audiences is a real one. However, as Lowenstein argues, the 'move to safeguard the idiom of survivors by treating their experience as "unrepresentable"' is equally problematic, since it

> evades the challenge of finding new idioms for that experience – it locks away survivor trauma inside an authentic moment in the past, free from the perilous present of cultural negotiation demanded by representation. What is preserved in such a move is the unquestionable authenticity of survivor experience; what is lost, I would contend, is the full possibility of that experience shaping our contemporary world. (5)

Through re-presenting otherwise erased, forgotten or suppressed historical traumas as immersive cinematic images, *The Nightingale* 'can be embraced as an artistic attempt to communicate what can neither be transformed into a shared experience nor transmitted in an undisguised manner'; because of this, it functions as a 'prosthetic memory' (Köhne, Elm, and Kabalek 12). For a memory to be prosthetic not only indicates that it is always already inauthentic, but a replacement for what has been lost, usually due to an experience of trauma. It is, in effect, a spectral memory, a gothic memory. *The Nightingale*'s relationship to the early nineteenth-century history of Tasmania functions in a similar way: the process of colonization not only resulted in the decimation of the Indigenous peoples, but also in the deliberate and organized suppression and erasure of Indigenous culture, language, and story. This prosthesis also applies to the film's imperfect analogy of colonial violence against Indigenous people with the liminal experience of a White Irish convict woman. That is, while the film treats its Indigenous actors, characters, and stories with careful respect, the narrative is always already framed as a white woman's story of oppression, transformation, and vengeance. The parallel is a problematic one: the attempt to conflate indentured servitude and slavery, Liam Hogan argues, is 'an obscene rhetorical move which decontextualizes and dehistoricizes the exploitation of both groups' (7). For instance, what the film prosthetically 'remembers' in its concluding scene is that its white convict woman gains a sense of freedom and a voice, and that its disenfranchised, unhomed Indigenous man is 'still here [...] not going nowhere'. The pair stand on a beach, facing the sunrise, so that the film explicitly evokes a sense of hope, of futurity and survival. At the same time, any informed (non-prosthetic) speculation regarding Clare and Billy's individual futures is far from hopeful. Clare will never reach the place of unfettered safety she describes to her daughter at the film's beginning, while Billy will never escape the colonial retribution for the murders he commits, nor return to a home and a people lost forever. Although the film had sought to align Clare and Billy as similarly disenfranchised and thus motivated to reclaim their agency, this comparison is destroyed at its conclusion since, as Larissa Behrendt points out, the Irish song Clare performs at this point is 'still a foreign, colonizing language that she is singing on [Billy's] traditional land. In the end, there is no way to escape your own complicity when you are part of the colonial system – no matter how powerless you yourself are'. Any disruption the pair have enacted is only temporary, and unable to rewrite the power imbalance that still exists between them. Perhaps more importantly, however, both Clare and Billy have been lured into the same monstrous cycles of systemic violence. Their acts of revenge do not end these cycles (Johnson 11), but merely ensure their continuation.

Both *The Babadook* and *The Nightingale* conclude with an emphasis on survival, however fraught or temporary that might be. The disconcertingly ambivalent status of Mister Babadook himself, Shelley Buerger observes, suggests the capacity for his disturbing return (43). Indeed, both Buerger (43) and Briefel (19–20) argue that Amelia must now behave as a mother or carer to the monster, feeding him, soothing him, and offering him shelter, literally becoming in one sense a monster-mother, or in another, a forced slave to the whims of the monster. Similarly, Clare in *The Nightingale* is profoundly changed by the violence she has enacted, witnessed, and been subjected to, such that both she and Billy have been pushed into monstrous behaviours they would not otherwise have entertained. In some ways we might see these transformations as inflected by the #MeToo movement, as

Gabrielle O'Brien suggests is true of Laurie Strode's figuration in the 2018 *Halloween* sequel, so that she is 'anchored in the context of being a survivor of male-inflicted trauma' (68), rather than simply an archetype of Clover's Final Girl. Clare and Amelia survive, to be sure, but their survival, as is also true of this iteration of Laurie, depends on their monstrous transformation. Even in these contemporary Australian films so centred on the female experience, the tropes of the Gothic resist their rejection or reinscription. Both individual and collective trauma are shown to profoundly change the female subject in ways that continue to contain and restrain her binary construction.

Works Cited

Alter, Ethan. 'Parental Descent'. *Film Journal International*, vol. 117, no. 11, 2014, pp. 24–32.

Aranjuez, Adolfo. 'Monstrous Motherhood: Summoning the Abject in *The Babadook*'. *Screen Education*, vol. 92, 2019, pp. 122–128.

Arrow, Michelle, and James Findlay. 'A Critical Introduction to *The Nightingale*: Gender, Race and Troubled Histories on Screen'. *Studies in Australasian Cinema*, vol. 14, no. 1, 2020, pp. 1–12.

The Babadook. Directed by Jennifer Kent, Screen Australia, 2014.

Behrendt, Larissa. '*The Nightingale* Review – Ambitious, Urgent and Necessarily Brutal. But Who is it For?' *Guardian*, 20 Aug. 2019. <www.theguardian.com/film/2019/aug/20/the-nightingale-review-ambitious-urgent-and-necessarily-brutal-but-who-is-it-for>.

Briefel, Aviva. 'Parenting through Horror: Reassurance in Jennifer Kent's *The Babadook*'. *Camera Obscura*, vol. 32, no. 2, 2017, pp. 1–27.

Box Office Mojo. *The Babadook*. <www.boxofficemojo.com/title/tt2321549/?ref_=bo_se_r_1>.

Box Office Mojo. *The Nightingale*. <www.boxofficemojo.com/release/rl2752022017/?ref_=bo_da_table_33>.

Buerger, Shelley. 'The Beak that Grips: Maternal Indifference, Ambivalence and the Abject in *The Babadook*'. *Studies in Australasian Cinema*, vol. 11, no. 1, 2017, pp. 33–44.

Clover, Carol J. 'Her Body, Himself: Gender in the Slasher Film'. *Representations*, no. 20, 1987, pp. 187–228.

Doro, Paul. 'Vengeance is Mine: Gender and Vigilante Justice in Mainstream Cinema'. *American Revenge Narratives*, edited by Kyle Wiggins, Palgrave Macmillan, 2018, pp. 227–244.

Dowd, A.A. '*Babadook* Director Jennifer Kent Returns with a Great, Harrowing Western, *The Nightingale*'. *AV Club*, 1 Aug. 2019. <www.film.avclub.com/babadook-director-jennifer-kent-returns-with-a-great-h-1836866037>.

Dowd, A.A. '*Under the Shadow* is a *Babadook* for War-Torn Iran'. *AV Club*, 10 May 2016. <www.film.avclub.com/under-the-shadow-is-a-babadook-for-war-torn-iran-1798189047>.

Fuller, Graham. 'Once Upon a Time in Van Diemen's Land: An Interview with Jennifer Kent'. *Cineaste*, vol. 44, no. 4, 2019, pp. 25–27.

Gibbs, Ed. 'I was Screaming All Day'. *Guardian*, 20 May 2014. <www.theguardian.com/film/australia-culture-blog/2014/may/20/the-babadook-iwas-screaming-all-day>.

Graham, Ben. '"She's Already Been Raped": Film Furore'. *Seniors*, 10 June 2019. <www.seniorsnews.com.au/news/cinemagoers-walk-out-and-yell-criticism-during-the/3749845/>.

Handler, Rachel. 'Jennifer Kent Doesn't Think *The Nightingale* is a Rape-Revenge Story'. *Vulture*, 1 Aug. 2019. <www.vulture.com/2019/08/the-babadooks-jennifer-kent-on-the-nightingale.html>.

Hills, Matt. *The Pleasures of Horror*. Continuum, 2005.

Hogan, Liam. 'Open Letter to *Irish Central*, *Irish Examiner*, and *Scientific American* about their "Irish Slaves" Disinformation'. *Medium*, 9 Mar. 2016. <www.medium.com/@Limerick1914/open-letter-to-irish-central-irish-examiner-and-scientific-american-about-their-irish-slaves-3f6cf23b8d7f>.

Howell, Amanda. 'Haunted Art House: *The Babadook* and International Art Cinema Horror'. *Australian Screen in the 2000s*, edited by Mark David Ryan and Ben Goldsmith, Palgrave Macmillan, 2017, pp. 119–139.

Hughes, Kat. '*The Nightingale* Review: Dir. Jennifer Kent (2019)'. *Hollywood News*, 25 Nov. 2019. <www.thehollywoodnews.com/2019/11/25/the-nightingale-review-dir-jennifer-kent-2019/>.

Ide, Wendy. '*The Nightingale* Review – A Whole New Level of Horror from *Babadook* Director'. *Guardian*, 1 Dec. 2019. <www.theguardian.com/film/2019/nov/30/the-nightingale-jennifer-kent-colonial-rape-revenge-drama-aisling-franciosi-sam-clafin>.

Ingham, Toby. '*The Babadook* – A Film Review from a Psychoanalytic Psychotherapy Perspective'. *Psychodynamic Practice*, vol. 21, no. 3, 2015, pp. 269–270.

Johnson, Travis. 'Hierarchies of Horror: The Violent Refrains of *The Nightingale*'. *Metro* 201, 2019, pp. 6–11.

Köhne, Julia B., Michael Elm, and Kobi Kabalek. 'The Horrors of Trauma in Cinema'. *The Horrors of Trauma in Cinema: Violence, Void, Visualization*, edited by Michael Elm, Kobi Kabalek, and Julia B. Köhne, Cambridge Scholars, 2014, pp. 1–31.

Kuhn, Annette, and Guy Westwell. *A Dictionary of Film Studies*, 2nd ed, Oxford UP, 2020.

Lloyd, Vincent W. 'The Post-Racial Saint? From Barack Obama to Paul of Tarsus'. *Sainthood and Race: Marked Flesh, Holy Flesh*, edited by Molly H. Bassett and Vincent W. Lloyd, Routledge, 2015, pp. 182–198.

The Loved Ones. Directed by Sean Byrne, Madman, 2010.

Lowenstein, Adam. *Shocking Representations: Historical Trauma, National Cinema and the Modern Horror Film*. Columbia UP, 2005.

Middleton, Jason, and Meredith A. Bak. 'Struggling for Recognition: Intensive Mothering's "Practical Effects" in *The Babadook*'. *Quarterly Review of Film and Video*, vol. 37, no. 3, 2020, pp. 1–24.

Mitchell, Paul. 'The Horror of Loss: Reading Jennifer Kent's *The Babadook* as a Trauma Narrative'. *Atlantis*, vol. 41, no. 2, 2019, pp. 179–196.

The Nightingale. Directed by Jennifer Kent, Transmission, 2019.

O'Brien, Gabrielle. 'Surviving Nightmares: Women in Horror'. *Screen Education*, no. 93, 2019, pp. 62–69.

O'Reilly, Nathanael, and Jean-François Vernay. 'Terror Australis Incognita? An Introduction to Fear in Australian Literature and Film'. *Antipodes*, vol. 23, no. 1, 2009, pp. 5–9.

Rayner, Jonathan. 'Gothic Definitions: The New Australian "Cinema of Horrors."' *Antipodes*, vol. 25, no. 1, 2011, pp. 91–97.

Scott, A.O. '*The Nightingale* Review: A Song of Violence and Vengeance'. *New York Times*, 1 Aug. 2019. <www.nytimes.com/2019/08/01/movies/nightingale-review.html>.

Sharf, Zack. '*Hereditary* First Trailer: Sundance's Most Horrifying Film is this Year's *Babadook* and *The Witch*'. *Indiewire*, 31 Jan. 2018. <www.ca.movies.yahoo.com/hereditary-first-trailer-sundance-most-140000307.html>.

Sims, David. '*The Nightingale* is a Harrowing but Worthy Watch'. *Atlantic*, 4 Aug. 2019. <www.theatlantic.com/entertainment/archive/2019/08/jennifer-kent-nightingale-review/595153/>.

Sleeping Beauty. Directed by Julia Leigh, Paramount, 2011.

Smith, Nigel M. '*Under the Shadow* Review: The Feminist Horror Film that Scared Sundance Silly'. *Guardian*, 6 Feb. 2016. <www.theguardian.com/film/2016/feb/05/under-the-shadow-review-feminist-horror-film-sundance-film-festival>.

Transmission Films. '*The Nightingale* Production Notes'. 2018. <www.transmissionfilms.com.au/uploads/media/THENIGHTINGALE_Production_Notes_Transmission_Films.pdf>.

Wilkinson, Alissa. '*Hereditary* is the Terrifying Arthouse Horror Film of the Year'. *Vox*, 10 Jun. 2018. <www.vox.com/summer-movies/2018/6/1/17408988/hereditary-review-toni-collette-milly-shapiro>.

York, Keva. '*The Nightingale* Roots Horror in Tasmania's Colonial History with a Tale of Revenge'. *ABC Arts*, 29 Aug. 2019. <www.abc.net.au/news/2019-08-29/the-nightingale-review-jennifer-kent-tasmanian-history-colonial/11450322>.

Zinoman, Jason. 'Home is Where the Horror Is'. *New York Times*, 7 Jun. 2018. <www.nytimes.com/2018/06/07/movies/hereditary-horror-movies.html>.

Zuckerman, Esther. 'Jennifer Kent's Follow-up to *The Babadook* is the Most Brutal Movie You'll See This Summer'. *Thrillist*, 10 Aug. 2019. <www.thrillist.com/entertainment/nation/the-nightingale-movie-director-jennifer-kent-interview-babadook>.

About the Authors

Jessica Gildersleeve is Associate Professor of English Literature at the University of Southern Queensland. She is the author and editor of several books, including *Christos Tsiolkas: The Utopian Vision* (Cambria 2017), *Don't Look Now* (Auteur 2017), and *The Routledge Companion to Australian Literature* (Routledge 2021).

Amanda Howell is a Senior Lecturer in Screen Studies at Griffith University. Her research on screen, gender, and genre has been published in journals such as *Camera Obscura, Screening the Past,* and *Continuum.* She is currently at work on *Monstrous Possibilities: The Female Monster in 21st-Century Screen Horror* (Palgrave).

Nike Sulway is a Senior Lecturer in Creative and Professional Writing at the University of Southern Queensland. Her research focuses on diversity and inclusivity in creative writing practice and research, as well as on fantasy and fairy tales, science fiction, and the weird. Her recent publications include the award-winning children's novel, *Winter's Tale* (Twelfth Planet 2019), and the novel *Dying in the First Person* (Transit Lounge 2016).

12. From 'Fixer' to 'Freak': Disabling the Ambitious (Mad)Woman in *Wentworth*

Corrine E. Hinton

Abstract

In 2013, Foxtel (SoHo) debuted *Wentworth*, the women-in-prison television drama and remake of *Prisoner: Cell Block H* (1979–1986). Season Two resurrects Joan 'The Freak' Ferguson, the prison's new Governor. While the disturbing and the disturbed are tropes common in both gothic texts and prison dramas, something more sinister lurks within *Wentworth* as viewers witness Ferguson's personal, psychological, and professional disintegration. Positioned within a feminist disability studies framework, this analysis reveals how *Wentworth* deliberately frames Ferguson as a revenge-seeking madwoman, conflating symptoms of psychiatric disorders that ultimately dehumanize her. By adopting the banal archetype of the madwoman as villain and leveraging disability as spectacle, *Wentworth* perpetuates patriarchal and ableist misconceptions about women in power and people with psychiatric disabilities.

Keywords: madwoman; madness; prison drama; psychiatric disorder; feminist disability studies; spectacle

In 2013, Foxtel (SoHo) debuted the women-in-prison drama, *Wentworth*, a remake of the soap opera *Prisoner: Cell Block H* (1979–1986). With its ominous prison landscape, terrifying characters, melodramatic suspense, and frequent themes of powerlessness, *Wentworth* exemplifies contemporary urban-industrial female gothic realism. Suspense-inducing plots by a host of flawed anti-heroines and grotesque villains help the series achieve the unpredictable surprises that keep its transnational viewers watching. Perhaps no other character in *Wentworth* epitomizes the grotesque villain like Governor Joan Ferguson (Pamela Rabe). While Ferguson's character begins

Gildersleeve, J. and K. Cantrell (eds.), *Screening the Gothic in Australia and New Zealand: Contemporary Antipodean Film and Television*. Taylor & Francis Group, 2022
DOI 10.5117/9789463721141_CH12

as 'the fixer', a formidable leader installed to overhaul the prison, she steadily devolves into 'the freak', exposing a flawed ethical code driven by revenge. Seasons two and three follow Ferguson's tumultuous tenure as Governor until her gradual psychological unravelling results in her imprisonment. Positioned within feminist disability studies, this analysis reveals how *Wentworth* deliberately frames Ferguson as the ambitious madwoman, conflating symptoms of psychiatric disorders that ultimately dehumanize her. By adopting the banal archetype of the gothic madwoman as villain and leveraging disability as spectacle, *Wentworth* perpetuates sexist and ableist misconceptions about women in power.

Wentworth as Urban-Industrial Female Gothic Realism

Wentworth reconstructs urban-industrial female gothic realism for contemporary audiences by trapping morally flawed women with sordid histories and violent tendencies inside the maze of Wentworth Correctional Centre. The series achieves the 'topophobia [...] central' to the 'Gothic and its haunted landscape' through themes of suffocating inescapability, danger, and powerlessness in a capitalist system (Marshall 770; Turcotte 127). *Wentworth*'s premier episode follows the perspective of hairdresser Bea Smith (Danielle Cormack), the show's initial protagonist. The naïve and fearful first-time offender is inserted into an 'alien place' and 'victimized by a powerful oppressor': an industrial system that parasitically capitalizes on her emotional, psychological, and physical labour (Turcotte 129). By tapping into 'anxieties and fears that [...] directly relate to female experience', *Wentworth* also assumes conventions of the female Gothic (Bailey 272). Although these fears are situated customarily in 'disturbing domestic spaces', Helen Wheatley credits nineteenth-century women writing about their work in the textile and iron mills as the source of American gothic realism (385). Thus, gothic realism may be inherently driven by women's experiences in any patriarchal system where 'threats to their physical safety and the constant surveillance under strict rules combine to create [...] control over [their] lives' (Marshall 777). *Wentworth*'s women are also subject to industrial oppression that extends beyond imprisonment and into their positions as forced labourers, sophisticatedly illustrated by scenes in the prison laundry, kitchen, and garden.

Gothic realism frequently achieves the *grotesque*, a key convention of the mode, by exposing what is undesirable in human nature. As a show 'depicted through a distinctly female gaze', as Kim Akass argues, *Wentworth* provides viewers with an uncomfortable look into the issues confronting women both inside and outside prison walls (qtd in Ford). Grotesque villains, 'who represent will and power in gothic fiction', are also central to gothic television because they make for ideal representations of what disturbs viewers (Novak 59). In traditional female Gothic, the villain is often male, but *Wentworth* modernizes the convention with its notable female villains. These villainesses are even more despicable, because they not only engage in 'exploitation of the powerless', they also violate the implied ethical code of their shared gender (Marshall 781). For example, Bea struggles to protect her daughter, Debbie (Georgia Flood), from the reaches of villain, Jacqueline 'Jacs' Holt (Kris McQuade). Holt manipulates her own son into seducing and murdering Debbie to gain power over Bea. Bea's debilitating grief and calculated revenge against her nemesis is just one storyline that establishes *Wentworth* as an example of urban-industrial female gothic realism.

Yet, not all of *Wentworth*'s villainesses are locked inside a cell; the series' most noteworthy villain is Governor Joan Ferguson, and her character over seasons two and three provides the subject of this analysis. Framing theory illustrates how the show explicitly guides viewers' perceptions through their portrayal of Ferguson through multiple personae, from masculinized boss bitch to the mental case. Critiquing the show's framing choices within feminist disability studies exposes how *Wentworth*'s adoption of the ambitious madwoman archetype sabotages representations of women in power and people with psychiatric disorders through the interpretations these frames intimate.

Framing the Ambitious Madwoman

The madwoman 'shape[s] how our culture understands illness, femininity, and normality', and the trope's extensive history in literary and popular culture has generated significant scholarly inquiry across disciplines (Garland-Thomson, 'Feminist Disability Studies' 1564). One version of this trope is the assertive but volatile, unethical madwoman of the workplace. This ambitious madwoman is often trying to gain or maintain power or position in careers from which women have been historically excluded, such as criminal justice, politics, or the military. Since the ambitious madwoman cannot fulfill her goals saddled by children, she is often childless or an aberrant (Walters and Harrison), ambivalent (Greer), or a bad mother (Lotz, 'Really Bad Mothers'). Her intimate relationships are non-existent, tumultuous, or abusive. She may be lesbian, bisexual, or asexual as a sign of her empowerment from, or her repudiation by, the heteropatriarchy (Rowe and Chávez; Schlichter). When the ambitious madwoman's unchecked emotions or uncontrolled mind make her dangerous, she becomes an ideal villain (Schultz and Youn). Rosemarie Garland-Thomson hints at the ways in which monstrosity and the grotesque are often metaphorically represented through 'appearance impairments' to bodies and minds like those implied by the madwoman ('Feminist Disability Studies' 1579). A central complication of the madwoman trope, then, is the dual coding of 'mad' as both anger and madness. When a woman's anger is falsely conflated with signals of mental instability, her power and competence as a self-expressive emotional being are questioned. Likewise, dismissing legitimate symptoms of untreated mental illness through the 'metaphoric use of madness' as irrational emotional outbursts 'erases or distorts experiences of disability' (Hillsburg 3).

To those ends, then, the madwoman is often a 'spectacle character', a term August Wilson coined to describe his characters with disabilities whose 'presence [was] troubling to power structures within their respective dramas' (McCormick 66). Disruption, a prominent feature of spectacle characters, acts as a mechanism of their empowerment and, simultaneously, their disempowerment. Jennifer L. Schulz and JiHyun Youn unearth three cinematic variations of female madness: madness as neurosis, monstrosity as ambition, and madness/monstrosity as failed motherhood. They find that 'the construction and cultural deployment of female monstrosity is [...] a project of subjugation that seeks to immobilize women of ambition and intellect, and leave them bereft of purpose [...] and ultimately, power' (Schulz and Youn 2). Hence, the ambitious madwoman-as-villain is abusive and abused, wielded for the sake of helping more sympathetic characters take their places as martyrs or heroes. She has no independent storyline and no future except imprisonment, obscurity, or death. These are indeed erroneous albeit robustly constructed pools from which audiences can draw their perceptions of psychiatric disorders and the people living with them.

Personae non gratae

As Governor of Wentworth, Joan Ferguson's monstrosity is signalled through the instability of her identity as she devolves from the methodical 'fixer' to the dehumanized 'freak' throughout seasons two and three. For Judith Halberstam, despite the evolving faces and bodies of gothic monsters, their power to horrify audiences relies, in great part, on their instability, unpredictability, and constant reconfiguring of Otherness. Ferguson's traits and behaviours, combined with the technical elements of camera, lighting, and music, work together to compose each of her monstrous personae: the masculinized boss bitch, the immoral manipulator, the violent predator, the dehumanized psychopath, and the mental case. As each of Ferguson's personae is removed, the Governor loses control of her prison and herself. Interlacing these personae are embedded fencing scenes and flashbacks that provide contextual clues about Ferguson's traumatic past and destabilizing present. Despite her previous traumas and the situations within the seasons that trigger traumatic responses, Ferguson is not framed rhetorically as a 'sentimental' character with mental illness, a construct that would encourage the audience to read her as 'sympathetic victim or helpless sufferer' (Garland-Thompson, 'The Politics of Staring' 63). Rather, as Vera Chouinard contends, Ferguson is visually and rhetorically signalled as 'monstrous' (793). Framing this typology within the work of Halberstam's cultural examinations of monsters, Chouinard explains that postmodern Gothic constructions of monstrous characters are those that generate fear through 'the façade of the normal', infiltrating a space and gradually 'work[ing] their way out' (793). By the season three finale, viewers are led to interpret Ferguson's choices as indicative of her fulfilling her ultimate role as psychopathic villain rather than as a woman whose behaviours are signs of a trauma-induced degrading mental state.

Act I: The Masculinized Boss Bitch

Starting with her season two debut, Ferguson steps into a familiar archetype for powerful women in leadership positions: the masculinized 'boss bitch'. The 'bitch' trope is an exaggerated characterization evolved from television's new woman of the 1970s (Ferguson; Lotz, *Redesigning Women*; Schmidt). The boss bitch was born from a fascination with and skepticism about career women in positions of power, especially in leadership roles within predominantly male-dominated professions including policing and criminal justice. Often, this tension is demonstrated onscreen through other characters' confusion about how to properly gender-code a woman leader or about how to leader-code a woman. For example, in analyzing Helen Mirren's Jane Tennison in *Prime Suspect* (1991–2006), Charlotte Brunsdon notes that 'the novelty of a female officer leading a murder investigation is signaled through the difficulty other officers have in addressing her' (384). Upending traditional patriarchal structures unapologetically, the boss bitch often finds herself in a 'discursively unmanageable position', where even the most basic of speech acts – giving orders to subordinates – 'queers her ability to exercise her agency through speech' (Kukla 447). Some boss bitches further adopt the 'masculinized boss bitch' archetype: strong professional women 'who have sacrificed their femininity and their niceness in their journey to the top' (Brunsdon 385). The masculinized boss bitch performs constructions of masculinity visually and/or discursively to secure her professional power untethered to the trappings of femininity. As such, she is Othered. Whether accomplished in the world of law like Annalise Keating (Viola Davis) in *How to Get Away with Murder* (2014–2020), in politics as the first female President of the United States like Claire Underwood (Robin Wright) in *House of Cards* (2013–2018), or in federal law enforcement like (double) Agent Nina Meyers (Sarah Clarke) in *24* (2001–2010), the masculinized boss bitch poses a greater risk for vilification than celebration on the small screen.

As Governor, Ferguson operates in ways that portray her as an assertive, unemotional leader with a desire for control, order, and obedience. Her tightly wrapped bun, pressed uniform, and authoritative posture affirm these traits. Ferguson's premier monologue in 'Born Again' transports viewers from watching her ready herself for her first day at Wentworth into her first briefing with the staff, and it sets the tone for how she perceives their place within the corrections system: 'Society has deemed these women defective, and it's our job to fix them. Not to pander, to befriend, to indulge, or to accommodate: we exist to *correct*. [...] Each and every person here will know their place. This is a prison, and we are in charge'. Her need for order is also signalled through nuances such as her tidy workspace. Technical aspects accentuate the Governor that *Wentworth* wants viewers to see. Her walk becomes one of her signatures – unerring, heavy, and deliberate – the length of her stride accentuated by a low-angled camera. Ferguson's body insinuates control of the room. When addressing her subordinates, she is typically positioned on one side of the shot with her staff looking at her – such as the staff meeting scenes in 'Born Again' and 'Boys in the Yard'. This configuration emphasizes a dictatorial nature that complements her indisputable position as Governor.

How others respond to Ferguson also highlights her initial persona. After Ferguson disrupts top dog Franky Doyle's (Nicole da Silva) drug operation within her first ten minutes on screen, Franky asks fellow prisoner, Liz Birdsworth (Celia Ireland), for information about the new Governor. Liz relays that Ferguson was transferred from another prison where she earned the nickname, 'The Fixer'. Ferguson applies the moniker to her philosophy about prisons and about people. Her need to 'fix' people is exemplified by her unsolicited mentorship of Deputy Governor, Vera Bennett (Kate

Atkinson). Vera speaks quickly, is indecisive, and avoids eye contact. Her passive, fumbling nature exaggerates Ferguson's precision and self-assurance. Physically, too, the women are foils of one another. Actress Pamela Rabe stands six feet tall, towering over 5'3" Kate Atkinson, emphasized as the pair are frequently shown together. The Governor's discourse also reflects self-control; she speaks at a lower register with little inflection, her lips and mouth moving only as much as necessary. Her speech is well articulated and free of any casual colloquialisms or contractions.

To code her demeanour as masculine, Ferguson is blatantly defeminized. While the other women personnel wear skirts, Ferguson wears pants and a blazer, buttoned and cinched to erase any noticeable contour from her breasts. Her face, with minimal makeup and no jewellery, rarely shows emotion. In the event viewers do not recognize these sartorial signals as strategies to obfuscate Ferguson's gender, two scenes help them see Ferguson as the inmates see her. In season two's 'Boys in the Yard', Sky (Kathryn Beck) paints a vulgar cartoon of Ferguson on a wall in the yard. Ferguson's likeness (including her bun) features a giant penis protruding from where her breasts would be accompanied by the label, 'FERG-ARSE'. During season three's 'Goldfish', the Governor's gender and sexuality are mocked when Lucy 'Juice' Gambaro (Sally-Anne Upton) accuses Ferguson of being the 'father' of Doreen Anderson's (Shareena Clanton) unborn baby. To the inmates, and by consequence *Wentworth* viewers, Ferguson's demeanour reeks of masculine aggression rather than feminine amicability.

Yet, Ferguson demonstrates compassion in some of season two's early moments. After inmates destroy Doreen's yard roses, Ferguson suggests they build a garden to 'give the women something to do' ('Born Again'). Ferguson agrees to Doreen's requests for resources to create the garden shed ('Whatever It Takes'), ultimately facilitating Doreen's interactions with Nash Taylor (Luke McKenzie). Nash, a Walford inmate who helps with the project, falls in love with (and impregnates) Doreen. Ferguson also shows an interest in mentoring Vera Bennett, telling her, 'You stick with me, and we'll achieve great things together' ('Born Again') in the opening episode of season two, and in the episode following, Ferguson invites Vera for drinks in her office so the two can get to know one another. The Governor raises a toast, vodka tonic in hand: 'Here is to trust: the basis of teamwork and to having someone who can share the load' ('Whatever It Takes'). The moment offers some hope for the women holding the two most powerful positions in Wentworth. As quickly as this collegiality develops, it is cast aside when the scene also gives viewers their first glimpse into Ferguson's next persona, the immoral manipulator.

Act II: The Immoral Manipulator

Ferguson's masculinized boss bitch persona persists until nearly the end of season three, but as early as episode two ('Whatever It Takes'), viewers learn to question her motives. In this second act, Ferguson unveils her cunning and opportunism. Her behaviours and speech shift as well, as do the technical aspects of production that frame her as the immoral manipulator.

As Ferguson and Vera indulge in vodka tonics after work in 'Whatever It Takes', Ferguson retreats to the backroom for refills. The camera shows Ferguson overfilling Vera's glass with vodka, while the Governor drinks only tonic water. A now-intoxicated Vera confesses to a brief romance with Officer Matthew Fletcher (Aaron Jeffery). During their time together, Vera learns of a sexual affair between Fletcher and Officer Will Jackson's (Robbie Magasiva) wife (Catherine McClements). In this moment, viewers begin to question Ferguson's moral compass. Vera is just the first of many people Ferguson manipulates. Soon after her onscreen arrival in 'Born Again', Ferguson calls Franky Doyle into her office to negotiate a mutually beneficial deal, and the seasoned inmate is sceptical of the Governor's intentions. As a character who viewers have known since *Wentworth*'s premier, Franky's scepticism keeps them from accepting the new Governor's proposition, or her character, as genuine. Doyle verifies those feelings when she tells her fellow inmates, 'Ferguson's a fuckin' player'. The Governor also converts Liz Birdsworth into an informant by convincing the older, motherly inmate that informing will help keep other women safe ('The Pink Dragon'). The inmates are not the only people Ferguson wilfully manipulates.

Some of Ferguson's manipulations of prison personnel are opportunistic plays toward ensuring her power as Governor. For example, in season two's 'Jail Birds', Ferguson is annoyed when Derek Channing (Martin Sacks), Regional General Manager of Corrections, arrives to conduct a review of the prison. Ferguson sees Channing's visit as an intrusion and suspects he may have ulterior motives (chiefly, having her ousted). To protect herself, Ferguson unearths something that she can use against him, confronts Channing with this career-ending information, and threatens to expose him unless he agrees to provide a 'sympathetic ear' to other members on the Board of Corrections. He acquiesces. Ferguson's intuition about Channing's motives was correct; Officer Fletcher, facing an unwanted transfer to another facility, has conspired with Channing. When Fletcher accosts Channing for an update, he learns the investigation has been 'put on hold'. An apoplectic Fletcher screams, 'She got to you, didn't she?' This sequence further reveals Ferguson as an immoral manipulator through direct observations of her choices and indirectly through her reputation as someone willing to threaten others to keep her job.

Ferguson also shows her ability to adapt her speech and behaviours as part of her cunning. When Ferguson's normally polished discourse errs, she does so in an intentional attempt to align herself with another character. In an effort to convince a despondent Susan 'Boomer' Jenkins (Katrina Milosevic) to surrender information about another inmate, Ferguson tries to get her talking: 'Hey, that Bea Smith, she got ya pretty upset the other evening at the phones, yeah?' ('Into the Night'). To a casual observer the change may not noticeable, but the calculating Ferguson considers every choice she makes. Debasing her professional discourse with clipped phrases ('you' to 'ya'), an informal greeting, and the confirmation-seeking 'yeah', to align herself to Boomer is a coercive tactic. Ferguson's body positions also shift as she enacts the immoral manipulator, and the camera work emphasizes these changes. Unlike her posture as the straight-backed, cross-armed masculinized boss bitch, the immoral manipulator hovers over the people she is threatening. Her height is often accentuated to create an enveloping effect. In 'The Pink Dragon', Ferguson visits Franky in solitary, her body consuming the entirety of the door frame. The light casts Ferguson's shadow on the inside of Franky's wall, making it appear as if she is surrounded by the Governor. In the scene, Franky is on the floor exercising and looks up to Ferguson from the lowest point, making Ferguson appear even more intimidating. Camera angles and Ferguson's position within the frame are leveraged to allow her to dominate the shot, just as she dominates people.

The Fencing Scenes, Part I

Viewers can investigate the inner workings of Ferguson's mind during several fencing scenes peppered throughout seasons two and three. Each scene provides actual and symbolic clues into Ferguson's decision making while accentuating her maliciousness, creating connective tissue across Ferguson's various personae.

At the end of season two's 'Whatever It Takes', Ferguson appears in her first fencing scene, a moment disruptive to the audience's experience when it appears without any discoursal guidance by the characters. The scene also takes place in an unfamiliar setting: a room lit by a row of windows along one wall, a mat, and a bench. Two fencers are mid-match, their sabres clanging to the aria, 'L'altra notto in fondo al mare', from Arrigo Boito's *Mefistofele*. In the opera, Faust makes a deal with the devil, Mefistofele, in exchange for reclaiming his youth. The rejuvenated Faust persuades Margherita to give her mother a sleeping concoction, so she can sneak out to have sex with him. The devil later deceives Faust, but Margherita is the victim. Accused of poisoning her mother and drowning the child she bore, Margherita sings 'L'altra notto in fondo al mare' from her prison cell, questioning her sanity. The musical choice is deliberate, a metaphor foreshadowing Ferguson's trauma and madness. As the vocalist reaches a crescendo, one fencer strikes. Ferguson removes her mask, pleased with her victory. Her opponent (Alex Menglet) nods his approval.

A second fencing scene occurs four episodes later in 'The Pink Dragon'. By this time, Ferguson is actively inhabiting both her masculinized boss bitch and immoral manipulator identities. This time, viewers can see Ferguson's face behind the hood as she faces off against a new opponent while the man from the first bout observes. Ferguson is victorious again, earning the man's praise and a reminder: 'Selecting the accurate time to start your attack is as important as the choice of attack. Yes? Draw their advance. Once you've lured them, parry and thrust'. Ferguson listens intently, the advice doubling as confirmation of the Governor's manipulative ways.

The fencing scene from 'Metamorphosis' provides further insight into Ferguson's decision making. Ferguson is on the attack but loses when she fails to capitalize on her opponent's vulnerability. Her frustration is visible as she rips off her hood and storms toward the bench. The familiar man enquires about her hesitation, and she justifies her strategy by positioning it within a moral argument: 'It was the sporting thing to do'. Ferguson's response shows she has a moral code and is capable of exercising it. Her coach discounts it as a flaw that jeopardizes victory. 'It was the weak thing to do', he corrects, 'the time to strike is when he's on his knees. A lesser opponent will rise up when given the slightest opportunity. You must be ruthless'. Ferguson applies her coach's advice to her leadership, as she mounts a counterattack against Franky Doyle. She hints that Franky may have an informant in her crew, capitalizing on the top dog's weakness by sowing seeds of deceit as a distraction.

Ferguson has learned to be relentless, to be ruthless, and to chuck morality for the guarantee of victory. The fencing scenes alongside the progression of Ferguson's character prompt the audience to consider the fencing coach's advice relative to Ferguson's strategy as Governor: consider when and how to strike for the greatest impact, 'lure' the subject in, initiate the 'attack', and do not stop until victory is achieved. His advice aligns with Ferguson's approach as the immoral manipulator: strategic, clandestine, relentless, and effective. Likewise, the scenes provide additional signals to the audience framing Ferguson as a likely villain, a role solidified as Ferguson enters her third act: the violent predator.

Act III: The Violent Predator

More than halfway through season two, viewers have come to question Ferguson's motives, and signs of a malevolence worse than bad decision making are starting to appear. Ferguson's persona of the violent predator shows a woman responding to people challenging her power through coordinating and committing violent attacks. In 'The Fixer', Ferguson threatens, authorizes, or commits violence three times against Doreen Anderson. Doreen's pregnancy has been discovered by prison personnel, and Ferguson feels betrayed. In one of the creepiest episode openings, Ferguson lets herself into Doreen's cell in the middle of the night to interrogate her about her rumoured pregnancy. Doreen denies the allegation, so Ferguson pulls on a tight-fitting black, leather glove and slaps her hard in the face. Later in the episode, Ferguson wants Doreen to name Officer Jackson as the father of her child, but Doreen refuses. Ferguson changes tactics, recounting the story of an inmate whose child was taken from her by a social worker. Doreen, angry at the thought of losing her child, attempts to stand up to Ferguson. Just when viewers think Doreen has reclaimed some ounce of power, Ferguson shoots back: 'There are other ways to lose a baby, Doreen'. Doreen remains unpersuaded, and at the end of 'The Fixer', a dead magpie flies through her cell's port door, the same bird she and Nash raised from a baby while working on the garden project together. The episode ends as Doreen falls to her knees and screams out in grief. While a dead bird, even a murdered bird, is on its own not indicative of a credible threat, Ferguson's behaviour is interpreted in concert with the threats and actual violence to which she has subjected the pregnant inmate. The pregnant body, itself a 'destabilizing' symbol 'between the inside and outside' in female Gothic, is vulnerable under any circumstance (Karlyn 11). But for an imprisoned woman whose child is also imprisoned with and *within* her, the pregnant body is made entirely defenceless. As such, threats against Doreen are inconceivable violations of human decency; having made such threats repeatedly, Ferguson begins her descent into the dehumanized psychopath.

Ferguson commits additional acts of violence against prisoners and orchestrates violence against some of her subordinates. She steals prescription medication from Vera and slips them to prisoner, Simone Slater, to murder her and make it look like a drug overdose ('The Pink Dragon').

She beats transfer inmate, Kelly Bryant, to keep her quiet about her past indiscretions at Blackmoor ('Into the Night'). When Officer Fletcher gathers too much intelligence on Ferguson from inmate Bryant, Ferguson has her henchman, Nils Jasper, run him over in the season two finale. Jasper, working under Ferguson's orders, also runs Officer Jackson off the road while on his motorcycle with nurse Rose ('The Fixer'). As the second season of *Wentworth* starts to come to a close, Ferguson becomes more violent, solidifying her status as the show's most formidable, conniving, and dangerous villain.

To complement her persona as the violent predator, the Governor's body movements become more dynamic and terrorizing. In season two's 'The Fixer', Ferguson walks around Doreen, fixated on her, stalking her as she conveys her disappointment and demands the identity of her baby's father. Ferguson also begins to move around the prison at night like a killer looking for prey, often lit only by single lamps from the prison's security lighting. To generate suspense around Ferguson's movement, the camera focuses on her legs and feet, surrounded by the space of a darkened hallway or dimly lit stairs. In season three's 'Knives Out', movement catches Franky's attention in the darkness of the solitary unit. She peeks out of the small glass window in time to see a frightened Jodie Spiteri walk by, held by the shoulder of a black-gloved officer. Only the officer's torso and arm are visible, but the camera rolls to slow motion in time to catch the nametag: Joan Ferguson. In addition to fracturing Ferguson's body through close-up shots, her violent predator persona is also accentuated by camera work that makes her appear and disappear seemingly from nowhere. Cloaked in conventions that mimic the haunted passageways of Victorian mansions, prisoners, staff, and viewers alike are incapable of tracking the elusive Governor.

The Flashbacks

Ferguson's behaviours in season two's 'The Fixer' catapults her from immoral manipulator to violent predator, epitomized most saliently by her mistreatment of Doreen Anderson. A series of flashbacks about Ferguson's past provides some rationale for Ferguson's misplaced mistreatment. While an officer at Blackmoor, a younger Ferguson had a secret relationship with prisoner, Jianna Riley, whom she promises to 'protect' ('The Fixer'). Like Doreen, Jianna becomes pregnant, and when Jianna laments her baby will grow up without a father, Ferguson promises Jianna she will not be 'alone'. When Jianna gives birth to her son, he lives with her in the prison until the Governor decides the baby is a 'disruption to the smooth running of his prison'. A social worker, a younger Will Jackson, arrives, and Ferguson watches him remove the child from Jianna's custody. Ferguson is inconsolable when she discovers Jianna has hanged herself in grief.

During 'The Fixer', Ferguson shares portions of Jianna's story but deliberately omits her own involvement; viewers must follow textual and visual clues to identify the experience as a source of significant trauma. Ferguson's commentary reveals that 'it was very traumatic' for the officer, who had 'naturally formed a very close bond' with the baby, to see him removed. Ferguson's trauma from losing Jianna and her son is substantiated further as she conflates these memories with Doreen's current experience. The frequency of the flashbacks – four in a single episode – convey importance, especially as each spends time with an aspect of Ferguson's past. The intimate bond Ferguson shared with Jianna, her promise to protect Jianna, the future she envisions for Jianna and her baby: Ferguson fails to realize these. Viewers can see the lasting impact of these failures on Ferguson as the Governor exhibits symptoms of struggling to reorient herself to the present.

Despite the impact they have on Ferguson's functioning, the flashbacks are not framed as a trauma designed to elicit sympathy for the Governor based on any guilt she may feel or grief she may still be processing; rather, they are framed as the incidents motivating the Governor's revenge plot against Officer Jackson. Ferguson's malice is confirmed when the final flashback is initiated during an interaction with Jackson. When he is arrested for damaging a vehicle (an arrest Ferguson orchestrates), Ferguson secures his release. During the car ride home from the police station, Ferguson tells Jackson, 'I don't want to lose the most valuable officer I have'. Viewers will not read the compliment as genuine, because Ferguson's expression, away from Jackson's view, mutates from a casual smile to a grimace. When Ferguson and Jackson ride together in silence, the episode's final minutes roll out to a cover of Tears for Fears' 'Mad World', foreshadowing the next persona to be revealed: the dehumanized psychopath.

Act IV: The Dehumanized Psychopath

The unveiling of Governor's plot against Will Jackson in tandem with her behaviours as the immoral manipulator and the violent predator cement Ferguson as the show's central villain. Yet, *Wentworth* does not stop at portraying her as the angry (mad), revenge-fuelled woman. Instead, viewers are instructed to trace her actions to undiagnosed psychopathy; Ferguson becomes the madwoman. These signals, located in Ferguson's behavioural changes as well as other discoursal indicators in the show, begin at the finale of season two and build throughout season three. The already defeminized, immoral, violent Ferguson mutates into the dehumanized psychopath, the consequences of which render her a monster devoid of any redeemable value.

The season two finale, itself directing viewers through its title 'Fear Her', lays some critical groundwork on which Ferguson constructs new attributes as the dehumanized psychopath. In separate incidents, Officer Fletcher and Bea Smith provide additional cues to viewers repainting Ferguson as a psychopath. After Fletcher learns about Ferguson's past, he confronts her: 'I know about Jianna, and what you did to those prisoners. You're not a Governor; you're a fucking psychopath'. At the end of the season finale, when Bea has been captured after escaping, Ferguson is waiting for her when the prisoner transport van arrives. As Bea heads back into Wentworth, she looks at Ferguson and sneers, 'Freak'. Bea's moniker is the last word the audience hears as the season wraps.

The language of the 'freak' and the 'psychopath' reappear in season three, ensuring viewers see continuity in Ferguson's newest persona. The prisoners adopt Bea's 'freak' identifier, framing the Governor as someone who does not inhabit a space of ablenormativity and, further still, someone who may not even be a person at all. 'Freak' has a long connection with the monstrous, an inescapable association with the spectacle performers with 'severe physical deformities and abnormalities' from the travelling freak shows (Grande 19). Later, when the women riot and assume control of the prison, the voice of Lucy 'Juice' Gambaro growls into the radio to assert their demands: 'Ferguson, you fucking freak, answer me' ('The Governor's Pleasure'). In 'The Long Game', Maxine (Socratis Otto) embraces the term, asking Bea, 'What are you gonna do about the freak?' The repetitive use of the disparaging identifier not only continues to separate the othered Ferguson from normative characters but also acts as a strategy to dehumanize her entirely.

While the prisoners take up the discourse of the 'freak', the prison personnel adopt the more clinical language of 'psychopath'. Importantly, the latter signifier comes from a new character with the expertise to wield it: Dr Bridget Westfall, the new prison psychologist and Ferguson's foil. Westfall is professional, credible, intelligent, and coded feminine with her visibly long hair, jewellery, exposed neckline, and bust-accentuating clothing. When the two debate the value of emotions, Westfall claims that being too emotional is better than not being emotional at all. Though Ferguson scoffs, she asks Westfall to explain. 'A deficit of emotion, particularly a lack of affective empathy would make you psychopathic', the psychologist replies ('Goldfish'). Westfall's comments are not just innuendo. In 'Freak Show', Vera wonders about Ferguson's motives, so Westfall points Vera to her session notes. Vera scours the doctor's records and locates Westfall's hypothesis about Ferguson's 'psychopathic indicators'. Taken together, the inmates' and prison personnel's discourse simultaneously diagnose, dehumanize, and condemn Joan Ferguson.

Notable alterations in Ferguson's behaviours, body movements, and her portrayal on camera depict a Governor losing control. The normally collected, unflinching Ferguson spends more time screaming at people and enacting more casual violence publicly. Her even tone becomes nearly unrecognizable as she screams at, and pushes, Vera out of Doreen's delivery room in 'Goldfish', and slaps her in 'The Living and the Dead'. During moments of frustration, Ferguson continues to act aggressively and in ways that deliberately create chaos of out order – behaviours that contend with the image created by the masculinized boss bitch. In 'Goldfish', for example, she destroys her own house: disorganizing her perfectly arranged silverware, smashing her glassware, and hurdling her fishbowl to the ground. In 'A Higher Court', she heaves a row of neatly arranged pencils against the glass wall of her office. She also begins resorting to childish ridiculing – a shift from her well-composed, biting insults. Ferguson calls her Deputy Governor 'delusional' when she wants to investigate Bea's overdose as an attack, but Vera ignores her. In the darkness, Ferguson surprises Vera mid-investigation, insults her intelligence, and spontaneously mocks her ('The Long Game'). In 'The Living and the Dead', Officer Fletcher stammers in denial when Ferguson accuses him of breaking into her office. Ferguson mocks the brain-injured Officer, waves her hands wildly, and shouts, 'Just stop! With the inarticulation, the slack jaw, and the Neanderthal gait'. Especially telling about these moments is that Ferguson marks disability as a weakness and the source of her mockery. Both Bea and Vera are disregarded for being defective (Bea is 'delusional', and Vera is 'stupid' enough to believe her). Likewise, Fletcher, whose 'accident' has left him with cognitive and mobility impairments, is disregarded and marginalized because his defects make him weak.

Wentworth also signals Ferguson's transfiguration from defeminized to dehumanized by infusing more Gothicism into the performative and technical elements. Her natural height, amplified throughout the series, starts to adopt a monstrous look through exaggerated shadows. Ferguson's presence is conjured through mysterious slamming doors and shadows that disappear around corners, such as the opening of 'A Higher Court'. She starts twisting her neck, as if attempting to loosen it from her spine. Her face animates in irregular movements, her twitching upper lips and teeth clenching distortedly. Inmates vocalize their concerns about Ferguson's humanness. When the Governor visits Bea Smith in the solitary unit, Bea chides, 'What sort of human being puts a person at risk just to prove a point?' ('The Governor's Pleasure'). Bea answers her own question later when she calls Ferguson a 'monster'. The dehumanized psychopath is imprinted successfully as Ferguson's next persona, because viewers have the ability to compare her volatile and irrational behaviours to those of the controlled, rational masculinized boss bitch. What viewers may not realize, however, is how Wentworth has been methodically building Ferguson toward her final persona as Governor: the mental case.[1]

Act V: The Mental Case and the Fencing Scenes, Part II

As the dehumanized psychopath, Ferguson is an evil, destructive villain who hurts others because 'she needs to see them hurt'. Her acts, while despicable, are constructed as rational choices driven by her insatiable desire to cause pain. As viewers become familiar with Ferguson's persona as the dehumanized psychopath, the final five episodes of season three contain revelations that convert Ferguson to mental case. The act of unveiling Ferguson's psychiatric disorder simultaneously becomes her undoing; that is, the moment she is revealed as 'insane' is the same moment she goes from a capably evil villainess to an incompetent mental case. Ferguson's persona of the mental case begins with a series of traumatic events in season three's 'Goldfish'. Thus, a thorough recounting of major events in the episode is necessary.

In the opening scene, Ferguson arrives home after work, and the audience sees her ritualized lifestyle. She methodically removes uniform items; her freezer is stocked with perfectly aligned shot glasses; and her refrigerator is filled with matching storage containers of microwavable food. She eats dinner alone, the mournful sounds of 'Stabat Mater Dolorosa' playing in the background. Ferguson stops eating upon discovering her goldfish is floating lifelessly in its bowl. She retrieves the body, pokes at the fish, and asks,

---

1   I do not use the term 'mental case' as a way to disparage people with psychiatric disorders or those living with mental health issues. Rather, the term reflects the mediatized representation of characters with mental illness or psychiatric disorders, as generated by repetitive, often hyperbolic, narratives and images.

'What's wrong with you?' Like other questions asked during season three, this one hints at implications beyond the immediate subject in the scene.

The next day, Ferguson meets with Westfall to discuss the rumours that she and Franky are engaged in an inappropriate relationship. During the conversation, Ferguson scoffs at Franky for being 'far too emotional for her own good'. Westfall tells Ferguson that a lack of emotion would make someone 'psychopathic', and the Governor finds herself introspectively conflicted. In the fencing scene that follows, Ferguson loses. Distracted by her conversation with Westfall, Ferguson asks her coach if he thinks her lack of emotion is a 'deficit in [her] that needs correcting'. Their conversation carries into a voiceover during which Ferguson admits, 'You've always taught me that to know your enemy, you must get inside their skin, become your enemy. But if you're enemy *feels*, is *emotional*—'. The man cuts in, explaining that emotions are a 'weakness', and Ferguson's 'greatest advantage' is that she is not 'hampered by emotions'. Detaching Ferguson from the humanness of emotional connection and weaponizing her apathy alienates her further, enhancing the Otherness necessary for contemporary monsters in gothic realism.

The scene cuts to Ferguson staring at her reflection in the window of her darkened office, her face barely illuminated by the external security lamp. She holds her gaze for a long twelve seconds of silence. The lighting, the stillness of her figure, and the silence generate a disquieting eeriness. When Ferguson finally turns away from the window, her reflection maintains its position like an apparition. Having experienced no other ghostly moments in the show's history, *Wentworth* viewers could easily dismiss the anomaly. But this leap from gothic realism to more Victorian Gothic, with the infusion of the supernatural, is deliberate, giving viewers visual cues as Ferguson's mental case persona is exposed.

Other clues to Ferguson's degrading mental state also appear in 'Goldfish'. Ferguson rekindles her fondness for Doreen and invites the mum-to-be into the kitchen for some ice cream. Watching from the shadows, Ferguson tells Doreen, 'Just as long as you enjoy it, Jianna, that's all that matters'. Doreen stops suddenly at the oblivious Governor's mistake but does not correct her. Further into the episode, Ferguson visits Doreen and promises to 'protect' her. Doreen allows Ferguson to touch her pregnant belly, reliving the same intimate moment she once shared with Jianna. Ferguson leans in as if to kiss Doreen, but Doreen's waters break. Baby Joshua is born healthy in the medical unit, with Ferguson by Doreen's side for the birth. While the Governor checks on the ambulance, Bea Smith enters the medical unit. Doreen tells her what she's learned about Ferguson and Jianna, describing the Governor's behaviour as 'weird and creepy', and concludes, 'she really is a freak'. Unbeknownst to them, Ferguson is listening on the other side of the curtain, seething. Doreen's ridicule, a reminder of her forced separation from Jianna intermingled with humiliation in being dehumanized once again, catalyses Ferguson's unravelling.

At the end of 'Goldfish', Ferguson returns home, enraged. She bangs her fists against the wall, kicks off her shoes, yanks her hair out of its perfect bun, and destroys the inside of her perfectly kept house. The man from the fencing scenes appears, trying to control her. She sinks to the floor and bangs her head against his chest, repeating, 'I'm a freak'. He strokes her hair, trying to calm her by refuting her claim. Her face contorts as she confirms, 'I am, Dad'. When Ferguson acknowledges to the man – who viewers now know is her father – that she accepts her identity as a 'freak', the label signifies her as both dehumanized psychopath and the mental case. The episode deliberately frames Ferguson's order-chaos, controlled-uncontrolled, human-nonhuman bifurcation through the bookends of the opening and closing scenes. Ferguson is, as she was upon Jianna's death, alone. Doreen's repudiation, in concert with reliving the birth of a son that is not hers, sends Ferguson into emotional turmoil similar to reactive psychosis.

Ferguson's madness fails her and, as such, it fails any goals in achieving patriarchal or ablenormative disruption without sacrificing the woman herself. Writing about another women-in-prison drama, *Orange is the New Black* (2013–2019), Lydia Brown asserts, that '[f]or as long as madness exists primarily as spectacle for neurotypical entertainment while reifying danger-ously ableist ideas of what psychiatric disability or madness *ought* to look like, the show cannot possibly do justice to people with any kind of mental disability' (178). The choice to prioritize the terror generated by the gothic madwoman over any stigma the archetype substantiates commits the same injustice: atypicality must surrender to neurotypicality, psychiatric disorder must surrender to cognitive order, feminine irrationality must surrender to masculine rationality. Unsurprisingly, most vilified characters with mental illness ultimately find themselves separated from their neurotypical counterparts, 'if not killed [...] then through incarceration' (Chouinard 793). Joan Ferguson, viewers are led to believe, suffers both fates in subsequent seasons. In the end, with its syndicated audience across more than 140 territories watching, *Wentworth* teaches audiences that when women attempt to gain or maintain positions of power, they must fail, disabled by their own hands or minds.

Works Cited

Bailey, Peggy Dunn. 'Female Gothic Fiction, Grotesque Realities, and *Bastard Out of Carolina*: Dorothy Allison Revises the Southern Gothic'. *The Mississippi Quarterly*, vol. 63, no. 2, 2010, pp. 269–290.

'Born Again'. *Wentworth*, written by Pete McTighe, directed by Kevin Carlin, season 2, episode 1, SoHo, 20 May 2014.

'Boys in the Yard'. *Wentworth*, written by Timothy Hobart, directed by Catherine Millar, season 2, episode 3, SoHo, 3 June 2014.

Brown, Lydia. '"You Don't Feel Like Such a Freak Anymore": Representing Disability, Madness, and Trauma in Litchfield Penitentiary'. *Feminist Perspectives on Orange is the New Black: Thirteen Critical Essays*, edited by April Kalogeropoulos Householder and Adrienne Trier-Bieniek, McFarland, 2016.

Brunsdon, Charlotte. 'Television Crime Series, Women Police, and Fuddy-Duddy Feminism'. *Feminist Media Studies*, vol. 13, no. 3, 2013, pp. 375–394.

Chouinard, Vera. 'Placing the "Mad Woman": Troubling Cultural Representations of Being a Woman with Mental Illness in *Girl Interrupted*'. *Social & Cultural Geography*, vol. 10, no. 7, Nov. 2009, pp. 791–804.

Devlyn, Darren. '*Wentworth*: Inside the Show's Global Success'. *Foxtel Insider News*. 2 May 2017. <www.foxtel.com.au/whats-on/foxtel-insider/showcase/wentworth/season-5/did-you-know.html>.

'Fear Her'. *Wentworth*, written by Pete McTighe, directed by Kevin Carlin, season 2, episode 12, SoHo, 5 Aug. 2014.

Ferguson, Mary Anne. *Images of Women in Literature*. Houghton Mifflin, 1973.

'The Fixer'. *Wentworth*, written by John Ridley, directed by Steve Jodrell, season 2, episode 9, SoHo, 15 July 2014.

Ford, Jessica. '*Wentworth* is the New Prisoner Conference Report'. *CST Online*. 4 May 2018. <www.cstonline.net/wentworth-is-the-new-prisoner-conference-report-by-jessica-ford/>.

'Freak Show'. *Wentworth*, written by Adam Todd, directed by Catherine Millar, season 3, episode 9, SoHo, 2 June 2015.

Garland-Thomson, Rosemarie. 'Feminist Disability Studies'. *Signs*, vol. 30, no. 2, 2005, pp. 1557–1587.

Garland-Thomson, Rosemarie. 'The Politics of Staring: Visual Rhetorics of Disability in Popular Photography'. *Disability Studies: Enabling the Humanities*, edited by Sharon L. Snyder, Brenda Jo Brueggemann, and Rosemarie Garland-Thompson, Modern Language Association, 2002, pp. 56–75.

'Goldfish'. *Wentworth*, written by John Ridley, directed by Kevin Carlin, season 3, episode 8, SoHo, 26 May 2015.

'The Governor's Pleasure'. *Wentworth*, written by Stuart Page, directed by Kevin Carlin, season 3, episode 1, SoHo, 7 Apr. 2015.

Grande, Laura. 'Strange and Bizarre: The History of Freak Shows'. *History Magazine*, Oct./Nov. 2010, pp. 19–23.

Greer, Amanda. '"I'm Not Your Mother!": Maternal Ambivalence and the Female Investigator in Contemporary Crime Television'. *New Review of Film and Television Studies*, vol. 15, no. 3, 2017, pp. 327–347.

Halberstam, Judith. *Skin Shows: Gothic Horror and the Technology of Monsters*. Duke UP, 2000.

'A Higher Court'. *Wentworth*, written by Stuart Page, directed by Catherine Millar, season 3, episode 10, SoHo, 9 June 2015.

Hillsburg, Heather. 'Mental Illness and the Mad/Woman: Anger, Normalcy, and Liminal Identities in Mary McGarry Morris's *A Dangerous Woman*'. *Journal of Literacy and Cultural Disability Studies*, vol. 11, no. 1, 2017, pp. 1–16.

'Into the Night'. *Wentworth*, written by Adam Todd, directed by Kevin Carlin, season 2, episode 11, SoHo, 29 July 2014.

'Jail Birds'. *Wentworth*, written by Timothy Hobart, directed by Steve Jodrell, season 2, episode 10, SoHo, 22 July 2014.

Karlyn, Kathleen Rowe. *Unruly Girls, Unrepentant Mothers: Redefining Feminism on Screen*. U of Texas P, 2010.

'Knives Out'. *Wentworth*, written by Pete McTighe, directed by Catherine Millar, season 3, episode 3, SoHo, 21 Apr. 2015.

Kukla, Rebecca. 'Performative Force, Convention, and Discursive Injustice'. *Hypatia*, vol. 29, no. 2, 2014, pp. 440–457.

'The Living and the Dead'. *Wentworth*, written by John Ridley, directed by Steve Jodrell, season 3, episode 11, SoHo, 16 June 2015.

'The Long Game'. *Wentworth*, written by Pete McTighe and Marcia Gardner, directed by Kevin Carlin, season 3, episode 7, SoHo, 19 May 2015.

Lotz, Amanda D. 'Really Bad Mothers: Manipulative Matriarchs in *Sons of Anarchy* and *Justified*'. *Television Antiheroines: Women Behaving Badly in Crime and Prison Drama*, edited by Milly Buonanno, Intellect, 2017, pp. 125–139.

Lotz, Amanda D. *Redesigning Women: Television after the Network Era*. U of Illinois P, 2006.

Marshall, Bridget M. '"There is a Secret Down Here, in This Nightmare Fog": Urban-Industrial Gothic in Nineteenth Century American Periodicals'. *Women's Studies*, vol. 46, no. 8, 2017, pp. 767–784.

McCormick, Stacie. 'August Wilson and the Anti-Spectacle of Blackness and Disability in *Fences* and *Two Trains Running*'. *CLA Journal*, vol. 61, no. 1–2, 2017, pp. 65–83.

'Metamorphosis'. *Wentworth*, written by John Ridley, directed by Pino Amenta, season 2, episode 7, SoHo, 1 July 2014.

Novak, Maximillian E. 'Gothic Fiction and the Grotesque'. *NOVEL: A Forum on Fiction*, vol. 13, no. 1, 1979, pp. 50–67.

'The Pink Dragon'. *Wentworth*, written by Marcia Gardner, directed by Dee McLachlan, season 2, episode 6, SoHo, 24 June 2014.

Rowe, Desireé D., and Karma R. Chávez. 'Valerie Solanas and Queer Performativity of Madness'. *Cultural Studies, Critical Methodologie*s, vol. 11, no. 3, 2011, pp. 274–284.

Schlichter, Annette. 'Critical Madness, Enunciative Excess: The Figure of the Madwoman in Postmodern Feminist Texts'. *Cultural Studies, Critical Methodologies*, vol. 3, no. 3, 2003, pp. 308–329.

Schmidt, Dolores Barracano. 'The Great American Bitch'. *College English*, vol. 32, no. 8, 1971, pp. 900–905.

Schulz, Jennifer L., and JiHyun Youn. 'Monsters and Madwomen? Neurosis, Ambition, and Mothering in Women Lawyers in Film'. *Law, Culture, and the Humanities*, 2016, pp. 1–21.

Turcotte, Gerry. 'Footnotes to an Australian Gothic Script'. *Antipodes*, vol. 7, no. 2, 1993, pp. 127–134.

Walters, Suzanna Danuta, and Laura Harrison. 'Not Ready to Make Nice: Aberrant Mothers in Contemporary Culture'. *Feminist Media Studies*, vol. 14, no. 1, 2014, pp. 38–55.

'Whatever It Takes'. *Wentworth*, written by John Ridley, directed by Kevin Carlin, season 2, episode 2, SoHo, 27 May 2014.

Wheatley, Helen. 'Uncanny Children, Haunted Houses, Hidden Rooms: Children's Gothic Television in the 1970s and '80s'. *Visual Culture in Britain*, vol. 13, no. 3, 2012, pp. 383–397.

About the Author

Corrine E. Hinton is Associate Professor of English at Texas A&M University, where she teaches writing, young adult literature, and the humanities. Her interest in contemporary Gothic television focuses on depictions of destructive, unruly women and anti-heroines.

Index

For Product Safety Concerns and Information please contact our EU
representative GPSR@taylorandfrancis.com
Taylor & Francis Verlag GmbH, Kaufingerstraße 24, 80331 München, Germany

www.ingramcontent.com/pod-product-compliance
Lightning Source LLC
Chambersburg PA
CBHW071514110726
47908CB00003B/830